THE TIME
OF
NOBLEST MIRTH

WENDY ISAAC BERGIN

ALSO BY
WENDY ISAAC BERGIN

The Piper's Story: A Tale of War, Music and the Supernatural

The Threshold of Eden

Lessons in the Wild

*In memory of Oliver Bennett "Ben" Foreman and
Richard Clostio, Vietnam veterans*

For Jacob Sweatt, veteran of Iraq and Afghanistan

And for all the soldiers, sailors, and saints

*But the Lord is the true God, he is the living God, and
an everlasting king: at his wrath the earth shall tremble, and
the nations shall not be able to abide his indignation.*

*Thus shall ye say unto them, The gods that have not made
the heavens and the earth, even they shall perish from
the earth, and from under these heavens.*

Jeremiah 10: 10–11

*Two Chinamen, behind them a third,
Are carved in Lapis Lazuli,
Over them flies a long-legged bird
A symbol of longevity;
The third, doubtless a serving-man,
Carries a musical instrument.
Every discolouration of the stone,
Every accidental crack or dent
Seems a water-course or an avalanche,
Or lofty slope where it still snows
Though doubtless plum or cherry-branch
Sweetens the little half-way house
Those Chinamen climb towards, and I
Delight to imagine them seated there;
There, on the mountain and the sky,
On all the tragic scene they stare.
One asks for mournful melodies;
Accomplished fingers begin to play.
Their eyes mid many wrinkles, their eyes,
Their ancient, glittering eyes, are gay.*

From "Lapis Lazuli," William Butler Yeats

CONTENTS

PROLOGUE

From the cabin where I write, I can see the still waters of the lake where so much of the story happened. Its calm surface, vast and quiet as memory, stretches out before me like history—my own and that of those I have loved, the narrative my mother recorded. On my desk rests the stained, ragged, handwritten manuscript she labored over for so long in the wilderness. Before it disintegrates, to preserve the past, I have transcribed it. The words of the story are hers, but I have added my own musings at beginning and end. I know she would not mind.

Imagine, at the end of the age, as night falls, a train traveling south at high speed across a flat, open plain. It rumbles across bridges; it passes through small towns and large cities; its horn rattles windows and rouses sleeping dogs. The wind of its passing bends the grasses and scatters dry leaves. The locomotive, sleek, dark, and powerful, projects a brilliant white beacon to light the way; it slices through the gathering gloom like a two-edged sword. The train is crowded with families and people of all ages and many professions. Some are brave, some are craven, some have never been tested; none know their final destination.

My name is Peter Brightman. When I was a child, I traveled on that train. There I met strangers who became my friends. One was a singer, a teller of tales. Some would say we met by chance. But there is no chance or luck. There is only Design, a pattern we walk in, whose scope is beyond our ken.

To keep me from fear and worry, this teller of tales told me the story of a prince, a princess, a birdcatcher, and of course, a dragon. (In every magical tale, as you probably know, dragons are *de rigueur*.) It wasn't long before these characters came striding out of the fairy tale into my life—even the dragon.

The dragon had the misfortune to come into his power at the end of an age. Swollen with pride and arrogance, he had free reign to slay whom he would, to gather gold and rubies, lands and peoples. He ruled. He breathed fire. He reveled in death and chaos and confusion. But his greatest hunger was for souls of men. (Although these, he discovered, were often a great disappointment.) Some of them he found slippery. They resisted chains, they overcame fear to rise out of his reach, and though he scorched them with flames, the fire simply burned away their dross and revealed a gold both imperishable and unattainable. (This enraged him.)

As time went on, he began to worry. He had not counted on the fact that the end of an age has its own dynamic; that the end was written before he came into being. As darkness swirled around the dragon and deepened, to his everlasting chagrin, his own fire ignited myriad candles. Even the smallest of them pushed away the dark and shone brilliant as a spark from the sun. In that light—because of that light—illusions shattered. Miracles happened.

And then came the thing that broke him: The universe laughed. It clapped its hands and had him in derision.

For you see, the culmination of an age, long awaited, is also long foretold. It comes; it will be. It is the time of noblest mirth.

PART I

CHAPTER 1

GIDEON

2026

The voices never left him. Chronic and oppressive as his persistent cough and shortness of breath, they hounded him: twelve of them, grinding him down day in and day out. For the entire thirty-minute drive home from Dr. Yousef's office, they jeered.

"You deserve it, jerk."

"Suffer, dungboy."

"Die in agony."

"But slowly—no quick death for you, Marine."

"Shut up!" Gideon shouted. Thankfully, he was alone in the SUV. Screaming at long-dead, invisible people would have otherwise earned him a straitjacket. It didn't help that the doctor, born in Texas of Iraqi parents, looked just like the enemy, the Alibaba bastards in Iraq and Afghanistan. Somehow he had survived the war, but now his X-rays revealed a new enemy, covert and insidious: a bulky, lopsided tumor growing in his left lung.

"Good news—you're a fucking dead man."

"Incurable—sweet." They cackled with laughter.

Dr. Yousef had outlined the treatment. "Six weeks of radiation, five days a week, starting a week from next Monday."

"The doctor lies. He is a bad haji, one of us. No treatment will help you."

"Go home and off yourself."

"No, suffer—writhe in agony, scream for mercy, Marine."

"No mercy for you, feces-face."

Gideon sighed. He would have to use all his sick days and vacation time, take a medical leave from the library. He turned into his driveway and cut the engine. He stared at the two-bedroom house he had bought in the village of Legend. Peeling paint, mildew, wood rot on the porch. Bald spots on the roof. Something needed to be done before the place fell into past-all-hope ruin.

Although he hated to admit it, for the time being he hadn't the strength or the energy to do it himself. Hard to believe he was the same guy who had trudged hours through the sands of Afghanistan bearing his "battle-rattle," ninety-plus pounds of equipment: helmet, flak jacket, supplies, and weapons. Gideon coughed into his elbow. If he survived the cancer, not to mention the ongoing war in his mind, it might be another year before he could even begin repairs. Maybe he should hire a handyman to spruce up the place.

"Why repair this dump? You're going to be six feet under soon enough."

"Die, murderer."

"The sooner the better."

"Hahaha—and no one will care. No woman, no children to mourn you, to weep and wail over your lifeless body."

"On that, I have to agree, you fucking bastards."

Although, once there would have been. But no, stay away from that dead end.

Five-thirty. With leaden legs and pain in his upper back, Gideon climbed out of the SUV and entered the house. Just the short walk across the yard and up the stairs to the covered porch left him gasping for air. He had little appetite, but he thought he'd better eat something to keep up what little strength remained. In the kitchen pantry, he found a package of spaghetti and a jar of pasta sauce. He set a pot of water on the gas stove, added salt, and turned the burner on high. He set the table for one and grabbed a longneck beer from the fridge. In the living room, he sat down heavily in his recliner to wait for the water to boil.

Five years out of the Corps, and he still felt lost. Re-entry into civilian life had been disorienting and almost as harrowing as the high-adrenaline, poised-on-the-brink-of-death daily existence of a Marine combat engineer. Most people pushing forty were settled into jobs and families; he was single and just starting out in the civilian world he had left at age eighteen. His exit from the military had been a whirligig ride with all the stability of a spinning top. The Corps had wrapped the string around him counterclockwise, turned him upside down and flung him out at high velocity. He hit the ground spinning in circles, mind whirling, wavering, expecting to topple and fall on his face.

He sipped the cold beer, thinking about the false starts he had made: auto mechanics, then medical technology. He finally enrolled in the library science program at the University of North Texas, grateful the GI Bill paid housing and tuition. He remembered his art history teacher, a young woman with spiky pink hair and a climbing rose tattoo encircling one arm, who gave a lecture on the architecture of bridges over the Euphrates River. She showed pictures of each bridge and discussed them one by one. As she described the third one, he raised his hand.

"Yes?"

"That bridge doesn't exist."

She snorted. "Well, of course it does." She pointed to the photo. "Here's the proof."

"It hasn't existed since late 2004, when I took it out."

After that, she told him not to come to class again. "You can follow the course online."

He rolled his eyes at the memory and took a long pull on the beer.

Once he got his degree, he applied for jobs at two different libraries in Texas. He got hired at the historic Carnegie Library in Jefferson, built in 1907. For a year he rented a garage apartment in town while he explored the area and waited to see if the job would really take. He discovered Caddo Lake, a place unlike any other, a mere twenty minutes away. After he and his boss, Marion Golding, agreed he should stay on, Gideon bought the house in Legend. With his salary alone, he couldn't have afforded it, but his monthly disability pay (PTSD) made it possible. He got a good price because it was in lousy shape.

He smelled something burning and remembered the pot on the stove. He dashed into the kitchen and found the water had completely boiled away. He turned off the gas and banged the stove with his clenched fist. "Can't do anything right."

"Idiot."

"Fool."

"Loser."

"Shut the fuck up!" *To hell with spaghetti.* While they laughed and jeered at him, he made a peanut butter and jelly sandwich. He wolfed it down standing at the counter.

Gideon guessed he could manage cooking and cleaning house, but he needed someone who could help him with yard work, painting, occasional heavy lifting, and small house repairs, all the things he once could have done himself. Everywhere else he'd lived, he would have run a newspaper ad, but the tiny town of Legend had no local paper.

Two days later, he tacked a "Help Wanted" ad on the post office bulletin board. He waited a week and got zero response. He decided his best bet was Chester LeBlanc, the chatty owner of Legend's Grocery & Grill. After work on a Wednesday in early June, Gideon paid him a visit at the restaurant.

Thanks to the lake, the grill could still provide food, but the sparsely populated shelves of the grocery store attested to the current shortages. At the counter, Chester took Gideon's order for a catfish po-boy to go. Gideon asked him if he could recommend a handyman.

Like a village innkeeper, ruddy-cheeked, short, chubby Chester knew all the locals and everybody's business. "Hmm. Well, I think your best bet might be Jaybird Alexander. He's a young black guy, about twenty or twenty-one. His dad Furnell was the best carpenter we ever had in these parts, and Jaybird worked with him from the time he was ten years old. But Furnell died last year. Complications from diabetes."

"Does Jaybird work full-time?"

Chester shook his head. "He could if he wanted to, but he's different from Furnell. Jaybird does a little painting and carpentry on a part-time basis. He keeps to himself and goes fishing a lot. That's part of his business; he sells catfish and bass to us and the Greek. Really small scale, but it seems to keep him going. And us, too. He could prob'ly use some extra work."

Gideon coughed into his elbow. "How do I contact him?"

Chester smiled. "Now that could be a problem since he don't own a phone. And he's hard to find. He lives in a cabin his dad built over there on Thatch Island."

"Do you know his address?"

"No, but he'll be comin' in tomorrow afternoon. Thursdays, he brings us the fish so we're stocked for the weekend rush—what there is of it."

Gideon nodded. Though it had dwindled with the hard economic times, the weekend tourist trade was still the lifeblood of the town and the store. "Well, I can't be here to meet him. I'm working in Jefferson and Thursdays are my late night at the library."

"I'll send him by your house on Friday evening or Saturday sometime." The cook appeared in the pass-through and handed Chester a brown paper bag. "Here's your po-boy. Enjoy."

"Thanks." The smell of fried fish from the warm bag made his mouth water. He coughed again and turned to go, but Chester stopped him.

"You got a cold?"

Gideon shook his head. "Allergies."

"Ah. Listen, Gideon, there's a couple things you should know about Jaybird."

"Such as?"

"Well, he don't work for just anybody. I mean, even if you offer him good money, he might not work for you. He turned down a full-time maintenance job at Caddo Cabins. He don't like Jack Dunham. Poor old Jack's not used to rejection—it really pissed him off. Wish I could've witnessed that scene." Chester laughed. "Just want you to know, your interview with Jaybird is gonna go both ways. If you don't meet his approval, that'll be all she wrote."

"Anything else?"

Chester pursed his lips. "Well, the boy's a little weird. Don't talk much at all and acts skittish around people. He's a loner, really."

Like me. "Is there something wrong with him mentally?"

Chester grimaced. "It's kinda hard to tell, since he's so tight-lipped and keeps to himself so much. He was in school with my son Jimmy. Jaybird wasn't the brightest kid, but he did manage to graduate."

Gideon didn't want a talker or a companion, just someone to help around the house. "As long as he does good work, and he's honest and responsible, he can be as weird as he likes." *And however weird he is, he won't be half as crazy as me.*

"Oh, he's a good worker, all right. I'll send him by."

"How am I gonna know when he's coming?"

Chester grinned. "You won't. He'll just show up."

The following Saturday morning, though he didn't feel like it, Gideon bestirred himself to wash his SUV. Its silver finish was superb for hiding the dirt, but shamefully, he couldn't remember the last time he'd washed it. The car, the house—hell, his whole life—was a case of neglect and disrepair, spinning out of control.

Dressed in shorts, T-shirt, and rubber flip-flops, he parked the SUV on the white shell driveway and did it the simple way: garden hose, sponge, and a bucket of soapy water. Midway into the job, as he bent down to wash the lower edge of the passenger side, he tensed. His combat instincts kicked in—he sensed a presence behind him.

Adrenalin shot through his veins—he stood quickly and pivoted to the rear, feeling slightly dizzy. He was slipping. Such a mistake in

Afghanistan would have likely cost him his life. He had grown soft and complacent, careless. Why hadn't he heard anyone approach?

A tall, slender black man stood near the rear of the car in the dappled shadow of the pecan tree. For just an instant, it seemed to Gideon that he was clothed in vine branches like a mythical forest creature. Pointed leaves made of light with bright, curling tendrils swirled and flickered around his head and shoulders. Over and above the smell of the soapy sponge in his hand, Gideon noticed a faint scent of cedar and pine.

It had to be a trick of the light. Either that or he was hallucinating. *It wouldn't be the first time.* He squeezed his eyes shut and shook his head to clear it. When he opened his eyes, the man hadn't moved. Gideon blinked rapidly until the picture made sense. At last he saw the khaki baseball cap, navy T-shirt, jeans, and white sneakers in the moving shadows, the electric bike parked on the grass.

Caught flat-footed and irritated by it, Gideon spoke loudly, with an edge in his voice. "Can I help you?"

"Are you Mr. Marsh?"

Gideon nodded, hoping he didn't look as foolish as he felt.

"Chester LeBlanc told me you might need a handyman."

His voice had a musical quality; like a bayou, it flowed deep and quiet and smooth. Gideon felt his muscles relax. "Oh, you must be Jaybird Alexander." Sunlight, filtered through the moving tree branches, flickered over his willowy form in varying patterns. Handsome, with large, dark eyes, ears set close to his head, and clipped hair, Jaybird stood with an almost unnatural stillness.

He looked Gideon in the eyes with an intelligent, probing gaze. He had the eerie sense Jaybird was reading him. Gideon coughed and gestured toward the one-story pier-and-beam house, frankly ashamed at how shabby it appeared. "The house needs a paint job, and some of the balusters on the porch need replacing. The wood has rotted. Eventually it's got to be reroofed."

Gideon waited for Jaybird to speak, but he said nothing. "I could also use some yard work on a regular basis, a couple of times a month.

I . . . uh . . . well, I can do it myself, but lately, I don't seem to find the time." He uttered the lie before he could stop himself. His voice trailed off as he surveyed the uncut grass and the flower beds choked with weeds.

Jaybird didn't react. Although he didn't smile, his presence did not seem unfriendly, just careful, almost measuring. Understanding, somehow.

Gideon found himself staring at the young man. Embarrassed, he coughed, and said, "I could pay a flat fee every month for the yard upkeep and twenty an hour for the painting and carpentry work."

They stood in the shade of the tree, but the June heat seemed to drain Gideon's energy. He was only thirty-nine, but at that moment, he felt winded and breathless as an old man. He wiped the cold sweat off his brow. "I know you do other work, so you can fit me into your schedule however you like. There's no hurry. And the money is negotiable."

"How long you been ill?"

Caught completely off guard, Gideon blinked rapidly. *How did he know? How* could *he know?* "You mean the cough?" he sputtered. "Ah, that's just allergies."

Jaybird bit his lower lip. Slowly and mournfully, he shook his head. "I'd like to help you out, Mr. Marsh, but I don't work for liars." He walked over to his bike, mounted it, and rode away.

Stunned, Gideon Marsh watched him go. He clenched his fist around the sponge he held, oblivious to the stream of soapy water that dripped onto his thigh and trickled down his leg to the ground that swallowed it.

CHAPTER 2

JOSHUA

2019

It is often in the wee hours that one ponders the profound. At 2:00 a.m. on a Friday in March, Joshua Brightman's profound had narrowed to one burning question: Was she honey or champagne? Honey: smooth, meltingly sweet, golden. *Doubtful.* On the other hand . . . he lifted a flute of Veuve Clicquot, closed one eye, and pondered: tart, tawny, effervescent. He held it against his mustache and let the heady smell and the spray from the tiny bursting bubbles tickle his senses and his schnoz. Much closer to the truth. Wholesome honey had no bad aftereffects. On the other hand, champagne, well . . . it laughed and sparkled so that one wanted more and more. He drained the glass. Ah, yes, one could drink a whole bottle. But woe followed in its train. Woe, woe, inevitable woe. One suffered the consequences.

And so he had.

A celebratory drink—or two—was well deserved after his debut concert with the New York Philharmonic. But somehow his celebration felt hollow . . . empty . . . precisely like this flute. That would never do. A little unsteadily—*tipsy-topsy, lost my popsy*—he filled it up again. *His popsy.* Well, actually he had lost much more than that.

He shook his head violently, like a dog shaking off water. *Ah, leave it—get your mind on the present.*

Tonight. It really didn't matter that he had got the chance via the back door. When Martha Argerich canceled, the orchestra's artistic director called his manager, Nathan Weiss. Thrilled to the marrow of his bones, Nathan rang him immediately, three days before the concert date of March 22. Having known Nathan since their high school days in Brooklyn, Joshua could hear the excitement and tension in his friend's nasal, New York voice. "Dude, it's one of her specialty pieces, the Prokofiev third. They don't wanna change the program. Can you do it on such short notice?" A complex, difficult work, it was a test of virtuosity and stamina: thirty minutes long, three movements, ending in a blaze of glory. More than just a vehicle for showmanship in Argerich's hands, and hopefully in his, it plumbed the depths of deep emotion.

Ironically, he had already bought a ticket to hear *her* perform the concerto. The legendary Argerich, probably the world's greatest living pianist, concertized mostly in Europe and Japan; she rarely played in the States. Her American fans would be sorely disappointed, making it a daunting task to please them. But the piece was in his repertoire—how could he pass up such an opportunity? He would have to dust it off, but he felt confident he could do it. Besides, the numbers were significant: 3/22/2019. Their sum equaled 46, and 4 + 6 = 10. Drop the zero and you get one. *Unity, primacy, a new beginning. Something he so desperately needed.*

"Yes, I can, Nathan."

That response had led to tonight's triumph: a minutes-long standing ovation and two encores. Afterward, he had had to wade through a throng of fans (mostly female) waiting by the stage door. Then there was the private party at Nathan's comfortable, roomy apartment on the Upper West Side with drinks, excited chatter, and a catered late-night dinner, a seafood feast.

Joshua lit a cigarette as he slouched on his sofa, at home in Brooklyn Heights. Too tired to shower, he had taken off shoes and tie, loosened the collar of his white dress shirt, and put his feet up. He wasn't alone; the champagne bottle chilling in its ice bucket kept him company. He topped off his glass again. He conveniently ignored the fact that before the weekend was over, he had two more performances to go.

Unfortunately, the triumph of a spectacular musical performance was just as enduring as a burst of fireworks over New York Harbor; its glory faded and fell in an instant, any remaining fire quenched by the dark, restless waters below. Dark and restless as his mind. Over a year now since she left—at his request—but despite her betrayal, a part of him still mourned. Gone, but not gone, she shadowed him like a familiar spirit. Li Ling, slender, elegant, and delicate as a flute of champagne. He observed the brimming glass in his hand. He recalled her scent, her smooth skin, the lightest amber, so intoxicating. But oh, underneath, a heart so cold—cold and deceptive, dangerous. He took another sip of the heady drink. *Let me drown in the waters of the Lethe, river of forgetfulness.*

He stubbed out one cigarette and lit another; he drew his head back and blew three smoke rings in quick succession. He watched them waver and rise to the high ceiling, expanding outward toward the crown moulding. Was it intuition, the slightest distrust, that kept him from proposing? They met when he accompanied her for one of her Juilliard recitals. Young and ambitious, they connected instantly as musicians, and as many musicians do, they shared a love of food, traveling, and languages. He helped her with English, and she taught him a little Mandarin. A native of Taiwan and a brilliant violinist, by the time she graduated she already had two years of concerts lined up. Their rapport, onstage and off, quickly deepened into an intense affair. Except for the end, he had been happy during their two years together.

His glass drained, he picked up the bottle to pour another and was surprised to find it empty. He had another bottle in the fridge, but he was shot—too tired to rise. The ashtray on the coffee table overflowed with crumpled cigarette butts. Bleary-eyed, he checked his watch: 3:44 a.m. He should go to bed. Joshua yawned, laid his head back, and slumbered.

He was playing the Adagio of the Emperor concerto. Beethoven's quiet, heartbreaking theme never failed to touch him. But this time the piano malfunctioned. The keys jangled, tinny and horribly out of tune, worse than a barroom upright on its last legs. Somebody ought to fire that incompetent ass masquerading as a piano technician . . . BRRRING—BRRRING—BRRRING!

The shrill, buzzing sound of the doorbell finally penetrated Joshua's uneasy dream. He woke with a foul taste in his mouth and a splitting headache. Disoriented, he blinked and rubbed the crusty sleep from his eyes. It was 11:30 a.m., and someone had shot a flaming arrow through his skull. He lay on the sofa, surprised to find himself still dressed in tux pants and dress shirt. Heaving himself up, he walked unsteadily to the door.

BRRRING—BRRRING—BRRRING! He ran a hand through his hair and licked his dry lips. "Who the hell is it?" he muttered.

"FedEx, package for Joshua Brightman."

What package? Must be some mistake—he hadn't ordered anything. He had been submerged in playing the Prokofiev for days, hardly coming up for food or air. He winced at the pain in his head, suddenly angry. "I didn't order anything, you idiot!" he shouted at the closed door.

"Well, somebody did. This package is addressed to Joshua Brightman, 145 Artman St., Brooklyn, New York."

He opened the door and balled up his fist, intending to punch the snarky bastard.

A skinny, bespectacled youth with a prominent Adam's apple stood there, holding a thin FedEx envelope. Dressed in black trousers and a purple uniform shirt, the boy gazed out from under the bill of a battered purple cap. He smiled a crooked, toothy smile. "Mr. Brightman?"

"Yes."

The toothy smile grew even wider. "Here's your package, sir."

Joshua took the thin rectangular envelope and peered at it. It was so light, it felt like its contents must consist of air. "You call this a package?"

The kid just stood there, grinning like a fool.

"Oh, right, hold on a sec." He returned to the parlor and found a bit of cash. The kid thanked him, dashed down the stoop, and left on a vintage blue moped. Joshua nodded sagely. "Courier on a retro bike." Maybe he was still dreaming. Maybe it was a prank and the envelope *was* empty.

Back inside, he peered at the label. Sure enough, it was addressed to him from a FedEx office in Brooklyn with no return address. He dropped the thin envelope on the coffee table. He'd open it later; the most pressing priority was to relieve himself. He dashed to the bathroom and peed with a grateful sigh. He rinsed out his mouth, washed his face, and found aspirin in the medicine cabinet. In the kitchen, he washed three pills down with a tumbler of water. He drank it all in a single go and groaned—the champagne had damn near slayed him.

Grimacing at the blinding pain in his head, he plunked a slice of bread in the toaster and brewed some coffee. While the toaster and coffee pot did their work, he changed into jeans, a T-shirt, and a gray NYU sweatshirt. Barefoot, he brought his cup and plate to the coffee table, where he munched and sipped while he stared at the anorexic package. Feeling slightly better, although the aspirin had yet to kick in, he lit his first cigarette of the day, took a deep drag, and opened the envelope.

Inside was a single sheet of yellow paper—a telegram! *What? Who sent telegrams nowadays?* He hadn't known it was still possible.

TELEGRAM

```
- urgent deliver without delay -
livrez immédiatement - liefern Sie
sofort - trasportare immediatamente -
entregue imediatamente -
```

```
Joshua Brightman
145 Artman St.
Brooklyn, NY 11201
USA
635941
SENT ON: 2019-Mar-22
Dearest Joshua, Wonderful concert!
Better than the last one I heard you
play. But you really should stop
smoking. Not good for your health.
Your friend
S
```

You really should stop smoking. He blew out the smoke he had just inhaled and burst into a spluttering cough, something he hadn't done since he sneaked his first cigarette in high school. *Who the hell sent this?* He searched the envelope and every last printed line, but couldn't find a name or a return address. Was someone spying on him? He glanced around the living room, peered at the tall windows that looked out onto Artman Street and turned back to eye the Steinway. *Crazy.* How did this telegram-sender—this anachronistic twit—know his personal habits? Mostly, he smoked at home or in hotel rooms on tour. *In private.*

Smoking soothed his ragged nerves. *Thank you, Li Ling, for making me a nervous wreck.*

Well, she could have replied, *you booted me out. It's your own damn fault.*

Agreed. But get out of my head, you beautiful, selfish deceiver.

He had quit smoking when he was twenty-four, during the time he lived in New Orleans. For the next seven years he lived tobacco-free, but after the breakup, behind closed doors, he turned to cigarettes as a comfort. He blazed through three packs a day. By 5:00 p.m. every day, the large ashtray on his Steinway held an Everest of stubbed-out butts. He smoked and practiced, practiced and smoked, inhaling enough chemicals and fine particles to encourage and cultivate in himself every kind of cancer known to man. Virginia Webb Artists, the firm who represented him, one of the biggest and best in New York, frowned on smoking; they urged their musicians to project a clean, wholesome image. Mostly he complied, but not always. *When was the last time he smoked in public?*

Oh. His shoulders slumped. *Last night.* After the concert, his fingers itched for a cigarette; his body craved that nicotine buzz. Unable to resist, he had lit up just before he stepped outside the stage door. The circle of waiting fans had certainly seen him before he ducked into the taxi to take him uptown to Nathan's.

He stared at the message. *Dearest Joshua.* Hmm—probably a woman. Young? Old? Somewhere in between? Females had outnumbered men in the stage-door crowd. Everyone had applauded and shouted congratulations. They waved their programs, eager for autographs. Chuffed by all the adulation, cigarette hanging from his lips, he had signed quite a few in a loose scrawl before he escaped into the cab.

Whoever the telegram's sender was, she had heard him play before, and she called herself his friend. *Your friend S.* Joshua sat back and tapped his lips with a forefinger. Sarah, Susan, Sharon, Sally, Scarlett, Sophia? *Shit—enough of this.* His head still hurt. *Why did she care about his smoking?*

He finished the cigarette and drank the last of his coffee. He was determined to figure this out. Something about the message played around the edges of his mind—something vaguely familiar. At the moment, he felt too miserable to pursue it. *Later,* he thought. *It will come to me.* In his experience, there was a direct correlation between deep thinking and hot water. Joshua headed for the shower.

After he had thoroughly steamed up the bathroom and washed all the dried sweat from the concert away, he shaved. He eyed his pale face and bloodshot hazel eyes, framed by the curling auburn hair. The bloodshot eyes he blamed on his late, drunken night, but his cheekbones stood out starkly in a drawn and thinner version of himself. He had clearly dropped a few pounds this week, preparing for the concert.

After he rinsed and dried his face, he dressed quickly. His headache had eased. He began to feel hopeful: there might be life after pain. In the shower, he had mentally run through a list of possible women, although he was sure none of them would have resorted to contacting him by telegram. Mobile phone addicts all, they would have texted, emailed, or employed some form of social media. No, this was someone original—someone who did the unexpected.

And then he smiled. *Aha!* He had a suspicion, an inkling. But she was just a—

His phone buzzed distantly. He finally found it on his bedside table. *Nathan.*

"Good news, my friend. Stellar reviews already posted online in three papers. I emailed you the links. Congratulations!"

"Thanks, Nathan."

"How ya feelin' this mornin'?"

Joshua laughed. "A little hungover, I have to say. One glass of champagne too many last night."

The silence on the other end surprised Joshua. "Nathan, are you there?"

"Yeah, dude, but you're makin' me nervous. I'm remembering that fiasco back in San Francisco, when you trashed the hotel room in a drunken fury. The next morning you showed up late, and the orchestra ran out of rehearsal time. You played the concert that night by the seat of your pants. Shapiro the critic found out and labeled you—"

"The Bad Boy of Classical Music." They spoke simultaneously.

"Yeah. Look, you gotta play again tonight and tomorrow. I know Li Ling threw you, but dude, you can't let your personal life jeopardize your professional reputation."

"Nathan, I know. We had this conversation back then, and I have not misbehaved since. I was on time and prepared for the rehearsal and the concert, as you well know. I just indulged myself too much last night—*after* the concert. I'll rest this afternoon. I'll be ready to go tonight."

Nathan blew out a noisy breath. "Joshua, I think you need to find a good woman and settle down. Soon."

"Spoken like a happily married man."

"Yes, I am. With kids."

Joshua winced. He hadn't told Nathan the whole story.

"And you should be, too. New York is a big sea, ya know. Lotsa fish in it."

Joshua rolled his eyes. "You sound like my mother, the matchmaker. I'll go fishing when I'm ready, Nathan, and not before."

"In other words, butt out?"

Joshua laughed. "Exactly." He cleared his throat. "By the way, a person of the female persuasion contacted me today—by telegram."

"*Telegram?* Who sends telegrams? Somebody born in 1920?"

"Don't think so. This person is nowhere near a hundred years old, and she attended the concert last night."

"Don't keep me in suspense. Who is it?"

"I'm not entirely certain, but I have a good hunch. Remember that girl—"

Nathan interrupted him. "Oh, sorry, man, gotta take this call comin' in. Rest up and do us proud again tonight!"

As Joshua pocketed the phone, he suddenly realized his whole mood had lifted. She had always had that effect on him. Smart, funny, and witty—what a precocious kid, twelve going on thirty. And her whole family had befriended him in a time when he had no friends. The fishing trip with them to Chef Pass had been one of the highlights of his life.

His stomach growled, and he realized he was famished. He decided to walk up to Montague Street for lunch: Middle Eastern food in honor of her family. He put on a jacket, clapped a Yankees baseball cap on his head, and left the house. He found himself whistling a hymn she had sung for him once, "Ye Holy Angels Bright." In the cool air, with the brilliant blue sky arching above him, his steps down the street were charged with an energy he hadn't felt for ages.

CHAPTER 3

JAYBIRD

2026

Jaybird Alexander tried not to put too much stock in superstition, but it was June thirteenth, and he had awakened that morning in his cabin with the knowing heavy on him: *blood, fire, and water.* He was supposed to trust in the Lord, and he did. *But dang it*—some kind of doom approached. Something dark and bloody—what or when, he didn't know. A persistent uneasiness, a lingering dread stayed with him all day. It stalked him on his trek through the woods. He moved as silently as possible through the trees toward the clearing. He was the hunter, but he felt like the hunted.

Jaybird knelt and waited motionless in the underbrush on the clearing's edge, just west of the lake. A headache pounded at his temples, and drops of sweat coursed down his back in the afternoon heat. As the minutes went by, only his eyes moved, searching the trees.

Across the clearing, a fat, reddish fox squirrel moved along a heavy branch fairly high up in a massive old live oak. Jaybird loaded his slingshot with a steel ball bearing the size of a grape. The squirrel came to an abrupt stop and sat upright; its tail shadowed its back like a question mark. Jaybird drew the pouch back by his ear and then released it. Blap! The squirrel never knew what hit him. He fell sideways off the branch, dead before he hit the ground with a dull thump.

Jaybird sprang up and retrieved the steel ball and the squirrel. He gripped its back right foot, took hold of the outside toe with the other hand, and quickly drew it back toward the heel, tearing the skin and exposing a white tendon. He threaded his stringer, a narrow, sharpened stick, underneath the tendon. He'd already bagged three other squirrels. The stringer was satisfyingly heavy with his catch for the day, four fat ones. He'd make a nice big squirrel stew tonight, with herbs, butter, a little flour, onions, potatoes, and tomato sauce. His mouth watered just thinking about it, a welcome break from his usual diet of fried fish.

With the heavy stringer in one hand and his slingshot in the other, he hiked back to his cabin through the Thatch Island woods. The small, unpopulated island (except for him) was his home and his refuge from people. Despite his pounding headache and a faint queasiness, he was sharply aware of all the sounds in the forest. He recognized the call of a mockingbird, a cardinal, and a mourning dove, underscored by the wind's soft music, humming through the trees.

Nudged by the breeze, the branches above him cast strange, moving shadows on the ground. Random patterns. Or was anything really random? He thought about Gideon Marsh, a man who tried to hide the shadows within him. *Shadow Man.* Jaybird sensed the illness in Gideon, the inner darkness of grief and guilt. It didn't faze him, but he wished Gideon had answered his question honestly. For all his anguish and illness, he seemed a decent man; Jaybird might have liked to work for him. Gideon Marsh had endured some kind of severe stress—a soldier maybe? His past had left him marked by blood, Jaybird was sure of it.

That took him back to the knowing. It resonated inside him, a discordant, troubling music. *Blood, fire, and water.* But this would not be a war, half a world away. No, it was approaching, a nameless, shapeless terror—here, close to home. *Dang it!* Something bad, something fearsome was coming. What it would be and when, he didn't know, but it would happen. Many people would grieve. As he came out of the shade of the trees into the bright, warm sunshine of a clearing, he shivered. He picked up the pace and hurried toward home.

CHAPTER 4

CONSTANTIN

2026

His father, Dumitru Lupei, was not really his father. Despite the fact that Dumitru was stocky, unattractive, a head shorter than his wife, and unable to pronounce the letter *r*, he clothed himself in arrogance. From under bushy eyebrows, he gazed imperiously at the world with dark, intense, hooded eyes. His face was dominated by a thick nose, and he wore his graying hair combed straight back. Although Constantin concealed it, he had always found the man repulsive. He was glad his father rarely touched him. Engaged in mysterious commerce on several continents, secretive but regarded as brilliant and charming by his business associates, Dumitru came only sporadically to the chateau. That summer, he had stayed from late June to August, far longer than usual. The prime reason was Grigori's birthday. Constantin's half-brother had turned thirteen on July 11, a rite of passage.

Constantin himself had entered this world in late September. Born under the sign of Libra, as his biological father before him (although of this he was completely unaware), he currently inhabited Adolescent Limbo, the netherworld between boyhood and maturity. He owned a magically shrinking wardrobe, courtesy of his erratic growth spurts. In a matter of weeks after the purchase of new clothes, his wrists stuck out from the shirt cuffs, and his trousers exposed his bony ankles to cold drafts. Neither oil nor water nor imprecatory prayer could tame the resilient new curl of his sandy hair. His nose, underscored by an unsightly crop of blondish fuzz, had grown too large for his face. Girls made him hot and cold. Drawn to them and fascinated by their hair, their scent, their soft bodies, he strenuously avoided them, fearful of rejection and convinced that he exuded as much sex appeal as a plucked chicken.

Despite his doubts and the raw intensity of his conflicting emotions, he possessed a patient, steadfast quality. He had borne a heavy burden all his life: the desire to know his real father, long since dead. He had never known him, and yet the loss was like the phantom pain of an amputated limb, aching in absentia. Keenly aware also that Dumitru preferred his natural son over him, Constantin rarely spoke of it and never complained.

Of those in his family, it was only Grigori who recognized Constantin's quiet strength. He relied on Constantin's forbearance, kindness, thoughtfulness, and loyalty, although he could never have articulated it in words. He simply trusted Constantin with all his heart. When he was sad, weary, or afraid, he rested on his brother's shoulders like a lamb carried by a shepherd.

When Constantin was twelve, Dumitru and his mother, Talyssa, had sat him down in the living room of the Swiss chateau and asked him if he wanted to know about his biological father. He stared at the crackling fire on the hearth, unable to utter a single word. After a moment, he simply nodded his head, keeping his eyes on the burning logs. Constantin thought it odd that Dumitru did most of the talking. His mother sat subdued with hands clasped in her lap and downcast eyes. According to Dumitru, Constantin's father had enlisted in the United States Marine Corps and died in Afghanistan in 2010, the year Constantin was born. Dumitru told him his mother and father had married too young; they simply made a mistake.

"The mawiage was bwief and unhappy. Once he left for Afghanistan, Talyssa never heard fwom him again. He never wote or called. She got a divorce and destwoyed all the photos and documents. Later, she found out he had been killed in action."

His mother uttered one sentence. "I hope you can understand, Constantin, how very painful it is for me to talk about my first husband."

"What was his name?" he asked.

Dumitru ran his tongue over his lips. "Gunnar."

"And his last name?"

Dumitru hesitated, then cleared his throat. "Woss."

"You mean Ross?"

"Yes, Woss."

Talyssa closed her eyes briefly and then rose abruptly. "I have a hair appointment in twenty minutes. I must leave now." Without a glance at either of them she hurried away.

Dumitru's hooded eyes followed her until the door closed behind her. Then he turned his dark gaze on Constantin and drew back the corners of his mouth in a rictus that passed for a smile. "Well, boy, that's the stowy. That's all we know. And that will have to be the end of this conversation." He cuffed Constantin roughly on the shoulder as he left the room.

For Constantin, the information had all the staying power of an appetizer. It didn't come close to satisfying his hunger; it only sharpened it and gave it more edge. There had to be more facts, more details about Gunnar Ross. But the knowledge that he could never meet him remained a gaping hole in his life. Sitting before the blazing fire, he determined to embark on his own personal quest. Surely there was much more to his father's story. He had the sense that Dumitru had worlds more to tell, but purposely refrained. As he stared into the fire that day, a steely resolve rose in him. He determined to find out everything he could about the man who had sired him, whether Dumitru wanted him to or not.

Like Dumitru, the lord of the manor, the fifteenth-century stone villa near Lac Léman concealed many secrets. Constantin discovered this in his own rite of passage, on an August evening when he was alone in the chateau. The family had been invited for dinner with one of Dumitru's business colleagues who lived in Cologny in a lakeside chalet. The man and his wife had two children a little younger than Grigori. With no kids Constantin's age, he expected the evening would be deadly boring and dull. He certainly didn't want to listen to two smug, rich old geezers gloat about their hostile corporate takeovers and obscene profits. In private he beseeched his mother to let him stay home, and to his relief, she permitted him. After the others left, he ate his dinner alone in the kitchen, a seafood salad with thick, crusty bread prepared by the new chef.

Afterward, he went to the library to find something to read, his first venture there since the previous summer. The beautiful room, with its large mahogany desk, two comfortable sofas, and high casement windows overlooking the garden should have been a pleasant and welcoming place, but its atmosphere tingled with malevolence.

The previous year, as he had approached one of the high windows to open it, he walked into a cold spot. It stopped him dead. The sudden drop of temperature felt like the heights of Mont Blanc in winter. Goosebumps formed on his bare arms. Suddenly he felt the pressure of a hand on his shoulder. The hair rose on his scalp and he squealed with fright. He jumped backward to escape, stumbled, and fell on his rump. He thought he heard faint laughter.

He scrabbled to his feet and ran from the room. The experience spooked him so badly he did not set foot in the library again for a year. When he asked his stepfather about it at dinner, Dumitru seemed incurious. "As you know, the chateau is vewy old; it has many quirks. It was vewy likely a dwaft from the windows, a gust of cold air." He sipped his red wine and dismissed the question. "I'm sure it was nothing at all."

A gust of cold air—on an August afternoon?

Older now, Constantin decided he wouldn't let "nothing at all" stop him from finding a good book. He entered cautiously and steered clear of the area near the casement windows. He hoped the cold spot had either dissipated or stayed in the same location. The volumes lining three of the walls included fiction and nonfiction in French, German, English, Italian, and some old tomes in Latin. He touched the spines of two of his favorites, books he had read many times over, Sir Thomas Malory's *Le Morte d'Arthur* and the French epic poem, *La chanson de Roland.* He browsed on the lower levels for a while amongst biographies, histories, a poetry section, the complete leather-bound works of Shakespeare, and a collection of books on World War II, including a copy of *Mein Kampf.* "Hmmph! Bad boy, Dumitru, bad boy."

He yawned over books on economics (*ugh*), and romance novels (*even worse*). Feeling discouraged, he glanced upward. The bookcases extended to within a foot of the beamed ceiling, where there was a gap above the top shelf. He decided to climb the movable ladder to see what titles Dumitru had placed highest up. On the very top shelf he found a section of German-language books on the flora and fauna of Europe. *Not too interesting.* To his left he saw a collection of books on alchemy and magic in the Middle Ages. *Better.*

He stretched to his left to pull out a book on medieval magic. Leaning precariously, he hooked the top of the spine with his finger and pulled. The book came out more easily than he expected, spewing a cloud of dust with it. Constantin sneezed so violently he lost his balance. To prevent himself falling, he released the book and grabbed the lintel above the bookcase with his left hand. With a resounding crack, the book struck the wood floor. Meanwhile, he teetered slightly, one leg swinging free, suspended between the ladder and the stacks. He gripped the two-inch lintel tightly. It creaked ominously, but held.

As his heart beat a loud tattoo in his chest, he regained his footing on the ladder. He glanced down at the splayed-out book on the parquet flooring, fourteen feet below. Better the book than his head, which would have split like a melon had he fallen. He slowly slid his left hand back across the lintel in the direction of the ladder. As he did, his fingers brushed against an object lying hidden in the space above the bookcase. Once he felt secure on the ladder again, curiosity took over. He reached above his head and over the lintel and felt around. He found a lone book, apparently discarded or forgotten. Wondering what it could be, he picked it up.

It was bound in dark cloth, so dusty he could hardly tell its color. No title or author. Clipped inside the back cover were several thin airmail envelopes. The one on top was addressed to Dumitru. *Very interesting, indeed.* Constantin's heartbeat quickened. He blew off some of the gray dust and opened the cover to a blank page, slightly yellowed with age. The next page was covered in a fine script. It was a diary or journal, written in French with an old-fashioned fountain pen, the kind with nibs. There was no name, but he suddenly recognized the clear, somewhat faded handwriting as Dumitru's. He had seen it in the occasional handwritten letters addressed to his mother and Grigori.

He was trespassing, and he knew it—but he forged ahead anyway. He held the book in sweating hands and read.

> *Patience. Nous avons un plan pour vaincre l'ennemi. Cela prendra du temps, des années peut-être, mais nous réussirons. Nous allons infiltrer leur gouvernement, leurs militaires, leurs tribunaux petit à petit. Ce que je ferai moi-même n'est pas encore clair. Mais ce sera ce que les Neuf décideront.*

Constantin spoke French fluently, but he read aloud, translating the entry to his native tongue: "Patience. We have a plan to conquer the enemy. This will take time, years perhaps, but we will succeed. We will infiltrate their government, their military, their courts little by little. What I myself will do is not clear yet. But it will be what the Nine decide."

Strange entry for a businessman to make. Questions arose thicker than the dust on the cover. Who are "we," and who is "the enemy"? "The Nine"—who are they? *Pretty damn mysterious.*

Well, mission accomplished: he had found some interesting reading, all right. The secretive Dumitru would reveal himself in his own words. Constantin ignored the whisperings of conscience and stuck the book inside the waistband of his jeans.

Thrilled that he might learn more about Dumitru, but horribly afraid that his stepfather might discover his snooping, he descended the ladder on shaky legs. He picked up the book on medieval magic, undamaged despite the fall. He decided to take that one with him too, in case anyone asked what he was reading.

He clicked his tongue. Too bad he hadn't found the diary sooner; he probably wouldn't have time to read it before he had to leave. His mother had already booked his flight to New York for the fall term. Well, he would just bring it along. Dumitru would never miss it. If the layer of accumulated dust was any indication, it must have lain there forgotten and undisturbed for ages.

He carried the books to his room on the floor above and set the magic book on his bedside table where it would be obvious. He turned on the lamp and picked up Dumitru's diary.

When he opened it, he realized the blank page actually had a small image at the top. He recognized it immediately; it was the great seal found on the back of every dollar bill. He studied it carefully. A circle enclosed an incomplete pyramid with thirteen steps. It was surmounted by an illuminated triangular capstone enclosing an eye. The capstone hovered above the pyramid, not yet settled in place. The Latin inscription above was *Annuit Coeptis*, the lower one was *Novus Ordo Seclorum*.

Five minutes later, with thanks to the internet, he had translated the Latin: *He has favored our undertaking*, and *A new order of the ages*. He also discovered that the eye was the all-seeing eye of Horus, an Egyptian god. *Strange.*

Why was this symbol, in plain sight of anyone who handled a dollar bill, a special feature of Dumitru's diary? His father loved money, no doubt about it, and he was immensely wealthy. Did the symbol mean money was his idol? But the symbol, in and of itself, did not really represent money. Why was it there? What did it mean? Constantin tapped the page with his index finger. Was the *He* who favored the undertaking supposed to be Almighty God or Horus? As far as he knew, Dumitru was an atheist.

Constantin shrugged. Perhaps the content would answer some of his questions. He turned to the first page. *C'est une journée d'hiver ensoleillée et je suis assis dehors dans le jardin. Ma main est au repos sur ma cuisse, les doigts tendus . . .*

> *It is a sunny winter day, and I am sitting outside in the garden. My hand is at rest on my thigh, fingers outstretched. A buzzing bee approaches and settles on my hand. I remain still. It senses the slightly sticky, sweet residue of the apple I have just eaten. As it navigates the uneven terrain of my fingers, I can see its small wings, ribbed and clear. They seem too small for its bulky, striped body, almost incapable of supporting it in flight. But despite my doubts, the bee, finding no nectar, flies away with ease.*
>
> *Moments later, a common house fly alights on my hand. Its wings extend well past its thorax, more in proportion to its body size than those of the bee. It rubs its back legs together and flexes its tiny, pointed wings. Its legs are thinner than eyelashes. I am not fond of flies; I shift my hand and it darts away.*
>
> *Wings. There are so many types: dragonfly wings, long, narrow and transparent; butterfly wings, tiny canvases of brilliant colors and astonishing patterns. Iridescent hummingbird wings whirring incredibly fast, up to two hundred beats per second. On the other end of the spectrum, the birds of prey: owls with*

wingspans of four feet or more, the powerful eagle's seven-foot span, and the eight-foot span of the California condor.

But all these wings pale in comparison to those of the fallen ones. I saw them in their lair beneath the city, where they sit in semi-darkness. Their grayish-black bodies thirty feet high, their eyes blood-red. When I, a mortal man, came into their presence, they rose and extended their wings—sixty feet or more. I dropped to my knees in dread.

You do not know true darkness until you have stood, mortal and afraid, in the presence of the fallen ones. They burn, these earth-bound stars, with the cold light of hatred and malice. Proud, rebellious, masters of guile, they hate their Creator and they long to see his creation destroyed.

As I do.

Led by the god of this age through millennia, their ancient warfare continues. They long for the day when he, the One who thinks he is omnipotent, will finally be overthrown. Watch and see: the end comes soon now. The human allies of the fallen—those who have direct contact—are few, but they are the most powerful men on earth. Each one has made his pact with the god of this world. Each one worships him, the prince of the power of the air.

I know, for I am one of their number.

I have earned my place. Our god requires complete submission in a series of escalating trials that culminate in a ritual of blood and sacrifice. Of this ritual I cannot and will not speak; I shudder to remember it. But submission to him is the gateway to incredible rewards: power, riches, knowledge beyond all telling.

Through him, the theater of the world is ours. And it is theater: it is all shadow play. Kings and queens, presidents, politicians, popes, priests, judges, media giants, bankers, and generals are puppets, every one. The words they speak are our words; they dare not speak anything else. They dance to our music. Otherwise they fall.

Constantin laid the book down on his lap and shivered, despite the warmth of the August night. Were Dumitru's words the ravings of a madman, a psychopath? Were these musings a sketch for a novel? Who was this Dumitru, the man he had known—or thought he had known—all his life?

The light, rhythmic tap of Grigori's footsteps ascending the stairs snapped him out of his reverie. The Lupei family had returned. Time had passed so quickly. He closed the diary and stuck it under his mattress.

Constantin inhaled deeply, then blew out his breath with a whooshing sound. He shook his head to clear it. He had two fathers: the biological one he had never known and the father who adopted him, whose ordinary appearance veiled some sort of secret life. Two enigmas, two mysteries. He intended to find out who they really were, even if his search led him to a place he did not want to go.

He pressed his lips together. Like the Arthurian knights of old, he had a quest, and he would follow it through, no matter what.

CHAPTER 5

SAM

2019

At the age of eighteen, Samantha Faris, daughter of the Deep South, swan dived into the Sea of Chaos otherwise known as New York City. Submerged in its icy, swirling waters, pushed by its currents, she floundered and flailed for at least a year before she surfaced. The city shocked her and took her breath away. The sheer volume and density of people and the endless, gray, towering buildings pushing against the sky overwhelmed her. She struggled with the idea that people lived in apartments their entire lives, disconnected from the land and nature. Astonished daily by the city's noise and frenetic energy, its horn-honking, riotous traffic, she watched the surging tide of taxis, cars, buses, and trucks whoosh by as she trod the wide sidewalks seeking employment and a place to live. She recoiled at the screeching subway trains and their dragon's breath, the hot, foul-smelling rush of air that preceded them into stations. Caught in the riptide of thronging crowds, she was taken aback by the aggressive nature of the inhabitants. Unused to their rapid speech patterns, she half-stammered in response to interview questions and the queries of impatient real estate agents. When she spoke at her slow Southern tempo and paused to think, they judged her dimwitted and interrupted her before she could complete her response. Even the edgy feel of the air itself, so different from the soft, warm humid caress of the South, seemed like an alien entity.

She had plunged herself into this urban sea ostensibly to attend The King's College in Manhattan, but that was only one facet of her true purpose. She turned down a full scholarship to Tulane in New Orleans, where her mother was an English professor, to live in New York because it was Joshua's hometown. Even though he forgot about her, even though he never knew how it broke her heart when he moved away from New Orleans, he remained to her a calling. Like a nun to the veil, her inner focus on him was intense and steadfast, never wavering. She didn't want to intrude on his life, but like a detective, a modern-day Sister Fidelma on the trail of a mystery, she intended to seek him out and observe him secretly.

She picked up his trail through the Virginia Webb Artists website. A little internet sleuthing revealed his address in Brooklyn Heights. (It thrilled her to know exactly where he lived.) For two years, she devoured every last tidbit about his career and all the latest gossip. It was not until her third year in the city that she actually saw him. She attended the Mostly Mozart Festival at Lincoln Center, where he was a featured soloist. With her heart in her throat, she simply observed him from afar and made no contact. That was the summer after he broke up with Li Ling. She knew about their romance and its unexpected end. As "beautiful people," young, photogenic, and immensely talented, they lived very public lives. Their entire relationship seemed to be a never-ending source of manna for "entertainment" articles.

When the breakup news came, she didn't get the whole story—no one did—since both principals refused comment to the media. She wasn't a bit sorry about their relationship's sudden demise. It simply pointed the way toward the declaration she had made years ago, on the very first day she met Joshua. With her mother and Sitti's permission, she had invited him to lunch at her house. At one point, she asked him if he had a girlfriend. When he said no, she said, "Good."

He laughed. "Why is that good?"

"Because I'm going to marry you." She spoke with utter certainty—to everyone's embarrassment but her own. She was twelve; he was twenty-four.

The night she learned the beautiful couple had gone their separate ways, she celebrated discreetly in her studio apartment. One Scotch neat (that's all it took), elicited a few wild whoops, a song and a dance. With something approaching wild abandon, she hummed "When the Saints Go Marchin' In" as she tripped the light fantastic 'round her 250-square-foot abode. She capped it all off with one standing backflip (she *was* an athletic type) to complete her personal shindig.

To supplement her college scholarships, she worked part-time as a server at Beiruti, a Middle Eastern café in Brooklyn Heights. Located on Montague Street, it was fairly close to her Park Slope apartment and only three blocks east of the Brooklyn Promenade.

When she read that Joshua would fill in on the New York Philharmonic's concert series, Sam immediately bought a ticket—not an easy task. The night of the concert, she arrived early and found her seat in the left rear of the hall (where she could see the keyboard). While she waited for the program to begin, she recalled the time Joshua played the Beethoven concerto in New Orleans, a very dark time for them both, after Eliot's death.

She had found the fledgling bluejay in her backyard and named him Eliot. She raised him in the house, knowing that she would have to release him someday. When the moment came, she took him outside, held him in her hands, and told him goodbye. Then, with a swift upward gesture, she released him into the air. He flew across the yard and landed on the wooden fence that separated her yard from Joshua's. A shot rang out and Eliot toppled backward into her arms, his breast a ragged, bloody hole. The shock took her voice away; she did not speak for over a month.

At Joshua's concert, she had sat between her mother and Dr. Leo in the jewel box theater. Leo tried to cheer her up with a one-sided conversation. He told her he had chosen seats on the left side of the theater so they could see Joshua's hands on the keyboard. He pointed to the nine muses, depicted in a beautiful ceiling mural, and told her their names: Terpsichore, the muse of dance, Melpomene, tragedy, Thalia, comedy, and so on until he got to the last one, Euterpe. "She's my favorite," he confided, "the muse of ice cream." With that, Leo came close to achieving his goal—if her depression had not been so deep, she would have laughed.

Joshua's distress, his bloodshot eye and swollen face, half-covered by a massive purple bruise, was much more visible. He played the concert despite the pain of a fractured cheekbone. Years later she learned that the same man who shot Eliot had also struck Joshua with the rifle stock—Billy "the Beast" Brightman, Joshua's father.

When the conductor entered, the crackle of applause brought Sam back from 2010 New Orleans to the present: 2019 and the New York Philharmonic. Mendelssohn's *Overture to a Midsummer Night's Dream* began with four quiet, shimmering wind chords. Sustained and unmeasured, they gave a glimpse of eternity. Vivid, lively music followed as Shakespeare's story of lovers, intrigue, fairy magic, and mistaken identities unfolded. The music brought to her mind Joshua's speculation, years ago, on the soul's journey, its beginning and ending in eternity and its short, impermanent sojourn on earth. At length, the piece ended with a slow, nostalgic theme in the strings: beautiful as a blessing in a sweet and perfect dream. All would be well. And finally, the high, pure chords: magical and timeless. The audience, Sam included, hesitated to applaud, unwilling to break the spell.

Her anticipation rose as the stage crew moved the piano front and center. When Joshua came striding out from the wings, his curly mane of auburn hair framing his pale face (no bruises this time), Sam's buoyant smile and the lightness in her heart practically lifted her off the seat. The piece began quietly with a lyrical clarinet solo, then strings and flute entered. But suddenly the piano came in with blinding speed, and together with the orchestra, like a pack of galloping thoroughbreds, the race was on. Joshua played with virtuosity and control, completely fearless. The audience broke protocol and applauded at the end of the first movement.

Next came a theme with variations, sometimes dreamlike and mysterious, sometimes shooting off sparks like fireworks. The final movement sizzled. The piece closed with a spiky theme, with tall chords, vertical as trees with shining notes flickering like shooting stars in between. The energy and speed, the brilliant interplay of orchestra and piano, took Sam's breath away.

The audience and orchestra members erupted in a roar. She was so proud of him, she thought her heart would burst. Joshua stood and thanked the conductor, the concertmaster, and acknowledged the orchestra with an upraised hand. He turned to the audience and a second roar went up. People stood and shouted "Bravo!" After the third call-back, he played an encore.

"Schumann," he said.

Sam had heard the piece before, but she didn't know its name. The audience, several hundred people, sat completely still, moved by the music's warmth and childlike simplicity. After that, they still wouldn't let him go, so he played another encore.

The orchestra concluded the concert with Rimsky-Korsakov's *Scheherazade Suite.* The program notes told how the Sultan, convinced that all women are false and faithless, (*so insulting*) vowed to put to death each of his wives after the first wedding night. But Scheherazade saved her own life by entertaining him with fascinating tales for a thousand and one nights. In the end, captivated by her tales, he renounced his vow entirely.

It was a night of fairy tales. As the sensuous, evocative music of "The Sea and Sinbad's Ship" washed over her, she daydreamed about meeting Joshua face-to-face again, nine years on from her childhood. He was the prince and she the princess. Surely they belonged together. Of course, if she was honest with herself, he was a prince and she was . . . a Bookworm-Turned-Impoverished-Student and Part-Time Server. So very romantic: Who could resist her charms?

Before she knew it, Scheherazade had spun all her tales, and the concert ended. No time to lose. She had already scoped out the stage door, where she would reunite with the love of her life. *Yalla, yalla, albi! Hurry, my heart!* She could hear Sitti's voice urging her. Her personal fairy tale would soon have its delicious denouement. Or so she thought.

The excited crush of fans who surrounded the stage door included some sexy, sophisticated New York babes with immaculate makeup, trendy hairdos, expensive jewelry, designer clothes and shoes, offset by a contingent of casually dressed, grubby young people, probably music students. Next to the sophisticates, Sam felt like a dog: a scruffy mongrel yapping at the heels of groomed and perfumed runway models. Their maturity and worldliness shattered her confidence. Her small size (5'2"), her cap of comb-defying black hair (she trimmed it herself), zero makeup, and the dowdy skirt and blouse she wore screamed *inferior!* She was twenty years old, a polite Southern girl, green and artless. Why would he even look at her?

Overcome by shyness, she knew she would not approach him—even if it had been possible. She stood on the crowd's outer edge, facing a wall of well-dressed backs. She might have had a chance to see him had she crawled forward between their legs. *What a great impression that would make.* Standing on her toes, she still couldn't see anything but the top of the stage door. Everyone, male and female, seemed to be at least six feet tall.

The door opened to a spate of spontaneous applause and shouts. "Mr. Brightman! Mr. Brightman!" People thrust themselves and their programs forward, hoping for an autograph. Hanging back to observe, she caught the barest glimpse of Joshua, a cigarette dangling from his lips (*What?*) as he signed programs. He would never see her, and if he had, it was doubtful he would even recognize her.

For her part, she had seen enough. She turned and walked toward the Lincoln Center subway stop with a sense of relief. With her fierce independent streak, she had never liked crowds—too easy for a herd instinct to take over; people under the spell would cease to think for themselves. As for those women—Sam puffed out her cheeks and blew a raspberry—to hell with them. She really didn't care about fashion or makeup or image. In her opinion, intelligence and humor always trumped physical beauty. She had wit and charm, and Joshua had truly enjoyed her company. Hopefully, he would once more.

But as she walked, doubts crept in. In New Orleans, he had seen her as a precocious little bookworm who could hold her own in conversations with grown-ups. If they reconnected now, it would be on a level playing field as two adults. In his eyes, would she still be unusual and unique? Or would she have lost her charm, like a child actor who flopped in adult roles? Would she be passé, like a prodigy who becomes old news at twenty-one?

Possibly. She shrugged. What would be, would be, but she wouldn't pass up the opportunity to see him again in person, no matter what. *If she could.* As she practically ran down the steps to catch the train at Sixty-Sixth Street, she devised a plan to contact him. Just as she got to the platform, she heard the brakes screech and felt the rush of stale, hot wind as the train entered the station. Good—she was in a yank to get home and send her message in her own way, with a little mystery. She wouldn't sign it. She smiled to herself; if she worded it just right, Joshua would figure it out.

The train doors opened and Sam stepped in, still enveloped by the magic from the concert. *Who knew what could happen?* After all, it *was* a night of fairy tales.

CHAPTER 6

ON CADDO LAKE

2026

"The wood of Cypress (*Cupressus sempervirens*) is almost imperishable; the gates of Constantinople, made of this wood lasted 1,100 years." So stated Daniel Oliver, Keeper of the Herbarium and Library of the Royal Gardens, Kew, and Professor of Botany in University College, London. Gideon researched his tome, *Lessons in Elementary Botany*, published in 1864.

Eleven hundred years. Gideon looked it up: the Romans held the city the Emperor Constantine had built, from AD 324 until the Ottomans, led by Mehmed II, successfully laid siege to it in 1453.

When he had a slow day at the Jefferson library, Gideon did a little more research. The cypress, native to ancient Persia (which included parts of modern-day Afghanistan) and the Levant, was the same tree Noah used to build the Ark. In ancient times, it was a symbol of immortality. *Sempervirens*, evergreen. Later on it was regarded as a symbol of mourning. Of course, during his time in Afghanistan, he had not seen cypresses, only desert. But mourning—oh yes. He still mourned. The sand had soaked up the blood of his brothers, while the stars gazed upon it impassively. And somehow, he had come out of it alive.

I hope you never experienced mortal combat, Daniel Oliver. Or the terrible guilt of surviving it. Gideon wondered what Mr. Oliver might think if he could be resurrected and transported across time from nineteenth-century England to present-day America, to Caddo Lake. The lake, which was not really a lake, straddled the Texas-Louisiana border. He paddled his kayak down a narrow waterway between two rows of the towering, stately bald cypress trees. Mysterious, bewitching, and unknowable as a woman, Caddo Lake enchanted him. At 26,800 acres, it was a watery woodland, a magical maze of ponds, bayous, sloughs, and interconnected channels. Alive with bird calls, buzzing insects, and the soothing, breathy voice of the wind in the trees, it was the one place he felt at peace.

He imagined giving Mr. Oliver a tour. "Welcome to Caddo Lake, Mr. Oliver, the biggest lake in Texas and home of the largest bald cypress forest in the world."

"And why are these cypresses referred to as *bald*, Mr. Marsh?"

"Because, sir, unlike most other species in the family *Cupressaceae*, the tree is deciduous; it loses its leaves in the winter. However, 'in these here parts,' as the locals would say, it never loses the Spanish moss, the greenish-gray, shawl-like mantles draped from the branches."

"I say, old chap," Oliver would surely reply, "it gives the place an air of mystery, like London, cloaked in fog."

"Indeed."

"Only crazy people make up conversations like that, fool."

"Deluded, you are."

Gideon rested his paddle on the gunwales, a little short-winded. He leaned back to conserve his energy and let the kayak glide. If he worked too hard he erupted into coughing fits. The morning interview with Jaybird Alexander had troubled him. To ease his mind, he had fled to the lake, where he hoped to find peace. But he could never escape the voices; they lived in his head.

The trees lining the waterway stood as dignified and solemn as a tribunal of gray-bearded mythological kings. With feathery, bright-green foliage above the branches and the draped moss hanging down, many of them stood over a hundred feet in height and six feet in girth. The base of each tree was surrounded by a crowd of strange, bony-looking "knees" that jutted up above the water. Some of the trees were ancient; cypresses had a five-hundred-year lifespan.

He wished the trees, like the gates of Constantinople, could hold off the enemy that had long laid siege to his mind.

"You'll never be rid of me, Murderer Marine. I'll wear you down 'til you lose your mind."

"Go away, small-town sheik, you false, honorless bastard. You hypocrite."

The bearded face of the village elder named Pazir had seared itself on Gideon's memory. He had spoken with him hundreds of times, visited his house, drunk endless cups of tea with the man. Pazir's face came to him at night when he woke in the wee hours: the long, slightly crooked nose in a narrow face with thick black eyebrows, the full lips half-hidden by the unkempt mustache and black, curly beard, threaded with gray. The glinting, deep brown eyes, so shrewd and calculating. Gideon paid the man for information. Pazir knew everyone in the village; he identified the good hajis and bad hajis for the Marines.

As a combat engineer, Gideon was responsible for route clearance and for breaching, clearing, and proofing minefields. "Engineer up!" was his call to action. If anyone saw metal or wires glinting in the sun, or any other suspicious objects, they radioed him. Gideon would question that Marine as to what he saw and where. Then the matter became his responsibility. While he checked it out and resolved it, the entire patrol, whether on foot or in trucks, stayed frozen in place.

First, he scanned the area with binoculars, looking for disturbed earth, wire or string, or anything out of the ordinary in a range of five meters and then twenty-five meters out. Once he spotted the anomaly, he used his metal detector to sweep the lane between the convoy and the object. If he discovered a land mine, he could blow-it-in-place or disarm it. If he found an Improvised Explosive Device (IED), the official policy was to provide security, back off, and call Explosive Ordnance Disposal. The problem was that EOD could take anywhere from eight to sixteen hours to arrive, and in the meantime, no one was allowed to move.

The official policy wasted critical time and stopped the operation's progress, so his squad ignored it. Gideon did the job himself. Once the metal detector identified the place where the IED was buried, he used a probe very gingerly, until he hit resistance. To uncover the device, he would dig down in the sand with the patience and delicacy of an archaeologist.

As the kayak's progress slowed, Gideon sat up and began to paddle again. His cough disturbed a great blue heron, hunting at the edge of the lake. The ungainly bird flapped its big wings and vaulted up with a long, screeching, unmusical cry: *Awwwwk!* At the edge of the channel where he had first seen the bird, Gideon noticed a few stakes: broken-off branches standing up about six inches above the ground, about the same diameter as his index finger. Each stake had a long piece of string knotted around it that disappeared into the water. Crabbing lines.

The string reminded him. Gideon had cleared a route through the desert not far from Pazir's village. Unfortunately, once a route was cleared, it could be backlayed: the hajis would come behind them and bury more IEDs or mines. During that period, they lost five men to IEDs. One picked up a children's toy just outside the village. When he pulled the string, it exploded and took off half his head. Four men died when their truck ran over an IED buried under a paved road.

At that time, Gideon noticed that the workmanship of the IEDs he discovered and disarmed pointed to a single maker. They had unique and identical knots. He thought it might be time for a conference with Pazir. It was very likely that someone in the village was the culprit, and since the elder knew everyone and everyone's business—for enough money—he could likely put the Marines on the bad haji's tail.

He and the interpreter paid a call. His interpreter, Ahmad, was a native Afghani nicknamed Bridge. In his early thirties, he dressed in Western clothes. Pazir, the village elder, always polite and dignified, welcomed them into his house, a flat-roofed building made of mud and timber. They walked up a steep staircase and met Pazir in a large upper room. He offered them cups of chai, the sweet, pungent hot tea central to the hospitality of the culture. Low cushions lined the walls, and various colorful rugs lay on the floor. The two windows had drapes, drawn to either side during the day and tied back with twine.

With Bridge's help, Gideon told Pazir there had been an uptick in the number of IEDs and asked him if he could get some intel for them. They needed to find the bad hajis who were laying the IEDs. While the elder and Bridge conversed, Gideon carefully studied the man and the furnishings, despite the fact that he had visited the elder in this room many times before. Close observation was an ingrained habit. He remained alert and keenly attentive to his surroundings, since his life and the lives of his men could depend on noticing the slightest details. Forty minutes later, after two cups of chai and friendly farewells, they left. Pazir said he would have intel for them in one week.

On the way back to "Alcatraz," their Forward Operating Base, Gideon made up his mind. He spoke little on the way back to the FOB, located on steep, high ground in the Land of Bad Haji. One week was far too long to wait; he didn't want to lose any more men. Two days later, to Pazir's surprise, Gideon returned alone. He brought a knotted string from an IED he had disarmed. He held it up beside the identical knot in the twine holding the drapes. He pointed to the same type of knot tied in the rug. He didn't need an interpreter to translate the panic in the man's eyes. When Pazir ran for the stairs, Gideon drew his 9mm pistol and fired a single shot. The elder pitched forward and slid down the stairs headfirst, leaving a trail of blood.

From then on, there was a sharp reduction in the number of IEDs surrounding the village. From then on, Pazir took up residence in his head.

That evening, Gideon visited his favorite bar and restaurant, the Alligator Gar, for a different type of solace. In the past year, the state had allowed the bars to remain open seven days a week. If he wasn't mistaken, he thought the government also supplied the liquor in this time of shortages. *Keep the people entertained* was their unspoken motto. Entertainment seemed highly desirable that night. If he drank and shot pool, he couldn't think about himself or the thirty radiation treatments soon to come. Better enjoy life while he could.

Gideon put his money down on the betting table. He wasn't a shark exactly, but he was confident. He hoped to whip their asses—the Greek, Reilly Mack, and that arrogant bastard Jack Dunham. He had watched them play eight ball before. They had twice as much bravado as skill. He hoped to take home the prize; the pot for the Saturday night tournament was three hundred dollars.

Apparently the Greek did too. Either that or it must have been a slow night at his restaurant, Marinos, across the highway from the Alligator Gar. The Greek had apparently left his wife in charge and walked over to kick up his heels with the boys. The fat man with his ragged, curling gray hair played as wild and sloppy as he looked. When he lost to Gideon in the first round, he said, "Well, I'll be damned. Lookit—the librarian can shoot pool with the best of them."

Gideon had never discussed his military service with his acquaintances in Legend. He let them think he was a book nerd; they had no idea he was a Marine combat vet who had served thirteen years in the Middle East. He detected a bit of envy in the Greek's tone.

"Pretty good for a Lie-berry Man, all right," echoed Jack Dunham with an oily smile. Weak-jawed, with lank, dishwater blonde hair, he watched his opponent carefully. "Old Gideon's not as girly as we thought. But I think we can still whup his ass." He hitched up his trousers, jiggling the drooping overhang of his belly.

"Let them insult you, fool."

"Why don't you take them out with your 10mm?"

"Why don't you take yourself out?"

"Stupid game, Loser—you'll never win."

Gideon coughed into his elbow and gritted his teeth; he ignored the voices and played his game. Jack, who rushed his shots and tightened up every time he hit the cue ball, was eliminated in round two. He cursed loudly, ordered a scotch, and sat down next to the Greek at the losers' table.

That left short, bald Reilly and Gideon.

"You're a real hustler." Reilly stroked his black, bushy beard. "How'd you learn to play like that?"

"My dad taught me. We had a table in the game room. I've been playing since I was tall enough to see over the edge." Gideon pointed at the table. "Your break."

"Hope he breaks your balls, Lie-berry Man."

"Does he have any?" They cackled with glee.

Reilly racked the balls and chalked his cue. On the break, he sank a solid. He sank three in a row before he missed a long shot to the corner pocket.

It was Gideon's turn. In an unhurried series of deft shots, he cleared the stripes from the table. All conversation stopped. He called the eight ball in the side pocket, while the other men seemed to hold their collective breath. One delicate bank shot later, he sank it. Victory.

"Well, shit," said Reilly.

"Pure luck."

"A fluke."

Gideon laughed and then coughed violently into his elbow. "Guys, let me ease your pain. The drinks are on me." With beers in hand, the four of them sat at a table near the bar. That was when they told him about a new "sighting."

"Sighting of what?" Gideon asked.

"Bigfoot," said Jack.

Gideon grinned. "You gotta be kidding. And besides, I thought Sasquatch roamed the Pacific Northwest—Washington and Oregon."

"Yeah, but we got his southern cousin down here," said Reilly Mack. "Over the years, there's been quite a few sightings around the lake. The Caddo Indians called him Caddaja, a man-eating monster."

"Stands to reason," added the Greek. "Caddo's a wilderness. It's vast and some of it's inaccessible, even by boat. It's perfect for Bigfoot."

The Greek spent his weekends cooking at his restaurant, this night being an exception, but the other two were going on an expedition the following Friday to get their own sighting, or so they hoped. "Why don't you come with us, Gideon?" said Jack. "Give you something to talk about down at the *lie-berry*."

He mispronounced it on purpose, to annoy Gideon. He succeeded. Against his better judgment, in order to make nice and be one of the guys, Gideon agreed to go. It would be an entertaining excursion before his radiation treatments began the following Monday. After that, he knew he wouldn't feel like it.

"If you need a gun, I can loan you one," said Jack. "We can give you a quick shootin' lesson that evenin'."

Gideon smiled. "Not necessary. And I've got my own rifle, thanks."

"Maybe one of them will get drunk and shoot you."

"Time for you to die, you piece of dog shit."

"All right!" They clinked their beer mugs together in a toast, and proceeded to plan the trip right there.

THE CHATEAU

2026

Every time he returned to school in New York, Constantin worried about leaving his mother and Grigori alone. Well, not exactly alone, since the fifteenth-century stone chateau housed a few invisible residents. Castle-like, it had thick walls, a tower with a spiral stone staircase, a vaulted stone cellar, wooden floors, oak ceilings, a walled garden with a pond and centuries-old trees. The first floor consisted of a large living room with a fireplace, a dining room, and a billiard room, with a kitchen in the back. The upper floors housed the library and ten bedrooms. Despite its medieval, storybook appearance, it was a troubled place, with frequent disturbances.

No matter how often the servants locked the French doors that led to the back garden, they seemed to unlock themselves during the night. Every type of lock, mechanical or electronic, failed. Strange occurrences happened elsewhere in the house, as well. His bedroom and Grigori's were on the third floor. They often heard the sound of running footsteps and children laughing on the unused floor above them. On several occasions during the eight years he lived there, Constantin had raced up the stairs to check, but each time, he found the hall and the guest bedrooms dim and empty of everything but dust and spider webs.

There was a high turnover in chefs, despite the fact that Dumitru paid exorbitant rates to keep them. It happened occasionally that as the chef prepared dinner, a hand would touch him on the back while a sudden ear-splitting whistle sounded just behind him. Claude-Henri, the last one to go, had been chopping vegetables when the ghost startled him. He jerked his arm reflexively and flung the chef's knife up with such force that it stuck in a ceiling beam twelve feet above. Still halfway embedded, no one had bothered to take it down. And Claude-Henri hadn't bothered to finish the meal that day. "*Merde—c'est tout. Je ne reste pas une minute de plus!*" White-faced, sweating, and breathing hard, nostrils flared like a racehorse straining for the finish line, he gathered his belongings and left. He texted Madame Lupei his resignation only after he had reached the safety of his own home.

In the dimly lit, dank stone cellar, a faint foul smell lingered, as of excrement combined with sulfur. Once, when they took Grigori's puppy, Dino, down the cellar stairs, the little dog had cowered and trembled pitifully all over. He had run back up to the door where he whined and scratched furiously to get out.

The fourth-floor bedrooms could have housed the chef, his helper, and all of the servants, but none of them dared to live on the premises. So at night after the servants departed, the family was alone. Constantin tried to puzzle out why his mother managed to remain unbothered by the place. Either she was insensitive to the eerie, oppressive atmosphere, or if she was aware of it, she refused to acknowledge it. He thought it was the latter, really. Her middle name should have been *Denial*.

Talyssa floated and bobbed on the surface of life like a red-and-white plastic fishing cork. Unaffected by tides and storms, she always rode the waves, popping to the surface, and never sunk for long. Unsure about her true feelings for his adopted father, the provider of all their material goods, Constantin was absolutely certain, however, that his mother reveled in the luxury of her privileged life, her social status, the clothes, the homes, and the seemingly endless wealth.

His brother was another matter. Like a barometer, Grigori sensed the atmospheric pressure and rose or fell accordingly. His nights tended to be stormy. A poor sleeper to begin with, he sometimes woke screaming and drenched with sweat from nightmares. He kept his bedside lamp on all night, since, as he explained to his mother, "Dino is scared of the dark." Daytime was better, but he begged off from school often; he had to stay home and comfort the puppy, who had frequent headaches, which only Grigori could detect. "*Dino a encore un terrible mal de tête.*"

One night that August, a week before he left, Constantin had awakened suddenly at 1:30 a.m. with an uneasy feeling. When he got up to check on Grigori, he saw a shaft of light shining into the hall from his brother's door. Grigori usually kept the door shut at night, so Constantin guessed he had gone to relieve himself. But the WC, like Grigori's bedroom, was unoccupied.

Where was he?

At that moment, Constantin's stomach growled, so he headed for the kitchen. Maybe a hungry thirteen-year-old had got there before him. Barefoot, he took extreme care to pad down the two flights of stairs silently, not wishing to wake his mother or Dumitru. He flipped on the light switch in the kitchen. The recessed lights reflected off the metallic surfaces of the refrigerator, the freezer, the stove, and the hanging pots and pans. Constantin circled the island to see if Grigori might be hiding behind it, but no one was there.

With his hunger trumped by growing concern, Constantin ignored his empty stomach and checked each of the first-floor rooms. His search of the billiard room and dining room turned up nothing, but to his relief, he finally found Grigori in the shadowy living room.

Wearing a T-shirt, blue pajama bottoms, and a white cowboy hat, his brother sat cross-legged in front of the fireplace holding out both hands toward the grate. Dino crouched beside him with his head on his paws and a worried expression in his eyes.

After Constantin switched on a lamp, he approached quietly and stood at the boy's left side looking down at him. "Grigori, what are you doing?"

He did not turn to look at Constantin; he showed no expression at all. "I'm keeping warm by the fire."

It was August. The fireplace was dark and cold.

Worse than that was the sound of Grigori's voice—small and high-pitched, like a very young child. Constantin's jaw dropped and a surge of fear washed through him. He leaned down and looked carefully at his brother. Grigori's dark eyes had a fixed and glassy stare. He suddenly realized Grigori was actually asleep—it wasn't the first time he had sleepwalked. But why had he spoken with the voice of a toddler?

"Why are you cold?"

"The room is always cold when they come."

"The library?"

"No, the underground place."

"The cellar?"

"No—way, way underground, where the tunnels are."

Constantin had no idea what he was talking about. "Who are the people that come?"

Grigori shivered and clutched his knees to his chest. "The ones in black robes," he whispered. "Shhhh! Be quiet, or they'll hear us. We need to hide." He squeezed his eyes shut, hid his face, tucked in his shoulders, and curled himself into a human cannonball. "I want to go home. I want to go home." His tiny voice was muffled.

Constantin stared at him in dismay. The boy was obviously immersed in a nightmare. He decided to play along. "I can take you home, Grigori."

He lifted his head. "You can? Do you know the way back through the tunnels?"

"Sure I do. Just take my hand, and I'll lead you home."

"Okay." Grigori held out his left hand to Constantin and like a toddler seeking comfort, sucked his right thumb.

Despite the apprehension he felt at seeing his thirteen-year-old brother assume the persona of a four-year-old, Constantin tried to keep his voice calm and reassuring. "Here we go," he said, taking Grigori's hand in his. Dino followed along.

"Will they catch us?"

"No, they won't. Don't worry, they'll never find us, and we'll be home and safe in bed very soon."

He led his brother up the stairs. "See, we found our way out of the tunnels, and we're almost there. You're going to be all right."

"Are you sure?"

"'Course I am. I'm your big brother, and I'm gonna take care of you. See, here's your bedroom. Now you're safe." Constantin pushed open the door and led Grigori to the bed. Dino jumped up onto it. "Just take off your cowboy hat and hop in."

Grigori laid the hat on the bedside table and climbed into the bed. "Will you stay with me a while, Constantin?"

"As long as you want." Constantin covered him with the duvet and smoothed Grigori's thick dark hair back from his brow. "Now close your eyes and go to sleep." The dog settled in at the foot of the bed.

Constantin waited half an hour, watching while his brother slept. He didn't think Grigori would get up again. He quietly closed the door and returned to his own room, where he tried to make sense of what he had just observed. Was Grigori caught in a nightmare, or had he relived something that had actually occurred? If it was only a bad dream, why had his brother regressed in age? He lay awake the rest of the night, trying to puzzle it out.

The next morning at breakfast, he tried to discuss it with his mother before Grigori appeared. But she laughed it off. "Oh, you know he has nightmares. I'm sure it was only a bad dream. Who knows what caused it. He might have seen a scary movie when he was little, and it just resurfaced. In his sleep, he talked like a four-year-old because the memory is from that time in his life."

Maybe. But maybe not. Constantin had never seen his brother act or talk like a toddler after a nightmare, and he had seen Grigori wake from bad dreams many times. Until last year, they had shared a room.

Dressed impeccably, with flawless makeup, his mother smiled at him. Her dark eyes, so like Grigori's, positively sparkled. She gave him an air kiss as a goodbye. "Going to shop for a leather handbag and shoes to match. Have a wonderful day, darling." She was a tall, willowy brunette, nearly always cheerful and carefree, with the kind of looks men noticed. Today, her thick, chestnut hair was gathered into a French twist to accent her shapely head. Constantin had seen men follow her with their eyes in restaurants, theaters, and public places. He too had always thought his mother beautiful.

Self-absorbed and completely unconcerned, she left without even checking on Grigori, who had yet to come down for breakfast. As Constantin watched her walk away, her beauty seemed to him diminished, brittle, plastic. Like a bright, shiny fishing cork, she floated on the waves. Did she ever give a thought, he wondered, to what lived, what stirred, in the depths below?

CHAPTER 8

ON MONTAGUE STREET

2019

On cloudless mornings, the rays of the rising sun move over the Brooklyn waterfront to bathe the city and its bridges in gold. In those moments, the towers of Manhattan seem to rise out of the water like a perfect mythical city. In that pure light, the city is transformed into what it will be. The spires of burnished gold foreshadow the kingdom yet to come.

Sam came there early on a weekend in May to break her fast. Sitting on a bench with the sun warming her back against the unseasonable cold, she ate an onion bagel slathered with cream cheese, and washed it down with a steaming cup of coffee. Afterward, she stood against the railing and tightened the scarf around her neck, while the breeze ruffled the curls of her dark, wayward hair. As she pondered her future, she gazed at the view she never grew tired of—the East River, New York Harbor, and the Brooklyn Bridge. An older witness, the Queen of the Harbor, held her torch steady and observed the new day as well: the gulls banking in the wind, the traffic on the sparkling water, the stirring of the city. She, too, waited (a bit more patiently) for the time to come.

Joshua's home lay within walking distance on Artman Street, exactly five blocks south and three blocks east. Sam's mind, like the needle of a compass, stayed fixed on his location. The temptation for her feet to follow true north nearly overwhelmed her, but with a stubborn effort of will she resisted. According to her rules of the game, she had made the first move; now it was his turn. If he was interested, he would find her and come to her.

It had been two months since his wonderful concert with the New York Philharmonic, two months since she sent the telegram. So far, she had received no response whatsoever. Of course she had made it difficult for him, but she thought he would have figured it out by now.

"You see, Joshua," she murmured to the East River and the seabirds gliding above it in the wind, "you were supposed to be overcome by an unrelenting curiosity as to the mystery woman's identity. By now, you should have used all your ingenuity and resources to find her." Sam touched her breastbone with one finger. "*Moi, monsieur.* Not the most beautiful or elegant, but surely the most intelligent, witty, and captivating of all the females you have ever known."

Alas, my dear, of Humility, you ain't the epitome. Always helpful, Sam supplied his side of the conversation.

She watched the white clouds gliding toward her, nudged by a brisk west wind. "You should have come upon me unawares at my university or my apartment and showered me with roses, chocolates, or season tickets to the Yankees." She remembered how he came over to her backyard at her invitation that first day. They had tossed a softball back and forth before lunch with Sitti and her mother. To her, he had been more dazzling than the sun.

Underneath her enduring fascination, her secret fears whispered. She couldn't entirely suppress them; they resounded in her head and ricocheted endlessly inside her skull as in an echo chamber: *What if he had figured it out and decided to ignore her? What if he already had a new girlfriend? What if Sam Faris seemed as interesting to him as . . . as that dog turd lying on the edge of the path?*

She released her grip on the railing and turned to go. Almost time for the lunch shift at the restaurant. She sighed. Maybe she would hear from him today. She kicked a crumpled candy wrapper. Maybe she would never hear from him again.

Before its latest incarnation as Beiruti, the restaurant had been called Capulet's on Montague. The name changed, but the floor plan did not. There was a long bar to the left as one entered, with booths lining the wall to the right. The main dining area lay farther in and down two steps, with eight tables and chairs. Beyond that lay the kitchen and storage areas. The sidewalk seating area outside was enclosed by a low iron fence. Each of the six tables had an umbrella affixed to the center.

Sam's lunch station that day was the bar area and the outside. She waited on a small, wiry, freckle-faced man at one of the outdoor tables, a customer, probably mid-thirties, she had seen before, but never served. He patted down his light-brown, kinky hair in a vain attempt to smooth it, but it sprang up again as soon as he removed his hand. The chilly breeze off the water swept right down Montague Street to the restaurant. The umbrella fringes flapped and the red geraniums in the containers just outside the fence danced in the wind. When she brought him a menu, he told her he was waiting for a friend. He asked for a cup of coffee to warm him up, and two glasses of water in his nasal, heavily accented New York voice. He wore a blue blazer over a white oxford shirt, jeans, and brown loafers. He cocked his head to the side as he glanced at her. "You look so familiar—haven't we met before?"

A pickup line, for sure. She mentally rolled her eyes, but kept a straight face. "You might have seen me working here at the restaurant, but other than that, uh, no, I don't think so."

"Hmm," he said, "I coulda sworn I'd seen you somewhere before."

Nice try, buddy, but you're too old for me. She noticed the gold band he wore. *And married.* Sam took drink orders from two young couples at another table in the *al fresco* section and walked inside to the bar to fill them. She went to get the drinks for both tables and an extra menu.

Like the other servers, she dressed in all black: slacks, long-sleeved button-up shirt, and non-slip shoes. Edward Boutros, the owner, had high standards for his waitstaff. He required them to memorize the menu and the daily specials and to memorize the orders. At peak times, it was quite a mental feat to do it perfectly.

When the friend arrived, about ten minutes later, he seemed out of breath, as if he had run to the restaurant. He had a medium build and a sophisticated look. He wore a gray blazer with black lapels over a white shirt and sharply pressed black slacks. His gray wool fedora was tilted so far forward it practically touched the top of his black sunglasses. He kept his face half buried in an expensive black scarf (cashmere?) to protect him from the wind, but above it she could see an auburn mustache and curling beard. Freckle Face leaned forward and spoke to him quietly and intently. Keeping an elbow on the table, the new guy nodded and stroked his mustache with thumb and forefinger. He never even glanced at her when Sam came up to the table. She set the water glasses down and laid the other menu on the table.

"It just struck me like lightni—" Freckle Face stopped speaking abruptly in her presence.

"I'll give you some time to look at the menu," she said. As soon as she was out of earshot, he leaned forward and resumed his rapid-fire chatter.

Sam took the orders of diners in the bar area before she returned to the table with the two male diners again. As she approached, Freckle Face glanced at her, then leaned over and whispered something to his friend. Sam had the distinct impression Freckle Face had made a joke at her expense. Suddenly self-conscious, she felt her cheeks flush. The friend, still stroking his mustache, kept his eyes on her until she reached the table, making her even more uncomfortable. At least she thought he did, but he still wore his sunglasses, so it was hard to tell.

She asked them if they would like anything from the bar or appetizers. Freckle Face asked her what appetizers she recommended. "The stuffed grape leaves with yoghurt and cucumber salad are excellent—almost as good as my grandma used to make."

"Oh, was your grandma Middle Eastern?"

"She was Lebanese."

His friend spoke. "Ze word *sitti* means *grand-mère* in Arabic, *n'est-ce pas?*"

Sam smiled at his accent. "Yes." Her curiosity piqued, she asked, "How did you know that?"

"Ah, zere are zo many Lebanese people à Paris."

Pa-ree. Sam smiled. "I see."

"We'll take the stuffed grape leaves," said Freckle Face. "What beers do you have?"

Sam rattled off the list for them. Heineken for Freckle Face and Stella Artois, naturally, for Frenchie. Before she left the table, they ordered the main course, as well. Lamb kebab for Freckle Face and chicken shawarma for Frenchie, tabouleh for both.

She turned in the order to the kitchen and picked up the draft beers at the bar. There actually *was* something familiar about Freckle Face. Could she have met him before? Maybe he hadn't been flirting. But where could they have met?

As she delivered food to other tables, she kept an eye on them. She guessed they were both mid-thirties, although it was hard to tell anything about Frenchie; all she could see was his hat above the sunglasses and his mustache and beard below, when his hand wasn't in the way. Unlike many diners who ignored their companions to fix their devoted attention and withering brains on the six-inch screens of mobile phones, the two men kept up a lively conversation. They radiated an excited air, as if they discussed some intriguing project. After they demolished the grape leaves, she brought their tabouleh and refilled their beers. When she brought the entrées, she asked them if they needed anything else.

"Where are you from?" asked Frenchie. "Your accent—you do not come from New York."

They barely glanced at the food; they seemed more interested in her than their lunch.

"No, I'm not from New York."

Freckle Face smiled at his friend. "Correct. I got a feelin' she's from the city of New Orleans. Is that right?"

"Yes." She was unimpressed—anyone familiar with New Orleans could recognize the accent.

"And you have a drop-dead gorgeous cousin named Lucy."

Sam's jaw dropped. "How do you know that?"

"Mademoiselle." Frenchie took off his sunglasses and removed his hat. His auburn, curly hair framed a very familiar face. His two laughing hazel eyes gazed at her. "Did you not live next door to a crazy pianist from New York named—"

"Joshua!" Sam could hardly believe it. "You rascal! You fooled me. I could hardly see your face—the accent and the beard! You never had a beard before—I didn't recognize you."

His grin was as wide as the East River. He stood up and held out his arms. "Samantha Faris, it's been a long, long time."

He drew her in and held her so close she could hear the rapid beating of his heart. "You're all grown up now. But since when do you communicate with telegrams?"

She grinned. "Well, now that I'm more mature, I gave up fishing poles and dangling notecards. I first considered the Pony Express, but I figured a telegram would suffice to get your attention. My mode of communication is only a half-century behind the times. By the way, when did you start smoking again? I thought I gave you the solution a long time ago."

Nathan interrupted. "Hey, don't forget about me—Nathan Weiss." He stood up and held out his hand. Joshua released her, and Sam shook his hand. "You may not know it, Sam, but I predicted you'd be as beautiful as Lucy, and boy, was I right!"

"Well, that's hyperbole if ever I heard it." Sam grinned, pleased, but doubtful it could be true. "And now I remember where we met. You came to Joshua's dinner party at Creole Louie's, after the hurricane and after Sitti died. You're his agent." She felt her face go pink from embarrassment. "Sorry I brushed you off, Nathan, I . . . uh, thought you—"

"No problem. Sad to say, but I'm an old married man now with two kids. I don't pick up girls anymore. But tell me, what was the solution to smoking? He needs it again."

She laughed. "I showered him with peppermints—the circular, cellophane-wrapped ones."

"Yeah, she threw them down from the tree and pelted me on the head."

"But, Joshua, how did you find me?"

"I realized pretty quickly that you were the one who sent the telegram. I did some research online, and found out you got a scholarship to The King's College. So I knew you were in the city, but that didn't lead me to you."

"What did?"

"Not *what*, but *who*." He gestured at Nathan.

Nathan took up the thread. "See, I knew Joshua was searching for you, Sam, and I wanted to help him, but I didn't really know how. I hadn't seen you since you were twelve years old, but I remembered Lucy vividly: the wavy black hair, the beautiful olive skin and classic high cheekbones." He laughed. "When I met her, my hopes soared, but they got shot down immediately when she mentioned her boyfriend. Anyway, as you know, I like this restaurant, and I noticed the same features in you, but it didn't connect until today."

"Why today?"

"Because it's the first time you waited on me. When I heard New Orleans in your speech, the light bulb came on. I told Joshua to get over here fast, because I thought I might have found you."

"I ran five blocks to get here."

"Which is why you were huffing and puffing when I came to the table."

"That, and too many cigarettes."

Sam pulled a peppermint out of her pocket and handed it to him. "Here we go again, Stubborn."

Joshua smiled. "I hope so. Listen, Sam, I know you're working now, but I want to hear all about what you're doing in New York, and all the news from New Orleans. Maybe we can get together later today after your shift and talk? When do you finish?"

"At four."

"Tell you what, I'll come back then, and we can take a stroll on the Promenade."

Sam floated through the rest of the afternoon. Her mind echoed with Mendelssohn's four quiet chords, timeless and perfect. Under her breath, she hummed the lovers' theme and smiled. At long last, with a little nudge from her, her prince had come.

What would be, would be.

CHAPTER 9

THE HUNT

2026

Gideon counted seven egrets flying just ahead of the boat, an aerial escort. Below them, their white reflections skated over the sheet of unbroken, blue-gray water. The slow, graceful movement of their wings, the smell of the water, the touch of the evening breeze calmed him. Even in the company of Jack and Reilly, Caddo Lake remained a reservoir of peace. Gideon guessed this serene, scenic ride would be the best part of the evening. No one spoke for fifteen minutes as Reilly steered the jon boat past Thatch Island to the north shore. Eventually, he turned the boat into a narrow inlet, cut the motor, and let it glide the rest of the way. He tied it to a rickety, abandoned pier, and the three men climbed out.

"This must be private property," said Gideon, adjusting his backpack. "There's a No Trespassing sign." He had no idea where they were, and he half wondered if the whole expedition was really an elaborate prank they had planned, revenge for beating them at eight ball.

"It *is* private property. It belongs to my uncle," replied Reilly. "We do a lot of hunting out here. C'mon."

Despite the heat, they all wore hats, long-sleeved shirts, jeans, and hiking boots. Jack and Reilly dressed in camouflage and carried shotguns. Feeling a little ridiculous, Gideon shouldered his backpack and carried his Henry lever-action .30-30 rifle.

"This is the general area where it was spotted around dusk," said Reilly, keeping his voice low. "Two guys were out here sittin' in their boat fishin' next to the old pier. They noticed movement at the edge of the water, and then they saw a hairy creature climb out of the water onto the shore. It disappeared in the woods, walking on two legs."

"I'll believe it when I see it," Gideon replied.

"Man, have some faith—there've been tons of Bigfoot sightings around Caddo Lake through the years," Jack reassured him.

"Maybe those guys were drunk and saw a black bear," suggested Gideon. "There are some around here. And besides, it's kind of hard to walk there." He pointed toward the trees. The woods were thick with briars, vines, and underbrush. "We might need a machete."

"To cut out your tongue, Marine."

"Slashing his throat would be better."

"No, we don't. There are some animal paths that lead through the brush," Reilly said. "Now shut your trap and follow me."

Jack followed Reilly on the narrow path, and Gideon brought up the rear. They ducked under thick vines, while briars pulled at their clothes and impeded their progress.

"Got to be some IEDs here."

"Go ahead—step on one."

Damn them. Gideon broke out into a clammy sweat. It was déjà vu—being on patrol in enemy territory. By the time they got to a pipeline clearing ten minutes later, his shirt was soaked.

"Right here's a good lookout spot," said Jack. "Be quiet and keep your eyes peeled." Staying concealed in the brush, they sat near the clearing's edges and waited, each man a little apart keeping watch in a different direction.

Birdsong, buzzing cicadas, and the occasional distant purring of a boat motor were the only sounds. Still, the quiet and peace didn't ease Gideon's rapid heartbeat and his heightened tension, taut as a tripwire. Worst of all, the memories flooded his mind, especially a scene he could never forget. One morning he and his buddy Myers had been kneeling on the sand, getting their gear ready for the start of an operation. A Humvee drove up and parked about a hundred feet away. Gideon smiled and nudged Myers. "Hey, look it's Guthrie." Colonel Guthrie liked to be present with his men in the field at the start of an operation. "Very cool," said Myers. It lifted everyone's morale to see him. The officer stepped out of the vehicle, directly onto a pressure plate. BOOM! The sound of the explosion deafened them.

They instinctively ducked and threw up their arms to protect their heads. Half a second later, Gideon looked up. Beside the wrecked vehicle, a pink mist hung in the air—Guthrie. It was Gideon's first experience with death, and he could never unsee it. It shattered his boyish delusions of war as a great adventure. The pink mist stayed with him, seared on his memory.

His heart hammered. His palms ran sweat. PTSD. Familiar and exhausting. His arms felt limp and leaden. At least he was separated from the others—he didn't want anyone to see him this way. After a while, the heat did its work; his eyelids drooped with drowsiness and he dozed a little.

He awoke with a start, disoriented. It took a moment to remember where he was. He located Jack and Reilly half-hidden in the brush, both of them a few feet away on his left. There was no sign of Bigfoot—this whole trip was a joke.

He let his thoughts ramble, and soon they found the well-trodden path. Where had Edie gone? Instead of a glorious homecoming after his tour of duty in Afghanistan, Gideon was greeted by an empty apartment stripped of rugs, furniture, even appliances. The only music was the buzz of a wasp underscored by the rhythmic drip of the kitchen faucet. Edie's note, taped to the bathroom mirror, told him how she had grown apart from him during his absence. She no longer loved him. And he shouldn't bother to search for her—he'd never find her.

When he questioned the neighbors, only one person told him anything of importance. Edie had been pregnant at the time she moved out. "She was showing. I'm guessing six months along," the woman told him.

A baby. Why hadn't she written to tell him?

The divorce papers arrived soon after, citing irreconcilable differences. Really? He thought their marriage was happy. But the fact remained—she had never replied to his letters. At least *he* had been happy—he loved her. But without a harsh word between them, she had simply disappeared. Of course, her father, the hard-nosed Marine officer, knew exactly where she was, but he stonewalled Gideon.

Betrayed and bewildered, he searched for months to no avail. The private detective he hired quit after three weeks. "Look, man, there are some powerful people who don't want your ex-wife to be found. They've burgled my house and threatened my life. The bastards killed my dog. You're paying good money, but it's just not worth it for me. Sad as it is, I'd advise you to give up the search and stay in the land of the living." He ran a hand through his hair. "In fact, if I were you, I'd think about going off-grid or changing my identity. These guys play hardball, and they've got infinite resources. There's so many ways to kill a man."

Ain't that the truth. Gideon knew all about killing.

Maybe Edie and the baby had assumed new identities; maybe her father had moved them out of the country to Costa Rica or Portugal, Scotland or South Africa. The big, broad world contained so many places where they could start a new life without him. It burned him that Edie took the coward's way out and never spoke to him directly. Except for her one handwritten note, all messages and correspondence came through her attorney. He smiled grimly—what a deluded fool he had been—before he left for his tour of duty, he thought she loved him as much as he loved her.

"No one loves you, loser."

"You shoulda died in the desert."

Yeah, I know. But I sure as hell don't want to die at the hands of the general or his hired assassins. Nor do I want to run scared.

And what of the child, his heir? He wouldn't recognize his son if he passed him in the street or sat across the room from him in a restaurant. Maybe he had a daughter. He wouldn't even know if she died—drowned or killed in a car accident, bitten by a venomous snake. If Edie remarried, did the new husband treat her child well? Questions without answers. It was as if they had dematerialized and been transported to the farthest reaches of the universe. Vanished.

A sudden hard jab in the ribs interrupted Gideon's thoughts. Reilly pointed to the left and put a finger to his lips to signal silence. His eyes, wide and glittering as brass cymbals, projected excitement and fear. In the fading light, Gideon struggled to see anything at all. But then motion caught his eye. A large, burly figure (*Hunter? Bear?*) crossed the pipeline clearing on a diagonal. It moved swiftly toward them from the far side.

Surely not. It can't be. They must have staged this.

The hairy, hulking figure, its color impossible to distinguish in the dim light, looked tall and immensely strong. And then on the evening breeze, they caught its putrid scent. Gideon grimaced. He felt the gut-churning fear of combat and gripped his rifle. The drifting stench unmanned Jack Dunham. He screamed and tore off through the bush in panic. Either he was a great actor, or he was scared shitless.

"Sonofabitch!" spat Reilly, and ran after him. His short, bulky form disappeared into the brush.

Gideon held his ground and looked back at the creature. Hearing the noise and the men's voices, it halted for an instant and then charged into the woods where Gideon lost sight of it. It fled into the trees about twenty-five meters from his hiding place. *Check 5 meters, then 25 meters.* His training kicked in. He remained still, gripping his rifle and listening to the dwindling sounds of Jack and Reilly's headlong flight through the bush.

After a few minutes, the only sound he heard was the moaning of the wind in the trees. He stood up, clicked off the safety of his .30-30, and eased his way into the clearing, hugging the tree line on his left. He moved as quietly as possible to the place where the animal had entered the woods. He scanned for tracks, but the ground was hard and dry, covered with pine needles and oak leaves. Holding the rifle against his shoulder, finger on the trigger, he peered into the darkening forest. He sniffed the breeze to catch any scent. Nothing—no sound or movement.

His Marine training had included tracking—of humans—but Gideon decided against following the creature into the woods. The sun had set, and he had only a few minutes until full darkness descended. He needed NVGs, night vision goggles, to do a proper job. Muscles tense, he quietly retraced his route to the animal trail where he and his fair-weather friends had parted company. Although a waxing gibbous moon rose low on the horizon, it wouldn't do him much good at the moment. He took out his flashlight and shined it on the path through the woods, hoping Jack and Reilly were waiting for him at the pier. He battled his way through the briars, making plenty of noise to scare away Bigfoot (or the man in the monkey suit) and any snakes out hunting in the darkness.

When he finally found the shore, the dilapidated pier was deserted. His "friends" had taken the boat and abandoned him. He took out his mobile phone. In its cold, puny light he read the words No Service. *Great.* It didn't surprise him—the signal reception on the lake was spotty at best. He would have to spend the night where he was.

Of course, he had spent hundreds of nights camped out on the sands of Iraq and Afghanistan in one Forward Operating Base or another. But tonight he had no tent. Didn't matter—he would make do. He set his backpack down and rummaged in it. Beneath the bottled water, energy bars, and apple he had packed, he found what he hoped for, a lighter left over from his former smoking days. For the next half hour, he gathered wood.

He got a small fire going and gradually fed it larger sticks and branches. He kept the .30-30 beside him, just in case. While he ate his meager supper by firelight, he thought about Bigfoot. Was it real—an unknown species of ape—or just a hoax perpetrated by people hungry for notoriety? Of course, the one possibility didn't exclude the other. He'd also read a theory that Bigfoot was a demonic entity, entering and leaving the earthly realm through portals. That explained the absence of dead Bigfoots. Incorporeal beings were incorporeal. While they manifested, they could seem as real as—

A sudden rustling near the water interrupted his thoughts. His flashlight illuminated two pairs of ghostly green eyes, low to the ground. Gideon laughed in relief—raccoons.

Maybe he could go after the creature in the morning. He had a talent for tracking, as he had shown on one long night in Afghanistan. The route from Camp Leatherneck to Camp Dwyer was a sixteen-hour journey at the best of times. They had been driving all day, but in early evening the traffic halted. The EOD had the long route blocked, and night was falling. The Marines decided to take a shorter, but highly dangerous route, a.k.a. IED Alley.

It was Gideon's job to clear the route, and he would have to do it at night, in violation of SOP. He got his equipment out. *This is the night I die.* He shrugged. If he got blown to shreds, it would be him, not his men.

The convoy followed him at a distance of 100 meters, out of the kill radius, as he went before them on foot with his metal detector. Wearing NVGs, he swept the road, back and forth. Very soon, he noticed the footprints: delicate, faint marks in the sand. He placed his own boots precisely on each imprint, never deviating.

The men behind him grew curious at his slow, careful progress, the way he carefully placed his feet, as if he followed something. They radioed him. "What do you see, man?"

"There's a trail of footprints."

"What? There ain't nothin' there but sand. No marks at all." Another man laughed. "He's puttin' us on, the bullshitter."

The metal detector gave out an audible tone. Everyone froze in place. As Gideon moved the detector slowly to his right, the volume increased. At the loudest tone, he stopped and then moved it ninety degrees in the other direction to help pinpoint the exact location. Satisfied he had it, he laid the metal detector behind him and took out his probe. When he found resistance, he dug, feathering away very thin layers of sand at a time until he uncovered the IED. He disarmed it. And the next one. And the next, and on and on.

He couldn't even remember how many he disarmed. Alone, ahead of the convoy in darkness, his fierce focus and tension took him out of normality into an otherworldly, almost hallucinatory experience. Under a full-starred sky, he danced with death, where any false step could be his last.

He worked more than eight hours, all through the night into the next morning.

Gideon watched the fire for a long time, immersed in memories. Fire was ancient and always new—elemental and fascinating. But what remained when fire burned itself out? Only ashes. Just like him inside. *Why hadn't he died that night? Why hadn't he died?*

The flames moved like wings, like a bird or an angel of fire. *O holy angels, comfort me. Take away my grief. Like the phoenix, let me rise again from the ashes.*

The fire burned lower, and at length his eyes grew heavy and drooped. He lay on a makeshift pallet of pine needles and rested his head on the backpack. He spent a tense, uncomfortable night near the fire with his rifle for company. Toward morning, he dozed off.

CHAPTER 10

REVELATION

2026

As he boarded the Air France flight from Geneva to New York, Constantin's inner tension was coiled tight and hard as a gun spring. He couldn't leave Switzerland fast enough. He wished a rifle could have fired him, like a supersonic bullet, directly to New York. But no, he had to endure a thirteen-hour journey with a stop in Paris. His only regret was to leave his mother and Grigori behind. He sat down in first class, pushed his backpack with its stolen treasure under the seat in front of him, and leaned back with a noisy sigh that turned heads his way.

During the long leg of the flight, from Paris to New York, Constantin hoped to sleep, to melt into oblivion for a few hours, but when he closed his eyes, he saw the navy-blue diary with its packet of letters. Too keyed up to sleep, he dug it out, thumbed through it at random, and settled on this passage:

> *At sea, far from land, especially on winter nights, one can see the stars so clearly. Watching them, I think of the fallen ones and their stargates. They have revealed to us the location of many of these hidden portals, some remote, some surprisingly close to civilization. Some call them wormholes or Einstein-Rosen Bridges.*

They are passages that in effect fold space together to connect distant points in the space-time continuum. Stargates (my preferred word) are believed to be theoretical. I know they are not; they are as real as the blood covenant—the scar delved in the palm of my left hand.

They are doorways for the Nine.

They are changing the world, but few realize it, and to what degree. The technology they have provided the military and scientific communities in the areas of weaponry, communications, and transport is revolutionary. Much of it has yet to be revealed to the populace at large. If it were, the common man would perceive it as magic.

Dumitru spent a lot of time on his yacht, Constantin knew. He also spent a lot of time thinking about the Nine, whom he had apparently encountered face to face. Were these writings just fantasy—fallen angels manifesting through portals, influencing men and events in the world? Everyone recognized the accelerated tempo of technological changes in computers and weaponry. Artificial Intelligence alone had advanced exponentially, to the point where some thought it could pose a danger to humanity, and the development of bioweapons was underway across the globe. Were the Nine the catalysts for it all? If so, the fallen ones seemed to be guiding the world—toward what?

He flipped a few pages and saw his mother's name.

In October of 2011, Talyssa conceived the heir to our two bloodlines. This of course was her function and the purpose of our marriage. To thank RH for his help, I invited him to spend two weeks with me on my yacht. No doubt he will accept. He is consumed with ambition and craves the company and contacts I provide, particularly the young, attractive females onboard, most of them not yet out of adolescence. Like caviar and champagne, my yacht is stocked with them.

The hidden cameras will record it all. Like so many other politicians and military leaders, he will be in my control ever after, the arrogant fool.

Constantin blew a noisy breath out through his mouth. *How repulsive—a mirror of the man who wrote it.*

His collar grew hot with anger. Was his mother some kind of breeder cow? The cold-hearted bastard regarded his marriage as though it were just another business transaction. What did that make poor Grigori, his sensitive, frightened brother? Was he to carry on the perversions of his bloodline? Dumitru was no loving father; he was a heartless, self-centered egotist who regarded other people as objects and used them for his own ends—including RH, whoever he was.

Constantin's stomach roiled in a mixture of anger and fear. Grigori was not safe around Dumitru. He recalled the episode when his little brother spoke like a toddler and described a scene in an underground place with black-robed men. Maybe Dumitru had already traumatized the boy in some kind of satanic ritual. He had no qualms about defiling other children—the conscienceless, puke-worthy pervert gloated about the young girls he used for pleasure.

Furious and confused, Constantin shut the diary and dropped his head into his hands. The existence of such evil struck him hard. He was only fifteen, self-absorbed as most adolescents, but this shook him out of himself. He didn't want to believe the scope and ugliness of such evil, and yet it seemed he must. This came from Dumitru. He couldn't just brush it off as the breathless, wacko delusions of conspiracy theorists.

Whatever the case, he longed to protect Grigori, to steal him away, but he knew he was powerless to do so. He shivered in disgust.

Forget about sleep. Grigori and his mother were alone now, subject to the whims of that creepy Romanian bastard, a five-foot-five embodiment of evil. There was nothing Constantin could do to help; he wouldn't even return to Switzerland until the Christmas break. Hopefully, Dumitru would stay away, taken up with his yacht-girls and business interests. Constantin's mind and emotions churned as he sat wide-eyed and troubled through the rest of the flight.

Tony picked him up at JFK and helped him load his bags in the car. "Welcome back to New York, kid—the best city in the world."

Constantin kept his voice light, not ready to share his anxieties with anyone. "It sure is." And he, a citizen of Europe and America, had had more room for comparison. The only other city Tony had visited was East Orange, New Jersey, to see his daughter and grandson. "Since it's Saturday, I told my mom to make sure the flight landed after opera time. Was it a good one today?"

Tony stuck out his lower lip, pulled down the corners of his mouth and shook his head in disgust, as if he had just taken a bite of moldy bread. "Nah—it was just weird. It wasn't live and it wasn't the Met neither. Some outfit outta Chicago, the Lyric Opera, I think. They did *The Turn of the Screw*."

"Never heard of it—oh, wait! Yes, I have, there's a short novel called *The Turn of the Screw* by Henry James. It's a ghost story about a governess and two young children at a manor house in England."

"Well, I can tell you the title fit. Inside of ten minutes, I definitely knew I was screwed. I shut it off."

As Tony turned northward onto the Long Island Expressway in the growing dusk, Constantin thought about *The Turn of the Screw*. The eerie atmosphere and events of the story reminded him of the Swiss chateau. Henry James's ambiguous story ended with the death of Miles, the young boy. He groaned internally, thinking of Grigori. Much had been made of Henry James's nineteenth-century tale, but Constantin's worries revolved around a living, breathing, very frightened thirteen-year-old boy.

In the pre-Switzerland days, from the earliest time he could remember, the family had lived in the Upper East Side brownstone on Ninety-First St. Even then, Dumitru's business interests kept him away most of the time. But when Constantin was eight, and Grigori had turned six, Dumitru moved the family to the chateau near Lac Léman. Dumitru also decided that Constantin should be educated in the States. As always, once Talyssa's husband decided on a course of action, she quietly acquiesced. She never stood up to him. So, with his parents in agreement, Constantin had returned to the private school in New York City. Grigori went to school in Switzerland. (Grigori always cried when he left; his mother never shed a tear.) For most of each fall and spring, he lived apart from his family in the brownstone, returning to Switzerland for the Christmas holiday and the summer breaks.

In New York, Constantin had the whole third floor to himself, while the servants, Tony and Stella Amore, a married couple native to the city, lived in the apartment on the fourth floor. Although Dumitru called them servants, to Constantin they were family. Tony drove him to school every day in the BMW, did small maintenance jobs, handled the house finances, and took care of Constantin's clothes like a valet. Stella cooked and cleaned. They spoke Italian with each other, but English to him in their heavy New York accents, compliments of their origins in Queens.

Blue-eyed, sandy-haired Tony was a man of average height who somehow managed to remain slender despite the daily diet of delicious pasta Stella served up. A hot-blooded Italian, his passions ran high for baseball, the horses, and opera. He kept statistics on every Yankee game and was a favored son of Off-Track Betting: he lost money on the horses regularly.

"I already laid bets on the Apocalypse," Tony confided once.

"With OTB?" Constantin asked.

"Nah, my bookie in Astoria. See, the Four Horsemen are gonna appear someday. Stella and her sister been yakkin' about it for years. The only question is when. I'm bettin' on 2027." He grinned. "I might as well be rollin' in dough when we head into the Tribulation."

Tony kept his schedule clear for three hours every Saturday afternoon so he could listen to the Metropolitan Opera's live radio broadcast. He adored the music of his countrymen: Verdi, Donizetti, Puccini, Rossini, and Bellini. He turned up the sound so loud in his apartment, the brass section could have parted his hair—it was like sitting in the third row of the opera house. Constantin had once heard the mighty hammer strokes of the Anvil Chorus all the way down on the first floor.

Once, when the Met scheduled Richard Wagner's epic Ring cycle—four operas on four consecutive Saturdays—it provoked Tony's wrath. To him, the composer was a Nazi poster boy, an anti-Semitic proponent of German superiority. Tony stomped around the house and fumed. He fumed best in Italian. "*Ancora Wagner, che rottura di coglioni! Un cazzo di musica di merda!*" He punctuated his outburst with a classic gesture.

Stella ignored him and pretended not to understand. She bent over a pot on the stove and stirred, but the color of her cheeks suddenly matched her tomato sauce.

Constantin grinned and listened intently, grateful for the Italian lessons. Soon a consummate swearer with a vast, colorful vocabulary, he could have held his own on the streets of Rome.

Stella Amore was a short, round-faced brunette, all curves, with a motherly, comforting manner and an infectious laugh. Once, when a neighbor, a young music student, asked her to take care of his cat while he was away for a week, she did. Upon the student's return to his small apartment, he found the cat in good spirits, a gleaming, spotless kitchen, and a pan of Stella's homemade lasagna in the freezer. That's the kind of woman Tony married.

Her diet of game shows, pasta, and homemade desserts (tiramisu, cannoli, gelato, or baba al rum), contributed to her pleasing plumpness and her mastery of odd facts. "Tony, did you know Babe Ruth kept cool by putting a cabbage leaf under his cap? He changed it every two innings." Tony rolled his eyes.

"Constantin, guess who invented scissors."

"Hmm. Cleopatra, probably."

"Close," she replied, always supportive. "It was Leonardo da Vinci."

True to her name, Stella Amore was a shining presence in his life—a star of love. Constantin felt more at home with her than with his own mother. Stella treated him like her own child; she gave him the warmth and affection he so needed. When he was younger and afraid of the dark, she read him stories at bedtime, tucked him in, and stayed until he fell asleep. She knew about night terrors; she had raised a daughter of her own, who had married and moved to New Jersey. A cheerful, sunny presence, Stella kept the house spotless and tended her indoor gardens, the array of ferns, ivy, ficus trees, and hanging baskets that warmed the house and brought the outside in.

That night, once Constantin and Tony were back from the airport, the three of them ate dinner together at the long, polished mahogany dining table on the first floor. The Amores ate with him at his request, as long as his mother and Dumitru were absent. To his parents, they were only servants, meant to serve the meal and disappear.

After dinner, he chatted with Stella as he helped her clear the table. Then he dashed up to his room and dug the diary out of his backpack, eager to read more and examine the letters without fear of discovery. He sat in the armchair next to the window, a favorite place at dusk. From there he often watched the lights of the city begin to shine, dispelling the darkness. But this night his mind was solely on what he might read next.

He leafed through the pages of the diary slowly, skimming the first lines of each page. When he found an entry beginning with the words

Ma femme, he had an energy surge equivalent to the consumption of two espressos with a half dozen macaróns. Wide awake, with a thumping pulse, he read:

> *My wife is like my top hat and tails. I take her out only on state occasions, a necessary prop. Most of the time, we live apart, quite amicably. I supply all her needs and more. Ours was an arranged marriage. In our circles, matchmaking is never about love; it is always about the bloodlines. Her real function is to supply my need: a son and heir.*

You're a cold-hearted bastard, Dumitru. "Your wife is a 'necessary prop.' *'Her real function is to supply my need . . .'* The more I learn about you, the more loathsome you become," Constantin murmured.

He closed the diary and unclipped the packet of letters, three in total, all addressed to Dumitru at the chateau. The return address (no name) for the first two was Washington, DC, but the third letter was postmarked Dallas, Texas. He carefully opened the first. It was written in an angular, slashing hand that heavily indented the thin paper, tearing it in spots.

04 JUL 2009
To DL:

> *Successfully recruited most of the top brass. Many in the DOD, Congressmen in both parties, key Cabinet officials, and two Supreme Court justices are in—convinced and confident of the direction we want to move the country. The money is fantastic—a great incentive. Some have purchased homes in countries without extradition, just in case.*

> *Just promoted to Major General—moving up the ranks of power quickly now. Awaiting further assignments from the Nine. Let me know.*

> *~RH*

"RH from Washington, DC." Constantin tapped the letter with one finger. *Who are you?* Was this part of the long-term plan Dumitru wrote about? *We will infiltrate their government, their military, their courts little by little.* Constantin shook his head in disbelief.

He opened the next letter.

27 MAY 2010
To DL:

It was a shock to me, as well, when she eloped with her Marine private. Now, at 18, she is pregnant. I know you are quite disappointed, but do not worry. Yes, I fully understand your concerns and purpose about the bloodlines. The plan will proceed—we will not be thwarted—she will abort this baby and she will marry you.

To answer your question, yes, it is an easy matter to dispose of the Marine. I have pulled strings—the peasant is assigned to the most dangerous missions in Afghanistan. I have also intercepted their letters to each other and monitored her phone calls. She is almost completely isolated. She has never cooked or cleaned for herself; she is not used to living in a drab apartment complex with only the television for company. She calls me twice a week—she is quite despondent and confused about his silence.

In the meantime, I continue to sing your praises: the wealthy, eager husband-to-be who is the friend of princes, billionaires, and the European aristocracy. I remind her of your properties in four countries, your love for her, (naturally in that order), and the privileged life she will lead as your wife. After a few more weeks of this conditioning, she will break. I know my daughter—I guarantee it.

~RH

The blood drained from Constantin's head so rapidly it made him dizzy. *RH—Richard Huffman. Grand-père, an agent of the Nine? Had he also been compromised by Dumitru's yacht cameras?* Constantin's face flushed with anger. *Grand-père* and Dumitru had conspired to break up his mother's marriage, and *Grand-père* had pressured her to abort the baby—him, Constantin. His mother had been *five months pregnant* in May of 2010.

But what a revelation. His parents must have had a good and loving marriage. Why else would she have become so confused and depressed by her husband's silence? The letter crackled when he slapped it against his thigh. *What kind of man destroys his daughter's marriage and schemes to murder his own grandchild?*

He slid the single sheet of paper back into its envelope. The question was: Who was more vile—his stepfather or his grandfather? With a sinking feeling in his stomach, Constantin opened the third letter, from an address in Dallas.

04 DEC 2010
To DL:

I feel relieved they are with you and out of the country now with new names, new citizenship. Consider waiting a year or two before you return to the house in New York. I don't antici-pate any trouble, but one can never be too careful.

We hoped the child's father, the peasant, would die in Afghanistan. How ironic that in the end, his death did not matter, because her will to resist us collapsed. She agreed to the no-fault divorce with hardly a murmur, so her intense fight to keep the child came as a real surprise to me, also. Wise of you to allow her that one concession. But she is well aware that if she violates any of the conditions of the marital agreement, she will lose all financial support as well as custody of any children born of your union.

In the meantime, I have obtained and destroyed all arti-facts of the previous marriage: photographs, the marriage certificate, the child's birth certificate, any documents relating to the former husband, and all memorabilia. Covering our tracks.

~RH

Constantin had been just over two months old when his grandfather wrote the letter. Stomach churning, he laid his head back against the chair, blind and deaf to the world, while his mind and emotions worked on two levels. *The peasant*—how condescending and arrogant they were. They had denigrated his father and deceived and manipulated his mother. Disappointed and overwhelmed, she had given in to them, but she had refused to give up her child.

Leaning on his desk, Constantin dropped his head into his hands, feeling regret and shame and sadness: he had completely misjudged his mother. *Talyssa had loved his father, Gunnar. She had also loved and fought for him, Constantin, her firstborn son.* He suddenly saw her in an entirely different light. She had suffered much, and yet she carried on with courage. No wonder she found it painful to talk about the past.

And what of his father? Had he died in Afghanistan? He reread that part: '*We hoped the child's father, the peasant, would die in Afghanistan. How ironic that in the end, his death did not matter, because her will to resist us collapsed.*'

His grandfather had sent Gunnar to his death. A major general, he had had the power to do it. His mother and grandfather had always told him his father was dead. But they had lied about so much. Was he to believe the testimony of his mother, who had been so clearly compromised? And *Grand-père* and Dumitru? Vipers inspired more trust.

The merest glimmer of hope rose in his heart, appearing intermittently and shining faintly, like a star glimpsed now and again through a moving cover of broken clouds. Could it possibly be . . . was it possible . . .

He slammed his fist against the arm of the chair and clenched his teeth. He wanted proof—proof that his father had died. And he intended to find it.

CHAPTER 11

SHADOW MAN

2026

It was still dark when he woke. *Blood, fire, and water.* The knowing lay heavy on him, and the dread of it was even worse. Jaybird rubbed sleep out of his eyes, then rose and slowly dressed for the day. He had eaten squirrel stew for two nights running, and the smell of it still hung in the cabin. He opened the front door to let in some fresh air. He heard the shrill, descending scream of a bluejay against the faint lapping of water. It cheered him up and he smiled. With a sharp whistle, Jaybird imitated his namesake's call, followed by its other characteristic song, a gentler, more musical *toolili, toolili, toolili.* A mockingbird chimed in. To amuse himself, Jaybird imitated the bird: *krrDEE, krrDEE, krrDEE—jeurrdi, jeurrdi, jeurrdi.*

He made a pot of coffee and filled his thermos. Afterward, he grabbed his fishing gear and tackle box. By the time he loaded everything into the jon boat, the sun had risen. Jaybird untied the boat from the short pier, started the motor, and headed north on a lake turned to shimmering gold by the eastern light. He smiled. Well, whatever else happened, he was a lucky man. Right here at his doorstep lay glory.

He headed for the cut where, long ago, a tin-roofed, wooden fishing shack had stood. The shack had disintegrated over the years, a victim of time and the elements, but the old fishing pier, at least most of it, remained. His favorite fishing spot.

Jaybird cut the motor when he was close enough to glide the intervening distance. He grabbed one of the pier's posts and tied the boat's painter to it. As he baited his line, he smelled smoke nearby. Then he heard a cough.

Here we go. He knew that sound. Shadow Man's cough.

Jaybird searched the shore and located Gideon, who sat on the ground rubbing his eyes. He waited for the other man to speak.

Gideon ran a hand through his hair and cleared his throat. "Good morning, Jaybird. I've been hunting Bigfoot."

"Uh-huh."

"It's the truth."

"You ain't known for tellin' the truth."

"Well, I am this time. We spotted him, too. Soon as that happened, my coward-ass buddies ran off without me. I was stranded out here all night."

"Uh-huh." Jaybird baited his line and cast parallel to the shore.

"Well, could you give me a ride back to town when you're done fishing?"

Jaybird reeled in the line and cast again.

"I can pay you," Gideon offered.

"Gotta stop by my house first."

As his stomach growled loudly, Gideon felt a flood of relief.

Ninety minutes later, he and Jaybird and Jaybird's morning catch of four big bass arrived at the cabin on Thatch Island.

On the pier, Jaybird tossed two fish at Gideon. "Clean these. That's your payment."

Using his pocketknife, Gideon set to work, while Jaybird quickly and expertly cleaned the other two fish right there on the pier. After they rinsed them off outside with a hose, Jaybird climbed the stairs to the covered porch and unlocked the cabin.

Inside, he wrapped the fish in plastic bags and put them in the freezer. The snug tin-roofed cabin was sparsely furnished, with a long, open room that served as kitchen and eat-in dining room at one end, and living room at the other. An open doorway led to the bedrooms.

"That's a dangerous book to keep in your house." Gideon pointed to the large-print Bible on the coffee table by the armchair and sofa. A harmonica rested on it.

The fine for owning a Bible was ten thousand dollars and two years in prison. Informers pocketed five thousand.

"How do you know I won't turn you in?"

Jaybird smiled. "'Cause you a liar, not an informer."

Gideon raised his voice slightly. "How do you know that?"

Jaybird ignored the question. He washed his hands at the sink and then tossed the bar of soap to Gideon. "Wash up. After I make breakfast, I'll take you back to town."

He didn't have to ask if his guest was hungry. Gideon scarfed up the fried eggs and ham with salty, buttered cornbread and washed the food down with two cups of strong coffee. He didn't speak a word until he had cleaned his plate.

"Thanks for breakfast," he said. "You know, I still need help around my house."

"I'm still waitin' for the truth outta your mouth. How long you been sick?"

"I'll tell you, as long as this remains between me and you."

Jaybird nodded.

"I don't know for sure when it began, but I was diagnosed with lung cancer earlier this year. I'm supposed to start radiation on Monday." Gideon's laugh was short and harsh. "Thank God it's not chemotherapy. Who can trust hospitals or the government? I won't take their poisons."

Jaybird's smile lit up his face. "Now that you come clean, Mr. Gideon Marsh, I'll be glad to help you out."

"But how did you know I was ill?"

He shrugged. "I get a knowing about things and people. It's hard to describe. I become aware of . . . I, uh . . . I just sense things."

"Yeah, well I wish your intuition could discover how to cure me. Then I wouldn't need radiation."

"There's a way."

Gideon raised his eyebrows. This he had to hear. Probably some natural remedy: okra fried in armadillo fat or turtle eggs pickled in Epsom salts. "Okay, so what way is that?"

"You got to get rid of all the darkness in you, Shadow Man."

"*Shadow Man*?" Gideon narrowed his eyes. "What darkness?"

Jaybird kept his face expressionless. "The anger, the unforgiveness, the bitterness and resentment." He paused and tapped his mouth with his index finger. "Oh, and the guilt. That's what's making you sick."

Gideon drew in a long breath and gazed up at the ceiling. "Well, Jaybird, ever since my pregnant ex-wife left me, you're damn right I'm angry, bitter, and unforgiving—who wouldn't be? And of course I've got guilt—I survived combat when so many of my brothers died." His voice broke on the last word.

Sudden anger flared in him, and he raised his voice. "And what about you, Mr. X-ray Vision, if you can read people like that, what are you doing living in this two-bit cabin on the backside of nowhere? Why aren't you making a fortune on TV—doing the talk show circuit and using your abilities to help mankind?"

"Prob'ly 'cause when I 'help mankind,' as you say, I get yelled at just like you're doin' now. Mankind don't necessarily wanna be helped. That's one reason I keep to myself."

"And what's the other?"

"I get sensory overload when I'm around too many people. I couldn't hardly stand to be in school. Couldn't concentrate in my classes for all the impressions I got from the other kids."

Gideon rubbed his eyes and sighed. "Look, man, I'm sorry I yelled at you. I'm tired and strung out from last night. I hate to admit it, but you're right about my anger and resentment. When my wife left, I was overseas in the military. She was expecting." He laughed bitterly. "Don't even know if she brought the baby to term. She just vanished without a trace. Never could find her. And then, somehow, I survived my tours in Iraq and Afghanistan, when so many of my brothers didn't."

Jaybird didn't comment. He rose from the table and picked up the harmonica. "This here's my MO."

"Modus operandi?"

"Mouth organ, Shadow Man. Here's a tune just for you." He sat down on the sofa and began to play.

It was a slow tune Gideon thought he'd heard before, but he couldn't name it. He watched and listened intently. He'd never heard anyone play a harmonica like that; the dude played like a pro. When the tune ended, Jaybird repeated it, but this time he added a bluesy feel with extra swirling notes at the ends of each phrase.

Gideon found himself rocking slightly in time to the music. He tapped his foot and smiled. "Who taught you to play like that?" he asked when it ended. "And what's the name of the song?"

"It's an old hymn, 'Just a Closer Walk with Thee.' Nobody taught me. This is my daddy's mouth organ. He played a little, but once I started, he stopped. I been playin' since I was four."

"Play another tune."

Jaybird sat back and lifted his eyebrows. "Didn't your mamma teach you any manners?"

Gideon grinned. "Okay, *please* play another."

He launched into a toe-tapping tune in an entirely different style. A march. Gideon recognized it.

"John Philip Sousa," he yelled triumphantly after Jaybird played the stinger at the very end. "I played that one in high school band."

"What instrument?"

Gideon held his left fist against his mouth and mimed a forward-and-back sliding action with his right arm. "Trombone."

"You got to know this one." Jaybird played again, slowly, with a rich organ-like sound.

Gideon smiled and sang along—on all of it.

> *Mine eyes have seen the glory*
> *Of the coming of the Lord;*
> *He is trampling out the vintage*
> *Where the grapes of wrath are stored;*
> *He hath loosed the fateful lightning*
> *Of His terrible swift sword;*
> *His truth is marching on.*
> *Glory! Glory! Hallelujah!*
> *Glory! Glory! Hallelujah!*
> *Glory! Glory! Hallelujah!*
> *His truth is marching on.*

After three more stanzas, Jaybird put down the mouth organ and gazed open-mouthed at Gideon. "How come you know all the verses?"

Gideon's laugh turned into a fierce cough. It took a moment for him to recover. "Oh, sorry—the singing did it. I have a recording of it on my iPod. Plus I heard it on every July Fourth and Memorial Day during my time in the Marines, back in the day."

"Julia Ward Howe wrote the words during the Civil War. But nobody sings it anymore."

"Of course not. Except for the Sousa march, the ten minutes you just played could earn you two years in jail."

"Yeah, well as long as you keep your trap shut, Shadow Man, I'm okay."

"Look, Jaybird, you'd better be careful about the Bible and those songs. There are paid informers planted in every community."

"Even here in little Legend?"

"Oh, yeah."

"How do you know that?"

"Let's just say I'm well acquainted with General Richard Huffman."

Jaybird's eyes grew large. "The second in command in Region VI! Whooee—what a bad dude. Compared to him, Bigfoot seems like Barbie."

Gideon coughed again and nodded. "That's what they say. He's six feet, six inches of malignant narcissism. And probably paranoid—hence the spy network. They pay the spies big bucks, with taxpayer money, of course.

"Who's the spy-rat in Legend?"

"I don't know for sure, but I'd put my money on Jack Dunham."

Jaybird pursed his lips. "No wonder he drives a BMW. He wanted me to be his maintenance man at Caddo Cabins, but I refused. He likes to cut corners, cut costs, and bend the law now and again. A slippery, slimy dude. I'd trust a 'gator 'fore I'd trust him."

"Yeah, he's one of the guys who left me stranded last night."

"Figures."

The sun was almost directly overhead by the time they left the cabin. They had worked out an agreement on the yard work and repairs Jaybird would do for Gideon.

On the trip back to town in Jaybird's old, rusty pickup, Gideon asked, "Why did you play me those tunes?"

As Jaybird followed the bumpy shell road to the far side of the island, he replied, "Because music has the power."

Gideon drew his brows down and stared at Jaybird. "What power?" The truck rattled across the old wooden bridge. Gideon wondered if the creaky one-lane suspension bridge might collapse under them.

"The power to lift you up, cheer you up, make you smile." Jaybird glanced at Gideon and grinned. "Spiritual therapy, Shadow Man. You need it worse than the physical kind."

Gideon thought about that for a few minutes. As they approached his house, he said, "Fishing is also therapy." It pleased him to see a tiny smile lift the corners of Jaybird's mouth. "So how 'bout taking me with you next weekend and showing me some good spots. I'll donate half my catch to your business."

Jaybird turned into Gideon's driveway and parked. He took so much time to answer, Gideon thought he would refuse. But as he opened the door to get out, Jaybird replied, "Friday evenin'."

Standing outside the open window, Gideon said, "What time?" But Jaybird put the truck in reverse and pulled away.

"Couldn't he just give me an answer?" Gideon muttered. After their long conversation earlier, he thought Jaybird had emerged from his shell, but no, the guy had clammed up tight and dug down into the sand, just like a bivalve mollusk. Gideon sighed as he watched the old truck and its enigmatic owner speed away toward the rickety bridge to Thatch Island.

CHAPTER 12

THE FUTURE

2019

As Joshua Brightman, the rueful expert on champagne, strolled north on Clinton Street toward Montague, he mused on the properties of honey. Thick and creamy, its color a beautiful amber or gold, honey's delicate flavor varies depending on the type of flowers the bees have pollinated. Its sweetness is sometimes floral, sometimes earthy, with hints of orange. A natural source of energy, it has antimicrobial properties and can heal wounds and burns. It is anti-inflammatory and has a soothing effect on coughs and allergies. It is known to boost the immune system.

Sam—beautiful, healing, sweet, and earthy. He had missed her without even being conscious of it. He sped up his strides, eager to meet her at the end of her shift. It had been ages since she was in the forefront of his mind. She was twenty or twenty-one now, all grown up. Almost the same age as L—

No, fuhgettabout it—not going there anymore. It was Sam he wanted to think about.

She wanted to be a writer, and she had that gorgeous, knockout cousin Lucy. Ha! He had led Nathan on about Sam. Told him about the sporty, athletic babe who lived next door—the one who declared she was gonna marry him. Joshua laughed: he never let on that Sam was all of twelve years old at the time.

Then out of the blue, nine years later, the telegram: *But you really should stop smoking*—the giveaway part. She must have been there after the New York Phil concert in the stage-door crowd—one of the few times he had smoked in public.

He crossed Joralemon Street and picked up the pace. He reminisced about their meeting, years ago, when he had just moved to New Orleans. Below the massive old mulberry tree that overhung the fence between their yards was a bench where he sat and smoked. He hadn't known about the little bookworm or about the tree platform in the top branches where she read. Annoyed by the smoke, she concocted a plan to admonish him. She lowered a notecard and pen on a fishing line until it dangled in front of his nose. Her message: *Would you please not smoke under my tree?*

He remembered their notecard-dialogue perfectly. He replied: *Who the hell are you?*

She reeled up the card.

My name is Sam. What is your name? Are you the piano player? By the way, please do not use cusswords like hell, damn, shit, fuck, or son of a bitch. That is not polite. P.S. You did not answer my question. Are you going to stop smoking under my tree?

My name is Joshua, and I am not polite, but I will consider your request. Yes, I am the piano player. Do you have asthma?

Asthma? I will have it if you don't stop smoking under my tree.

If you don't have asthma, then why does the smoke bother you?

It gets in my eyes while I'm reading. Smoking is not good for you, but don't worry. I have the solution.

At that point, she pelted his head with peppermints. Then as now, she had her own way of communicating—completely original. That's how he knew it was she who sent the telegram. As he turned left onto Montague he spoke with the proper New Orleans accent. "What a *chahmah.*"

On the Promenade, they set their coffee and take-out boxes on the bench between them. Sam brought warm falafel, pita bread, and two pieces of baklava. Her ever-healthy appetite amused him: a locust swarm out of Pharaoh's Egypt could not have consumed the meal as fast and systematically as she did. With utter disregard for the Promenade's spectacular views, Joshua focused his attention solely on her. He ate slowly while he listened and watched her expressive face and gestures: the flawless light-olive skin, high cheekbones, slightly hooked nose in an apple-shaped face, the intelligence and warmth in her dark-brown eyes. Beautiful, she was.

"Are you still a bookworm?"

"Of course. Libraries have been and remain my home away from home. When I depart this life, I hope to be buried in the Bodleian." She ate a falafel in two bites and sipped her coffee.

He laughed. "Well, Oxford will have to bide its time, 'cause I won't let you depart now, Samantha-the-Bookworm Faris, not until I get to know the grown-up you. Tell me all about your life here in the city and all the gossip from New Orleans."

They had resumed their old camaraderie effortlessly. Sam, saucy, cheerful, and articulate as ever, seemed completely at home with him. Her natural ease and good humor seemed unchanged. She carried on her part of the conversation as if they had never parted. For Joshua, the only unsettling note was the fact that now, for the first time, he saw her as an adult, not a precocious child. Like a man slowly adjusting binoculars to bring an image to perfect clarity, he had to refocus his mind to perceive her truly and clearly in the present. He shared the bench with a Sam who was new to him, a most charming, attractive, and unselfconscious woman.

He vividly remembered the day she invited him to lunch with her mother, Sitti, and Eliot the bluejay. During the meal, Sam asked him if he had a girlfriend. When he answered no, she said, "Good."

He laughed. "Why is that good?"

"Because I'm going to marry you."

Sitti exclaimed "*Albi!*" and clapped her hand over her mouth in embarrassment. Her mother, Diana, laughed and shook her head. "Sam, you are twelve years old."

"Almost thirteen. Well, it's the truth. I'm going to marry him when I get old enough."

Surprised as he had been, Joshua hadn't laughed. He had been struck by her utter certainty, her sincerity and earnestness. Now, here they were nine years later. His past experiences with Samantha Faris had taught him one thing: *Never mind sugar and spice and all things nice. This girl—no, this woman—was a firecracker.*

The small college she attended matched her conservative, Christian upbringing. Sam's mother, an English professor at Tulane, had brought her up in the Episcopal Church, although Sitti and Sam's father Joseph had been Syrian Orthodox. "I'm an English major. My scholarships are not enough to cover all the cost, so that's why I'm working at Beiruti. And please thank Nathan for that over-the-top tip."

"Will do." Joshua breathed in the fragrance before he took a bite of the baklava. "Mmmm. Almost as good as Sitti used to make."

Sam smiled. "She was a wonderful cook."

"And an even better healer." He had met Sam's family at one of the lowest points in his life. In debt from school loans and the purchase of his Steinway at age twenty-four, he couldn't afford his own apartment, so he lived at home with his parents, Amy and the Beast. Brooklynites transplanted to New Orleans, they had struggled to adjust to the climate and culture.

Billy "the Beast" Brightman, an attorney for Leviathan Oil, had lived up to his name. An aging ex-athlete, domineering and verbally abusive, he disapproved of—well, practically sneered at—his son's musical career. Joshua's suppressed anger toward his father festered into obsessive, violent thoughts, compulsive counting, and a germ phobia. The skin of his hands stayed chapped and red from constant washing.

His neighbors—Sam, her mother Diana, and Sitti—provided a haven of peace and acceptance for him. Their warmth, affection, and respect helped counteract his miserable home life. When he learned of Sitti's reputation as a healer, he summoned the courage to ask her to lay hands on him and pray for him. To his surprise, she had already seen through him and discerned his problems. She promised she would. The moment came just prior to her death. Her prayers plus his own forgiveness toward his father and mother exorcised his demons and healed him of his obsessive thoughts.

"How is my former landlord?" Dr. Leo DeLuca had been Sam's other neighbor. When the tensions between Joshua and his father grew intolerable, the Beast kicked him out. He had nowhere to go until Leo suggested his garage apartment at an extremely low rent. Joshua accepted the kind offer.

"He and Mamma got married."

"Did they?"

"Yes, about a year after you left. Leo adores her. He moved into our old house, and now he rents out his house and the garage apartment."

Joshua listened, letting Sam do most of the talking, while on a deeper level in his mind, his thoughts took flight. In their meeting, in this very moment, he wondered what futures awaited. What would come from this?

He thought about the future that had been stolen from him, about his child, the son or daughter Li Ling had aborted without telling or asking him. The child that would have interfered with her career. An entire future, a life, vanished.

He had not told anyone what had happened, but he would tell Sam someday.

As she talked about her mother and Leo, Uncle George and Lucy, he listened attentively. To his musician's ear, her sweet voice soared like a pure and agile flute with the depth and warmth of true silver. Like a melody, it rose and fell in counterpoint to the orchestra of the city: the voices of passersby, the shouts and laughter of children, the hum of a bicycle's tires, birdsong, the noise of traffic, the blare of a car horn, and the cries of seagulls borne on the wind that rustled the new spring green of the sycamores behind them.

And to his mind, that was not all. Below them, undergirding everything, hummed a deep and profound music, beyond the range of hearing: the movement of the earth itself, the coursing music of the sun, the moon, the stars—ever-present, but unperceived by mortal ears. The intricate, perfect clockwork of the universe proceeded as it should—as it always would—while above them arched the blue air, where Heaven reached down to enfold Earth.

He mused on all this as he observed the quicksilver play of emotions and expressions in her glimmering eyes, in the movement of her small hands. Peace moved through his body, slowing his pulse and the rhythm of his breath. Here with Sam, on this bench, he had found the center of the world, the still point of its turning. *Home.* What Sam had known years ago, he knew now. A new future had arisen; it simply would be.

They talked for hours as the earth turned and the sun moved westward. Joshua watched the golds and reds of receding day peek out from under the blue clouds of dusk, while the lights winked on in the skyscrapers, comforting and warm against the impending darkness.

Later, he walked Sam back to the train stop at Borough Hall. Before she left, they exchanged phone numbers. He hugged her in parting, holding her gently against his chest, reluctant to let her go. She lifted her head and kissed him on the cheek. The chaste, warm kiss set his pulse galloping like a racehorse. He stroked her hair with one hand, kissed the crown of her head, and then released her. He watched her until she disappeared down the stairs into the station.

On his long walk home, he thought about the date, May 4, 2019. A most significant day—the day of their reunion. He reverted to his former obsessive-compulsive habit; he converted the date to numbers, 5/4/2019, then added them together. Their sum was 30.

Thirty. Joshua smiled. *A very good number.* Thirty equals 3x10: three, the number of divine perfection, multiplied ten times. The words of the *Shema* came into his mind, absent from his lips for so long during his depression over Li Ling's betrayal.

Hear, O Israel: The Lord our God is one Lord:
You shall love the Lord your God with all your heart and with
all your soul and with all your might.

He followed it with his personal prayer: *O Lord, thank you for this day, for bringing Sam back into my life. Help me to be the man you mean for me to be. Help me to protect and defend Sam all the days of our lives. Our lives together.*

He walked on, while the earth revolved and sang its way through space, while other planets and all the stars stayed their courses in a universe ever-expanding. Surrounded by the music of the earth and the music of the spheres, he imagined he could hear the turning of the age.

PART II

THE GENERAL

Monday, September 21, 2026

He waited all morning for the news. At midday, he was too keyed up to contemplate eating. Finally, just after noon, the story broke. The chyron running on national news networks proclaimed it: *BREAKING NEWS – Flight 2211 crashes into Caddo Lake, number of casualties unknown.*

Part one, accomplished. With sweating palms, he waited and watched, hoping the key component of the mission had succeeded. The phone call from one of his men on the scene came through at 15:40 Central Time. His whole life turned on the two words spoken: "No survivors."

Wasted—the fool was wiped off the face of the earth. Nothing could stand in his way now. The thrill of it stirred his blood; he felt himself go hard. Power was the ultimate aphrodisiac.

He poured himself a scotch and drank it neat as he regarded himself in the mirror above the fireplace mantle. He lifted his glass in a celebratory toast. "Here's to the new governor of Region VI." He knocked back the rest of the fiery liquid and turned to his desk. The Nine had laid the plans long ago, but now he had to activate them. Exultant as he was, General Richard Huffman still had a lot of work to do.

WARNING

2026

He was eight years old and all alone at the edge of the high diving board. Constantin's stomach fluttered; fear and indecision paralyzed him. The wind raised goosebumps on his body. He shivered and dithered, eyes riveted on the blue water of the pool ten feet below. Should he jump or climb down the ladder to safety? Step forward or step back?

The older boy behind him grew impatient. "Are you gonna stand there all day? Jump, you little turd."

Then, as now, Constantin gathered his courage and jumped. At dinner with Tony and Stella, he took the plunge. "Tony, how can I find out about my dad?" He was almost sixteen; he wasn't a little boy anymore, and he wanted answers. Better to know than not, no matter what he might discover.

Tony held a forkful of lasagna suspended halfway to his mouth. He wrinkled his brow. "Mr. Lupei?"

"No, my biological dad—he was in the Marine Corps in Afghanistan. Dumitru is not my real father." *Thank heavens.*

"Oh, right. Well, you could start with military records. Your grandpa's a general; he ought to be able to get some information on him."

Oh, his grandfather had plenty of information; he just chose to withhold it all. Constantin dared not tell the Amores what Dumitru's diary revealed. "I'm sure he can, but will he? He disliked my dad. He thought he was a bad husband for his daughter. Ha! He thinks Dumitru is the best thing that ever happened to my mom—a hero, somewhere between Charlemagne and Tarzan."

"Well, how do you see him?" asked Stella.

"Dumitru? He's like Dracula merged with Elmer Fudd. Suave, charming, dark, Eastern European—but short, and as you know, he can't say his R's." Constantin dropped his voice an octave and mimicked his stepfather. "Let's go fow a wide, Gwigowi."

Stella laughed explosively, spewing bits of lasagna across the white tablecloth. She clapped her hand over her mouth. "Constantin, I'm so sorr—"

"And the top of his head only comes up to my mom's shoulder. He's a midget."

While Stella's shoulders shook with laughter, Tony nodded solemnly. "A very powerful, very wealthy midget."

"Yes, vewy." Constantin rolled his eyes. "Anyway, I know enough about *him*. My *dad* is the mystery man. For God's sake, they didn't even tell me how he died."

"Can you check the military records online?" asked Tony.

"Yes and no. As next-of-kin I can, but in order to check, I need his complete name, service number, and social security number. All I know is he was killed in 2010, the year I was born."

"What was his name?" asked Stella.

"Gunnar Ross, and I don't even know if that's his whole name."

"Gunnar?" said Stella.

"It's Scandinavian—Swedish, probably. The last name Ross could be Scottish or French from Normandy—I looked that up. I think I probably got my hair and eye color from him."

The landline rang, and Tony hurriedly rose to answer it. Landline calls were often from Europe, either Switzerland or London, or wherever Dumitru's business interests took him. Constantin and Stella halted their conversation and ate their lasagna and salad in silence while Tony walked quickly into the parlor, at the front of the brownstone to answer. The kitchen and dining room were at the back of the house. The furnishings and Persian carpets dampened the sound of Tony's voice and made his words indistinguishable. In any case, he spoke very little.

When he returned to the table, Stella said, "Well?"

Tony blinked rapidly and transferred his gaze from his wife to Constantin. "It was the General."

Constantin raised his eyebrows and smiled. "*Grand-père*? Huh—speak of the devil." For him, it was no longer a figure of speech.

Tony did not return his smile. "He called to warn us."

Stella, caught in the act of lifting her fork to her mouth, halted it in midair. A chunk of meat filling dropped off and fell onto the white tablecloth. She didn't even notice; she drew her eyebrows together in concern. "Warn us—about what?"

Tony pulled on his nose in a nervous gesture. "Well, I'm not sure exactly, but there is some kind of military action going down this week—"

Stella's eyes grew wide. "In New York?"

"Yes. He told me to stock up on food and water immediately. After tomorrow, we're not to leave the house."

"For how long?" Constantin asked.

Tony shrugged. "He said not until he notified us." He tugged on his nose again. "But he did say I should buy enough supplies for a month."

"A month! What about school? I can't miss that many days."

"Constantin, I'll bet the schools will have to shut down when this happens. It's going to be some kind of emergency, but he didn't want to give me details." Tony laughed. "You know—he's a general. Everybody's supposed to follow his orders without question. As the poet said, *Ours is not to reason why, ours is but to do or die.*"

Alone in his room after dinner, Constantin looked up the quote. Tony had got the sense of it right, but not the exact wording. It came from Alfred, Lord Tennyson's poem "The Charge of the Light Brigade." The poem described a famous incident during the Crimean War at the Battle of Balaklava in 1854. Six hundred British cavalrymen, armed only with lances and sabers, made an almost suicidal charge against Russian artillery. Following orders unflinchingly, despite the overwhelming odds, they rode into a valley where they faced devastating fire from three sides.

> *Half a league, half a league,*
> *Half a league onward,*
> *All in the valley of Death*
> *Rode the six hundred.*
> *"Forward, the Light Brigade!*
> *Charge for the guns!" he said:*
> *Into the valley of Death*
> *Rode the six hundred.*
>
> *"Forward, the Light Brigade!"*
> *Was there a man dismay'd?*
> *Not tho' the soldier knew*
> *Some one had blunder'd:*
> *Theirs not to make reply,*
> *Theirs not to reason why,*
> *Theirs but to do and die:*
> *Into the valley of Death*
> *Rode the six hundred.*
>
> *Cannon to right of them,*
> *Cannon to left of them,*
> *Cannon in front of them*
> *Volley'd and thunder'd;*
> *Storm'd at with shot and shell,*

Boldly they rode and well,
Into the jaws of Death,
Into the mouth of Hell
Rode the six hundred.

Constantin's imagination filled with the sounds of pounding hoofs, ear-shattering explosions, the screams of men and horses. His breath came quickly; his heart hammered. His father had been a soldier in Afghanistan. How had he died? Had he and his company been hopelessly surrounded by the Taliban and slaughtered like the men of the Light Brigade? Had he stepped on a mine or been killed by a suicide bomber? He had to find out, and he would not stop until he did. He had to know all he could about the man whose very blood ran in his veins.

He sat at the desk in his bedroom and opened up his laptop to search the internet for any mention of his father, something he had done many times before. After another fruitless search for his father's name, he made a shot in the dark. He entered two words: *casualties Afghanistan.* To his wide-eyed astonishment, he got a hit. "Ha!" he shouted. "I cannot believe it!"

The Afghan War Fatalities website consisted of a comparison chart that listed the dead soldiers' names first, followed by rank, date of death, and age. It included the place of death, cause of death, and hometown of each individual. There were hundreds of pages, beginning at the year 2021 and proceeding backward in time. As he scrolled through the pages to the year 2010, he realized Afghanistan had become the graveyard of the world. Soldiers from many foreign countries had died there: American, British, Australian, Danish, Norwegian, Polish, Russian, French, Turkish, Italian, German, Canadian, Dutch, Romanian, and Estonian. Some had died in non-hostile circumstances, by drowning or vehicle accident. But most had succumbed to hostile fire: small arms, bombs, IEDs, rockets, suicide car bombs, or land mines.

Certain he would find his father's name, Constantin sat on the edge of his chair in anticipation; his knees jiggled, and his heart pounded with excitement. When he got to the year 2010, the listing began in December and went backward through the year, month-by-month to January. He scrolled slowly through each month, but did not see the name Gunnar Ross. Determined to find it, he read through the names again. He counted 295 casualties in that year, but only four Texans, each of them Hispanic. That stumped him for a moment. Where was Gunnar Ross's name? Either he had missed it, or the person responsible for uploading names had made a mistake. He scrutinized the entire list carefully a third time. Nothing. Then he backed up and checked the names in 2009. Still nothing. He scrolled forward into 2011. The name was nowhere.

By then, it was 1:45 a.m. He gave up and closed the laptop. He rubbed his eyes and slumped back in the chair. Despite his fatigue, his mind whirled with possibilities. Either someone had omitted his father's name . . . or . . . he could hardly bear to think it—his mother and grandfather had lied to him. *Had they withheld the truth all these years?* He scarcely breathed. *Why?* Why would his grandfather hide the truth? Suspicion and anger swirled in his heart, like clouds of smoke shot with flames. Had his mother loved a criminal? Did they concoct the story of a noble war death to keep the ugly truth from him? Was his father a murderer, a thief, a child molester, alive and rotting somewhere in a Texas prison?

He rubbed his tired, itchy eyes. Surely there would be a few lingering online references to Gunnar Ross if he had committed some sort of heinous crime. *No, no, no—it couldn't be.* He had searched diligently so many times. He crossed his arms and looked up at the ceiling, thinking.

Suddenly, in an epiphany that stopped his breath and shot adrenalin through his veins at the same time, Constantin knew the blinding and stupefying truth—*he is alive. My father is not among the casualties—because he is not dead.* He drew in a deep breath, held it, and then exhaled noisily. Flushed with nervous energy, he got up and paced rapidly back and forth. Wild hope rose in his heart, like a phoenix arising out of the ashes. It mounted on such powerful wings, he thought it might tear him apart.

Gunnar Ross walked this earth now, just like Constantin himself. He would find him—that would be his quest. He would not give up until he did.

He was certain they had lied to him, his mother and grandfather—and Dumitru. He didn't know why, but someday he would. Whatever the reason, it would keep—that could not be his focus now. He clenched his fists and made himself a vow. He would find his father even if he had to walk through enemy gunfire to do it.

He had no idea just how prescient he was.

C H A P T E R　1 5

BIGFOOT

Friday, September 25, 2026

Toilet paper is insignificant when the larder is stocked, but when nature calls and one has run out of it, it suddenly becomes a priceless commodity. Gideon, sitting upon the commode and lacking said commodity, considered the alternatives: corncobs, leaves, dry grass, stones, or—the hand. *Shades of Afghanistan.* Fatigued, his ribs aching from coughing fits, he really didn't want to drive to the grocery store. On a slow day at the library, he had read an article on the history of toilet paper. Across time and in various lands, people resorted to animal furs, sticks, seashells, and snow. *No thank you.* In ancient Greece, they used *ostraca* (his favorite choice): pieces of broken ceramic inscribed with the names of enemies. *Oh, yeah*—he would have gladly covered his ex-father-in-law's name in excrement.

But lacking all the above, he dragged himself to the SUV, drove to the Grocery & Grill, and bought an eight-roll bundle. When he got home that Friday at 4:30, he wondered why Jaybird's battered pickup was parked in front of his house. Gideon pulled into the driveway and got out, holding his precious cargo under one arm.

Jaybird leaned out of the driver's window and called, "Ready to go fishing?"

Gideon had completely forgotten about it. His radiation treatments had begun the same day as the horrific plane crash five days ago, on Monday, eclipsing everything. A 767 had exploded and fallen out of the sky into Caddo Lake. The crash made national and international news headlines. Consequently, the village of Legend had tripled in size. All the hotels in Jefferson and along the major highways were filled with federal and state investigators, reporters, and camera crews.

Some of the locals had helped with recovery efforts, but Gideon had not. He had taken a medical leave from the Jefferson library that week. The radiation sapped his energy and took away his appetite. He spent his time resting, reading, listening to music, and feeling generally miserable. Unlike most people, he had avoided the lake. He had no desire to gawk at plane debris or body parts. He'd seen enough of that in the Middle East.

Gideon walked over to the truck. "Are you sure you want to go out to the lake this soon after the plane crash, Jaybird?"

"What's the matter? Scared?"

"Wimp."

Jaybird nodded. "The place I'm takin' you is far away from the crash site. I stayed away and worked in town this week. After mowin' your yard, I did some maintenance at a house over by Karnack. Now I need to catch up on fishin' for myself."

"Has it calmed down out there?" Gideon had seen the TV reports on the recovery efforts at the height of the operation. Helicopters and boats had buzzed over the scene, while divers probed the depths below to recover human remains and plane parts.

"The feds and TV crews left yesterday morning. All the vultures disappeared, too."

"Vultures?"

"The ambulance-chaser types who wanted to watch. The show's over—they're gone."

Not certain he wanted to go fishing in the lake after a major tragedy, Gideon stood frozen. Images swarmed his mind: the pink mist, a boot lying alone with the foot still in it, a young man eviscerated by shrapnel, intestines dangling from the bloody wound. Cold sweat soaked him.

"It shoulda been you that died."

Gideon nodded and whispered, "I agree."

"What was that?"

Gideon didn't answer.

Jaybird had not told Gideon about his premonition of blood, fire, and water, even though it had come to pass—trauma and death, a burning plane falling out of the air. He understood Gideon's reluctance; he practically read his thoughts. In some way invisible to the eye, the tragedy seemed to have stained the water.

"I got a feelin' you're shell-shocked from the military service."

Gideon drew a deep breath and released it. "Yeah, I have PTSD. I saw too much blood and death. I wish I hadn't."

Jaybird spoke softly. "Life goes on, Shadow Man."

Gideon met his eyes. "Yeah, I know it does." *But there are times when it would be easier to die than to live.*

"You ain't never had fried catfish as good as I make it." Jaybird's grin was lopsided.

Gideon's laugh broke the somber mood.

Jaybird smiled. "The thing is, you gotta catch those damn suckers first, 'fore you fry 'em."

"I can see the logic in that," he replied. "Hold on a minute. Let me change clothes and get my gear."

Shadows grew long as they passed the inlet where the old fishing pier was located, where Gideon had spent the night alone. To his great relief, he saw no signs of the plane crash on the journey—no debris or gruesome remains. Turning east along the north shore, they arrived at a little bay, maybe sixty feet across. Curving parallel to it on land lay a shallow, semicircular clearing.

"This is an isolated area," Jaybird told him. Two long spits of land, wooded with tall trees, curved around the bay like crab claws. It had a private, protected atmosphere. Jaybird cut the motor and dropped an anchor. It was suddenly very quiet.

They baited their lines with the live worms Jaybird had brought and threw them in. Sunset was around 7:15, so they had a good two hours to fish before dark.

In companionable silence they waited for the fish to bite. It was the same time of day as Gideon's previous adventure. After a few minutes he asked Jaybird, "What do you think about Bigfoot? Have you ever seen him? You've lived here all your life, haven't you?"

Jaybird lifted his eyebrows and pursed his lips. "All my twenty-one years, but I ain't seen anything like that."

"Oh." Gideon's disappointment was evident in his tone.

"But my daddy did." Jaybird grinned. "Back in the day, when there were less people around. He told me he saw Bigfoot once. Happened before I was born. He was sittin' in his boat, fishin' close to the shore like we are, around dusk. Out of the corner of his eye, he saw movement on land, something big. At first, he thought it was a deer, but it was way too big and walkin' fast on two legs. It was hairy all over—dark-colored. Coulda been a bear, but bears are scarce 'round here, and black bears ain't the size of grizzlies. This thing was a hulk.

"He said he forgot to breathe. He watched it for close to a minute, until it walked back into the woods. Scared him real bad. From then on, he took a shotgun with him in the boat, and he never walked the woods without some kind of firearm."

A sudden tug on his line startled Gideon—he jerked and cried out in surprise. "Oh!" It came out high-pitched, like a girl. Embarrassed, he bent his head and reeled. As he pulled the catfish out of the water, Jaybird grabbed it with a net.

"Nice one." Jaybird unhooked the fish and plopped it in the ice chest. Two minutes later, Jaybird got his first catch, a foot-long catfish. He was gleeful. "All right, man. We're in luck—those suckers are bitin' now."

They threw in their lines again, and as they waited, Gideon asked, "You know, the night I spent out here alone, I did see a creature that looked like Bigfoot. It was about this time of day. Whatever it was, it sure spooked my two buddies. Do you know where your dad spotted Bigfoot? What part of the lake?"

Jaybird laughed. "Yeah, it was somewhere around this little bay. Probably because nobody lives around here. Those encounters, at least the ones I've heard of, seem to happen out in the boondocks. A lot of hunters have seen strange animals around Caddo Lake."

In less than an hour, Jaybird hooked three more catfish and Gideon two. As the sun sank below the tops of the trees, the temperature dropped and the wind picked up. Gideon hadn't brought a jacket. "About ready to go?" he asked. He was exhausted from the radiation treatments, and goosebumps covered his arms.

"One more cast," Jaybird replied. He baited his line and threw it in.

The sound of the splash was overpowered by the crashing noise of something big charging through the dry woods. A doe broke out of the trees to their right and bounded across the clearing. It disappeared into a thicket on the left.

"Runnin' scared," said Jaybird.

"From a hunter?"

"Nah, too early for that. Deer season starts in November. Cougar, maybe."

A rabbit, following the same track as the doe, shot out of the brush.

What came next stunned them both. A bulky brown figure on two legs stumbled out of the dark woods into the fading light of the clearing. Shaggy-haired, head down, it walked with a halting, uneven gait favoring one leg. It carried a long stick in one hand and babbled to itself in a low voice.

"Holy shit," Gideon blurted in a hoarse whisper, "it's Bigfoot!" But it was a much smaller version than the creature he saw previously. A juvenile, maybe?

Until he spoke, the creature had not seen them, but at the sound of Gideon's voice, it gave a loud cry, almost a bellow, and turned toward them. It picked up its pace and growled. Gideon suddenly realized neither of them had brought a gun.

Jaybird dropped his fishing pole and grabbed the slingshot he always kept with him. He dug out a ball bearing from his jeans pocket and loaded. Facing the oncoming creature, he stretched out his left arm and pulled the pouch back with his right. Just as he released, Gideon jostled his arm.

"Dang it—what you doin'?" Jaybird yelled, as the steel ball flew wide of the mark.

It didn't seem to matter, since the creature stumbled and collapsed face first on the ground anyway.

"Jaybird, it's not Bigfoot. It's a man, and he's in trouble. I think he's hurt."

A low moan escaped from the prostrate figure.

"Come on—let's go see. He needs help."

With a paddle, Jaybird maneuvered the boat close to the shore. He looped the painter around a young cypress tree and tied it securely. They climbed out and cautiously walked the thirty feet to the prone figure. His curling auburn hair hung dirty and matted almost to his shoulders. He wore a brown-leather bomber jacket. Although it was ripped in places and dirty, it must have cost a bundle. No shoes, though. His bare feet were torn and bloodied.

Gideon spoke softly, "Hey man, we're here to help."

The man lay still and limp and gave no response.

Gideon wrinkled his nose at the scent rising off him, a mixture of stale sweat, body odor, and blood.

"Jaybird, help me turn him over."

When they rolled him over onto his back as gently as they could, they saw scratches on his face and hands, as if he had walked through a bramble patch. One ankle was quite swollen, sprained maybe, but other than that they couldn't see any major injuries.

"Let's take his jacket off," said Jaybird. "Maybe he's got injuries we can't see."

Once they removed the bomber jacket, Jaybird pointed. "Look, something's off about his shoulders. They don't look right." They unbuttoned the man's shirt and opened it. The left side of his torso was covered in old bruises, now purple-edged and yellowing. "Whooee," said Jaybird, "he's beat up. And now I see the problem."

"Yeah. Both shoulders dislocated." Gideon ran his hand over the man's arms and collarbone. He gently flexed the arms. "There aren't any obvious breaks. I think I can relocate the shoulders, but let's get him back to your house first and give him some food and water. His ribs are showing; he's half-starved."

"Yeah, the sooner, the better. Before he comes to."

Thin, bearded, with scratches and mosquito bites on his face, the man could have been twenty or forty. His eyes were half-closed.

Gideon touched his forehead. "I think he's running a fever. Jaybird, do you have a first aid kit in the boat?"

"No, it's at the house. Let's get him to the boat."

They draped his jacket over him and carried the unconscious man to the edge of the lake where they laid him flat on his back. "He's probably dehydrated." Gideon glanced down at the gaunt, disheveled man. "I hope he wakes up soon. Do you think he's a tourist who got lost in the woods?"

"Could be—it wouldn't be the first time that happened around here. He coulda got lost, wandered in circles, and got disoriented. Maybe he fell into a ravine. There are some deep ones back in the woods."

"Or maybe he climbed a tree and fell out of it. If he grabbed onto a branch in the midst of a fall, his own weight could have dislocated his shoulders. And a fall would explain the swollen ankle. Hopefully it's just a sprain, and hopefully he'll tell us his story when he wakes up."

Before they lifted the man into the boat, they checked his jeans and jacket for identification. Except for a quarter, the pockets were empty. There wasn't room to lay him flat in the bottom of the jon boat. Jaybird propped him up in the front section while Gideon moved in behind him on the seat. He put his legs on either side of the man's torso, and leaned the head against his stomach.

Once they were set, Jaybird took his place at the back of the boat, gunned the motor and headed full throttle for home.

GRACE

Friday, September 25, 2026

Sam refused to fly—not even when the airline offered her and Peter first-class tickets, *gratis*. She could have flown from New York to Dallas (Region VI) in under four hours, but instead, she took a two-day train trip. Her days of jet-speed journeys at 35,000 feet had ended. She felt far safer traveling at 90 mph, six feet above the rattling rails and the earth from which she was formed. If she ever had to go to Europe, for her it would be the modern equivalent of the *QE2*.

Four days after the plane crash that took her husband's life, along with Eric Tecken and that of every other living soul on board, she set out on a journey to the place where it happened. For most Americans, the popular governor's death eclipsed all the others, occurring just a year and ten months after the 2024 election.

The election had resulted in major changes. At the outset of his second term, President Puddinghead consolidated the fifty states into ten regions. Ten governors would be much easier for him to control than fifty state legislatures, she suspected. With the states dissolved into regions, state driver's licenses became obsolete. The new obligatory National ID included a photo, the owner's name, address, date of birth, and social security number. It also included embedded biometric data: face and fingerprint.

Under Puddinghead, the government moved farther and farther away from the inspired, original vision of the Founding Fathers. Tecken, the governor of Region VI, had been the only governor courageous enough to fight for the Constitution and the rights of the people who elected him. Once, the dire effect of his death on the nation's future would have been the subject of Sam's op-eds for weeks. Now she could only watch from the sidelines, wordless and calcified, as inarticulate as stone.

The one compulsion that penetrated her benumbed state was the desire to see the site of the crash. It would be some kind of connection with Joshua—as close as she could come to him in his final moments. It was the last place his eyes had seen, and she wanted to see it, too. Afterward, she would visit her mother and Leo in New Orleans. At that point, she would have to make some major decisions.

She and Peter boarded the Amtrak train at Penn Station at mid-afternoon. Their trip from Region II (formerly New York and New Jersey) to Region V (Minnesota, Wisconsin, Michigan, Illinois, Indiana, and Ohio) was a colossal adventure for Peter—he'd ridden on the subway, but never on a passenger train. Like a miniature Magellan, he explored the inside of their Viewliner bedroom. He climbed up onto the seat, slid off, climbed up again, stood on it, played with the air vents, investigated the bathroom and shower. Sam offered him a cup of chocolate pudding after his exertions. Post-pudding, he climbed onto the seat once more and, with sticky fingers, traced his name on the large window.

Somehow, despite the fog and apathy clouding her mind, Sam knew she ought to use the next forty-eight hours to map out a strategy for survival. She had lost her husband and her job as a featured writer for the *Atlantic Star* on the same day, and unless she found a highly lucrative position very soon, it was only a matter of time before she had to sell the house in Brooklyn Heights.

Sam had worked for the conservative paper for five years, ever since she graduated from The King's College and married Joshua. It had been one of the few independent bastions for conservative writers, but as stars are wont to do, it had gone out blazing. It managed to survive internet censorship by the liberal tech giants, but an unruly mob brought it down.

Rioters, those accomplished name-callers and self-righteous vandals, swarmed outside the building. They shook their fists, consulted their three-word dictionary, and screamed at the staff: "You fucking racists! You fucking fascists!" The word *debate* did not appear in their dictionary; they thought it meant something one attached to fishing poles. Rational arguments caused them to break out in hives. Anyone with an opinion different from their own deserved to be stomped on or shot. Gathering facts or actual statistics interfered with their primary pastimes: hurling bricks and setting fires.

They burned down the building on Atlantic Avenue where the online newspaper had its offices. For a small company, it was a mortal blow. Lacking the resources to recover, the management notified Sam of the decision to close on the same morning Joshua left for Houston.

She gazed at the dark curls and innocent blue eyes of her son with pity. *Your country teeters on the edge of tyranny, and your father will never come home.*

Clutching his woolly lamb and speaking in whispers, Peter watched the broad waters of the Hudson River. "See, Albi, there's a white motorboat, a big ferry, and two sailboats." *Albi* was an Arabic endearment meaning *my heart*. Sitti had called her that, and she sometimes called her son by that name, so Peter had adopted it for his lamb.

He pointed, to make sure Albi didn't miss any of the sights. "Where do you think they're going? Maybe Daddy's on one of them. He said he'd come home in four days. He said it."

Sam's heart sank. No explanation she gave Peter helped. He wanted his daddy back, and that was that. When the boy grew tired of the view, he played with his toy cars and trucks on the shelf just inside the window. As he talked and hummed to himself, Sam mused on her dark secret. She harbored the tiniest hope that there was a mistake. Without a body as conclusive proof, she couldn't—no, she *wouldn't*—truly believe Joshua was dead. If the lab came up with DNA evidence from a body fragment—she winced to imagine it—well, then she would have to accept it. She told no one—neither friends nor family—that she continued to pray for him.

In the meantime, she still had to deal with financial realities. With a heavy heart, she weighed her options. To stay in New York, she would have to land a job with a salary high enough to compensate for the loss of her husband's income. The brownstone's steep mortgage, due the first of the month, threatened to slice her in two like Poe's pendulum, "a crescent of glittering steel," hissing through the air.

On the other hand, she could return to New Orleans and its lower cost of living. She could probably rent Leo's house at about one-third of her current mortgage. Or she and Peter could live in the garage apartment, cheaper still. She would have to find a new job. Some relief might come from Joshua's life insurance policy. When the company settled the claim, she would have a few months leeway. She hated the thought of profiting from his death—Joshua would want her to use the funds, but it still seemed like blood money.

The vibration of the train and the regular thrumming of the rails lulled her as she watched the Hudson River glide by. The river—time's metaphor. It flowed on and on. No one could stop it and bring back the past. But in memory, as in the Book where all is recorded, the past remains.

Joshua's proposal on June 4, one month after they met again at Beiruti, scandalized friends and family alike, but fulfilled Sam's prediction. (It wasn't too stressful for him. He was certain of her answer, since she had said *yes* nine years before.) To beat the Louisiana heat, they got married at 7:00 a.m. on July 13, in the backyard of her mom and Leo's house. The wedding party on Sam's side consisted of her mother and stepfather, Uncle George and Aunt Cat, her cousins Michael and Lucy, and their spouses. Joshua's parents attended: plump, teary Amy and the ever-critical, hulking Billy. Lucy was Sam's matron of honor, and Nathan stood up for Joshua.

The pianist played for his own wedding; he recorded Schumann's *Kinderszenen*, thirteen short pieces as a prelude. Leo played the music on his top-of-the-line audio system and piped it into the backyard. The roses and geraniums bloomed for them, the morning birds sang, and the breeze hummed its own music. The trees danced, and the sun rose like a bridegroom, rejoicing to run his course. Sam, slim and straight in white satin, glowed like a candle flame. Joshua wept.

As they stood before the priest, the sun's first rays touched their heads, her dark hair garlanded with a simple chaplet of greenery and pink rosebuds, his hair like burnished copper. When it was the rabbi's turn, the risen sun bathed them in gold and scattered diamonds on the dew-laden grass.

She and Joshua fasted before the ceremony. Afterward, they had the wedding breakfast at Marigold's Bistro: Eggs Benedict, bacon, *crêpes* sweet and savory, strawberry shortcake, café au lait or Irish coffee.

Sam's special wedding gifts included Sitti's small sterling silver cross, saved for her by her mother; the approval and love in Diana's blue eyes; Leo's heartfelt embrace of Joshua; the smell of Uncle George's cigars (he smoked one before and three after the ceremony); cousins Lucy and Michael—their teasing and jokes, their clear delight in welcoming Joshua into the family; her mother-in-law's kiss; and the tears of joy in Joshua's hazel eyes.

Then, as now, she felt the rightness of their marriage—they belonged together. It had always been true; it was the unshakable foundation of her life. They flew back to New York later that afternoon. That night, Joshua told her why he had chosen the date: 7/13/2019 = 32, 3+2= 5. Five, the number of grace.

"After my father killed Eliot the bluejay, you went into such a deep depression you ceased to speak. When Sitti ran in the house to call for help that day, she fell and broke her hip. After my family had caused untold injury to yours, your grandmother, on her deathbed, prayed for me and healed me. That taught me the meaning of grace. And best of all, today you married me." He paused and took a deep breath. "Words cannot express how complete I feel when I am with you, Sam. Our marriage, to me, is like an anointing with oil, a shower of undeserved goodness and immeasurable peace. Grace means favor to the unworthy. The unworthy being me."

"No," she said, and stopped his mouth with kisses. The mystery that followed, where two become one, was as old as humankind, as new as the moment, and as tender and thrilling as any bride could wish.

If only she could have kept him home, kept him from the doomed flight. If only she could somehow call him back.

Joshua had been en route to Texas to play a weekend of concerts with the Houston Symphony. His successful substitution for Martha Argerich with the New York Philharmonic five years before had boosted his career in America and Europe. The flight had not been completely booked, but according to the airline's seating chart, Joshua and five others had sat near the epicenter of the explosion near the back of the plane. Eric Tecken's first-class seat hadn't saved him.

Although many bodies had been recovered and identified, those of Joshua and the other five were yet to be found. Sam and those families lived in limbo; they all had to wait for DNA evidence to identify their loved ones, and no one knew when, or if, that would come in.

"Why are you crying, Mamma? Albi wants to know." He tapped the nose of his one-eyed lamb, whose once-white curly coat was currently grimy gray.

Sam drew her gaze from the view of the river. She hadn't even realized she was weeping. "Oh, I'm just missing Daddy a little." She took a tissue from her pocket and wiped her face.

"Albi wants to know if we'll see him at the lake where we're going? Will he take us for a boat ride?"

His hopeful eyes broke her heart. He still did not comprehend that his father was gone forever. How could he? She had trouble with the reality of it herself. "No, not this time, honey."

To distract him, she asked if he was ready to eat. "This is a special part of our adventure, Peter. There's a whole car that's just for dining." She held out her hand and he grasped it with his sticky fingers, still coated with pudding. "Uh, let's wash our hands first, and then we'll go eat."

"Albi, too? He can eat my salad."

"Yes. Albi, too." Getting Peter to eat vegetables was the least of her worries now.

After his dinner of macaroni and cheese (plus two bites of peas) with ice cream for dessert, Sam gave him a quick bath. When Peter's eyes grew heavy, she tucked him and his ragged lamb into bed. She kissed him goodnight and then recited William Blake's poem. Peter knew it by heart and joined in.

> *Little lamb, who made thee?*
> *Dost thou know who made thee,*
> *Gave thee life, and bid thee feed*
> *By the stream and o'er the mead;*
> *Gave thee clothing of delight,*
> *Softest clothing, woolly, bright;*
> *Gave thee such a tender voice,*
> *Making all the vales rejoice?*
> *Little lamb, who made thee?*
> *Dost thou know who made thee?*

Peter yawned and his eyes fluttered shut. "Keep going, Mamma." He hugged Albi while Sam continued softly:

> *Little lamb, I'll tell thee:*
> *He is called by thy name,*
> *For He calls Himself a Lamb.*
> *He is meek, and He is mild,*
> *He became a little child.*
> *I a child, and thou a lamb,*
> *We are called by His name.*
> *Little lamb, God bless thee!*
> *Little lamb, God bless thee!*

By the time she finished, he had fallen asleep.

Their route led north to Albany, and from there east to Buffalo. The train would hug the southern coast of Lake Erie most of the way to Chicago. As the train sped into the night, she mused on life and death: a baby's first breath, the last gasps of the dying, the alpha and omega of mortality. Joshua had told her of his anger and grief when he discovered Li Ling had aborted their child. When Sam told him she was expecting, his anticipation and deep delight matched hers—like a bell, she had resonated with it.

Lulled by the rocking train, she closed her eyes and remembered her mother's words: *Children come at the appointed time.* The way the pregnancy changed her body and formed a new living being within her—completely independent of her will—had astonished her. Her body carried out its business efficiently. Like a bemused bystander, she observed the process in quiet amazement. By the ninth month, as she looked down upon the half-globe that had supplanted her formerly flat abdomen, trepidation raised its head. A whole lot of baby would have to exit soon, with only a very small opening as the portal. How would that work?

In fact, it almost didn't. It was a long, hard labor, and the baby had the umbilical cord wrapped twice around his neck. He struggled in the birthing; he wasn't getting enough oxygen. The doctor made a quick decision, and the next thing she knew, they raced her gurney down the hall to the operating room. Dazed with fatigue and pain, she watched the ceiling lights flash by.

One emergency Caesarian later, she was a mother. In the recovery room, they laid her son in her arms. One of the nurses helped Sam bare her breast, and the infant clamped on for dear life. She could not stop smiling. She watched her tiny boy in wonder.

In an earlier time, in different circumstances, her baby could have died, or been born with brain damage due to lack of oxygen. But thanks to the modern hospital and the doctor's skill, he lived and thrived. Only much later did it occur to her that perhaps the dark forces that control this world had wanted the child to die.

That evening, after her mother, Leo, and Joshua had left, she lay in the private room, alone for the first time with Peter. As she touched the incredibly soft, silken skin of his face, he reached for her hand and enclosed one finger in his tiny fist. His head was slightly misshapen from the difficult birth, but the doctor had assured her it would round out in a few weeks. She studied the wisps of dark hair crowning his skull, the long black lashes, the close-set, perfect ears, the strong nose and the eyes, still indeterminate in color, peering out at the world—a place of danger and wonder, good and evil. A melody came into her mind as she watched her son. *He's got the whole world in his hands.*

"As the Lord holds his creation, so I hold you." She kissed him softly on the forehead. She and Peter were the center of the world, the only world she wanted. She bent her head down and breathed in his musky scent of milk and flesh. The solid weight and warmth of him grounded her, gave her comfort. She wanted to prolong this moment, this oneness forever, to delay his trajectory into the world, away from her. Like a fledgling bird, he would someday leave the nest. Even so, she knew it was her duty to make him strong and independent so he could.

Sam roused herself from all the memories and came back to the present. In the tiny bathroom, she took a shower then changed into her pajamas. They would reach Chicago sometime around noon the next day. There they would change trains and continue the sad journey south to Texas, to Joshua's watery grave. Physically exhausted and emotionally worn out, she climbed into bed with Peter, hoping for the respite of sleep without dreams.

CHERUBINO

Saturday, September 26, 2026

As is often the case with adolescent males, Cherubino's troubles sprang from his newfound infatuation with women. When the panicked pageboy jumped out of the second-story window, fleeing discovery by Count Almaviva, his heart pounded wildly. He landed dead center on the mattress positioned backstage, in the sure and certain hope that his dramatic flight would simply lead to his dressing room in the opera house.

It did, but as in all things earthly, complications do develop.

Mezzo soprano Katie Lamb had just completed her part of Act II as the hormone-driven teenager in Mozart's *The Marriage of Figaro*. The trouser role required her to dress and act like a young man. When she leapt down off the stage set, she had no idea her flight had just begun, a flight that would take her from the Chicago Lyric Opera's Saturday matinee to a place she never wanted to go.

With performance adrenaline driving her, she wended her way backstage and charged upstairs to the hallway. She quickly tapped in the four-digit code to enter the dressing room. The mirror and brilliant lights reflected her enormous smile and the sheen of perspiration coating her face. She exulted over the thunderous applause the aria

"*Voi che sapete*" had received and the audience's laughter at the comic hijinks of Act II.

Katie studied herself in the mirror. In the white puffy-sleeved shirt, red vest, yellow knee-pants, white hose, and black shoes, she did indeed resemble a lanky adolescent boy. Her life as a farm girl and the years of roughhousing with her two brothers had given her a physical confidence that had made the twenty-eight-year-old perfect for the role of Cherubino. In the latest reviews she had been praised both for her acting and singing. It amused her that her realistic onstage male swagger attracted female admirers who contacted her by social media.

"Sorry, girls. I'm in the market for a guy."

She sat down at the dressing table and used a tissue to pat away the perspiration, careful not to smear her makeup. Through the theater's backstage sound system, she could hear the cast and orchestra in the act's long, rousing finale. She smiled to herself—the performance was going really well.

Suddenly, she heard a voice coming from above and to her right. "Take your backpack and exit the theater through the loading dock now."

Startled, she quickly glanced back over her right shoulder, but no one was there—she was alone in the dressing room. She drew her brows down in concentration. The voice was not an announcement—it had not interrupted the brilliant music of the second act finale, still playing through the overhead speaker.

Exit the theatre in the middle of the opera? She might as well ditch her budding career—the company would fire her on the spot. There were still two acts to go. Was this someone's idea of a prank? That must be the answer—it would be just like Hugh Murray, the roguish baritone from London who sang the role of Figaro.

She jerked involuntarily when she heard it again. "Take your backpack and exit the theatre through the loading dock now!"

This time the voice was louder and more commanding. *Insistent.*

How could it be Hugh? She could hear him singing the title role onstage. Katie's hand trembled as she dropped the tissue on the dressing table. Was she losing her mind? Hearing voices? Was the voice real or in her head?

Well, she wouldn't play along. It had to be some kind of a joke. How could she leave? She couldn't go AWOL in the middle of a performance. She sat back and took a deep breath. That was when the wooden chair began to rock back and forth. She gasped and clutched the chair arms. Looking up, she met her own frightened eyes in the mirror. At least she could see the movement of the chair—no hallucination there.

"Take your backpack and exit the theatre now!" Louder still.

What the hell? She was thoroughly unnerved. Well . . . all right. She could play along, at least temporarily, and maybe everything would sort itself out shortly. She had the fifteen-minute intermission and time after that before her entrance in Act III. She stood up and the chair ceased to move. With trembling fingers, she grasped her backpack. Feeling ridiculous and anxious at the same time, she grabbed her street jacket, just in case, and left the dressing room.

She hurried downstairs to the loading dock and pushed open the human-sized door beside the massive metal loading dock doors. To her dismay, it was raining heavily outside. She donned the denim jacket over her costume and dug a worn, purple Vikings cap out of her backpack. (A rebellious Wisconsonite, she disliked Green Bay.) "Go, Minnesota," she murmured as she drew it on. She picked up a rubber doorstopper from the floor and wedged it so that there was a narrow opening, not too obvious, for when she had to get back in.

As she hesitated just outside the doorway, she heard the burst of applause that signaled the end of Act II. *Am I nuts? What am I doing here?* Convinced she was an idiot, she turned to go back inside. At that moment, she heard a loud, startling *pop-pop, pop-pop-pop!*

She'd shot enough quail in Wisconsin to know gunfire when she heard it. *Coming from inside the theater.* A wave of fear made her whole body quake. A terrorist attack? What was going on?

Then she heard the screams.

That decided her. She took another step onto the sidewalk just outside the building and swung her head rapidly both ways. To the north, an army tank blocked the intersection. *A tank? Were we at war? Was this an invasion?* Armed soldiers, booted, wearing camouflage and blue helmets, swarmed around the front of the opera house. *Oh, my God.* Heart hammering, she stepped out into the pouring rain and walked quickly in the opposite direction. She feared running would draw too much attention, the last thing she wanted. Like a magician's rabbit, she needed to disappear . . . to where?

The driving rain soon penetrated the denim jacket and soaked her knee pants and hose, chilling her. Water seeped into her black patent-leather shoes, between her toes. Every step she took made a squishing sound. Cold, irritating droplets found their way under her collar and down her back. Shivering and afraid, Katie Lamb pulled down the bill of her cap, lowered her head, and headed south on Wacker Drive. At West Madison, she turned right and crossed over the river on the Lyric Opera Bridge. She immediately turned left onto S. Canal Street, and from there it was a straight shot to Union Station. It took a matter of eight minutes.

She took out her mobile phone to call the stage manager and check on the other singers, but there was no signal. *Why not?* Katie heard more gunshots and shouts up ahead. When she saw soldiers coming toward her, she ducked into the Great Hall of Union Station, hoping Chicago's grand, secular cathedral would give her asylum. Frightened, but hiding her fear by assuming a role as she did on stage, she strode confidently into the crowd with a male swagger. If there was an invading army about, she certainly didn't want the soldiers to think she was a woman. She thanked God for her height, athletic build, and her tomboy past. As a mezzo soprano, she drew on her roles of Hansel in *Hansel and Gretel* and Octavian in *Rosenkavalier*. She knew how to be convincing as a young man onstage; now she had to have the same panache in real life.

With a long, confident stride, she moved quickly through the crowded hall. She had no idea where she was going, or what she was fleeing, but she hoped to lose herself in the maze of people until she could figure out what was happening. The straps of her backpack dug into her shoulders. Stuffed with energy bars, nuts, dried fruit, and crackers, her collection of ten silver spoons, a money clip choked with cash in case the banks closed, gold and silver jewelry, comb, toiletries, makeup, and an extra pair of underwear (green), it was her survival cache. Her friends mocked her, but now Katie the prepper was vindicated. She stuck her mobile phone in an outer pocket, hoping at some point it would no longer be a piece of electronic junk.

She found herself humming a tune, and raised her eyebrows when she recalled the words: *Lead me, O thou great Jehovah, o'er the world's tempestuous sea.* She murmured, "Lord, I'm not kidding. I have no idea what to do or where to go."

"Get on the train to Dallas." Again, coming from above and to the right, the voice surprised her. Katie glanced over her shoulder, but at this point she didn't expect to see anyone. And of course, at that moment, there was no one near her.

She stopped at a large electronic sign listing departures and arrivals and checked her watch. The next train to Dallas left in five minutes. *Now what?* She didn't have time to purchase a ticket. She'd just brazen it out—board and pay for it once she was on the train. (She hoped that would work. If not, her next stop might be jail.)

She walked quickly downstairs to the platforms and found the train. She glanced back as distant shouts reached her, and a flood of frightened people spilled over the top of the stairs and charged down in her direction. She stepped aboard, caught in a surreal dream. She was supposed to be singing the third act of the *Marriage of Figaro*, but now, flushed out of the opera house by an apparent military massacre, guided by a voice from above, she boarded a train to Texas and fled the city.

RELOCATION

Like giant, misshapen snowflakes strewn by the wind, luminous white patches dotted the shore and lake as dusk descended. Gideon's stomach clenched as the boat approached Jaybird's Thatch Island cabin. He suspected it was plane debris that had drifted west, pushed by wind and water, although the cleanup crews really shouldn't have missed that much.

Jaybird killed the motor, guided the boat to the pier, and secured it. Gideon picked up one of the white oblong pieces on the pier. Relieved, he realized it was not plane debris at all, but some sort of notice. Multiple copies littered the area. He folded it in half and stuck it in his back pocket. He would read it later.

The injured man was looking up at him, wild-eyed. "Hey, dude, you're all right—I'm glad you're awake," Gideon said. "Jaybird, he's conscious."

Jaybird knelt on the pier beside the boat and gazed at the stranger.

"Where am I?" Though the man spoke softly, Gideon noticed some kind of accent.

"You're in Legend."

"Legend?" He squinted as if he was trying to focus his eyes or his mind, or both.

"Yeah," replied Jaybird. "Let's talk when we're inside. First, we need to get you outta the boat and into the house."

To avoid pulling on his arms, Gideon grasped him by the waist and lifted him. The man groaned in pain, and the boat rocked, making it awkward and difficult, but they finally got him up onto the pier. He was too weak to walk on his own. "Jaybird, let's grab him around the torso, so we don't hurt his shoulders."

Supporting him on either side, they half-carried him into the house. He could hardly put any weight on his injured ankle. Gideon wrinkled his nose at the sharp, sour stink of him. They sat him down on the sofa, and Jaybird brought him a glass of water, which he drained. "I've got some leftover gumbo I can heat up. It's prob'ly best to start him on liquids instead of solid food. There's enough for all of us."

While the gumbo heated, Gideon helped the man take off his jeans so he could examine his lower body. His legs were bruised but sound, and only one ankle was swollen. "Can you move your ankle?"

He nodded and flexed his ankle. "Hurts, but I don't think it's broken."

"Your shoulders hurt?"

"Oh, yeah."

"They're both dislocated, but we'll try to fix that later. What's your name?" Gideon asked.

The man shook his head and blinked; his hazel eyes were wide with fear and confusion. "I don't know . . . uh . . . I can't remember." He shivered.

"Huh, maybe you had a concussion. Do you remember hitting your head or falling?"

"No. Just wandering in the woods, hungry. My mind . . . my memory . . . it's all blank." He shook his head. "Everything runs together. I . . . uh . . . don't know why. I don't know what happened."

"Well, don't worry. We'll figure it out soon, I'm sure. My name is Gideon, and this is Jaybird. It's his cabin."

Jaybird brought a light blanket to cover him. "After you eat," he told the man, "Gideon will try to fix the shoulders and then we'll put you in the tub to clean up."

To Gideon, he added, "Epsom salts. It'll sting some of those bites at first, but it would be good for him to take a real long soak. It'll prob'ly help the ankle, too."

While Jaybird and Gideon wolfed down full bowls of gumbo and rice, the stranger slowly ate half a bowl of the broth with a little rice and drank more water. The food seemed to revive him; his cheeks took on a rosy hue.

"All right, now that you've got some food in your stomach, we'll clean you up a bit. Jaybird, can you bring me a basin of warm water, some soap, a washcloth and a towel—and some ibuprofen." He turned his head away and coughed.

Jaybird gave the stranger two ibuprofen. "Sit over here on this kitchen chair."

While they waited for the ibuprofen to take effect, Gideon sat on another chair facing the young man and gently bathed his face and his shoulders. "All right, sit up straight and hold your right arm by your side. Hold onto my forearm with yours. Take some deep breaths and just relax. I'm going to massage your shoulder first, over your collarbone, then the deltoid and finally the bicep."

With just a little massaging, the muscles relaxed, and the shoulder popped back into place. "There it goes."

"Oh man, that feels better."

"Wow, that took less than a minute," said Jaybird. "Where'd you learn to do that?"

"I saw the medics do it in Afghanistan. The Cunningham technique." Gideon bent the arm across the man's chest and then flexed it up and down. "All right?"

"Yes, seems fine. Thank you."

Gideon coughed into his elbow. "Now the other one."

Afterward, Jaybird ran a bath with Epsom salts. They helped the stranger out of his underwear and eased him into the tub.

"Here's a towel and washcloth," said Jaybird. "Prob'ly best to soak a long time before you wash."

"Thanks." He winced a little at the heat and the sting when the water covered his scratches. He crossed his arms over his chest and laid his head back.

"Yell when you're ready to get out," said Jaybird.

As the water enveloped his body, he gasped as the salt found its way into all his scratches and abrasions. His ankle throbbed. The only thing sharper than the smarting saltwater bath was fear. Was he insane? Was he hallucinating? What was his name, his history? He had lost himself. He closed his arms over his chest in a protective manner and tried to think, but his thoughts swirled and flapped like torn, ragged banners in a maelstrom.

How can a grown man not even know his own name? How long had he wandered in the woods, alone and confused, and why? Where had he come from, and where was Legend? Who were these men who had found and fed him, the young black guy and the white man with the nagging cough?

He had no answers—only questions. He was a man without a history. His whole life, or all he could remember, was the long, aimless wandering in the woods. Headache, thirst, throbbing pain. He remembered eating very little: a few rotten wild plums and dandelion leaves. His strength had waned a little every day. As he grew weaker, the boundary between reality and hallucination blurred. He had held onto one thing in the long, waking nightmare: he didn't want to die. He survived on lake water and obstinance.

He remembered waking up on the forest floor, face down. He hurt everywhere. He opened his eyes and watched a line of ants march across blackened leaf debris, onto his hand. They disappeared under the cuff of his jacket. He brushed off the ants, rolled over, and groaned in pain. He did not know where he was or how he had got there. Surrounded by thick underbrush, he looked up at a dense canopy of trees hung with ropy vines. The chill air was damp, foggy. It felt like early morning. Not fully awake, he lay there on his back an interminable time, as though he had snagged himself in a bad dream, just on the cusp of consciousness. In the neverland between sleep and waking, his mind rambled, confused and agitated. Surely this was a nightmare; he would wake up and find himself home. But where was home? His head ached. His shoulders and ankle hurt. He closed his eyes and slipped back into oblivion.

The light woke him. While he slept, sunshine had dispersed the fog, and bright shafts of light pierced the leafy canopy, warming him. He was thirsty; he had to pee. His head still ached, and he felt a sharp pain when he moved his arms. He sat up and grimaced. "Oh, God." Barbs of pain behind his eyes and in his shoulders impaled him and took his breath away. He leaned forward and gazed bleary-eyed at his left ankle. It was twice the size of the other one and the swollen skin had a bluish tinge. He was able to move it gingerly. Only a bad sprain, he hoped.

He slid on his backside over to a young pine tree. He grasped the trunk with his left hand for leverage and support. Oh, man that hurt—something was wrong with his shoulder. When he put his weight on his good leg to help him rise, a sharp pain in his foot made him yelp. He had stepped on a briar growing at the base of the tree. Why was he barefoot? How had he lost his shoes? Sitting on the ground, he scraped up pine needles to cover the thorny vine, and then tried again. He struggled up, awkward and hurting, but he got to his feet. He held onto the tree, swaying slightly, engulfed by waves of pain, eyes closed.

Leaning on the tree, he unzipped his fly and relieved himself. His stomach growled. He checked his pockets for anything to eat. He found two cellophane-wrapped peppermints in one jacket pocket and a quarter in the other. No wallet, no clue to his own identity.

He found himself in an alien world. He had no memory of this place. He recognized nothing—no landmarks, nothing at all to tell him where he was. When he tried to think back beyond waking in the forest, he came up against a frightening, impenetrable darkness. With every passing moment his anxiety grew, until his heart pounded in his ears. Eyes squeezed shut in blind panic, he hugged the pine tree like a terrified child holding onto his mother's knees. It seemed like hours before the anxiety attack passed and his heartbeat slowed.

Still holding onto the tree trunk for balance, he relaxed his grip and looked around. Was this what a newborn felt like—ejected identityless into the strangeness of the world, with its only memory a dark womb? A mysterious wall lay between his present and his past. He could neither penetrate it nor climb it. A blank—full stop.

He unwrapped a peppermint and popped it into his mouth. It was small comfort, but as a little piece of reality, it made him feel better. Then he noticed the gold band on his left ring finger. He had a wife; he was someone who had bought peppermints; he had money in his pocket. He had to have come from somewhere—even if it all eluded him. Surely in time he would remember. He peered in each direction. Now what? Woods were woods. No street signs, no billboards. Where was food? Where was water? Where were other human beings who would help him?

He leaned down and grabbed a fallen tree branch. Using it to support his bad leg, he began to walk haltingly in the direction where the undergrowth was thinnest. He had to ignore the pain and move. He was certain of only one thing: if he stayed here, he would die.

While the stranger soaked, Jaybird and Gideon got their catch out of the boat. Under the porch light, they rapidly cleaned and gutted the six good-sized catfish and rinsed them off. Jaybird brought the fish in the house, wrapped them in plastic, and put them in the freezer. They washed their hands and sat down for a minute.

That was when Gideon remembered the piece of paper he'd picked up on the pier. He slid it out of his back pocket and unfolded it.

09/25/2026 - Region VI
Mandatory Relocation Notice

All citizens of Region VI are ordered to report to the nearest post office by 11:00 p.m. this evening for Relocation Assignments. Bring National ID. Each individual allowed one suitcase for personal items.

Imprisonment of up to 15 years and $10,000 fine for non-compliance.

Authorized by Gen. Richard Huffman, Acting Region VI Governor

"Relocation assignments? What the hell are they talking about? Look at this, Jaybird."

Jaybird quickly read the notice. "Relocation at eleven o'clock?" He glanced at his watch. "Man, that's three hours from now. Is this some kind of political round-up?"

"Could be. Governor General Huffman is a megalomaniac. His lust for power knows no end." Gideon's tone was bitter. "But I don't think he could make this kind of drastic policy decision on his own." Gideon scratched his head. "Eric Tecken, who died in the plane crash, was the last conservative governor in the ten regions. Unlike Tecken, Huffman has no scruples—his allegiance is to himself. He will be the willing tool of the powers-that-be." He looked around the room, "Where's the TV—let's turn it on."

"Ain't got one. This'll have to do." Jaybird walked over and flicked the switch on a clock radio on the kitchen counter. The male voice on the radio announced, "Notice to all citizens of Region VI: You are ordered to report by eleven p.m. to the nearest post office for Relocation Assignments . . . "

"Same wording as the paper we got. Try another channel," said Gideon.

Jaybird tried every station he could. FM and AM—it was all the same. Each station broadcasted a repeating, automated loop. No music, no commercials, no commentary, no explanation: just the monotonous announcement.

"Wait a minute," said Jaybird. He disappeared into one of the bedrooms and came back shortly with a Red Cross emergency radio. "Just checked on our friend." Jaybird smiled. "Mr. Bigfoot's sound asleep in the tub."

He held up the small, windup radio. "This thing can pick up shortwave broadcasts from all over." He extended the antenna and vigorously rotated the black handle on the side, producing a whirring noise. "This charges it up," he said. "It sounds like the old-fashioned eggbeater my mamma had." He kept on for a minute or so, until he sweated with the effort.

"Let's see what we got." He set it to shortwave and fiddled with the tuning dial. The radio crackled with static, but from one bandwidth to another it produced no voices, only high-pitched whines and static.

"Do you think it's shot?" Gideon asked.

"No, I know it works."

They got more static as Jaybird carefully rotated the tuning dial. A man's voice suddenly emerged from the white noise. " . . . roadblocks, with troops and tanks . . . " Then they lost the signal.

They locked eyes. "Keep trying," said Gideon, indicating the radio. "Before we figure out what to do, we need the whole story. But I, for one, have no intention of following General Richard Huffman's orders."

Jaybird's eyes widened, and he blew out an audible breath. "Me neither." He slowly shook his head. "No way."

FLIGHT

Constantin padded his back with three pillows and leaned against the headboard of the double bed. He had just eaten a Frisbee-sized cheeseburger with a mountain of fries in the hotel restaurant and topped it off with cherry pie and ice cream. The food and his fatigue from the trip made him drowsy, but he still wanted to read more of Dumitru's diary. He knew he would have plenty of time on the train trip to Dallas the next day, but his curiosity prodded him and wouldn't let him rest. Or at least not yet. He opened the book.

At last—the trap is planned and in due time it will be sprung—in the last bastion, save Israel—in the nation most critical to conquer, where power resides: America. Everything hinges on the United States. Once America is subdued, the world shall be governed by one leader with absolute control.

Europe is ours long since. The leaders of the EU are puppets in league with each other, all dutiful servants of our god. Though their member states appear as separate entities on maps, their individual sovereignty is simply an illusion. Like blocks of salt thrown into the sea, those countries will soon dissolve into the whole, our New World Order.

The Judeo-Christian foundation of the Western world is crumbling. Hitler dealt the death blow to European Jewry, and now, less than seven decades later, most of those who call themselves Christians are Christian in name only. They have no real spiritual power. Their numbers diminish; they wither away like leaves on a dead tree. In Europe, one wonders how many true believers remain. Churches are converted into mosques, nightclubs, restaurants, bookstores, breweries, and—how laughable—even skate parks. When put to the test, how many Christians will choose martyrdom over conversion to our god?

Very soon now, we shall see.

Constantin laid the slim, clothbound book in his lap. Written many years earlier, it was evidence of a very long-term plan, indeed. In the intervening time, actual events had taken the direction his stepfather foretold.

But the passage he had just read puzzled him. Why would the powers-that-be—if this emanated from the powers-that-be and wasn't some sort of megalomaniac fantasy—why would they target Christians? Did Christians pose some sort of worldwide power threat?

Constantin laid his head back against the headboard and laughed. Maybe he underestimated the Christ-followers: Who knew what havoc those savage gangs of English choirboys could unleash? Their piercing high notes might overcome whole armies, mow down artillery, and cause fighter planes to fall from the cerulean sky.

And don't forget the Hebrews. Israel and America harbored violent hordes of Torah-toting rabbis and yeshiva students with their yarmulkes and bouncing side curls, those rapacious aggressors. If their shofars had the power to knock down walls in ancient Jericho, well, with a group effort, they could quite possibly shift the earth on its axis. Yes, indeed, the Judeo-Christian ruffians apparently scared the crap out of the elite.

Constantin scratched his head. But what, really, was at the heart of their fear? The elite did not live in dread of a weaker force; they feared a power greater than their own.

His only point of reference was Stella Amore; she was the one Christian he knew. Well, there was Tony, but he didn't seem as strong in faith as his wife. She went to Mass every Sunday, and sometimes on other days—Feast Days. She prayed the rosary every day. She was hell on spiders, flies, dust bunnies, and dirty dishes, but where people were concerned, Stella was as ferocious as a butterfly.

So if the Christians themselves did not inspire fear, it had to be their leader, Jesus Christ. Constantin had heard the name used as an expletive many times; he himself had spat it out in anger. But Christians all over the world revered his name.

Jesus Christ was a man, a Jewish man. He also claimed to be God.

Constantin had never really considered the man. He had read and thought about other famous men: baseball players, opera stars, William Shakespeare, J. R. R. Tolkien, Nikola Tesla, and Winston Churchill. But he had not considered the one man whose birth became the dividing point of history, the one man for whom Gothic cathedrals had been built, endless hymns had been written, and for whom countless martyrs had been crucified, beheaded, or burned at the stake. Quite a résumé.

Throughout time, temples had been erected for other deities: temples to Baal and the goddess Ishtar in ancient Syria. There were Hindu temples and Buddhist temples all over the world. But neither Buddha, nor any of the millions of Hindu gods, nor Baal, nor Ishtar had become *the* pivotal figure in history. The years were reckoned according to that one nativity. It was 2026—as many would say, *Anno Domini*—the year of the Lord. Maybe it was time to learn about the Lord who was feared by the most powerful entities on earth.

Constantin yawned, weary from traveling. He had paid for the bus ticket in cash at the Port Authority Terminal. His twelve-hour trip from New York to Pittsburgh had worn him out and given him a colossal backache, but he was sure it had given him a head start over any electronic tracking. He flew from Pittsburgh to Chicago and took a cab to the historic hotel. The interior wrought-iron railings and gleaming mahogany paneling reminded him of London. Of the two elevators, only one worked, and it took its time, clanking as it ascended. It was charming in an old-fashioned way, a survivor of a more elegant era. No plastic key cards here: he opened the door with the real metal deal. Small, but cozy, the room was surprisingly quiet despite the fact that the hotel was situated in the heart of the city.

After a good night's sleep, he intended to treat himself to a late birthday breakfast and a matinee performance of *Le nozze di Figaro* at the Lyric Opera. But his pleasure in striking out on his own was shadowed by guilt. While Tony and Stella had spent the previous day buying supplies to prepare for the military action the General had warned them about, Constantin had slipped out of the house and made several ATM cash withdrawals. That night, after they went to bed, he stuffed his backpack with clothes, took the diary, the cash, and his Swiss ID, and headed for the Port Authority. To help cover his tracks, he left his National ID (US) behind. He felt like a cad for leaving them, and he hoped they would come to no harm if there was violence or some kind of offensive operation in New York.

He had blocked Tony's calls—he knew he had worried the Amores and possibly imperiled their employment. Dumitru would hold them responsible. They were probably frantic now that he had been missing two nights. But what else could he have done? They would never have let him leave on his own. Neither the Amores nor anyone else knew the urgency in his heart to discover the truth about his father. Since the only one who could really give him the necessary information was General Huffman, his grandfather, Constantin intended to pay him a visit.

Somehow, he would make it up to Tony and Stella. The blame was his alone, and he would tell Dumitru just that.

He yawned and roused himself to take a shower. Afterward, he changed into his pajamas and crawled under the bedcovers. He breathed a short prayer. "Jesus the Christ, if you are there, help me find my father." He closed his eyes and fell asleep almost instantly.

He slept late the next morning. When he finally forced himself to rise from the warm, comfortable bed, he remembered the date was September 26, his sixteenth birthday. He dressed for the occasion in khaki slacks, a blue button-down shirt, and a navy-blue blazer. His sneakers didn't quite match his outfit, but in his situation, comfort and mobility trumped style.

A glance out the window revealed a gray day with low, scudding clouds. He checked the weather on his phone—eighty percent chance of rain. He decided he had better protect the diary from the damp; it had become his most valuable possession. He wrapped it in the white plastic lining from the bathroom trash can and stuffed it in his backpack with everything else. He checked out and went into the hotel restaurant, adjacent to the lobby. He set his backpack in the booth beside him and quickly perused the menu. When the waiter came to take his order, he pointed to two different breakfasts.

The waiter leaned forward to see. "Yes sir, did you want the strawberry and whipped cream waffles with bacon, or the goat cheese and avocado omelet?"

Constantin grinned. "Both, with extra bacon and a bottomless cup of coffee."

"Umm, are you expecting someone to join you? Should I bring more silverware?"

"No, I'm alone." As the words left his mouth, he realized their truth, exhilarating and frightening at the same time.

"Yes, sir. Do you want cream and sugar with your coffee?"

"Just cream. Have to watch my calories."

The waiter put in the order and remarked to the chef, "It's always the skinny ones who eat the most."

Constantin started with the omelet, and had the waffles for dessert, enjoying his freedom as much as his breakfast. When he finished, he had one more coffee refill and lingered at the table. With his iPhone he checked the opera schedule, the train departures from Union Station, and the walking directions to each. The opera matinee began at two. There was a train leaving for Dallas at 1:45 and another at 5:30. He figured he could make the 5:30, since Union Station was only a seven-minute walk from the opera house. Pleased with his research and improvised itinerary, he burped discreetly, paid his bill in cash, and left.

It took twenty minutes to walk to the Lyric Opera House. He was glad of the blazer, since the Windy City lived up to its reputation. The strong, chilly breeze with the smell of water in it ruffled his hair and drove the covering of thick, gray clouds to the east, like a relentless border collie nipping the heels of its flock. Constantin hoped he would find the opera house before the rain found him.

When he arrived, he saw a most welcome sight. A young man outside on the sidewalk waved a ticket above his head. "Ticket for sale! Ticket for sale, lower balcony!"

"What's your price?" Constantin asked.

"Seventy-five."

He took out his money clip. "I'll take it." *Excellent—not traceable.* He paid the young man, placed the ticket in his blazer pocket, and walked into the fine Art Deco building as the first few drops of rain spattered the steps.

Inside, he presented the ticket and received a thick, glossy program in return. He headed to the lower balcony, where he found the restroom. Therein, with a sigh of relief, he let fly an impressive amount of bodily fluid (28 seconds, steady), thanks to his bottomless cup of coffee. As he left the restroom, he passed an Emergency Exit door with a crash bar. Tony always said, "When you go into a new place, kid, case the joint and find the exits. If a fight breaks out, you can get the hell outta there fast." *Done, Tony.*

He found his aisle seat, about halfway up the balcony and placed his backpack underneath it. He had decent leg room, firm cushions cradling his back and bottom, and a very good sightline to the proscenium stage. Impressed by the height of the ceiling and the size of the space, he admired the calming bronze, green, and gold of the interior, set off by the deep red carpet.

From the program, he discovered the Ardis Krainik Theatre was named after a mezzo soprano who became the general director of the Lyric Opera of Chicago. It was the second-largest theater after the Met, with about 3,500 seats. The lofty ceiling was actually twelve stories high.

He knew how much Tony would have enjoyed being here; he would have understood every word of Lorenzo da Ponte's Italian libretto. Guilt stung him like a dart. Tony, who was surely trying to locate him before too much time passed, would soon be forced to contact Dumitru and Talyssa. Constantin silently vowed he would explain it all, apologize, and exonerate Tony at some future point, probably when he arrived at the General's house in Dallas—about twenty-four hours from now. It would be all right—everything would work out perfectly.

To distract himself from his sins, he opened the program to the pictures and biographies of the cast and artistic team. He and Tony had heard Hugh Murray, the English baritone cast as Figaro, on one of the Met's live Saturday broadcasts. In that production of *The Magic Flute*, Hugh Murray had sung the comic role of Papageno. Constantin looked forward to seeing him in person. The role of Susanna would be sung by an American soprano, Lindsey Bell, whom he did not know. She was a question mark, to be swiftly answered in the opening duet with Figaro. The trouser role of Cherubino was an attractive, blonde American mezzo with a gap between her front teeth, Katie Lamb, in her debut performance with the Lyric Opera. In Geneva, he had seen the spectacular Alice Coote as Cherubino. He doubted if Katie Lamb or anyone else could top the bar Ms. Coote had set.

The hall filled with people who settled into their seats as curtain time quickly approached. In the pit, the musicians warmed up in a pre-performance orchestral stew, practicing passages and excerpts, oblivious of the audience and one another. The resultant concoction of sound included bits of flutey, reedy woodwinds, blasts of brass and tympani against violin volleys, cello chatter, and booming basses. Sheer cacophony.

When the conductor entered and the applause rose and died the orchestra played together: sixty individuals became one living entity. Their collective sound coalesced into the famous overture. Somehow, through Mozart's magic, the breathless, lively music portrayed effervescent excitement and intrigue. It drew smiles from the faces in the audience (including Constantin's) and set the atmosphere.

The story begins in early morning on the wedding day of two servants, Figaro and Susanna, and concludes the same evening. They must foil the plans of their aristocratic employer, the philandering Count Almaviva, who schemes to exercise his "feudal right" to bed Susanna first, to the betrothed couple's deep distress, and that of his wife the Countess. In less than twenty-four hours, the tale traverses a world of human emotions and follies, schemes and schemers, plots and counterplots. There is revenge, jealousy, infidelity, forgiveness, and true love, suffused with beauty, nuance, and psychological depth by Mozart's sublime music.

What a birthday present: *Perfetto!*

To Constantin's delight, Hugh Murray as Figaro lived up to his expectations. By turns amorous, perplexed, and angry, the barrel-chested baritone was as fine an actor as a singer. His wife-to-be, the small, spunky Susanna, matched him with an equally strong stage presence. A small-waisted, attractive brunette, her real name, Lindsey Bell, was fitting; she sang with a pure, clear, ringing tone. Cherubino should have looked like a fourteen-year-old boy, and did. The tall, slender Katie Lamb, had a convincing male swagger. To his surprise, her performance matched that of Alice Coote. With her own cornsilk hair pulled back and gathered at the nape of her neck, she wore a red vest over a puffy-sleeved white shirt with bright yellow knee pants and white hose, the perfect picture of an eighteenth-century pageboy.

Katie Lamb wasn't too busty either. As a connoisseur of female mammary glands, Constantin knew that a bosom too large spoiled a trouser role, no matter how well the character acted. With a purely clinical interest, of course, and a discriminating eye, he scanned Katie's chest, as he had those of Susanna and the Countess. Although the Countess's nose was too large and she had no waist to speak of, she owned two luscious melons in the breast department, with spectacular cleavage. Thankfully, Cherubino's chest appeared as flat as his own, making it easy to believe she was a guy. *She must have been a real tomboy growing up.*

In the second act, as part of an elaborate plot to foil the lecherous Count, Susanna and the Countess disguise Cherubino as a girl in the Countess's room. He is supposed to impersonate Susanna in a rendezvous with the Count that night in order to trap him. But before they can finish dressing the boy, the Count knocks at the door and throws them into a panic. Cherubino hides in a closet. The jealous Count suspects his wife is hiding a man there. Ultimately, Susanna takes Cherubino's place in the closet after she engineers Cherubino's escape. He jumps out the second story window and runs away. The tension builds until the Count and Countess, Figaro and Susanna, as well as Basilio, Bartolo, and Marcellina sing a final, complex septet in which all their inner thoughts and conflicts are made known, but left unresolved.

As the applause at the end of Act II began, Constantin did not join in. He grabbed his backpack and practically ran down the aisle—his full bladder demanded it. He exited the performance hall, rounded the corner, and burst into the men's room. He peed hard in relief (24 seconds). As he zipped up his trousers, he thought he heard firecrackers popping in the theater.

No—gunshots!

Then screams.

He didn't think twice—he dashed out of the restroom, ran to the Emergency Exit, and hit the crash bar. Whatever was going on, he wanted out of it. As the door closed behind him, Constantin found himself on the lower landing of a two-story metal staircase. It led down to an alley on one side of the theater. Cold rain pelted him as he scrambled down to street level.

He grimaced as he heard more muffled screams and shouts punctuated by gunfire from inside the building. Shielded from the street to his right by a huge metal garbage container, he peered around its edge. Armed soldiers with their backs to him blocked the entrance to the dark alley. He recognized the blue helmets of UN troops, which completely puzzled him and gave the scene an air of unreality. He would flee first and ask questions later.

Keeping close to the wall, he sidled away from the soldiers to the back of the opera house. He turned left into another very narrow alley and skirted the back wall. This alley opened up onto a main street. He sheltered in the alley a moment and reconnoitered. To his left, he could see the great metal doors and raised platform of the theater's loading dock. Beyond that were more troops, trucks, and tanks in the street that fronted the building.

Tanks? A "military action," his grandfather had warned. Apparently not just in New York.

The soldiers had blocked off traffic in front of the opera house. Some stood watch, while others herded people exiting the theater onto trucks like cattle: dressed-up old ladies, young women, men in suits and sport coats. They pushed and prodded them, shouted orders.

Where were they taking them and why?

Suddenly, a young man in a white shirt vaulted over the edge of the truck and tried to run away. Instantly, one of the soldiers shot him in the back. The man stumbled and collapsed on the street as a red stain bloomed and spread across the back of his shirt.

The brutality of it stunned Constantin. His knees shook. Fear bordering on terror immobilized him and rooted him to the sidewalk. Breathing fast and shallow, like an animal panting in shock, he felt cold sweat drench his armpits and run down his back.

He was alone in a strange city without help or support of any kind.

He couldn't think straight, nor could he remember how to get to the train station. Maybe he could catch the earlier train to Dallas. He took his iPhone out and punched the keys, but it was dead. *Damn it—why? He had fully charged it last night.* He stuffed the useless piece of junk in his blazer pocket.

Now what?

He glanced to his right down the street, gray and dimmed by rain. In the distance, he saw a spot of color moving away from him, a patch of yellow with white below. He suddenly recognized the lower half of Cherubino's costume: knee pants and hose. The mezzo soprano, still dressed for the stage, was also fleeing the theater. Even if he didn't know her, she was the only familiar person in his surroundings. She seemed to him like Hope—the one ray of light in a darkening and very frightening world.

He darted out of the alley and followed after her.

She had a good head start; she was at least a block and a half ahead, and her long, rapid strides ate up the sidewalk. He had the barest glimpse of her blonde ponytail under a purple baseball cap. Her backpack and denim jacket covered her upper body, but the knee pants and hose were unmistakable.

He had to watch his step on the slick cement. Puddles dotted the sidewalk and streams of water poured out from the gutters. He broke into a run, afraid he might lose sight of her, and the gap between them closed somewhat. As his feet pounded the pavement and his breath became labored, he wondered at himself. He had no idea where she was going or what he would do or say once he caught up with her. He just followed a blind instinct to go where she went.

"Oh, crap." She turned right down a different street, and he lost sight of her. Panic, hot as a gushing geyser, erupted in him. Dodging passersby, light poles, and dogs on leashes, he increased his pace. He made it to the corner in time to see her crossing a bridge over the river.

The cross-traffic prevented him from following. He halted at the intersection before the bridge. Frustrated and half-panicked, he jogged in place. At a break in the oncoming cars, he charged across the street and leapt the curb onto the bridge. He stumbled as the toe of his sneaker caught an uneven edge in the sidewalk. He lost his balance and went sprawling, face-first. He heard a clatter and watched his iPhone skitter across the pavement toward the edge. It slid under the railing and plunged into the river.

Merde.

Well, nothing he could do about it. If anyone tried to trace him through his phone now, they'd think he was fish food at the bottom of whatever river that was. He scrambled up and glanced at the muddy streaks on his khakis and blue blazer. He'd deal with that later. In the meantime, Cherubino had gained ground on him again. He broke into a run. The rain and the increasing number of people on the sidewalk made it difficult to keep her in sight. She turned left onto the first street after the bridge.

Constantin turned the corner shortly after, but she was still half a block ahead of him. Sweat ran down the sides of his face, and he had a stitch in his side. He could see a massive whitish building looming ahead, its exterior porticos and elegant colonnades probably made of limestone. Two-tiered, like a giant's wedding cake, it took up the whole block. Cherubino stopped short in front of the building to gaze ahead at something he could not see. Then she fled into the building and disappeared from his sight.

Like a predator stalking its prey, he dashed after her.

To his astonishment, she had led him into Union Station—right where he wanted to go. He ran under an arched roof, a barrel-vaulted ceiling of skylights, between supporting marble columns with leafy capitals. Her path led him through an enormous waiting area where travelers waited on wooden benches.

She stopped to read an electronic sign listing arrivals and departures. Then she looked at her watch and bolted away. Constantin also paused to read the sign. The train to Dallas departed in four minutes. He had time to make it. In the meantime, Katie Lamb had vanished. He didn't know where she was headed, but he had to catch the train to Dallas. Feeling wistful and somehow bereft, he guessed he'd probably never see her again, except on an opera stage somewhere. A phrase popped into his mind, and he blushed: *Sweet sixteen and never been kissed.*

He followed the signs to the correct platform, crestfallen and resigned. His goal was in sight, but his heart ached and his sneakers seemed to be weighted with concrete.

CHAPTER 20

AN UNEXPECTED GUEST

In a last burst of self-indulgence before her austerity measures kicked in, Sam had booked another bedroom on the leg from Chicago to Dallas. Still wounded and raw over Joshua's death, she craved the cocoon of protection a private room afforded. While she could, she wanted to wrap herself in the white gauze of privacy and solitude.

As they settled into their new room on the Texas Eagle, Sam could hear the voices and footsteps of passengers in the narrow corridor. The overhead speaker crackled to life, and the conductor announced there would be a slight delay in departure. "Due to a national emergency, we are taking on additional passengers as required by UN troops. Thank you for your patience. We will be underway in about a half hour."

National emergency? UN troops? What was he talking about? Alarmed, Sam glanced out the window and saw a surging crowd of people herded from behind by a few blue-helmeted soldiers bearing arms. *Foreign soldiers.* She quickly tried to access the news on her phone, but there was no service. At the same time, she heard raised voices and the sound of footsteps in the corridor. Suddenly, someone rapped three times on the door. Sam pushed the privacy curtain aside but kept the door locked. On the other side of the glass stood a tall, slender young person with an anxious expression.

He or she—Sam couldn't tell—had the currently in-vogue androgynous look, emphasized by heavy mascara, eye liner, and rouge, and a short blonde ponytail. His fashion sense was eclectic, to say the least—he dressed like a time traveler caught between two worlds. His clothes appeared to be twenty-first century above the waist—backpack, baseball cap, and denim jacket—and eighteenth-century below— yellow knee pants, white hose, and black patent-leather shoes.

Probably some kind of weirdo. "Yes?"

"Uh, hello, I'm one of the extra passengers. There are no coach seats left, so I wondered if I could possibly share your room?" Even his voice was androgynous—low, but somehow girlish. His anxious eyes were a startling blue, and when he respectfully doffed his baseball cap, his cowlick, a wayward strand of very blonde hair, popped up and made him look like he was fourteen years old. He clutched the strap of his backpack with a white-knuckled hand and shifted his weight nervously from foot to foot, as though he had an urgent need to pee.

While Sam tried to figure out what she should do, Peter rushed up beside her and asked, "Mamma, what's his name?"

His question elicited a broad smile. "My name is . . . Ka . . . uh . . . Cherubino."

Sam didn't believe the name for an instant, but she found the young man's gap-toothed smile charming. It projected a certain innocence, which helped calm her fears.

"Beano!" exclaimed Peter.

The smile widened in relief, revealing a mouthful of white, but crooked teeth, a throwback somehow disarming in the age of orthodontists and compulsory braces. He stopped his rocking motion to focus on Peter. "Yes, my friends call me Beano. And what's your name?"

"Peter." He proudly held up five fingers. "I'm five years old." He introduced his ragged lamb. "And this is Albi."

The stranger gave a European half-bow. "Nice to meet you, Peter and Albi."

Sam decided to allow him in. Better to share the room with an inexperienced adolescent than a grown man who could overpower her. She would leave the curtain open until she felt she could trust him, but she doubted she would sleep tonight. Taking a deep breath and mentally crossing her fingers, she unlocked the door and said, "All right, you can come in."

"Thank you!" As he stepped into the small room, relief shone out of his eyes like a lighthouse beacon.

"I'm Sam."

"She's my mom, Beano," explained Peter.

"I see."

"Listen," said Sam, as she locked the door, "do you know what national emergency they're talking about? What's happened?"

"Well, I—"

"Me and Albi are hungry, Mamma."

"All right, we'll go to the dining car and—"

Before Sam could finish the sentence, a voice on the speaker interrupted her. "Passengers, this is Commander Kirov with the United Nations Peacekeeping forces."

He spoke loudly with a strong Russian accent. "The train is under our control, as are all ten regions within the United States. Your president has been deposed, and General Arthur Pierson has invoked martial law in every region. The country is undergoing a massive reorganization. You are being transported to Camp 615 in Texas, where you will be processed and given your relocation and work assignments. You will stay in place until the time we reach our destination. If you try to leave the train now or at any point on the journey, you will be shot by one of our armed guards. Thank you."

Thank you? Sam felt as if a giant had played tee ball with her head and knocked it into an alternate universe. Barely breathing, with downcast eyes, she tried to comprehend what had happened. A military coup? Was this the United States of America? Had the train bypassed Chicago and taken her to Caracas? Venezuela would make more sense. She lifted her head and locked eyes with Beano. They stood frozen, reading each other's confusion and dread, too full of emotions, too burdened with questions to speak.

Peter tugged on Sam's hand. "Mamma, can we eat now?"

His question chilled her. Sam's mouth worked, but no words came out. She had no food, and who knew when they would next be able to eat in the coming hours? Everything spun out of control; she couldn't even protect her child from hunger.

Beano set his backpack down on one of the seats. "Guess what, Peter. I've got something in here for you."

His eyes brightened. "What?"

Beano rummaged around and pulled out a rectangular cellophane-wrapped bag of crackers and cheese and a red, child-sized box of raisins. "How about some crackers and raisins?"

He nodded his head vigorously. "Me and Albi like crackers and raisins."

"Here you go." She unwrapped the crackers for him and opened the box of raisins.

Sam's eyes burned with sudden tears; she was so grateful she couldn't even speak. She lifted Peter onto the seat, where he ate, still enveloped in the security of a child loved and protected, undisturbed and unburdened by worry or fear. He was the only one in the room oblivious to the fact that in an instant, their security had been shattered, and everything had changed.

During their southward journey, as the minutes and hours ticked by, Sam and Beano talked quietly and guardedly until Peter fell asleep, around eight-thirty, just before the brief stop in St. Louis, when even more people were forced onto the train. The conversation was awkward at first, a slow probing of each other's identities and life history.

"Let's start with names," suggested Sam. "I'm Samantha Brightman. And I know Beano or Cherubino is not your real name. So what is it? If we're going to face our doom together, we might as well be honest with one another."

"Okay. My real name is Katie Lamb—"

"Oh, so you *are* a girl. I wasn't entirely sure."

Katie smiled. "That's a good thing in a way. I'll explain, but first have an energy bar." She rummaged in her backpack and came up with two, one apiece. She unwrapped hers, and after chewing a moment, she continued. "I grew up on a Wisconsin dairy farm, where I used to sing to the cows seven days a week. I don't know how much it helped the herd, but that plus the church choir developed my voice. Now, I'm a professional opera singer at the beginning of a long and illustrious career." She broke into a great gap-toothed grin and laughed. "At least that's my hope. But on the way here, with soldiers everywhere, I didn't want to be taken for a woman. A few hours ago, I went AWOL from the stage of the Lyric Opera of Chicago, where I sang the role of Cherubino, the pageboy in *The Marriage of Figaro.*"

Sam smiled. "Ah, Cherubino, yes. I've seen that opera. That explains the name, the makeup, and the knee pants."

Katie touched her face. "Oh, goodness, I forgot about the stage makeup." She laughed. "It always looks bizarre up close, doesn't it?" She paused for a moment. "Normally, I would've washed my face and changed into street clothes, but the opera was only halfway over when I left. I went back to my dressing room after the last duet in the second act, just before intermission. I heard a voice out of the blue telling me to leave the theater through the stage door."

Sam wrinkled her brow and drew her head back. "What do you mean—*a voice out of the blue?*"

If Katie hadn't seen Sam's silver cross, worn openly in this time of Christian persecution, she would not have divulged the truth. But she believed she could trust the small, dark-eyed woman with the true story. "I can't explain it. All I can tell you is that no one else was in my dressing room. I was alone, and the voice didn't come over the in-house sound system. I could still hear the cast and orchestra in the second-act finale through the speaker. The voice said, 'Take your backpack and exit the theatre through the loading dock now.'"

She shrugged. "I thought it must be some kind of elaborate prank by another singer in the cast, so I ignored it. But then the voice came back more insistently. I refused to budge. The third time, the voice repeated the message, really loudly, and the chair I sat in began to rock back and forth, as if to pitch me out of it. That was the clincher—I grabbed my backpack and jacket and practically ran down to the stage door. I figured I had time to go out and still come back for my third act entrance. When I got to the door, I heard the applause when the second act ended."

She dropped her head and shook it slowly from side to side. "I felt like a fool and decided to go back upstairs. But before I could re-enter the building, I heard gunshots and screams coming from the theater. My insides turned to jelly. I felt a rush of adrenaline and my whole body quaked. I've never been so scared in my life. When I stepped out onto the sidewalk, I saw tanks and armed soldiers at the front of the opera house. So I turned in the opposite direction and walked away quickly with my head down."

"How did you end up on this train?"

"It was raining, and I was chilled, so I headed for Union Station, which is only a few minutes' walk from the opera house. As I approached the station, I saw more troops ahead, coming toward me, so I ducked in and hoped to hide in the crowd. I had no idea what to do or where to go next, so I prayed the Lord would lead me. Then the voice said, 'Get on the train to Dallas.'"

"Huh, must've been the Lord guiding you all along," said Sam. She clutched Sitti's small cross with one hand. "But why did you knock on our door?"

"This is the car I boarded, and your room is at the end of it—I couldn't go any farther." Katie shrugged. "So what about you, Sam? Where are you headed?"

"Hmmph—I wish I knew. I didn't think my life could get any more difficult, but it just did." She squeezed the bridge of her nose with thumb and forefinger, then exhaled noisily. "I was traveling to Texas to visit the site of a plane crash where my husband Joshua died."

"Oh, my gosh." Taken aback, Katie laid a hand over her mouth. But the name sounded familiar. "Joshua Brightman?" Her eyes lit up. "The pianist?"

"Yes."

"Oh, I heard him play the first Tchaikovsky concerto with the Chicago Symphony last year." Katie beamed. "What a wonderful musician. As I recall, he was a very attractive guy. Didn't he have some kind of nickname?"

Sam rolled her eyes. "Yes, the Bad Boy of Classical Music."

Katie nodded emphatically. "That's the moniker." She glanced down as if she was afraid to meet Sam's eyes. "I read about that plane crash—no survivors. I'm so sorry."

"Thank you. He was also a wonderful husband and father. I'm on this train because I wanted to see Caddo Lake, where he died. After that, Peter and I intended to visit New Orleans, my hometown, to see my mother and stepfather." She shook her head. "But now everything's changed, and . . . " Sam's voice trailed off.

"How did you meet Joshua?" Katie prompted. Although she was curious, her main motive was to converse, to keep their fears at bay. "I mean I know he was a New Yorker."

Sam smiled wanly. "Yes, from Brooklyn. His family moved to New Orleans in 2010, when his father, who is an attorney, got a job with an oil company there, the one responsible for the Gulf Oil spill. They bought the house next door to my family's home." She smiled. "We met in my backyard."

Katie grinned, trying to lighten the atmosphere. "Was it love at first sight?"

"Actually, for me it was. I was twelve years old." Sam laughed. "He was twenty-four at the time I determined I would marry him."

"Ha! Really? You were just a kid."

"Yes. I embarrassed my whole family when he came to lunch one day, by declaring my intentions."

"Looks like your prediction came to pass. But he had to wait for you to grow up."

"Well, that's not how things worked out."

Katie's eyes widened; she dropped her jaw and drew down the corners of her mouth. "You mean you were a child bride?"

Sam laughed. "No, of course not. About a year later, in 2011, he moved back to Brooklyn to pursue his musical career. I was just a kid to him, and he forgot about me. He fell in love with a beautiful, talented violinist named Li Ling, a star pupil at Juilliard. He accompanied her on one of her solo recitals, and apparently *that* was love at first sight. Eventually they became engaged, and she moved in with him.

"I think they lived together for almost two years, and during that time, her career as a soloist took off. They set a summer wedding date in 2018, but Joshua broke it off a month beforehand."

"Why?"

With Joshua's death, Sam felt free to reveal the secret he had confided only to her. "She concealed a pregnancy from him and aborted the baby. A child would have interfered with her concert career."

Katie winced. "Oh, gosh. How painful."

"And dishonest. It broke his heart. He didn't date anyone for a long time after."

"Well, how did you come back into the picture, Sam?" Katie prodded the conversation forward to avoid thinking about her future in an internment camp. Or Peter's future. She couldn't begin to imagine Sam's level of dread.

"I moved to New York to go to college and decided to approach him after one of his concerts, but I lost my nerve. So I sent him an unsigned telegram."

"A telegram? I didn't know that was still possible."

"He figured out I had sent it, and we got together after that."

"And what's your profession?"

"I'm a writer."

"What kind of writer?"

"The worst kind."

Katie's agile mind immediately filled in the blank: *uh-oh—porn scripts.*

"An unemployed one."

Katie slapped her hand over her heart. "Oh, good."

Sam looked at her quizzically.

"Uh . . . um, I mean that's too bad."

"I'll say. For the last five years, I wrote for a conservative newspaper in Brooklyn. It cratered after protesters—a.k.a. rioters—burned the building to the ground. Since the company was underinsured and the management didn't have the funds to rebuild, they folded. So, I'm out of a job."

"When did that happen?"

"Last Monday, September 21—the same day Joshua's plane exploded and crashed."

Katie put her hand over her mouth. "Oh, my gosh, and now a military coup to boot."

Sam sighed and looked out the window, feeling a familiar heaviness descend on her heart as the light of day dissolved into darkness.

Suddenly, Katie was at a loss for anything comforting to say. A great fatigue overwhelmed her, and she stifled a huge yawn. "Sorry, Sam, I'm fading. Let's talk more tomorrow. It's been quite a day for me. I've gone through a metamorphosis that would shame a butterfly. I began as a mezzo soprano, a girl playing a boy, then transformed into a war zone fugitive, after which I crashed a private room on a Texas-bound train, and now I'm heading for my new role as an inmate in some kind of internment camp."

Playing along, Sam snapped her fingers. "And in no time at all, you'll be relocated, given a work assignment, and march onward to new adventures."

Katie rolled her eyes, "Oh, what fun that'll be. I don't suppose there are too many employers in dire need of an opera singer dressed in drag."

"You never can tell," replied Sam. "Who knows? Maybe at the camp, you can sing the bad guys to sleep and allow us all to escape." She smiled. "Never underestimate the power of music. And speaking of sleep, we better get some while we can. Peter wakes up awfully early."

"By the way," asked Katie, "when do we arrive in Texas?"

"We were supposed to arrive at 11:30 a.m. tomorrow, but we're already delayed by an hour or more, so maybe by one o'clock, I guess." Sam rose and stretched. "Up, Katie. We have to figure out how to make your bed. I have a feeling the train staff is not gonna help us tonight."

CHAPTER 21

RECONNAISSANCE

The night was cool and damp, with heavy clouds obscuring the full moon. Dressed completely in black, Jaybird approached Gideon's house from the rear. He had avoided the roads, riding his electric bike on narrow pathways through the woods. He knew all the shortcuts. When he neared Gideon's house, he dismounted and walked the bike close to the perimeter of trees. Watching carefully, and taking his time, he ventured cautiously into Gideon's neighborhood, still off-road. In the darkness, he moved through deserted yards. A few homes had porch lights burning, but he saw only one or two lighted windows. He guessed most people had already packed a single suitcase in obedience to the edict and assembled at the post office. It was 10:30 p.m.; the deadline was only a half-hour away.

No siree—he and Gideon would never follow those orders, but before they bolted, they had to know what the hell was happening. As soon as he scoped out the situation and gathered supplies, he'd hightail it back to the cabin, and they'd make their plans to go off-grid.

Jaybird parked the e-bike behind Gideon's detached garage, between its back wall and the azaleas that grew up against it. He'd left Shadow Man to babysit Bigfoot while he sneaked into town. The bike would be all but invisible hidden there in the darkness—as he hoped he would be on his hike to the tower. He was glad of the black hoodie he wore over his hunting vest in the chill darkness. He had stuffed the vest pockets with a flashlight, his slingshot and ammo, binoculars, nylon rope, a folding knife, and the key to Shadow Man's house. After he climbed the water tower, he'd pick up some extra clothes for Shadow Man and Bigfoot—they were about the same size. He would also collect Gideon's guns and a few other essential items.

The amnesiac dude was a puzzle. His origins were mysterious, but the sudden vision Jaybird had when he observed him was even more so. The dude's heart was shaped like a harp, but the music that came from it was not audible—it was visible. Jaybird saw it as a changing series of geometric constructions, pure and perfect, that enfolded him. Like kaleidoscopic images, they flowed around him in an ever-changing mantle, some elegant and complex, like Middle Eastern mosaics, with curving, sinuous lines. Others were simple: crosses, stars, flower-like patterns. Jaybird had never seen anything like it, and it baffled him. When he told Shadow Man about the harp-shaped heart, Gideon said, "Like Harpo Marx."

"Who?" Jaybird drew a blank.

"One of the Marx brothers. They were American actors and musicians who starred in comedy films way back: Groucho, Chico, and Harpo. Groucho always wore a greasepaint moustache and carried a cigar. Chico played piano, and Harpo, who never spoke, played the harp. We could call him Harpo."

"Nah, I like Bigfoot better. Think he'll remember who he is and tell us his real name?"

"Hope so, eventually." Gideon shrugged. "Who knows, maybe he's some kind of musician."

"Well, he ain't a rapper or a rock star."

"How do you know?"

"No tattoos, piercings, or purple hair."

"Country and Western?"

"Don't make me laugh, Shadow Man. He don't sound hillbilly, like Alabama or Tennessee. You cain't be Country and Western without the raaht accent." Jaybird rolled his eyes. "Oh, I hope to God he ain't an opera star."

Gideon laughed. "I guess we'll know if he suddenly bursts into song and it's all Italian."

Despite his taut nerves on this dark night, Jaybird smiled to himself as he remembered their conversation.

Wearing moccasins, he kept to the shadows as he eased his way, slowly and quietly through the backyards, two blocks west to the water tower, the highest point in sleepy Legend. But Legend didn't doze that night; there was enough noise to keep the deaf awake and cover any sounds he might make. Dogs all over town barked and bayed. Sirens wailed, and men shouted in the distance, while red and blue rotator lights reflected eerily off the underside of the heavy cloud cover.

The tower stood north of town in a cleared, grassy lot behind the elementary school and just off Clementine Street. The post office, ground zero for the assembly of all citizens, lay three blocks south and one block east, between Dewey St. and Crocker. From the tower, Jaybird would have an overview so he could get an idea of what was going down. As a teenager, he had climbed it many times.

When he reached the open area surrounding the white tower, he lay prone on the damp grass and crawled to its base. There in the darkness, he waited a few minutes, all his senses primed to detect anyone approaching. He crawled to the narrow ladder attached to one of the big metal supports on the north side and started to climb. By the time he got to the top, his leg muscles burned, and despite the night's chill, sweat trickled down his back. He climbed up and over the railing and immediately dropped down and lay flat on the circular walkway, beneath the spotlights that illuminated the town's name, LEGEND, in red paint with a black lightning bolt intersecting the top of the G.

Hmmph—we're getting zapped by a lightning bolt right about now, for sure.

He crawled around to the south side of the tower where he would be able to see the tiny post office. The town—a village, really, population

250—was laid out in a simple grid. Tonight the atmosphere felt malignant. The spiritual burden produced a physical heaviness in him. With his interior sight, Jaybird saw the town veiled in a malevolent, roiling black cloud, streaked with blood. It stank—it made him sick to his stomach.

He wanted to know what was taking place, and yet he didn't. It was like the time a hunter shot his dog Bouncer by mistake. When the dog yelped, Jaybird ran through the woods to the place where Bouncer fell, even though he was desperate to bolt in the opposite direction. Same thing now. He had to find out, but the prospect filled his mind with dread.

He took a deep breath and forced himself to lift his head. His eyes were drawn to the flashing lights at each end of town. He took out his binoculars. Eastward, to his left, he saw a roadblock next to Legend's Grocery & Grill, where Jefferson Highway came to T at Lake Street. With the store lit up, he wondered if Chester was there standing behind the counter as always. At this time of night, the lake itself was invisible, just a vast patch of darkness beyond the lights. He made out two state trooper vehicles with their red and blue rotator lights and two Humvees blocking the intersection.

Dang it, they got dogs, too. Four armed soldiers stood there, and a fifth one held a German Shepherd on a leash. He could make out the white UN logo on the soldiers' helmets. *UN troops? What the hell?* The other roadblock lay much closer, two blocks straight ahead at the entrance to Legend, where Jefferson Highway intersected Clementine. The blinking yellow light was practically washed out by the brilliant flood lights on the troopers' cars. Two Humvees blocked the intersection. More UN soldiers, but he couldn't see their faces clearly—he wondered if they were all foreigners.

"Man, I don't like the look of this," he muttered, shaking his head.

Jaybird trained the binoculars on the Cypress Street post office, one block south of the main drag and about halfway between the two roadblocks. Instead of cars, the asphalt parking lot was crowded with people standing in clusters, their suitcases beside them. He couldn't believe his eyes: the perimeter had been secured with a barrier of razor wire coils. Soldiers with rifles at the ready patrolled outside and inside the perimeter. There was one narrow entrance, a checkpoint at the front where he watched new arrivals show ID and then enter. A soldier with a laptop perched on a temporary barrier appeared to check each person off.

Four big military trucks waited on the side streets, the kind with high railings around open cargo areas in the back. At the moment, the trucks were empty, but Jaybird had a pretty good idea what the cargo would be. He turned his attention back to the people inside the parking lot. The soldiers had separated them into three groups at the far end of the lot, backed up against the razor wire: men, women and children, and the old and sick, those who sat in wheelchairs or held onto walkers. He knew the four trucks, even if overcrowded, would not be enough to carry away 250 people. A wave of nausea came over him.

Turning to his right, he scanned the area past the roadblock, just west of town. The red and white lights of the Alligator Gar shone on a deserted parking lot. The one vehicle parked across the highway at Marinos, the Greek's restaurant, was the owner's blue Ford pickup.

He turned back to the post office where a Humvee had driven up with two soldiers in front. The two in the backseat held rifles. After a brief discussion with the officer who seemed to be in charge, the driver pulled away. As the vehicle turned into the neighborhood, the soldier riding shotgun spoke through a bullhorn: *"Warning, warning, warning! You have ten minutes to report to the post office. Ten minutes. Last call."*

Not an American voice: the foreigner had some kind of accent Jaybird couldn't identify. He watched the Humvee cruise slowly up and down the streets. It didn't take long for them to cover the whole town, since Legend consisted of the three-block business section on Jefferson Highway, nine blocks of houses like Gideon's on small lots, and a scattered number of small-acreage homesteads farther out.

"Warning, warning, warning! You have ten minutes to report to the post office. Ten minutes. Last call."

In the meantime, at the post office, one of the cargo trucks had backed up to the narrow opening. The soldiers herded the men forward. They clambered up into the truck at gunpoint. They were forced to stand until they were packed in so tightly no one could move. The truck drove one block north to Jefferson, turned left, and headed west. Keeping it in his sights, Jaybird saw they had opened up the roadblock to let the truck pass. He watched its red taillights speed away into the night.

The Humvee making the warning announcement came into his view. It slowly followed the truck's route. It turned in at the Greek's, then a black BMW pulled in beside it. He knew that car—Jack Dunham. Jaybird saw a heavyset man open the door and step out from the restaurant. Probably the Greek. Dunham got out of his car. The soldiers stayed in the Humvee. Jaybird could tell there was some discussion, but it didn't last long. The Greek took a step forward and pointed his arm at the Humvee. The doors opened and one of the soldiers stepped out. Almost immediately, Jaybird saw two muzzle flashes and heard the slightly delayed reports. The big man staggered and fell in a heap onto the asphalt. A woman charged out of the restaurant door. Two more flashes and reports. She collapsed. Jack Dunham just stood there for a moment, looking at the two bodies, then he got in his car and left. The Humvee had already driven away.

Jack Dunham, you shit! They killed the Greek and his wife, and you just left them there.

"Dang it!" His hands shook so badly he had to put the binoculars down. He squeezed his eyes shut and lay prone, resting his forehead on his arm. Maybe the Greek had tried to argue with the soldiers. He must've believed he still had some rights, that he still lived in the United States of America. Jaybird groaned. Not anymore: the Land of the Free just died right in front of his eyes.

Feeling queasy, Jaybird lifted the binoculars to gaze at the post office. The women and children stood in a shuffling line, herded toward another cargo truck. Two soldiers prodded them forward. He saw a young blonde boy, maybe ten years old, make a sudden dash for the opening at the front. One of the guards lunged forward to try to catch him, but the boy dodged him. Just as the boy reached the open space, the Chinese officer stepped forward, blocking the opening. The man struck the boy in the head with his fist, and he crumpled to the ground. The officer drew his revolver and aimed down; Jaybird saw the muzzle flash. A woman with long, blonde hair, probably the boy's mother, broke loose and ran toward her son, arms extended. He could see her open mouth. The officer fired again. She jerked back and dropped in her tracks.

Jaybird put down the binoculars and vomited. He retched four times until his stomach was emptied. The streams of hot, brown vomit splattered on the open grid beneath him, most of the liquid and small chunks passing through. Shaking, and covered in cold sweat, he spat to clear his mouth. His nose ran with clear mucus. He wiped it on his left shoulder. *Heartless, merciless sonsabitches.*

But it wasn't over yet. He crawled backward, away from his vomit and its stench, and trained his binoculars on the post office again. He watched them load the rest of the women and children. The truck drove off, following the same route west as the one bearing the men. He heard rifle fire in the distance and wondered if the soldiers in the roaming Humvee had shot more people who tried to protest, or if they'd begun shooting stragglers in the outlying areas instead of picking them up and transporting them to the post office.

He knew many of the homesteaders; he had done work for them from time to time. Mick Turner, the grouchy old Vietnam vet who kept to himself, lived on five acres north of town. He owned a small arsenal—he'd put up a battle, for sure. Roger Fannett's property was next to Mick's. Roger worked offshore for Leviathan Oil. He was gone a lot, leaving his wife and two young kids there by themselves. Jaybird hoped Roger was home now. *If not, Lord Jesus Christ and his angels, protect them.*

He zeroed in on the post office again. They had saved the smallest group for last—all the old people and handicapped. There were only about twenty of them. He could see the white heads clearly. He recognized Seth Mason, the young guy with cerebral palsy, slumped in his elaborate wheelchair. His mother tended him and homeschooled him. Seth couldn't walk on his own or speak; he used an iPad to communicate. Jaybird knew Seth; he'd been mowing Mrs. Mason's yard since he was thirteen. Sometimes, in good weather, if it wasn't too hot, she put Seth out on the porch. He always smiled at Jaybird and waved his good hand; he seemed so pleased to see another guy at his house. But now Seth was there alone—no sign of his mother.

The old people began to line up and move toward the cargo truck. The soldiers pushed and prodded them. One soldier standing in the bed of the truck dragged a fat, white-haired lady in and then shoved her toward the cab. She stumbled and fell. Then he pushed a frail-looking old man after her. Jaybird was suddenly glad his father was dead. He didn't have to suffer this, or worse, watch it happen and be unable to help.

Seth's wheelchair rolled to the truck and stopped. One of the soldiers lifted him out of the chair. He was so thin, Jaybird guessed he probably weighed less than a hundred pounds. The soldier tossed him upward, like a bag of bones, to the guard in the back of the truck. But instead of catching Seth, the soldier sidestepped, and let the boy fall flat on the hard bed. His body bounced.

"Oh, God." Jaybird's stomach muscles contracted. "You cruel bastard." He lay prone again, head on his arms, and wept. Frustration, anger, and pity swirled and boiled in his heart. He ground his teeth and was surprised to hear a low growl. It took him a moment to realize the voice was his own. His hands hungered to grip a high-powered rifle. He wanted to waste that sonofabitchin' soldier in the truck bed. See his ugly head explode.

He wiped his eyes and forced himself to look up again. Through the binoculars, he watched the truck leave the parking lot and then turn right on Jefferson Highway. *East? Why were they headed east? Nothing there but the lake.*

He watched the taillights move toward the roadblock at the Grocery & Grill. The truck stopped briefly and then turned left on Lake Street—north, the same direction as Thatch Island.

Half-dazed from the swirl of emotions, he knew it was time to leave. Nothing more he could do here. He and Shadow Man had made the right decision; they needed to cut and run, pronto, to avoid capture at all costs—if that was possible. He pocketed the binoculars and scrambled over the railing to the ladder. He descended quickly and dropped to the ground. He crawled across the open, flat area surrounding the tower and retraced his steps to Shadow Man's house. He let himself in the back door with the key. Using the flashlight, he went through the kitchen to the living room.

He played the light over the tall double bookcase against one wall. Kneeling on the floor, as Shadow Man had instructed, he grabbed the lower edge of the central connecting panel and felt for the hidden lever. He pressed it and heard a faint click. He hooked one finger under the lip of the panel and pulled gently. Jaybird smiled. *Pretty damn cool—a hidden gunsafe!* The narrow panel, about a foot wide and tall as the bookcase, slid toward him soundlessly and smoothly, exposing a tactical shotgun, a .30-30 lever action rifle, and two handguns. Jaybird removed the firearms, four packs of ammo, a first aid kit, and four packaged Mylar blankets, each one folded into a packet the size of a man's wallet.

He laid the firearms on the floor and slid the panel back into place. In the hall closet, as Shadow Man had told him, he found a large black backpack hanging from a hook inside the door. He returned to the living room and quickly loaded the boxes of ammo into the backpack. The shotgun, at only 26 inches, fit easily stock-down into the largest compartment. "Perfect." The gun was completely hidden. He laid the Mylar blanket packages and the handguns in the bottom next to the shotgun's stock.

Using the attached sling, he hoisted the .30-30 behind his right shoulder, and with the backpack in hand, he entered Shadow Man's bedroom. Searching in the chest of drawers, he gathered socks, underwear, T-shirts, and jeans. He found two plaid flannel shirts in the closet and a pair of hiking boots. He stuffed the clothes in the backpack, cushioning the shotgun, the revolver, and the pistols. As Jaybird left the room, he noticed the digital clock on the bedside table read 11:35.

In the bathroom, he collected all Gideon's aspirin and ibuprofen, bottles of Betadine and hydrogen peroxide, a tube of antibiotic ointment, and a roll of sterile gauze. Back in the living room, he saw a full bottle of Jameson's Irish Whiskey on a side table. *Whoa, can't pass that up.* He grinned—that was damn sure worth the extra weight.

He exited through the kitchen and locked the door behind him. Easing in sideways between the azalea bushes and the garage, he stuffed the boots and the whiskey in the bike's saddlebags. Time for the homeward journey.

Still cautious, but less apprehensive than when he came, Jaybird wheeled the bike into the woods and onto the narrow trail. The backpack and rifle were mighty heavy on his shoulders. It gave him a new respect for soldiers who carried this kind of gear on long marches. Under cover of the trees, he mounted the bike and bumped along the uneven track, inhaling the scent of pine, cedar, and damp earth. It was quiet in the woods. The sound of the sirens had stopped, and he only heard one lone dog barking in the distance. Hopefully, the soldiers had moved out after the roundup.

He could smell the lake before he reached it. He dismounted and walked the bike to the edge of the woods bordering Lake Street. He was just a half mile north of the roadblock. He glanced to the right, toward the Grocery & Grill, but the flashing lights and the Humvees were gone. *Well, that's good news.*

Suddenly a flurry of rapid gunshots broke the silence. *Now what?* The reports carried clearly across the lake, harsh and loud, erratic and wild as a pack of Black Cat firecrackers thrown into a bonfire. He couldn't identify the exact location, but he tried to count the reports. Gripping the handlebars, he counted thirty-nine before they ended. But there could have been many more, all fired simultaneously.

"Man, what went down there?" he muttered.

Grinding his teeth, he waited motionless in the shelter of the trees, watching the road in both directions. It seemed like years before he heard a motor and saw headlights approaching from the north. He laid the bike down and stood stone still beside the trunk of a pine tree. The rattle of the truck grew stronger until it passed right in front of him. It was the east-bound cargo truck that had ferried away the old people and poor, broken Seth Mason.

His heart sank. He saw three soldiers in the cab, but the back of the truck was empty.

CHAPTER 22

NOMADS

Sam woke on Sunday morning while it was still dark. She had slept fitfully, due to her unwelcome bedfellow—fear. She was also squashed against the wall by Peter the bed-hog, who lay spreadeagled. But her son's proximity gave her both comfort and warmth. For a Southern girl, the New York winters were a trial; in Brooklyn, she slept buried under a sheet, a weighted blanket, a hand-woven wool blanket, and two quilts. Katie's presence in the bunk above was also a comfort; a companion made the uncertain future a little easier to face.

Her greatest fear was for Peter. With Joshua gone, her son, so vulnerable, was all she had. How could she protect him in the days to come? Would there be food and clean water at the camp? Would the soldiers take him from her—would they consider him useless and therefore expendable? Images of Auschwitz loomed before her mind's eye. She thought of those in WWII who had been transported in cattle cars against their will, all the mothers with their babies. They too had been relocated and given work assignments. Some had been starved and beaten, experimented on, raped, and murdered. Many of their children died.

Would this new regime create a twenty-first-century American holocaust? Who would live and who would die? She thought about the gas chambers and the unspeakable cruelty of the Nazi guards and shuddered. Whoever the UN troops were, they were not Americans; they would not have the same compassion or mercy as Americans.

She squeezed her eyes shut. How would the foreign men treat the women? Katie had a point—young, attractive women were perfect prospects for rape. Sam gagged. Every muscle in her body tensed. *Oh, Joshua, if only you were here. We wouldn't have been on this train at all.*

The window lightened with the gray light of dawn—the dawn of a day she didn't want to face. At least they had the morning, a few more hours, before they disembarked—to where? She hoped Katie could stay with them as long as possible.

Her bladder was so full it hurt. She sat up and moved gingerly so as not to disturb Peter, who still slept soundly. She shut the door to the tiny bathroom as quietly as possible. After she relieved herself, she went to the outer door and pushed the privacy curtain an inch to the side, expecting to see into the corridor, but something gray blocked her vision. She glanced up and saw the back of a man's head. He had thick, straight hair, black as her own. His broad back and gray overcoat blocked her view. When she opened the curtain a little more to the right, she could see past his shoulder. The corridor was jammed with people. A frail-looking, white-haired couple sat on the floor, heads resting on their drawn-up knees. A woman with dark circles under her eyes stood huddled with two adolescent girls, her daughters probably. They swayed slightly with the movement of the train. With blank expressions, in studied self-containment like big-city subway riders, they faced down and avoided eye contact.

She realized those in the corridor must have been forced onto the train at St. Louis. She let the curtain fall back into place. When she turned around, Katie sat at the edge of the top bunk, watching her.

"The corridor is packed with people," Sam whispered. "They've overloaded the train."

"I'm surprised they haven't pounded on the door and made us take in extra people."

"Well, there's more room out there than in this tiny bedroom," Sam replied. Again the image of cattle cars packed with human cargo crossed her mind. "At least we only have six or seven hours to go, and not days."

"Days?"

"I was thinking about—"

Someone knocked on the door. They froze.

Rap, rap, rap. "Hello?" queried a feminine voice. "Please open the door. May we use your restroom?" *Rap-rap.*

"Mamma!" Peter sat up and rubbed his eye with his fist.

Sam picked him up and held him.

"Just a minute," she called out to the woman at the door. "We're getting dressed." Then she whispered, "Peter, come, let's go pee-pee right now, and then Beano, too. There are a lot of people out there who need to use the restroom after us."

After they completed their bathroom business, they dressed quickly. "Let me open the door," said Katie, "while you hold Peter." She grasped the handle, pushed the curtain aside, and opened the door a crack. "Okay," she called out, "let's do this in an orderly way. One at a time."

A line of women, old and young, stood in the corridor. An elderly woman with a shock of pure white hair entered first. Her face was worn, but beautiful and distinctive, and her carriage upright. With a direct, blue-eyed gaze she said, "Thank you so much," in a clear, projecting voice. "It'll just be women for the most part . . . well, except for the big jobs, if you know what I mean. The men are peeing into the metal recycling bin at the other end of the corridor."

"Well," whispered Katie, while the woman used the facilities, "I guess you could say that's a relief in more ways than one."

Sam smiled and glanced thoughtfully at the closed restroom door. "Did you notice what a self-assured air that woman had? She seems in control of the situation, like she's walking on granite even though the rest of the world is at sea. And she looks very familiar. I'm sure I've seen her somewhere before."

"I don't think I have," said Katie. "But she carries herself confidently, like a dancer or a model maybe."

The woman exited the restroom and thanked them. She was followed by nine more female visitors. Sam hoped the toilet wouldn't back up.

When all the women had finished, Katie shut and locked the outer door again. They stripped the beds and returned the seats to their original positions. By then Sam's conscience bothered her. "Katie, I think we should let the old couple have our seats. You know, the white-haired older woman who knocked on our door first. She and her husband must be in their seventies. We can sit on the floor for a few hours."

Sam made the offer to the elderly couple, who gladly accepted. They introduced themselves as Bertil, "but everyone calls me Bertie," and Susannah Falkenberg, from St. Louis. They had intended to travel to Chicago to see their son Edward. But the soldiers forced them onto the train going the opposite direction, along with all the other people waiting on the platform.

Above a swollen nose, Bertie had an ugly black-and-blue shiner. "When my husband argued with the soldier who demanded we board the train, the man struck him in the head with his rifle butt. Bertie fell and hit the platform hard. It's a wonder he didn't pass out or break any bones."

Bertie smiled. "I'm just a hardhead, Susannah."

"Mamma says I'm a hardhead, too, Bertie," announced Peter.

Everyone laughed.

"That's 'cause you are," said Sam and tousled his hair. She introduced him to the Falkenbergs. "My son, Peter."

"It's a pleasure to meet you, Peter. How old are you?" asked Susannah.

"Five."

"Precocious, isn't he?" said Bertie.

Sam nodded.

"And my name—"

"Is Beano!" Peter's high-pitched exclamation finished the sentence for Katie.

She laughed. "Well, consider that my nickname. My real name is Katie Lamb. I boarded the train unwillingly too, in Chicago." She gave a little bow to all. Peter immediately imitated her.

Bertie nodded. "Nice to meet you all. Well, everyone, Susannah and I are exhausted. We didn't sleep well in the corridor. Would you mind if we closed our eyes and rested here a while?"

"I don't mind, Bertie," said Peter. "If you don't rest, you might get cranky."

Bertie laughed and patted him on the shoulder. "You're exactly right about that. And thank you for letting us borrow your seats." They both closed their eyes and leaned back. Two minutes later, they were fast asleep.

In the meantime, Katie spread a blanket on the floor to make a cozy nest at the feet of the Falkenbergs. "We're going to camp out, Peter," she said, keeping her voice quiet. "Want to make a tent?"

His eyes lit up. "Yeah."

"Okay, you sit in the middle between your mom and me. We'll be the tent poles." They sat on the floor and placed pillows behind their backs, while Katie draped the other blanket over her head and Sam's. They put her backpack and Sam's carry-on beside them. In the close space, the blanket covered them entirely and made a very satisfactory tent.

Peter laughed and clapped his hands in delight. "I like this, Beano. But what do we have for breakfast?"

"I've got just the thing." She dug into her backpack and pulled out three strawberry breakfast bars.

"Thank you so much! I cannot believe how much food you squirreled away in that backpack," remarked Sam. She unwrapped her bar and Peter's. "I think it's really a magic portal to a food warehouse."

Katie smiled. "I wish. Singers need comfort food, and lots of it."

"Are you a singer, Beano?" asked Peter.

"Yes."

"Will you sing a song for me today? I like music. Did you know my daddy plays the piano?"

Sam sighed audibly.

Katie glanced at her briefly, then answered her son. "I do—I heard him play once, Peter. And I will sing for you; it will be my pleasure. But let's wait until Bertie and Susannah wake up, okay?"

"All right."

After they ate, Sam rummaged in her carry-on bag and pulled out two toy cars, a blue and white one marked *Police* and a tiny red fire truck. She also found two containers of chocolate pudding she had forgotten about. At least she could help out in the food department, before she and Peter decimated Katie's supply.

The two women scooted farther apart, to give Peter more space. He reclined on his side and played with the cars. Then Sam asked, "So what is life like for an opera singer?"

"Well, the hours are late, the pay is so-so, but the singing is glorious. It's a nomadic existence; two to three weeks in whatever city, bouncing around the country like a ping-pong ball."

"Yes, Joshua did that too. I guess it's the price professional musicians always pay. I remember reading that music and poetry are the hallmarks of nomadic peoples. The visual arts, painting, sculpture, and architecture, came from the sedentary tribes who cultivated the land. And a tension has always existed between those two ways of living."

"If you ask me," said Katie, "the sedentary tribes are winning. Apart from professional musicians and reindeer herders, there aren't very many nomadic peoples left on the earth."

"Except we're all nomads now."

"True, but we carry our music and poetry with us."

"Mamma, I have to pee-pee."

Sam laughed. "Had enough philosophy, Peter? Okay, we'll let you out of the tent." She lifted the edge of the blanket and opened the restroom door for Peter. He closed it behind him. Then Sam confided in her new friend, "Katie, I'm so worried about Peter in this situation."

Katie leaned toward Sam. "Of course you are—I am too. I've been thinking about that. Maybe we can prepare him a little by making it an adventure."

"What do you mean?"

"Well, what if we told him a story? Something along the lines of *The Magic Flute*. Are you familiar with it?"

"I saw it at the New Orleans Opera when I was a kid. The trials by fire and water, right?"

"Exactly. I could adapt the story for Peter and teach him a song that might help. It might strengthen him for whatever is to come."

And who can know what is to come? Sam sighed deeply and bit her lower lip. "Yes, it would be good to prepare him a little without frightening him. Children have such powers of imagination . . . " Her voice trailed off.

They heard the restroom door open. Sam lifted the edge of the blanket, the tent's side panel, so Peter could crawl in.

"Do you like camping out like this, Peter?" asked Sam.

"Uh-huh."

"Well, we're probably going to do some more camping out when we get to Texas."

"At the lake?"

"Um, we're not going to the lake right away. We're going to an actual camp, where we might live in a real tent, or maybe a cabin—a house with some of the other people on our train."

"With Beano and Bertie and Susannah?"

"Maybe—I hope so. But we won't know exactly until we get there." Trying to veil her worry and fear, she smiled at her son. "It's going to be a great adventure."

CHAPTER 23

RETURN TRIP

With the instincts and patience of an experienced hunter, Jaybird bided his time; he let at least fifteen minutes pass before he ventured out onto Lake Street. Problem was, the night crawled with hunters. To avoid becoming the prey, he would have to be wily as a coyote, elusive as a fox. Finally satisfied that all was quiet, he quickly walked the bike across the street to the edge of the lake and daubed the back reflector with mud. He dared not use the headlight. He wore his own camouflage—he smiled to himself—*sometimes, it do help to be black.* In addition to his skin, his dark clothes would blend in with the night and the road's black asphalt.

He kept to the far-right edge of the street and mounted the bike. Even riding at top speed, about 30 mph, he knew it would take him ten minutes to get to the Thatch Island Bridge. Thankfully, this stretch was unpopulated: forest on the left and lake to the right, with no adjoining roads. He kept a close watch, peering ahead and glancing at the rearview mirror often, but the darkness of the overcast night remained unbroken by headlights.

The thought of crossing the bridge worried him most. Although it was unlighted, he would be visible to anyone on the water or on the road. Despite the chilly night air, he felt sweat trickling down his neck, and his stomach still felt queasy. He sensed some danger he could not see, something he hadn't anticipated. *Listen to yourself, Jaybird. Trust your gut.*

When he got to the bridge, instead of immediately making a right turn onto it, he dismounted the bike and quickly walked it into the cover of the trees on the opposite side of the road. He waited there for something—what exactly, he didn't know—but his sixth sense cautioned him to bide his time. The buzzing of cicadas and the croaking of tree frogs kept him company. The strong smell of pine resin mixed with the dank smell of the lake filled his nostrils. His muscles were bunched and rigid from tension; his shoulders ached from the combined weight of the rifle and heavy backpack.

A harsh new note joined the loud buzzing of the cicadas. He closed his eyes and focused on what he heard. *What the hell was it?* He tilted his head to the right and scratched his scalp. As he did so, he glanced up and saw the source of the buzzing. He inhaled sharply and froze. The thing was a lot bigger than a cicada, and it turned his blood to ice. Like a mechanical insect, showing two red lights in front, two green lights in back, with a pulsing white light underneath, it flew a jerky zigzag pattern over the bridge from the island, directly toward Jaybird.

A drone. *Dang it—those suckers had cameras that could read heat signatures at night.* Jaybird hugged the pine tree so hard he almost merged into the trunk. He should have known. With drones, the military could save manpower and spy on vast areas day and night. That made the odds of avoiding discovery pretty dang dismal. In fact, if the infernal thing had come from the island, chances were that his cabin, with Shadow Man and Bigfoot in it, had already been discovered. How soon before the military sent out a patrol boat to capture them?

The drone's eerie mechanical flight suddenly stopped. It hovered over the road not thirty feet from him. Jaybird's heart pounded so hard he thought it might be audible to the drone sensors. He broke into a fearsome sweat. Had it sensed him? If the thing was armed, he'd soon be a dead man.

Suddenly, quite near, he heard a thrashing noise. His muscles jerked and contracted in fright. Then he heard a scrabbling, clattering sound on the asphalt. Two panicked deer broke cover. He saw the drone shift position and prayed the camera had detected them and not him. Their lifted tails waved like white flags of surrender as they dashed headlong up the road, away from the buzzing drone.

After a moment, the drone continued its flight south. Jaybird breathed a sigh of relief, but far across the dark expanse of water, he saw the colored lights and erratic flight path of another one spying on the road south of the lake. He needed to warn Shadow Man, so they could disappear into the wilderness ASAP.

He wanted to bolt like the deer, but he gritted his teeth and forced himself to wait until both drones vanished toward town. When all was quiet, he mounted the bike and headed over the bridge. He was pretty sure he and Shadow Man had only minutes to escape before somebody came after them. And from what he'd already witnessed, that somebody would be armed and merciless.

Once he got past the bridge, Jaybird left the road. He kept to the island's winding backwoods trails. He'd grown up on Thatch Island; he could've navigated them blindfolded. The one existing road, an uneven, pitted single lane paved with oyster shell, ran parallel to the shoreline and dead-ended at his cabin. But he was too spooked to travel on it. He would be much more exposed and vulnerable on the white shell road, both from above and from any observers on the lake itself. Weaving through the trees would take him longer, but it also protected him somewhat from spying drones.

When he arrived at the back of the cabin's clearing, he stopped in his tracks. No lights in the windows. Alarm bells went off in his head. He halted inside the tree line just behind the old tin-roofed shed where he stored his tools and lawnmower. Still as a deer on high alert, he watched the cabin; he listened and sniffed the air—all senses vigilant to detect any sign of movement or danger. Had somebody captured Shadow Man and Bigfoot already? Were they gone? Jaybird guessed about fifteen minutes had elapsed since he saw the drone. But of course the drone had flown over the island before that, maybe thirty minutes ago.

Did an ambush or a slaughter await? The house remained still and silent as a coffin. Maybe they had left. Maybe they were dead. Only one way to find out. Jaybird set the heavy backpack on the ground and leaned it against the shed. He lifted the loaded .30-30 from his shoulder and gripped it with sweaty hands. He flicked off the safety. If anyone was lying in wait inside the cabin, that sucker was as good as dead.

Bent at the waist, he moved quickly across the backyard, footsteps muffled by the dew-laden grass. He reached the back of the cabin and held himself perfectly still against the wall, listening for any sound from inside. All he heard was the wind sighing in the trees and the rise and fall of the cicada chorus. He crept around the corner, ducking under the bedroom and living room windows until he was flush with the front wall and he could see the front yard and the lake.

His mouth dropped open. It wasn't what he saw that amazed him—it was what he didn't see. Where was his truck? And the dock was empty—his jon boat had vanished. The door to the house hung open as if the place had been long since abandoned. *What the hell?*

Now, the worst part—he had to enter the cabin. *Shadow Man and Bigfoot—please don't be dead.* Hands greasy with sweat, he gripped the rifle and stepped up onto the porch. Waited. No sound, except the squeak of a hinge when the door swung slightly, nudged by the evening breeze. It was his home, but the odd circumstances changed the familiar into the strange, like a nightmare. He pushed the door all the way open and crossed the threshold.

As he entered, the soft, rawhide soles of his moccasins, molded to his feet, moved soundlessly over the wood floor. He heard the pounding of his own heart in his ears and the high-pitched whinny of a screech owl close by in the woods. Holding his breath, he glanced left to the living room and right to the kitchen. He breathed out a sigh of relief—no bodies there. But he still had to search the bedrooms and bathroom.

The screech owl whinnied again, much like a horse, as he took the small flashlight from his hunting vest pocket. He clicked it on and held it left-handed, while he gripped the .30-30 in his right hand. He padded over to the sofa and shined the light behind it, just in case. The narrow beam of light illuminated only gray cobwebs, dust balls, and a dead June bug.

He crept cautiously into the hall, where all the doors stood open. Directly ahead, he could see the bathroom was empty. Light reflected back at him from the mirror. He lifted his head when the owl whinnied four times in a row. Strange. A pair, maybe, calling and answering?

At the doorway of his room he shined the light on the neatly made double bed, the pine dresser, and the small doorless closet that held his jeans, shirts, and shoes—all undisturbed. At this point, Jaybird's intuition told him he would find nothing in the spare bedroom either. As he checked to be sure, his mind shifted to the insistent call of the screech owl. He heard it coming closer. He shone the flashlight into the spare bedroom, gave it a cursory glance, and then returned to the living room.

He stopped in his tracks and raised the gun to his shoulder.

A man stood in the doorway, hands raised high. "Take it easy, Jaybird. It's me, Gideon."

"Shadow Man. You mean it's you, the screech owl."

"The very one." Even in the darkness, Jaybird caught the glimmer of white teeth, bared in a smile.

"I'm impressed." Jaybird took a deep breath and lowered the rifle. "Wanna tell me what the hell is going on here? Little details like where's the truck, my boat, and our friend Bigfoot?"

"I will, and I wanna hear about the roundup in Legend, but first, did you bring the clothes and supplies?"

"Yeah, got it all. I left the bike and backpack in the woods next to the shed. Hey, man, did a drone fly over the cabin?"

"Yes, unfortunately." Gideon's smile vanished. "That's why we gotta book it. I'll go get the gear. You stuff a backpack with a change of clothes. As soon as you're done, we fly. We'll swap stories later."

Gideon led Jaybird to the clearing where he had hidden the pickup truck. They carried all the medical supplies, clothing, and firearms to the truck, about thirty feet into the woods north of the house. They took very little food—they would hunt and forage once they got away. The pickup truck was not visible to any drone, protected as it was from above by the spreading branches of a live oak.

"I turned off the house lights, then hid the truck and the boat so the place would look abandoned. I figured they would send surveillance drones, just like we did in Afghanistan."

"God damn you Americans."

"Murderers."

Gideon struggled to keep his face impassive despite the voices.

"Well, you got that right," Jaybird said.

"The best we can do is to stay away from the house and this whole area. The boat is not far from here. I dragged it up on the shore and camouflaged it with branches. Bigfoot is waiting there for us. We've got to get out of here tonight and find shelter somewhere. We won't survive long in the open, nor will our amnesiac buddy. You know the area, Jaybird. Any ideas?"

"There's a rundown old hunting shack in the woods, maybe five miles from here. It's gonna be a long walk for a dude with a sprained ankle."

Gideon coughed. "He'll make it—he just has to carry his own weight. We'll carry the rest."

CHAPTER 24

DESTINATIONS

The train might have been his mother; he rode within its living embrace. Its hypnotic humming filled his ears; its steady vibration rocked him. Absolved of responsibility, suspended from reality, he drifted. The line between dreaming and waking blurred. He floated like an infant in the womb, while he was projected forward into a destiny he could not even imagine.

The train had taken on passengers well past its capacity in St. Louis. Constantin had given his seat to an old lady. He and many others sat on the hard floor. He half-dozed at one end of a coach car. Knees drawn up, he hugged his backpack and rested his head on top of it. His body bumped and swayed with the motion of the train.

It was night. Frantic, he ran down a dark tunnel, seeking Grigori. He came to the entrance of a vast cave where a circle of men dressed in black robes chanted in front of a fire pit. Behind the blazing fire, shadows twisted and writhed. Suddenly they coalesced into a gigantic winged figure. The chanting ceased abruptly, and the men fell to their knees with faces to the ground. Constantin suddenly recognized Dumitru at the front, with Grigori beside him. When Dumitru shoved the boy toward the fire, the creature rose up and spread its black wings until it seemed to fill the cave. In a swooping motion, it enveloped not only Grigori, but the entire planet.

Constantin awoke with a start. Like a terrified rabbit thumping the ground, his heart knocked against his sternum. Dry-mouthed and shaken by the nightmare, he blinked rapidly. He rubbed his bleary eyes and wiped the slick sweat from his brow. An anxiety dream, that's all it was. Constantin feared for Grigori's safety. As long as Dumitru stayed away, as he did most often, Grigori would be all right. *Someday, little brother, I'll come back. I'll take you away from that creepy pervert, so you don't ever have to be afraid again. And I'll take my mother away, too.*

But the dream had larger implications. The winged creature—one of the Nine, a fallen angel, maybe—had somehow enveloped the entire world in darkness. Did the fallen ones really exist and interact with men such as Dumitru? Could such evil actually overthrow the world and control it?

Outside, the day dawned, gray and murky as depression. His destination was Dallas. The country was in turmoil, and Dumitru, if not one of the orchestrators of the coup, surely rejoiced to see it happen. He had written about the planned overthrow of America at least fifteen years ago. And *Grand-père*—how big a role did he play in the coup? He had warned Tony beforehand. According to his letter to Dumitru, he had helped infiltrate the government with traitors. And of course, he and Dumitru had worked together years ago to deceive and coerce his mother. The whole idea of running to General Huffman for the truth about his real father suddenly seemed foolish to Constantin.

Still, he had to try. Dallas was only a few hours away. Soon he would see *Grand-père*. He had to know the truth. Somewhere he had read: *The truth will set you free.*

The truth. That was his real destination.

The woman Constantin had chased through the streets of Chicago and given up for lost traveled in a private room two cars behind his coach. Katie

Lamb sat in a makeshift tent facing Peter Brightman and his mother, Sam. "While we're traveling, Peter," she said, "I want to tell you a story about a good and brave prince named Tamino, who had a great adventure." She hoped to entertain Peter, but she wanted badly to distract herself and Sam, at least for a little while, from the ominous circumstances.

Peter sat between his mother's outstretched legs. Holding Albi in his arms, he leaned back against her body, like a man in an easy chair. He gazed expectantly at Beano.

"One day Prince Tamino set out on a journey to find a princess. As he walked through a forest, before he had gone very far at all, he met a big snake."

"Ecch! I don't like snakes. Neither does Albi."

"Me either, but there are snakes in Texas."

"Big ones?"

"Yes, and little ones, too."

"Was Tamino's snake a big one?"

"Yes, indeed. It was green with black spots, and it scared him because he didn't have a weapon to fight it. No sword or gun."

"What did he do?"

"He called for help, and help came. A birdcatcher hunting in the forest heard his cries and came running. The birdcatcher saw the snake and pulled out his trusty slingshot. He put a stone in the pouch, pulled it way back and then let go. *BAM!* He hit that snake right between the eyes."

Peter laughed. "He killed it dead, didn't he?"

"Yep, he sure did. Dressed all in forest green, with a hat made of feathers, he had a small musical instrument hanging around his neck. 'My name is Papageno,' he said. 'Who are you and why are you here in the forest?'

"'I am Prince Tamino.' He bowed in his white princely shirt and blue princely pants. 'Thank you for saving my life, Papageno. I am searching for a princess, and if I can find one who is pretty, charming, and kind, I will marry her. Do you know of one?'

"'I do,' replied Papageno. 'We birdcatchers roam the forest and the birds tell us many things—even secrets, sometimes.'"

Peter disagreed. "But birds can't talk—well, except for parrots."

"True," Beano replied. "But birds have their own language, and Papageno could understand it, and he could sing it, too."

"Oh!" said Peter. "Mamma had a pet bluejay named Eliot when she was a girl."

"I did," said Sam, "and I can assure you that Eliot had his own way of speaking."

Beano explained that the forest birds had told Papageno about a lovely princess named Pamina and had given him a picture of the princess. He showed it to Tamino. Imprisoned by the evil wizard Sarastro at his castle, Dragon's Cry, she needed rescuing. When Tamino saw her picture, he fell in love with her on the spot. "'She is beautiful, and there is such kindness in her eyes,' he said."

"Did she have blue eyes and blonde hair like you, Beano?"

"No, Peter. Like your mom, she was small and beautiful with kind brown eyes and dark, curly hair."

"Did the prince look like my dad? My dad has green eyes and kind of messy, reddish hair. He forgets to comb it sometimes."

"How did you know? Tamino looked just like your dad. What do you think Papageno looked like?"

"Hmmm." Peter wrinkled his nose and scratched his head. Then his eyes brightened. "I know—he looked like Isaiah."

The prophet? Beano widened her eyes. She imagined a robed, bearded man with a staff. Finding herself on uncertain ground, she looked to Sam for help.

Sam grinned. "Beano doesn't know Isaiah, Peter. You'll have to tell her what he looks like."

"Well, Isaiah is chocolate, and I'm vanilla. He has black eyes, curly black hair, and very brown skin. He's my best friend in kindergarten."

Beano nodded. "You guessed right! That's exactly what Papageno looked like."

Peter nodded solemnly. "I thought so. Okay, then what happened?"

Although Beano loosely followed the plot of *The Magic Flute*, she simplified it quite a bit. She improvised from moment to moment, no problem for her. She and her younger brother Jake had spent hours making up stories to entertain themselves as they did their chores in rural Wisconsin. At night in their shared bedroom, they lay in their bunk beds and created more stories to make each other laugh.

"Tamino said, 'Take me to Dragon's Cry, Papageno, so I can rescue the princess!'

"Now Papageno knew the way to the castle, but he was afraid of Sarastro, who was ten feet tall and very mean. So he did a very bad thing—he lied. He said, 'Sorry, Prince, I don't know the way.'

"Tamino got so upset he almost cried. He sat down on the ground at the base of a big oak tree and put his head in his hands. 'How will I ever rescue her, if I can't even find her?'

"Just then, Papageno cocked his head to one side. 'I hear music.'

"Tamino lifted his head. He heard it too, a high, sweet singing somewhere above them. When they looked up, they saw three young boys sitting on the lowest limb of the tree. The funny thing was, they hadn't been there moments before.

"Here's the song they sang." In a quiet voice (not at all like an opera singer), Beano sang a simple little tune:

> *We three young boys, fair, gentle and wise,*
> *Along the way, will be your guides.*
> *Follow our counsel and ours alone,*
> *And at the last, you will come home.*
>
> *Papageno, do not lie!*
> *Lead the prince to Dragon's Cry.*
> *In prison there, the princess waits.*
> *Tamino brave will open the gates.*

When you need us, you may sing us;
Just five notes—the music brings us.
Papageno, play the tune you know;
Listen well: do, re, mi, fa, sol.

Be brave, no matter what the test,
Fear not, and always do your best.
Arise and go, with courage strong.
Farewell, goodbye, we'll meet 'ere long!

"And just like that—" Beano snapped her fingers, "—the three boys disappeared."

Sam leaned forward. "I think they were angels." She dug into her carry-on and pulled out a small book. She turned its pages, searching for something.

"Maybe so," said Peter.

"Tamino stared at Papageno. 'So you *do* know the way to Dragon's Cry! Why did you lie to me?'

"Papageno blushed. He bowed his head and whispered, 'Umm, well, I don't like fighting. I really don't.'

"'But the princess is in prison. We must free her at whatever cost.'

"'Hmmph,' said Papageno, 'that's all well and good for you. The princess will be so grateful, she'll probably fall in love with you. But what reward will I have?"

"Tamino said, 'I'll bet there are other fair maidens in Sarastro's prison. I'm sure he only steals the very prettiest ones. They too will be grateful for their freedom.'

"Papageno smiled. 'Do you think I might find a nice little wife, too?'

"'I'm sure of it,' declared the prince. 'And besides, if we're in danger, you can play the tune you know to call the boys. But what tune is it?' asked Tamino.

"'The one I play on my little flute.' He pointed to the instrument hanging around his neck."

"What did it look like?" asked Peter.

Beano found an envelope in her backpack and sketched quickly. "Like this."

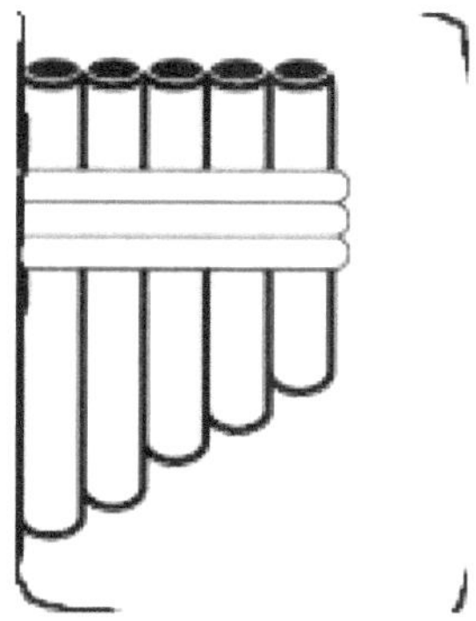

"Oh, I see," said Peter.

"Papageno blew the pipes from largest to smallest, and they produced five clear notes." Katie sang, "*Do, re, mi, fa, sol.* Can you sing that, Peter?"

"You sang G, A, B, C, D."

"I did, you little stinker. You must have perfect pitch."

Peter imitated her flawlessly. "*Do, re, mi, fa, sol.*"

"Do you play piano already?"

"Yes, but not as good as my dad. He has perfect pitch, too."

"Would you like to learn the whole song, Peter?"

He nodded his head vigorously. "Yes!"

Peter's excellent musical memory enabled him to learn the song in ten minutes. As soon as he finished singing the entire song, he said, "Mamma, I'm hungry."

Sam smiled. "I've got just the thing. I forgot I had these in my carry-on." She took out the containers of chocolate pudding and two plastic spoons. "Here you are, Peter. Beano, would you like some pudding?"

"Why, thank you." She smiled. "Musicians are always ravenous after performing."

"And I quite enjoyed that performance," remarked Bertie Falkenberg. His voice surprised them all. "Knock, knock, knock. May I come in?"

Sam lifted the edge of the tent cover. "Bertie—you're awake."

He leaned forward, stuck his white-haired head under the blanket, black eye, swollen nose and all. He grinned. "I recognized the tune from Mozart's opera."

"Did you?" said Beano. "I've simplified the story, but that part's from—"

"The first act, with the three spirits and Tamino and Papageno, right before they start their quest."

"Do you know this story, Bertie?" asked Peter.

"I do indeed. It's one of my favorites, and Beano is doing a wonderful job of telling it to you."

"Are you a musician?" asked Katie.

"No, I'm a doctor, retired. I was an internist at Barnes-Jewish Hospital in St. Louis for many years, but I've always been a big opera fan. I've seen many productions of *The Magic Flute*. The last two were in St. Louis and Houston. Now it's my turn to be curious," he continued. "What's your connection to opera?"

Peter piped up. "Beano's a singer, Bertie."

From her sitting position on the floor, Katie smiled and bowed theatrically from the waist. "Correct: an opera singer, a mezzo soprano. In fact, I'm still in costume. Yesterday afternoon, I sang Cherubino at Chicago Lyric Opera. Midway in the production, the . . . uh . . . " She glanced at Peter and hesitated. "Well, when the current events took place, I was warned, in an unconventional way, to leave. I looked out the loading dock door and saw the street in front of the theater swarming with troops, so I absconded."

"A runaway mezzo—a most unusual voice type." Bertie grinned.

"True. I ended up on this train and in this room by chance."

"Not by chance," objected Sam. "Not with the type of guidance you had."

Katie glanced at her. "Yes, well, you may be right about that."

"Nice costume, by the way," said Bertie. "Knee pants, hose, red vest. You're the perfect eighteenth-century pageboy. So Cheru*bino* is your alias."

"Yes, Beano for short. At least for the time being."

"May I come in, too?" asked Susannah.

"Oh, what the heck," said Sam. "Let's just take down the tent and talk." She removed the overhead blanket and wrapped it snugly around Peter.

Bertie immediately sat upright and stretched. "Oh, that's better," he said. "My back is killing me."

From her place on the floor, Sam gazed up at Susannah. "You didn't sleep long. I hope we didn't disturb you."

"No, the older I get, the less sleep I seem to require. Five or six hours is enough, and I did doze off for a while in the corridor last night."

Sam couldn't keep her eyes off the older woman's face and her shock of pure white hair. At last she gave in to her curiosity. "Susannah, you look so familiar. I wonder if we've met before?"

"A frequent question." Susannah smiled. "I'm an actress. I've played character roles in many plays and a few films."

"*The Piper's Story* was the latest, both play and film," Bertie said.

"Oh, I didn't see the play, but I saw the movie," said Sam.

Susannah nodded. "I was cast in the same role in both."

"Ha!" Sam grinned and pointed a finger at Susannah. "Now I remember. You were the Scottish grandmother!"

"Aye, wee lassie, tha's correct. Barbara was the name. A feisty one from Edinburgh, she was." Susannah's hazel eyes sparkled as she turned on the accent.

Peter's mouth dropped open. "You sound so different."

A flash of light from outside drew their attention. The gray morning had darkened considerably, and the train charged ahead into a rainstorm. They heard thunder and watched fat droplets spatter against the window. Occasional lightning flashes, brilliant as strobe lights, illuminated the heavily wooded, rural countryside.

Katie's story had distracted them all and lightened the heavy atmosphere in the room, but now grim reality surged back. As Sam watched the storm, she wondered about the greater storm upon them—the takeover of a constitutional republic by an unknown military force. The train moved them ever closer to what bleak future? It was morning, but she feared night was upon them.

GLIMMERINGS

He swam just below the surface. The sun warmed his back and his bare buttocks. Shafts of early-afternoon sunlight pierced the clear water of the quarry pool at a sixty-degree angle. Curious about its depth, he swam down deep with open eyes and tried for a long time to follow the downward-slanting sunrays, but in the darkness below, he could not see the bottom. At last, he faced upward, kicked, and broke the surface, gulping air in relief. Down below, where the sunlight did not warm the water, the icy cold had gripped his body like death, seeking to drag him down.

He brought his legs up to the warm surface water and swam parallel to the quarry's flat, dark-gray granite edge where his clothes and sandals rested. He drew his pale, muscled arms and hands together and then pushed outward to each side repeatedly in a lazy breaststroke. The gold band on his left ring finger caught the sunlight and reflected it, gold to gold. Old Sol poured his light over and into the pool, making the waves rippling out from his exertions sparkle with myriad miniature suns.

The warm sunlight, cool, sweet air, and the womb-like enveloping water filled his senses. He closed his eyes and relaxed; he merged with it. He felt part of it all, and he was filled with a deep peace. *All shall be well, and all manner of thing shall be well.* In that moment, he knew it to be true.

He woke.

Vermont summer. It was more memory than dream. He had been there—he was certain of it. There was something else he remembered; he'd had a vague sense that someone else had been present. Not in the quarry pool, but she was there on the periphery, just out of sight.

She. The wedding band. His wife? He had been married, at least at the time of the dream/memory, and he had visited Vermont in the summer. He was a thirty-something New Yorker—the accent was unmistakable, as Gideon had pointed out. Those facts currently summed up his entire identity. He still didn't know his own name.

Where was his wife now? Why was he in Texas? Gideon and Jaybird had found him wandering near Caddo Lake, but his identity was still a mystery, locked within himself in a safe with the key gone missing. Perhaps he would find the key, open the strongbox, and recover himself in one fell swoop. Or maybe his identity would emerge piecemeal from dreams or sudden recollections.

Who was he—who could he have been? His mind ticked through a list, as though he was a boy again, wondering who he would be when he grew up. *Rich man, poor man, beggar man, thief / Doctor, lawyer, Indian chief.*

To amuse himself, he created his own list: *Soldier, sailor, fireman, priest / Painter, rock star, mythical beast.*

After all, they called him Bigfoot.

He mulled over the list. *No, certainly not a lawyer.* He shook his head. That had been his father's profession, one he never wanted to emulate.

Ah! Another fact had surfaced: *his father was a lawyer.* How many young, married New Yorkers could there be with attorney fathers who visited Vermont in the summer? Answer: *beaucoup*—a whole slew. But he felt hopeful: the clues to his identity had begun to rise, bubbling up from a hidden spring.

He lay wrapped in a Mylar blanket on the dusty floor of a one-room cabin, long since abandoned and now in the last phase of its existence, simply marking time until it disintegrated into a rotting heap. But at least its roof was still intact, and it gave some protection from the elements. Narrow rays of sunlight pierced a multitude of cracks in the eastern wall and warmed him. Gideon and Jaybird were out either hunting or checking the traps they had set. Breakfast would likely be roast rabbit or fish.

He was pretty certain his former life had not included roughing it like this. They had been holed up here for weeks, from late September to November, carrying water in buckets from a creek, sometimes trekking back to the lake to fish. At the lake's edge they were at their most visible and vulnerable. Like wild animals, they went there only at dawn or dusk.

Now that he had gained back weight and strength and his ankle was better, they were teaching him to hunt. Being outdoors most of the time helped him forget himself and all his anxieties for a while. But on the hunts, the best distraction of all was Jaybird, their leader; he was a veritable magician.

He had never imagined a slingshot could be a real weapon. But in Jaybird's hands it was a near-silent instrument of death; he wielded it with confidence and amazing skill, like David the shepherd boy. In addition, the young black man seemed to have a sixth sense about locating his prey. He knew their habits and their haunts. He could identify their tracks and spoor, and he had the patience to sit silently for long periods, moving only his head and eyes, alert for any motion in the brush. Jaybird zapped his targets—rabbits, doves, and squirrels— about eighty percent of the time.

"How can you be so accurate with that thing?"

"Bigfoot, I grew up poor. We saved our rifles and ammo for bigger game, deer and hogs." He tapped his slingshot with one finger. "Been huntin' with this since I was seven years old. It's the perfect weapon now when we gotta be careful about drawing attention to ourselves. There are eyes and ears out there, and a rifle report carries a long way in the woods and over water. But I feel a little better now we ain't seen a drone in over a week. I think it's gonna be okay soon to use the rifles huntin' deer."

Jaybird and Gideon had taught him how to skin and gut small game, and how to scale and gut fish. During the last few weeks, he had gotten more efficient at those tasks, and it made him feel like a solid contributor. He had his doubts about gutting a deer, but he sure looked forward to eating roasted venison.

The nights had turned colder, so he was glad for the fire pit Gideon had dug under a tree at the edge of the clearing. The opening was about a foot across and the pit itself two feet deep, widening out toward its base to accommodate more wood. The eight-inch hole angled diagonally toward the main pit provided airflow. The result was a fire pit that burned really hot, and whatever smoke it produced was dispersed by the tree above it.

"You didn't learn that at no library, man."

Gideon's laugh turned into a coughing fit. "No, Jaybird, I learned that in Afghanistan trying to keep the enemy from shredding my ass. At least we've got more cover here than in the desert. We'll use the fire pit the same way we did there—very early in the morning or at dusk."

"Library? What's he mean?"

Gideon coughed into his elbow. "After I left the Marines, Bigfoot, I got a degree in library science. I worked at the public library in Jefferson, a small town about twenty minutes from Caddo Lake and the mighty metropolis of Legend."

"What's the population of Legend?"

Jaybird gave the statistics. "Oh, about eighty people, twenty dogs, forty cats countin' the stray ones, fifty cows, and two hundred chickens. Chickens got the majority. We do what they say."

The New Yorker laughed.

Gideon smiled. "Good work, Jaybird, you finally got a laugh outta him."

"Yeah, one of the head chickens is Jack Dunham. He thinks he's a rooster, but he ain't. The way he stood there and didn't lift a finger to help the Greek and his wife the night of the roundup . . ." Jaybird shook his head. "That ain't even chicken—that's chicken shit."

Gideon and Jaybird had told him about the relocation during their sojourn in the woods. They intended to live off the land until they could think of a better plan. His situation could have been much worse—he might have died alone in the woods, or if others had found him, he could have been consigned to a relocation camp. After spending weeks with them, he trusted them; they were good, decent men. But he worried about Gideon's chronic cough. According to Jaybird, he had lung cancer. Gideon had only one week of radiation before the relocation, not enough to kill the tumor—just enough to make it mad, according to Jaybird.

He stretched and yawned. His friends would soon be back with the morning's catch. He would go with them on the deer hunt that evening. He laced his fingers together over his chest and watched dust motes floating in the light, flecks of gold. Transfixed and suspended in light—not a bad place to be. Perhaps on a universal scale, the worlds were like dust motes, held and warmed in celestial glory.

Spider webs floated like interior clouds or hung like gray Halloween beards from the bare rafters. Stirred by the cool morning breeze, coming through cracks in the wall, he watched them sway like dancers. He suddenly realized he heard music. An orchestra played in his head: French horns, oboes, and strings. Three melodies in triple time, each strong and independent, fit together in a wonderful unity. The jolly, rhythmic bass, confident and powerful as an engine, drove the piece smoothly and surely forward. A second melody joined the bass: two French horns, in tones of pure gold at the top of their range, played a soaring theme; it rose and arched in noble splendor above the joyful, dancing bass. Now oboes and strings, in freedom and astonishment, like a flock of white doves suddenly released, joined the chorus, exulting in flashing, rapid rhythms above it all.

The music lifted his heart; it took him far from his troubles. He smiled—he wanted to know the man who had written it. The composer—whoever he was—must have touched the gold, the everlasting delight, at the heart of the universe. Wordlessly, the sublime music affirmed that the world sprang forth out of an overflowing joy, that nothing, now or ever, could extinguish it. He hoped so—maybe somewhere in time to come, all wrongs, all injury, all hurt would stand redeemed and transfigured, at once whole and well and new. Though flesh cannot perceive it, he thought, the eyes and ears of the spirit know the very fabric of life is exultation.

Who was the composer? He huffed in exasperation; he couldn't remember his own name, much less anyone else's. But those were small matters compared to the deep peace that filled his heart: *All would be well, and all manner of thing would be well.*

The shrill call of a bluejay roused him: "Aaaay—aaaay—aaaay!" Three times. During the weeks at the camp, Jaybird had taught him that call and those of the cardinal and mourning dove. He discovered he was a natural mimic.

He sat up and whistled. "Aaaay—aaaay—aaaay!"

Jaybird popped his head in through the door. "Pretty good, Bigfoot. Got two rabbits for you." He held them by the ears. "Time to rise up and show off your skinnin' skills." He held up two round, orange fruits in the other. "Found a wild persimmon tree, too. We gonna dine well today."

The music kept running through his mind as he cleaned the still-warm rabbits. When he finished, he brought the silvery carcasses to the fire pit. Jaybird salted the rabbits first and then impaled each one lengthwise on a long, sharpened stick. He placed each stick into Y-shaped branches he had stuck in the ground on either side of the crackling fire.

"Well, Bigfoot, you seem cheerful this mornin'. Nice tune you're hummin'. Your mission is to watch our breakfast here and turn each spit now and again, so the bunnies don't burn. You might have to hold onto the—"

"Handel!"

Jaybird almost fell off his haunches. His mouth dropped open. "Whoa, man. Don't scream it in my ear. That's right—hold onto the handle."

"No, not that handle—I mean *Handel*. Georg Frideric Handel." He grabbed Jaybird by the shoulders and shook him. "I remembered something, Jaybird. Handel is the composer of the piece I've been hearing in my head all morning."

"Hmm, don't think I know him. Prob'ly not a rhythm and blues man."

"He's one of the greatest composers ever. See, that tells me something about myself—it's a clue. I must have listened to his music so much it stayed with me, and not only the tune. The piece was written for strings, oboes, and horns. I can hear the whole orchestra in my mind."

"Well, you likely a musician, dude. I saw it around you."

Bigfoot wrinkled his brow. "What do you mean? What did you see around me?"

"Music. 'Cept not notes and such. It was like shapes and forms flowing. I saw circles and star-like figures, simple and complex. Kinda like a kaleidoscope, but somehow, I knew it meant sound." Jaybird laughed. "Pretty weird stuff, huh?"

"I'll say. Do you see darkness around Gideon? Is that why you call him Shadow Man?"

"Yeah. I knew he was sick the first time I met him. But back to you—here's the weirdest part. Your heart was shaped like a harp."

Bigfoot raised his eyebrows. "You think I played the harp?"

Jaybird threw back his head and laughed. "How should I know, man? I just saw what I saw." He pointed at the roasting rabbits. "Right now, you're not a musician, you're a chef. Time to turn the handle, man, 'cause them coneys startin' to burn. Get to work. We got to eat well so's we got strength for the big hunt today."

CHAPTER 26

THE DRAGON

He was afraid because they were afraid. The grown-ups tried to hide it from him, but he knew. Mamma held onto her silver cross all the time and hardly smiled. Her mouth pulled down and her eyes looked worried. The lines on her face had gotten deeper. When Bertie and Susannah whispered to each other, which they did a lot, Bertie would say something and then Susannah would bite her lip and nod. When she whispered back, Bertie looked sad. He would shake his head slowly.

In the distance, Peter saw lightning flashes strike the ground over and over. Maybe a great dragon hidden in the clouds shot fire from its mouth at the earth. Maybe it was aiming for the train. After each flash, a thunderous roar made him jump. Sheets of rain hid the landscape and washed against the windows of the train. The dark morning seemed like night.

"This storm reminds me of what happened when Tamino and Papageno reached Sarastro's castle, Dragon's Cry," said Beano.

Peter turned from the window to gaze at her. "What happened then?" he asked, eyes wide.

Beano's story made him feel better. It made that scary alone-in-the-dark feeling go away for a while. He wasn't alone, and he wasn't in the dark, but something was wrong with all the grown-ups—he didn't know what—and that made it worse. He knew they were afraid of something fierce and bad, like the monstrous dragon in the clouds.

"They arrived cold, wet, and hungry, in a pouring rain, just like this," said Beano.

To Peter's relief, when he searched Beano's shining blue eyes, he saw no fear or worry there. He leaned toward her and reached for her hand. Her grip was so warm and comforting. He knew he could trust her; like a superhero, she would protect him, no matter what.

"A dragon guarded the castle gate. Papageno's knees trembled so badly, he could hardly stand up. 'How—how—how can we ever get past the dragon?' he asked. 'We'll be eaten alive before we ever enter the castle.'"

Somehow it made Peter feel better that the prince and the birdcatcher were frightened, too. The scaly, ugly dragon roared and blew out a whoosh of fire that turned the raindrops into a giant cloud of steam. That's when Papageno played his pipes—*do re mi fa sol*. Flying out of the steam cloud in a small wooden airship, sort of like a homemade helicopter, the three boys suddenly appeared. They didn't seem one bit afraid of the dragon or anything else, and they sang this song:

> *In Sarastro's realm, danger is near,*
> *But have courage, men, and never fear.*
> *Go forward soon, without delay;*
> *These gifts will help along the way:*
>
> *Food and wine to keep you warm,*
> *Bells and flute shield you from harm.*
> *Goodbye! We'll meet again 'ere long.*
> *Safety lies in music and song!*

They handed Papageno a small set of silver bells in a box with a wooden crank, and they gave Tamino a magic flute. Then they sailed away in their airship. The bread, cheese, and wine the boys had given them warmed them and gave them new energy.

When the dragon saw the prince (who looked like Peter's dad) and Papageno (a grown-up, woolly-haired Isaiah) coming, he stood up and swung his ugly old head from side to side. Smoke rose out of his nostrils, and a wedge of fire shot out of his mouth.

Papageno's knees shook. "'Don't you think we can find a princess somewhere else—where there's no dragon guarding the gate?'

"'Maybe so,' said Tamino, 'but I don't want just any old princess. I'm here to rescue Pamina.'

"'Drat,' said Papageno. 'You would be a hardhead.'"

"Like me and Bertie," said Peter.

"Exactly!" Sam and Susannah spoke at the same time.

When everyone laughed, the cloud of fear in the room vanished—because of Peter's remark. He felt proud of himself for that. Then Bertie prompted Katie, "Carry on! Carry on with the story."

"'Well, how can we get past the dragon?' asked Papageno. 'My slingshot won't even put a dent in him.' He was sure the dragon would breathe fire on him and burn him to a crisp."

"What happened next, Beano?" Peter had to find out how they would get past the dragon. In his mind, the prince was his dad, and his dad would never let a dragon stop him.

"Papageno played his magic bells. He turned the crank and they rang with a pure, clear sound. Suddenly, the dragon clasped his two scaly hands together and moved his clawed feet up and down in time to the music. He closed his eyes, raised his tail, and whirled around like a ballerina—the most awkward and clumsy ballerina ever.

"While his eyes were shut, they hurried past the dancing dragon and entered the castle. Tamino opened the castle door for the birdcatcher and quickly shut it behind them. Papageno followed as the prince dashed up a stone staircase. They raced up three flights of stairs before they stopped for breath.

"'Do you know where you're going?' asked Papageno.

"'To the tower at the top of the stairs, where the princess is imprisoned.'

"'How do you know that?'

"Tamino huffed. 'That's how it works in fairy tales.'

"'Are we in a fairy tale?'

"'Of course,' replied the prince, "and in this tale, the good guys win.' He grinned and clapped Papageno on the shoulder. 'That's us.' Then he shot up the stairs in a mad dash.

"'I sure hope you're right,' muttered Papageno.

"A few minutes later, huffing and puffing, they arrived at the top of the staircase and the door to the tower room. The wooden door had a little barred window in it. They saw two people inside. One was the princess—the one who looked like your mom—but the other one . . . oh, my goodness! She was green—her eyes and her hair—and her skin was lumpy and bumpy as a pickle.

"Papageno stared at Tamino. 'I thought you said Sarastro only kidnapped the most beautiful princesses. This one bears a striking resemblance to the Waxy Monkey Tree Frog, green and ugly as they come.'"

Peter laughed. "Did he make that up?"

"Papageno, the nature boy? Nope. The Waxy Monkey Tree Frog is an amphibian that spends its life in the treetops of South America. But Papageno didn't want to marry a frog.

"Tamino said, 'Well, maybe she's the kindest, sweetest person you could imagine on the inside.'

"Papageno shook his head and gazed at the green girl. 'I'd rather try my luck with a Gila monster. Maybe marriage isn't such a good idea after all.'

"Tamino tested the door handle. It was locked. 'Well, let's not get ahead of ourselves,' he said. 'Before we worry about marriage, we have to figure out how to open this door.'"

Beano yawned and stretched. "That's a good place to stop," she said.

Peter scratched his head. "Are we in a story, too?"

His mom answered. "Yes, we are."

"Is there a dragon in it?" He was sure there was, but he wanted them to say it.

Everyone seemed to freeze in place, and no one answered. The humming of the rails and the beating of the rain against the windows filled his ears.

Finally, Beano answered. "Yes, there is."

Susannah said, "I've acted in many plays, Peter, and I can tell you, every story must have a dragon. The dragon's presence creates danger and excitement. The hero must stand up to the danger to prove his courage; it inspires him to do great deeds."

"The dragon propels the story forward," added Bertie.

Peter wrinkled his nose. "What do you mean?"

Bertie thought for a moment. "He's like the motor of a big truck. If you lift the hood while it's running, the engine is hot and roaring, pistons are firing, and sometimes it shoots out smoke—kind of scary, but all of that has to happen so the truck can go forward. It makes it possible for the driver (or the hero) to reach his rightful destination."

"What do you think, Mamma?"

"I think we can't let the dragon defeat us. 'Let courage rise with danger, and strength to strength oppose.' That's from a hymn. Do you know what it means, Peter?"

"Not really."

"It means the scarier it is, the braver you have to be," said his mother. "And if the enemy is strong, you've got to be strong, too."

"Let courage rise with danger." Peter spoke slowly and thoughtfully. "Does that mean I can't be afraid?"

"Not at all. People who are not afraid don't need courage. Courage is the strength to face danger in spite of fear—not to run away. Will you remember that?"

"I'll try. But, Mamma, are you afraid sometimes?"

"Yes, we all are. But we will go forward and be brave."

Peter lifted his chin and touched his chest with his pointer finger. "Then I will, too."

In that moment, her eyes lost their worried look, and she seemed very proud of him.

"Good boy." His mother leaned over and kissed his cheek. "Don't you worry—that old dragon will never defeat us."

ASSIGNMENT

Region VI Headquarters

The phone call came in at 3:00 a.m. The General was furious when his aide woke him. "Who the hell is it?"

"Dumitru Lupei." The aide, who thoroughly disliked the General, had the pleasure of watching the blood drain from his face. Richard Huffman sat up on the edge of the bed and put his feet on the floor. He took the proffered phone. "Hello, Dumitru." With an impatient, abrupt gesture as if he swatted a fly backhanded, he dismissed the aide.

"Genewal, we have a pwoblem."

It had better be a damn gnarly one, dwarf, if you have to wake me up at three in the morning to tell me about it.

"My diawy is missing from the libwawy of my chalet in Geneva."

The General rolled his eyes. *So what, Elmer Fudd?*

"It contains the outline of our plans."

Richard Huffman disliked most people, but he particularly despised the pint-sized billionaire, who had duped him long ago. Unless he toed the line, Dumitru threatened to expose him with the damned yacht video. He felt his blood pressure rise. *Get to the point, Shrimp.*

"In them I mention the Nine."

The fallen ones. His stomach dropped like an elevator in free fall. Sweat popped out on his brow and cold fear made his hands tremble. "Dumitru, what does this have to do with me?"

"It has to do with Constantin. He found the diawy and stole it. I suspect he took it back to New York when he weturned for school. So, Genewal, it is now your job to locate him ASAP. When you find him, I want that diawy back. It contains highly sensitive information. I want him interwogated and, if necessawy, silenced."

Silenced? He would have to murder his own grandson?

"And believe me, Genewal, if you cannot or will not do it, we will wemove you from your curwent position. Do you understand me?"

"I do. But it's going to take some time to find him. The country is in chaos."

"I don't give a goddamn. Find him soon, Genewal. Your life and position depend upon it."

The line went dead. *My life?* If his fist could have reached Switzerland, Richard Huffman would have smashed Dumitru's face in and reveled in the blood and broken bones. Oh, how he hated the man. He bristled at taking orders from anyone, much less such a ridiculous twerp.

He rubbed the sleep out of his eyes. Though they inhabited opposite ends of the physical spectrum, they were twin souls: members of the ruling class, alpha males, lords of domination and control. Dumitru's authority lay in his vast wealth and his connection to the fearsome Nine. The General's authority lay in his powerful military rank and in his intense, imposing physical presence.

Grudgingly, he admitted to himself that he would have demanded the same thing in Dumitru's place. Given the choice between power and love, Richard Huffman knew he would not hesitate for an instant. If his grandson stood in the way, Constantin's life was forfeit, and Dumitru Lupei knew it.

CHAPTER 28

DRAGON'S CRY

They had finally outrun the worst of the thunderstorm. The deluge had diminished to a light drizzle by the time the train reached Texas. They passed directly through a small-town station without even slowing. Sam and Katie watched the deserted platform fly by.

"What town was that?" asked Susannah.

"The station sign said Zabach," answered Katie. "Never heard of it, but then I don't know anything about Texas, except rodeo and the Houston Grand Opera."

Odd name for a town, Sam thought. She would have looked up its origin and meaning, but her iPhone was dead. "Whoever's driving this train must be in a hurry to reach Dallas."

But five minutes later, to their surprise, the train slowed down. Eventually, it came to a halt with a screech of brakes. Sam scratched her head. "Maybe the conductor realized he missed the station, and we'll back up."

Bertie shook his head. "Doubtful. They'd have to have another engine at the back of the train to do that."

They all peered out at the seemingly endless piney woods of East Texas. Susannah glanced at her wristwatch. "It's almost two-thirty. I wonder how long it'll be to Dallas?"

They heard an outer door open, and one of the guards shouted, "Everyone off the train! Now! Bring belongings with you."

"Mamma, can a train run out of gas?" Peter's brows drew together in worry.

Sam smiled at him. "That's a good question, Peter. I guess it could happen. Do you think that's why we stopped?"

He nodded vigorously and clutched his ragged lamb.

"Could be," Sam answered. "But maybe they just want us to get some exercise. It'll be nice to be out in the fresh air. But I think you should go to the bathroom first."

In fact, they all took Sam's advice. Susannah and Bertie had no luggage, so they walked out first, after the crowd of people in the corridor departed. Katie hefted her backpack, lightened considerably from when she boarded, since she and the others had consumed much of her food cache. She smiled at the little boy. "Peter, why don't you hold my hand, so your mom can have both hands free for that big suitcase?"

He clutched his lamb under one arm and put his hand in hers. They left the small compartment just ahead of Sam, who negotiated the bulky suitcase out the door, through the narrow corridor, and down the steps of the railcar. Since there was no platform, the distance to the ground from the steps was great. She lowered the bag a few inches, but fearful she might overbalance and fall, she let it drop. It hit the light-colored ballast with a thump and keeled over on its side. Sam hopped down and righted it.

As they stood wondering what came next, the clouds broke and the sun appeared. The bright Texas sunshine converted the damp midafternoon into an eighty-degree sauna. Though their prospects remained cloudy, at least the brilliant blue sky cheered them. A loose line of armed, blue-helmeted UN soldiers stood between the passengers and the pine forest bordering the tracks. Sam looked left and right, puzzled as to why they had stopped and disembarked in the middle of nowhere.

A middle-aged passenger in a rumpled gray suit seemed to read her mind. He asked a soldier, "Why are we—"

The soldier raised his rifle, threatening to strike him with the stock. "Shut up, man!" The veins in his neck stood out. "You not ask questions. You move—fast. Dat way!" He gestured with his rifle toward the front of the train.

Why do they seem so angry? she wondered. Every soldier she could see was Asian—Chinese, probably. The blue helmets with white lettering identified them as UN peacekeeping troops. *Peacekeeping? Hardly,* thought Sam. In their presence, all peace had fled.

The passengers' footsteps crunched across the slope of crushed ballast stone lining the tracks until they stepped onto the flat grassy area flanked by the trees. They headed west, in the same direction the train had moved. Sam and Katie walked abreast with Peter between them, just behind Susannah and Bertie. Sam couldn't see past their backs, so she had no idea where they were headed.

After they trudged past four railcars, she saw the long column of people turn to the right and move into the trees. Her heart thumped wildly, and she broke into a cold sweat. Images of WWII massacres flitted through her mind. Were they marching to their deaths? Would they have to dig their own graves? Dread for Peter seized her as she glanced down at his curly dark hair. It would be agony to see him suffer. Silently, she addressed her Maker: *Dear God, if we have to die here, let it be quick.*

When they reached the point where the column turned north, to the right, she saw the fire lane, a wide, cleared, grassy area between the trees. She relaxed a little. The line of passengers stretched ahead, flanked by soldiers. The open, grassy area was level, and it had been recently mowed, making walking easy.

To keep her mind from fear and panic, Sam focused on the calling of the woodland birds. She heard the familiar scream of a bluejay, the sweet song of a cardinal, *cheer-cheer-cheer, birdie-birdie-birdie,* and the varied chirping of a mockingbird. But a sudden loud chuff followed by a clanking sound made her jump. She glanced behind her. The empty train began to move slowly down the tracks. As she walked on, pulling her suitcase behind her, she heard the train pick up speed. Its destination was Dallas, but where she and the others were headed, she had no idea.

The line of soldiers stretched out on either side of the long column of people, herding them like horseless cowboys on a cattle drive. "Faster!" they urged. Fatigued from the all-night train ride and lack of sleep, they forced themselves to pick up the pace. After a short time, Peter's face wrinkled up and reddened. Tears leaked from his eyes. "Mamma, I can't walk any faster. I'm tired."

Sam knew she could carry him a while, but she had no idea how far or how long they would walk. Katie could help, but it would eventually exhaust both of them. "Lucky you, Peter. You get to ride on my suitcase. Katie, can you put him on it while we're walking?" They couldn't stop and impede the people behind them. If they did, she feared the angry guards might beat them or shoot them.

"Good idea, Sam. Sure, I can." With the energy of a big, healthy farm girl, Katie swooped down and lifted the little boy in mid-stride. "Oh, you're lighter than a sack of chicken feed," she told him. She hoisted his forty pounds with ease, and she kept her balance as though she did that sort of thing every day. "I'm gonna set you down on the top of the suitcase, Peter. Face your mom and stick your legs through the handle."

He managed to do it. Sam glanced behind her as Peter settled on the suitcase.

"Good, now hold on tight to the big brown strap between your legs." She gently took the lamb from him. "Here, let's put Albi inside your shirt so you can use both hands to hold on." She helped him tuck in his shirt. The lamb made a lump against his chest.

"Don't want you to fall off. Got it?"

"Yes, Beano." He gripped the handle and adjusted his bottom to find a good balance. "It's bumpy," he said.

"You're in Texas now," replied Katie. "Gotta ride that bucking bronco."

"What's a bronco?"

"It's an ornery horse that tries to throw off its rider. But it's not gonna throw you off, is it, little man." She made it a statement, not a question.

"Nope, not me or Albi either."

"I didn't think so, not a tough guy like you."

Sam leaned forward slightly to counterbalance the added weight. "Thanks, Beano." She was so grateful to the singer for entertaining Peter, for generously sharing her food, and for her buoyant good humor, the antidote to the cloud of fear that threatened to overwhelm them all.

Katie grinned at Sam. "No problem." She patted the little boy's shoulder. "Hey, Peter, where were we in the story?"

"In the tower where the princess and the green frog lady were."

Marveling at Katie's powers of invention, Sam listened to the tale in an effort to keep her own fear at bay. Speaking quietly, Katie explained how Prince Tamino and Papageno unlocked the door to rescue the brown-eyed, dark-haired princess. (So like Sam herself.) When a guard came up the stairs, the music of Papageno's magic bells put him to sleep, and they used the guard's key to open the door. It was love at first sight for the prince and the princess. On one knee, he pledged his life to free her from prison and the evil Sarastro.

Meanwhile, Green Girl, a.k.a. the Waxy Monkey Tree Frog, flirted with the birdcatcher. She wanted him to kiss her. When Papageno got up the courage to do it, his kiss broke the spell the evil Sarastro had laid on her. Green Girl vanished. In her place stood a young, beautiful, tawny-skinned girl. Her shining eyes were a dark, liquid brown; her black hair formed a close, curly cap around a most lovely face, and her teeth were straight and white. In fact, she looked a lot like Papageno himself. Delighted, Papageno kissed her again, but this time with all his heart.

They ran out of the castle and found themselves in a courtyard with a great fountain at its center. They should have hurried away, but they stopped and stared at it, fascinated. Life-sized sea creatures ringed the center where the water gushed out: dolphins, seahorses, sea serpents, beautiful mermaids with shell collars, all entwined around a huge statue of Neptune, the bearded sea god. In one hand he held a trident, a long spear with three sharp points, and in the other a conch shell.

Sam glanced behind her at Peter. Perched on the suitcase and gripping the strap tightly, he kept his eyes riveted on Katie as she continued.

"Tamino tasted the cool water, but he spat it out in surprise. It was salt water. Pamina told him it was connected through an underground channel to the sea.

"Tamino's eyebrows rose in wonder. 'How strange, and yet how marvelous. The sea lies a thousand leagues eastward.' He gazed thoughtfully at the turbulent green water. 'What could be Sarastro's purpose?'

"'That you shall soon see!' The booming bass voice startled them all.

"To his everlasting shame, Papageno squealed like a girl. They whirled around to find Sarastro looming over them like a cliff. He must have been ten feet tall. His steel gray armor reflected the sun, except for the black dragon insignia on his breastplate, which seemed to swallow the light. His long black hair hung to his shoulders under a gray helmet, and he carried a huge sword. He could have sliced their heads off in one stroke.

"'My fountain has a special purpose for thieves.'

"'Thieves?' Tamino glared up at the giant. 'We came to rescue the princess and Papagena, whom *you* stole from their homes. *We* have stolen nothing.' Tamino pointed a finger at Sarastro. 'You really should let us go now. Otherwise, we might have to kill you. We don't want to do that if it's not necessary.'

"'You insolent varmint!' Sarastro's roar almost deafened them. 'Count yourself lucky that I don't stomp on your head this minute. Kill me?' Sarastro raised his eyebrows and laughed. 'You've got some nerve.' But even though he sounded confident, Tamino read the glimmer of uncertainty in his eyes."

Peter wrinkled his nose. "But Beano, how could they kill Sarastro?"

As Sam sweated and trudged ahead with aching shoulders, she smiled. *A very good question.*

Beano replied, "Well, Tamino had no idea. He was bluffing—trying to scare his enemy and make him unsure. And he knew one important fact."

"What's that?"

"Sarastro was a bully, and bullies are really cowards at heart." Katie smiled. "They act tough, especially around people who are smaller. But if you stand your ground and fight, they will turn tail and run. Will you remember that?"

Peter smiled and swung a fist. "Punch 'em in the nose."

Sam grinned. *That's my boy.*

Beano laughed. "Exactly." She continued her story. "Tamino looked up at the giant Sarastro and spoke in a firm voice. 'And we don't want you to kill us. So isn't there some other way to settle this dispute?'

"'There certainly is.' Sarastro stuck out his lower lip and pulled on his black beard. 'You must undergo trials by fire and by water. If you survive them both, I will let you go freely.'"

Sam took a deep breath. *Listen well, Peter. Our trials are coming, once we reach the camp.*

"'I will do it,' said the prince.

"'Ah, but the princess, Papagena, and this ridiculous birdcatcher must also undergo the tests.'

"The women immediately agreed, but Papageno hesitated, mostly because his teeth chattered uncontrollably, and his knees knocked together so he could hardly stand up."

"He wasn't a fighting man," said Peter.

Beano and Sam laughed. "Not at all, but he did manage to nod his head in agreement. As soon as he did, Sarastro pointed his sword at them and shouted, 'Dragon's fire consume you!'

"A wall of fire taller than their heads whooshed up and encircled them with a deafening roar. Its searing heat threatened to burn them to ashes. The only thing they could hear above the crackling of the fire was Sarastro's booming laughter. They closed their eyes and huddled together, certain they would soon die—all but Prince Tamino. He said, 'Be brave and follow me.' He put the magic flute to his lips and played a noble and solemn march. The fire seemed to retreat a bit; it didn't seem so hot. This encouraged Tamino. Still playing, he walked forward right into the flames!"

Peter's eyes grew wide. "Did the fire burn him?"

"Not one bit. He passed through the wall of fire and the others came right behind him. Sarastro quit laughing then. Furious that they had passed the trial by fire, he cried, 'Let the sea swallow you!'

"Suddenly, Neptune, the bearded god in the fountain, came to life. He raised his trident and blew a loud blast on the conch shell. The green seawater surrounding him bubbled furiously and rose. All of the stone creatures in the fountain awoke. The mermaids brushed back their long, dark hair and swam with the serpent. The water gushed over the sides of the fountain in a cold flood until the entire courtyard was awash. In just seconds, the icy water covered their ankles and knees. It soon rose up to their waists and chilled them to the bone. Dolphins circled them, leaping and diving, while Neptune and Sarastro threw back their heads and laughed.

"As the water rose, Tamino shivered, but he declared again, 'Be brave and follow me.' Only Pamina's head and shoulders were visible above the green, foamy water, but she kept her eyes on him. He lifted the flute and played the calm, majestic melody. Tamino began to circle the fountain.

"They noticed the water seemed a bit warmer. Little by little, it dropped to their waists, then to their knees. The sea creatures quickly swam to the fountain where they and Neptune once more turned to stone.

"The prince and princess, Papageno and Papagena had passed the trial by water. The courtyard dried up, and Sarastro gave them their freedom."

"Hurray!" said Peter.

Sam smiled. "I second that. Oh, looks like we're changing direction." The column of passengers turned right onto a double-track dirt trail. As she made the corner, Sam was able to see ahead. "Maybe that's our destination." A two-story red brick building loomed in the distance.

Every step brought them closer to the stronghold of a real-life Sarastro where the dragon lay in wait for them. What would their own trials by fire and water be? Fear rose in Sam's throat like bile, but she bit her lip and straightened her back. Time to take her own counsel: *Let courage rise with danger . . .*

DEER HUNT

They set out on the deer hunt at 4:00 and followed narrow animal trails through the thick underbrush of the wooded, hilly terrain. Gideon had the .30-30 rifle slung over his shoulder; Jaybird carried the tactical shotgun loaded with buckshot, and they entrusted Bigfoot with Gideon's 10mm pistol. He had bought it after he left the military; he wanted a semi-automatic with more stopping power than a 9mm. "I don't think you'll need it, but just in case," Gideon told him. He showed Bigfoot the magazine and how to draw back the slide to reload after firing. He allowed him one practice shot. Bigfoot missed the pinecone, but hit the tree trunk beneath it and to the left.

"Not the best training, but we can't waste the ammo, and we can't afford to advertise our presence. The only reason we're taking a chance with guns today is because the drone surveillance has eased off." Before they set out, Gideon instructed Bigfoot once more. "Keep the safety on, keep your finger off the trigger, and don't point it at us."

As the day cooled off and the shadows lengthened, they followed Jaybird silently in single file. Bigfoot, with the handgun tucked in his jacket pocket, brought up the rear. A woodpecker tapped its irregular cadence high up on a nearby tree trunk as the evening breeze rustled the leaves above them. They walked about twenty minutes across the uneven terrain until at length they climbed a ridge overlooking a clearing. Jaybird had them take a knee behind a massive fallen oak with bare branches. In a state of decay, it had clearly lain there a long time. It wasn't as good as a deer blind, but it gave them cover.

They watched and waited. The plan was for Jaybird to take down the deer with buckshot. Gideon would follow up with the rifle if need be. They told Bigfoot to observe and learn. That was fine with him. Although a few memories had surfaced, he had no recollection of hunting, fishing, or camping—at least so far.

Jaybird and Gideon rested the muzzles of their guns against the fallen trunk as they knelt behind it. Keeping their eyes just above the trunk, they scanned the clearing. A squirrel darted out into the open, rapid motion to sudden stillness, stopping with raised tail. Suddenly, Bigfoot remembered standing inside a house, several feet back from an open patio door. He saw a grassy back yard enclosed by a wooden privacy fence where a bluejay alighted and perched. Beside him, a swarthy, bald man seated in a living room chair raised a rifle and aimed at the bird.

Engrossed in his vision, Bigfoot never saw the doe walk into the clearing below them. "No!" he screamed.

Jaybird fired in the same instant, but the startled doe lifted her tail, wheeled, and bolted. He aimed just behind her shoulder, but hit her toward the rump, wounding but not killing her. "What the hell's wrong with you—screaming like that?" Gideon's face flushed with anger. "Now we gotta trail a wounded animal to finish her off."

Bigfoot blinked rapidly, startled out of his vision. "But I saw—"

"I don't give a shit what you saw. Don't ever do that again." Gideon coughed and spat on the ground in disgust. "Stay here until we come back."

Jaybird and Gideon clambered over the tree trunk and raced down the ridge toward the clearing, with Jaybird leading the way. Bigfoot watched them cross the clearing diagonally and disappear into the woods, following the blood trail. Having no experience, he had no idea how long it would take them to find the doe and put her down. Once they found her, they would have to skin and gut the animal. That would probably take less than an hour.

A cardinal landed on one of the bare oak branches just a few feet away from him. It brought his mind back to the bird in his vision. The bald man shooting from inside the house was his father. He had cried out, "No!" and lunged at the gun to stop his father, but too late. His father had killed the bluejay.

He reversed position and sat with his back to the trunk, facing the forest. Strange that the sight of a squirrel would trigger the memory. He scratched his head. *Ah, yes.* His father had baited squirrels with nuts, piling them in the backyard. He would open the patio door and sit concealed several feet back inside the room, rifle in hand. When the squirrels came to eat the nuts, he used them for target practice. Sometimes he let the carcasses lie there for days.

And the bird? Why had he cared so much about the bluejay? After a moment, it came clear in his mind, as if a fog had lifted. The bird belonged to the little girl next door. She found the fledgling when it fell out of the nest and raised it as a pet. She loved the bird—Eliot the bluejay—and she had decided to set it free.

Since no squirrels took the bait that day, his father, impatient, noticed the bird and shot it instead. His attempt to disrupt the shot infuriated his domineering father, who brooked no criticism or opposition. His father sprang out of the chair and clubbed him in the face with the wooden stock. The blow broke his cheekbone and concussed him.

Bigfoot drew out the 10mm pistol and stroked the smooth, gray metal of the five-inch barrel. He ran his fingers over the rough, textured surface of the grip. His father had loved guns, but he had felt very uneasy around them, at least at the time of the memory. He laid the gun down in his lap and rested his head against the trunk of the fallen oak.

His memories had begun to surface. Like pieces of a jigsaw puzzle, they were oddly shaped individual bits—a large picture shattered into fragments. None of them made sense alone, but once a few of them interlocked, the picture would emerge rapidly in ever larger sections. He hoped his recollections would come more quickly as time passed.

Drowsy from the long walk and his riled-up emotions, he gazed idly at the forest through half-closed eyes. Sudden motion drew his eye. A sapling about fifty feet away, its base obscured by the underbrush, swayed back and forth. He opened his eyes fully and sat upright, trying to analyze what he saw. It wasn't the wind or else all the trees would be moving. The sapling stopped quivering, and then he heard a crashing sound that steadily increased in volume. Something—probably a deer—advanced toward him rapidly through the thicket.

He rose to one knee to watch it emerge from the trees. The crashing sound grew very close. Suddenly a bulky, blackish-brown animal barreled out of the woods almost directly in front of him. A bear? No—he saw the white, curved tusks. A huge wild hog. He cried out in fear. A rush of adrenaline put springs in his legs as he leapt to his feet. With no time to run and the log behind him, he faced the animal. The hog growled aggressively, clicked its teeth, and charged. It struck him with surprising force, knocking him off balance. He fell backward and hit his head a glancing blow against the tree trunk. The pig charged a second time, head down. With a quick upward thrust, it gored him in the thigh. The pain seared him and took his breath away. Flat on his back, with the pig standing above him, he remembered the gun in his hand. He flicked off the safety, pointed the barrel toward its chest and fired twice. The hog screeched and fled.

That was all he could do. The burst of adrenaline evaporated, draining him of all strength. He laid his head on the ground and watched the canopy of branches waver and spin. *How odd*, he thought, as a black and endless vortex sucked him down.

The deer's blood trail made tracking her easy. Jaybird figured she was way ahead, since he had wounded her high on the rump, and she ran unimpaired. The trail led uphill to the next ridge, and then downhill where it disappeared at the edge of a slough. He pointed into the mud. "See, she entered the water here. Dang it, Shadow Man, we ain't gonna catch her. We can't follow her into the water. By now, she coulda swum clear across. We'd have to skirt the edges of the slough and hope to recover her trail somewhere, but it sure ain't gonna happen in the dark." The sun had dropped below the treetops.

"Yeah, and we gotta go back and collect Bigfoot." Gideon lifted his hat off his head by the bill and swatted his thigh with it, exasperated. He looked out over the placid water framed by tupelo gum trees and moss-draped cypress. "Whatever possessed him to yell like that? We just lost a week's worth of food."

"Hope you starve, asshole."

"Or maybe you could eat bullets."

"Uh-huh. Nothin' to do about it but cry." Jaybird turned down the corners of his mouth and rubbed his eye with the knuckles of one hand. "Boo-hoo."

Gideon laughed, in spite of himself.

Then they heard two shots at a distance in close succession.

"Appears we ain't the only hunters in the woods."

"Either that or Bigfoot decided to take down a deer all by himself."

"I doubt that," said Jaybird. "We better hightail it back, just in case."

At the clearing, out of caution, they decided to stay concealed in the trees and skirt around it. They had a short climb to reach the top of the ridge and the fallen tree where they had left Bigfoot. But at the base of the ridge, Jaybird stopped Gideon. He spoke very quietly. "Somethin's wrong."

"How do you know?"

Jaybird shrugged. "Just got a feelin.'" He knelt in the brush and motioned Gideon to do the same. Then he imitated a bluejay's call. "Aaaay—aaaay—aaaay!" He repeated the shrill, descending pattern three times.

No response. "Don't like this. If he's there, he knows he's s'posed to answer."

Now what? Gideon's stomach muscles tightened and his palms felt sweaty. With a wave of his hand, Jaybird beckoned Gideon to follow him up the hill. When they reached the fallen oak, they found Bigfoot lying face-up on the ground with his eyes shut.

"Look at that," said Gideon in relief, "he fell asleep with the 10mm still clutched in his hand."

"He ain't sleepin'," said Jaybird. "He's hurt." Through a ripped place in his jeans, they could see blood on his left thigh.

"Holy crap, you think he shot himself and fainted?"

Jaybird knelt down and examined the wound, a deep gash about six inches long toward the outside of the left thigh. "No, I don't think so. If he shot himself, it would be more likely in the right leg or the inside of the—" He lifted his head and sniffed. "Hold on." He swiveled his head slowly and fixed his gaze on a dark heap barely visible through the underbrush. "If that's what I think it is . . . Stay here, Shadow Man." Carrying his shotgun, Jaybird walked cautiously about ten feet into the brush. He aimed the shotgun downward and prodded something with his foot. Then he threw back his head and laughed. "I cain't believe it. Say it ain't true!"

"What?"

"Bigfoot done redeemed himself. He killed a wild hog 'fore it could kill him. The pig must have stuck him in the leg, and then he shot it. Whooooeee! Never mind the deer—we gone dine on pork for a week!"

ZABACH

I have come to the shocking realization in the last few years that I am unable to think for myself. Although I am still able to decide if I'll have a hamburger or sushi for dinner, and I can choose what earrings to wear and on which side I should part my hair, my impaired ability to think seems to apply particularly to the political sphere. Of course, I am not the only one afflicted. I suspect this rather sudden ailment has affected nearly half of the citizens of this country and many in Western Europe as well.

Thankfully, the other half of the population remains unaffected by this problem. Among those who can and do still think for themselves are the journalists for the great newspapers, those pundits who host television and radio news programs, and the majority of Hollywood celebrities. With forbearance and great understanding, they have all adjusted to the new situation. You see, in times past, newspaper, radio, and television journalists reported the news objectively. But now that I can no longer think for myself and make informed decisions, those writers, commentators, and celebrities have, in charity, with a sense of noblesse oblige, cast aside objectivity. Why? For the very reason that if simply given the facts, I will very likely draw the wrong conclusions. To alleviate this problem, they now write articles and give interviews to tell me what and how I should think.

This has made life so much easier. I don't have to check facts, read the Constitution, or study the issues any longer. Now I can lie back, eat bonbons, and tune in to find out what my opinion is. If I don't get it from a news program, a famous Hollywood actor or two will fill me in.

Sam had total recall of the pieces she had written. The beginning of the last op-ed reeled out before her mind as on a screen. The seed of satire is anger, and Sam had it in abundance. She kicked the red dirt of the trail, thinking about the arrogance and condescension of those in power toward the American people and the baseless propaganda that now passed for journalism. The so-called "elites" and their controlled media had brought America to her knees. Regimes that deceived the people and stifled all dissent led to one place. She had no illusions; she and this group of random people were targeted for persecution and death. How many times had this same scenario played out in the course of history?

The atrocities of WWII in Europe attested to that—the persecution and slaughter of Jews, political dissidents, and so many others. More recently, internet rumors warned that certain federal agencies had prepared camps for "domestic terrorists." They had supposedly outfitted shopping malls, schools, and even some of the old WWII internment camps to imprison American citizens the government deemed dangerous: Christians, Jews, political dissidents. Ridiculous, of course. *Ha-ha: American concentration camps. Not in a million years.*

The people trudging through the Texas heat at gunpoint weren't laughing now.

Sweating and weary, they followed a double-track dirt trail still damp from the rain. The forest fenced them in on either side. After a five-minute walk, they came to a cattle guard.

Sam warned her son. "Hang on tight, Peter!"

He laughed as the suitcase bumped over each round steel beam in turn.

They marched on into a cowless cow pasture enclosed by more pine trees and a barbed-wire fence. Was the lone building ahead part of the town of Zabach? Sam wondered. *Zabach, Zabach, what do you hold for us? What does your name mean?*

She knew in the sorting and labeling to come, she would be classified as a domestic terrorist; she was a Christian who had written for a conservative newspaper. With a host of others, she stood on the losing side of the coup, a very dangerous place to be. And a coup was in progress—why else would law-abiding Americans be rounded up and guarded by foreign soldiers within the United States? Why else would they be herded like cattle at gunpoint, deprived of their rights?

She feared the coup had dealt a death blow to the Republic. There would be no more elections of any kind—the world's ruling elite had successfully shot down the Eagle. They had eviscerated the Constitution and destroyed the system of government that had shone like a light to the world for so many years. It galled Sam bitterly. Like her grandfather, a WWII vet, and all her family, she loved America.

But coup or no coup, she believed the problem lay much deeper than the political turmoil on the surface, as bad as it was. The true conflict was spiritual: the ancient, ongoing battle between light and darkness. *The law of the Lord is perfect,* Sam thought; *it does indeed rejoice the heart—because its pillars are love and truth, righteousness and liberty.* Obedience to this law was the path of life. But the Creator gave human beings free will. (Even the angels had free will, and the most splendid of them all chose rebellion.) The opposition, led by that self-deluded angel, the Adversary, was founded on pride and envy, lies and fear: the very elements of dissolution.

To this day, Sam thought, *obedience to God's law by individual human beings or governments brings peace and stability. Disobedience, as it did throughout the ages, manifests in sin and chaos and death. And here we are, immersed in chaos and soon to face death.*

But, as it had been foretold, the long arm of God's justice would manifest one day. Evil might reign for a time, but it would not last forever. *Justice*, Sam thought, *like time and space, is intrinsic to the fabric and order of the universe.* Though it tarry, one day Justice would arise in splendor, like an angel wielding a sword of fire, the downstroke sudden, breathtaking, irreversible as lightning. She knew she might never see it come to pass, but nevertheless, its inevitability strengthened her to face what she must. For the time being, it would sustain her.

The track through the cow pasture ended at a gate where they crossed another cattle guard and came to an actual road. They turned right onto the narrow asphalt lane that ran between the east side of the pasture and the red-brick school. Its bare red-dirt yard was enclosed by a high fence. Guard towers stood at either end: platforms on metal supports with waist-high walls and covered roofs, manned by more soldiers with guns. Between the towers, she counted seven long, narrow temporary buildings with tin roofs. Barracks, she was sure of it. The school had probably been built a century earlier, similar to the high school she attended in New Orleans.

"That fence doesn't look too secure," Sam remarked. Its horizontal wires were spaced about six inches apart. "What are all those knobs by the posts?"

Bertie turned his head toward her and spoke softly, but distinctly. "It's an electrified fence. Those are insulators made for extra high voltage. Should you touch it, you will fry. See how the top of it angles inward? That's not to keep people out; it's meant to keep prisoners in. Welcome to the School of Really Hard Knocks. Or maybe I should say *Shocks*."

The column of people slowly snaked around the school to the front, where they came to a halt. Sam asked Bertie, who was at least a foot taller than she, if he could see what was happening ahead. He leaned left and right and craned his neck.

"No, I can't, but I think this is our destination. I'm guessing they will process each person before anyone enters. If it's like most government operations, it'll be a monumental cock-up and take twice as long as it should."

Sam smiled wanly—she admired his humor. She wondered if she had any humor left. Since the stationary queue lay parallel to the school, she distracted herself by studying the building. A wide, cement staircase led up to the main entrance, two tall wooden doors under a central archway. The school's name, Zabach High School, carved in white stone letters, stood out in relief at the top of the arch. As best she could tell, it faced east, with the entrance flanked by north and south wings. She counted twelve tall windows on each wing, six on each floor.

The school had clearly been prepared for this political roundup. It made sense, in a way. Schools were built to handle large groups of people, with many rooms, lockers, large bathrooms, showers, gymnasiums, and cafeterias. Some had specialized shops with carpentry and welding equipment. Many had stadiums; places where crowds could be corralled. She leaned to her left and looked past the school to the north. Sure enough, there it was; she saw the tops of the grandstands and tall stadium lights.

Handy. Throw in barracks, guard towers, an electric fence, and *voilà*: a school became a prison. So economical, too—no need to build new ones from scratch, and available in every community, urban or rural. America, from the mountains to the prairies, from sea to shining sea: *Prison-Landia*.

Movement above caught her eye. Black against the blue sky, two vultures with outstretched wings glided in slow circles above the school. *Waiting for the feast?* For as sure as the sun had begun to set in the reddening west, Sam knew blood would flow here. Every revolution resulted in genocide. The twentieth-century Lords of Slaughter—Hitler, Stalin, and the all-time winner Mao Zedong—had shown the world how to execute, torture, and starve their citizens by the millions.

Now she walked a path that would have been unimaginable in America just a few years ago, a path that people in so many other countries had walked before. Zabach High School might very well be her Auschwitz. She wondered how many other Americans found themselves in the same situation—herded like cattle into makeshift concentration camps.

The queue inched forward. They passed the school's main entrance gate and the sidewalk that led to the central arch. A soldier stood with his back to the closed gate and motioned them to keep moving. Sam saw Bertie whisper something to Susannah. Then he turned his head and spoke to her. "They're moving us toward the stadium. That must be the gulag's processing center."

The corners of Sam's mouth lifted in the barest smile. *The gulag—Bertie had that right.* She admired her new companions. Bertie still had a sense of humor, and Susannah, tired as she must be, marched straight-backed with her head held high. Cheerful Katie, a complete stranger until last night, walked just behind Sam, keeping an eye on Peter while improvising an elaborate fairy tale to entertain him. Their presence strengthened her. Though Joshua's absence was like a hole in her heart, thanks be to God, she wasn't alone. She took a deep breath and resolved to stand tall—all five feet, two inches of her—no matter what.

As they shuffled past the high school and across a grassy area toward the stadium, Sam heard a faint mewling sound. It quickly crescendoed to a wail. *Oh Lord, a baby.* She felt instant sympathy for the mother. It made her wonder how many other children besides Peter and the baby there were among the passengers. She had only seen two teenage girls so far.

Somewhere up ahead, the baby continued to wail and sob in short bursts, a highly irritating squall. Few sounds could equal its annoyance factor, especially when it happened in public. She hoped the woman wasn't traveling alone. As the crying continued, she heard a man shout. The words were garbled and incomprehensible, but the tone was ugly. Her stomach muscles clenched, and she glanced back at Peter. The corners of Katie's mouth pulled back, and her blue eyes, dark with apprehension, locked with Sam's. As tension rose, people in the queue murmured among themselves, a low-level white noise under the baby's bawling.

The child reached a new level of distress, high-pitched, wild and hysterical. Sam knew the mother must be frantic to calm it. Suddenly, she heard a different male voice shout, "Leave her alone!" Then several men shouted, a woman screamed, and Sam heard two rapid gunshots. The baby's wailing ceased abruptly. All murmuring stopped, and an ominous silence descended.

Susannah gripped Bertie's arm with one hand and clapped the other over her mouth. Her husband bowed his head and shook it sorrowfully.

"Mamma, what happened?"

The dreaded question. Sam's heart seemed to tumble into a bottomless pit as she searched for a reply. Should she lie? *Not sure, but don't worry, honey, everything's all right; we're going to be fine.* Or tell the truth? *The world as we know it is falling apart, and the new people in charge would just as soon kill us as look at us.* She answered with the surface truth, the bare facts. "Honey, I don't know exactly. None of us can see way up there at the front of the line."

"Here, Peter," said Katie. She offered him a handful of peanuts. "Eat them slowly, one at a time, so they last."

He took them from her with a smile. "Thank you." He examined each peanut and concentrated on the task. He never saw the sheen of tears that magnified the blue of Beano's eyes.

CHAPTER 31

SURGERY

Shortly after Gideon and Jaybird found him lying wounded beside the fallen tree, Bigfoot regained consciousness. He described how he and the wild hog had surprised each other, and how he had shot it twice at pointblank range. Gideon helped him sit up and gave him water. With his knife, he carefully slit the jeans above and below the cut. Then he cut away the fabric on both sides to keep it away from the gash. He rinsed it as thoroughly as possible with drinking water. "Once we get back to the camp, we'll dress your wound better," he said. "Think you can walk?"

"I'll try." Bigfoot cried out once and grimaced as Gideon helped him up. "I'm sorry about the deer—the squirrel in the clearing triggered a horrible memory . . . "

"No problem, Bigfoot. You can tell me about it on the way back to headquarters. Put an arm around my shoulder."

"Ha—*Headquarters*." Bigfoot smiled and rested his weight on Gideon. "Lead on, O Captain, my Captain."

Gideon laughed and glanced over at Jaybird, who cut and sliced deftly with his knife, field dressing the hog. "See you back at HQ."

"I'll follow soon's I can. I'm gonna take the best parts of the hog and leave the rest to the scavengers. I'll be done in about twenty minutes." He grinned. "Bigfoot, my man, you done good. This here's a sow— much better eatin' than one of them stinkin' old boars."

Back at headquarters, to cut down on the roasting time, Jaybird sliced the meat into small bits and salted it. He had taken the hindquarters, shoulders, and the tenderloin from the back. His mouth watered as he impaled the pieces on a stick and set them up to roast.

In the meantime, Gideon gave Bigfoot water with a couple of ibuprofen for the pain. He rinsed the wound again with salt water and some hydrogen peroxide. "It's as clean as I can get it."

Bigfoot sipped water. "Are you gonna wrap my leg? The flap of skin just flops down."

"I think I'd better try to sew it up first."

Bigfoot's eyes grew wide. "Really? You mean I got extra pain to look forward to?"

Gideon laughed and patted him on the shoulder. "Don't worry, I got the best kind of anesthetic."

"And that is . . . ?"

"Jameson's Irish Whiskey, single malt, 80 proof."

"Where did that come from?"

"Jaybird collected that and some medical supplies from my house the night we found you. We knew we'd have to bug out, so we tried to prepare."

"When will you stitch me up?"

"Tonight after supper."

They feasted that night. The juicy persimmons with their mildly sweet taste complemented the strong, almost nutty taste of the pork. They spoke little as they sat beside the fire pit and ate the meat off the skewers in the cool of the evening. Their fatigue from the hunt combined with their full stomachs to make them drowsy.

"Let's take a rest," said Gideon, "and then we'll do it."

"Do what?" asked Jaybird.

"Operate."

"What you talkin' about?"

"I'm gonna sew up Bigfoot's wound."

Jaybird raised one eyebrow and gazed at Gideon doubtfully. "You some kinda doctor?"

"No."

"You ever done something like this before?"

"Sure, lotsa times."

"Uh-huh." Jaybird didn't believe him for an instant. "Lotsa times? Like when?"

"Like every Thanksgiving when I sewed up the turkey to keep the stuffing from falling out. Same thing, a flap of skin."

Jaybird raised his eyebrows.

"Well, skin is skin."

Jaybird gazed at the man sitting on the other side of Gideon. "Yeah, but he ain't a turkey."

"No, but unless you want to do it, I'm all he's got."

Jaybird exhaled a burst of air that puffed out his cheeks and glanced skyward. "Lord, help us."

Gideon and Jaybird lay down inside the cabin and fell asleep almost immediately. Gideon, whose energy was sapped by the cancer and his chronic cough, regularly took two-hour afternoon naps, but he needed more rest after the exertions of the hunt. Bigfoot lay awake longer, wondering about the ordeal to come. But at last he too dozed. They slept for two hours.

"Let's get to it," said Gideon. He knew Bigfoot needed a tetanus shot. Feral hogs and their tusks were not known for cleanliness. But if they took him to a hospital, they would risk incarceration in one of the "relocation camps." He didn't want to risk it. He set his mind on the task at hand. First, he searched his backpack. "Ah, here's the essential thing." He pulled out the bottle of Irish whiskey. Then he drew a compact canvas case out of a side pocket. "Ta-da! My first aid suture kit."

"You're prepared, man. Better than a Boy Scout."

Gideon handed the bottle of whiskey to Jaybird. "You administer the anesthetic while I prepare the wound. Remember, it's only for the patient, not the nurse."

"Nurse! You callin' me a nurse?"

"That's right, Florence Nightingale. Do your best."

About three-quarters of an inch deep, the gash ran vertically along the outside of the thigh for six inches or so. A loose flap of skin hung down from it. It had to be stitched, but Gideon needed Jaybird's help to do it. He rubbed his hands with a little whiskey, threaded the needle and then sterilized it. He cleaned the area around the wound with alcohol wipes from his suture kit.

In the meantime, Bigfoot downed three shots of whiskey. He grimaced and then smiled. "Oh, man, that's good. Warms me all the way down." He lay back on a Mylar blanket. "I'm guessing this will be the best part of the operation."

"May your pleasure be greater than your pain," replied Gideon. He might as well have said, "Enjoy your flight," to a man about to make a swan dive from a high rise into rush-hour traffic. Pain awaited, very bad pain. "After Jaybird soaks this washcloth in whiskey, put it in your mouth and bite down hard. Try not to move while I'm stitching. Jaybird, sit on his legs to keep them still, and shine the flashlight on the wound. I'm gonna do one stitch at a time, tie it off, and then do the next. Take this forcep in your other hand and press the edges of the wound together. We'll start on the end closest to the hip."

Jaybird grunted his assent and took the tweezer-like, stainless steel instrument.

"Grab the wound here." Gideon pointed to a place about two inches from the top edge of the cut. Bigfoot inhaled sharply from the pain. Gideon eyed the gaping wound, said a silent prayer, and pushed the needle through the skin.

THE MOUTH OF HELL

The sun had sunk below the horizon by the time they reached the stadium parking lot. The only vehicles parked there were three tan Humvees and two odd-looking trailer trucks with chunky cabs. Sam guessed the larger trucks served to haul personnel and equipment. At one end of the lot, close to the stadium, a black tarp covered an odd structure shaped like an upright ladder with an ironing board attached to it.

In the fading light, she noticed movement to her right, underneath the stadium bleachers. Two men, bent-backed, used shovels to dig a large hole. Facing each other, about eight feet apart, they stood knee-deep in the hole. The thin, sandy-haired younger man wore a blue shirt and khaki slacks, while the other, a bald man, had on jeans and a white, long-sleeved shirt that stood out in the gloom. He dug much more quickly and efficiently than the younger man. A lone soldier stood beside them. To her dismay, she saw what looked like two piles of laundry on the ground beside the hole, one large and one very small, side by side. Her heart sank; she knew they weren't laboring to bury clothes.

As she watched, the young man mopped his brow with a white handkerchief, and then seemed to look directly at her. He lifted his head and did a double-take, open-mouthed, as if he recognized her.

"Katie, do you know that young guy digging the . . . uh . . . under the bleachers? He's staring at us."

Katie gazed back at the young man. "The teenager? No, I don't. Maybe he recognizes Susannah."

The moment ended when the guard spoke sharply to the young man, who dropped his gaze and resumed digging.

Sam mourned internally—the bloodshed had begun, even before they entered the prison camp. If the guards could kill a mother and child in cold blood, Sam knew there would be little hope of mercy. Cruelty reigned in concentration camps; the world had seen it many times before. She was glad of the oncoming darkness; it hid any signs of slaughter. She purposefully avoided scrutinizing the ground as they approached the stadium. She wanted to shield Peter and herself as long as she could.

Just then the stadium lights came on. A few feet ahead stood two small tables where soldiers with laptops screened each individual. Beyond them, she could see the crowd split into two lines, each moving through a different entrance gate into the stadium proper. The system reminded Sam of airport security, except there were no conveyor belts or scanning machines for scanning luggage because no luggage was allowed; all personal items had to be discarded. Piles of suitcases, briefcases, backpacks, as well as iPhones and computer equipment lay to either side of the two queues. People entered the stadium with only the clothes on their backs.

"Have your National ID ready," shouted one of the guards at the head of the line. He held a pistol in one hand.

Susannah and then Bertie went to the left table. At the table to Sam's right, a large, bespectacled Chinese soldier questioned an Asian man. The soldier had a strong accent. They spoke loudly enough for Sam to overhear them.

The soldier glanced at the man's National ID and then studied his face. "Adam Chen from St. Louis, Missouri. Do you speak Chinese?"

"No, only English and Spanish. My parents are Chinese, but I grew up in Venezuela. They didn't teach me Chinese because they wanted me to learn the native language. I moved to the States for college."

"Occupation?"

"Musician—violinist, to be exact—and I'm not giving up my instrument." He tightened his white-knuckled grip on the violin case in his right hand and glanced at the pile of suitcases and other belongings off to the side. "It's very valuable."

The soldier sat back in his chair and smiled. "I have an interest in music. May I see it?" He held out his large hands.

Adam Chen reluctantly laid the case on the table. The soldier carefully opened it and peered at the instrument, head nodding. "Very nice." After a moment, he shut the case and latched it.

Glancing up at the musician, he adjusted his glasses and said, "So, Adam Chen, don't worry. I will take care of your very valuable violin." He grinned and gripped the handle. "It will burn brightly in my personal fireplace."

With an incoherent cry, Adam Chen charged the table with hands outstretched, whether to grab the instrument or throttle the soldier, Sam couldn't tell. Immediately, a nearby guard smacked the back of Chen's head with his rifle stock.

Sam winced at the sharp crack.

Chen dropped onto the table, stunned. The bespectacled soldier shot to his feet and shoved him away. His body slid off the flat surface and fell in a heap on the ground.

"Fool, don't ever touch me again," he shouted, red-faced with fury. "Next time, you die." He grabbed the violin case, walked a few paces toward the pile of belongings and hurled it onto the heap.

"Take the fool away," the soldier ordered. The guard put a yellow wristband on the groggy violinist, hauled him to his feet and shoved him toward the right door. Weeping and unsteady as a drunk, Adam Chen staggered through it and disappeared from Sam's sight.

"Next."

Holding her breath, Sam walked forward on wobbly knees with Peter still perched behind her on the rolling suitcase. *Here we go, into the mouth of hell.* She presented her ID to the fuming Chinese soldier, who scanned it with a card reader. His startling blue eyes, magnified by his glasses, projected ill-humor. He scowled at her. "Religion?"

Sam's eyes narrowed. *The very first question. He got right to the point.* "Christian."

He tapped a single key on the laptop. "Profession?"

"Writer."

His fingers tapped on the keyboard. "Employer?"

"Currently unemployed."

He gave her an irritated glance. "Most recent employer?"

"The *Atlantic Star.*"

That perplexed him. "What is that?"

"A UFO."

He blew out an impatient breath. "Do not waste my time—"

"An online newspaper."

"Where?"

"Brooklyn, New York."

"Any other skills?"

"Editing, cooking." *Praying.*

"Marital status?"

Sam hesitated. "Umm, married."

"Where is your husband?"

None of your damn business—no way she would tell him anything about Joshua. "Obviously not here."

He glared at her with a sour expression, like a man with severe heartburn. Then he focused his gaze on her breasts and moved his eyes slowly to her face, clearly ogling her.

She stood stone-faced, refusing to react to his deliberate provocation. *Drop dead, lecher.* She wished she knew how to say it in Mandarin.

Peter chose that moment to clamber off the suitcase. He stood beside her, clutched her hand tightly, and sneezed.

"Is this your son?"

"Yes."

"Name?"

Peter spoke for himself. "Peter Joseph Brightman."

The soldier transferred his cold gaze to the boy. "Age?"

"I'm five years old."

The man grunted and reached down into a box beside the table. He set two lemon yellow plastic bracelets on the table. Sam saw a number and imprinted barcode on each. He scanned the first one and entered the number by hand. Sam guessed the barcode was her new ID, since he tossed her National ID card into a box below the table. "Left wrist."

He attached the bracelet to her arm, and then scanned a second one for her son. "Your arm, boy." Peter obliged. Once the man attached the bracelet, he barked, "Go to the line on the right. And by the way, if you remove the wristband, we remove the first finger of your right hand." It was the second time Sam saw him smile.

"Suitcase over there." He pointed to the pile of abandoned belongings.

Sam set the suitcase near the fallen violin. She glanced uneasily at the yellow wristband. Now that they had been labeled like dry goods, Sam wondered where they would be stocked. She and Peter walked past armed guards and the processing tables to the back of the line on the right. Susannah and Bertie had already arrived.

"You got yellow, too," said Bertie, holding up his wrist to show her.

Sam nodded. "Looks like everyone in this line did." She read the six-digit number stamped in black beneath the barcode: 615-348. She pointed to the band on Peter's wrist. "What's your number?"

"615-349."

Sam remembered the announcement on the train: *You are being transported to Camp 615 in Texas, where you will be processed and given your relocation and work assignments.* Camp 615, inmates 348 and 349—their new identities. That much she knew, but what did the color-coding mean?

The queue of people entering the stadium on the left was much longer. They wore blue wristbands. Were they the sheep of the new regime, the favored ones who gave approved answers: atheists, communists, politically correct supporters of the coup? Blue for them and yellow for the Christians? She watched the people in each line shuffle forward toward gates that led into the stadium itself. Above the high wooden fence surrounding the playing field, she could see the top of a goalpost and through the gates, a patch of mown green grass with faded-white yard lines. Christians in stadiums—not a happy combination, as ancient Rome had proved.

Christ's words to the apostle Peter resounded in her mind. *When thou wast young, thou girdedst thyself, and walkedst whither thou wouldest: but when thou shalt be old, thou shalt stretch forth thy hands, and another shall gird thee, and carry thee whither thou wouldest not.*

Here she was, where she surely did not want to go, a place of trial and testing, a place of suffering. She thought about Sitti, who bore her last illness without complaint. *The patience of the saints: they know the outcome, they see beyond the evil and suffering of the present world, with faith they endure the unendurable.*

Sitti had borne the worst with a calm resolve. Sam hoped she could do it, too.

But Peter was her Achilles heel. She clasped his small hand in hers. She thought about the women whose children had been tortured and murdered in the concentration camps of WWII. How did they bear it? How could she? She took a deep breath and fought off the python of fear that coiled itself around her heart. *I will not be afraid. I will not be afraid. One step at a time, one day at a time. The Lord is my Shepherd. He preparest a table before me in the presence of my enemies.*

The sheep and the goats. Sam blew out an impatient breath through her mouth. In this context, she hoped she was lined up with the goats. She surely didn't want the current regime's approval. Whether it was to keep up her spirits or just blow off steam, she commented on the situation in her best she-goat bleat: *"Baaaaaa!"*

"Sheep or goat?" Katie the farm girl had quietly joined the queue behind Sam.

"Goat. At this point, I refuse to be a sheep."

"Good choice." Katie knew the voice of rebellion when she heard it. "I'm with you."

Peter gave the thumbs-up sign. "Me, too, Beano."

Katie Lamb laughed, and the bright sound, clear and musical, floated up past the harsh, glaring lights to the heavens where the stars had emerged, points of light, serene and unmoved, keeping their eternal watch.

CHAPTER 33

MAX

Gideon and Jaybird rode in the bed of a pickup truck with their backs to the cab. Bigfoot lay flat on his back between them. It was a relief to rest their aching bodies and feet. After two days of carrying Bigfoot on a litter, they had finally trudged out of the woods. During the long, difficult trek they had given Bigfoot a new name, Max Grandpied. They had also perfected the tale they would tell.

Their trek out of the woods had become necessary when, despite Gideon's best efforts to prevent infection, Bigfoot's wound became red and swollen with pockets of pus. They knew they had to get him medical help. They made a litter out of saplings and rope and lined it with a Mylar blanket. Once they got the newly christened Max Grandpied to a hospital, Jaybird and Gideon planned to disappear into the woods again.

They flagged down the truck from the side of the road near Marshall. Gideon told the driver the injured man was a tourist from New York named Max Grandpied. The New Yorker had hired him and Jaybird as guides for an extended hunt. After the feral hog gored Max, they realized he needed medical help, so they took the closest route to civilization. The driver, Chuck Broussard, seemed suspicious and questioned them about Max's missing ID. They told him Max had lost his ID in the woods.

Seemingly satisfied, Chuck agreed to take them to the hospital. But as soon as he climbed into the truck's cab, he made a phone call and spoke to someone for at least ten minutes.

Aware of the extended conversation, Jaybird said, "Shadow Man, I got a bad feelin' 'bout that man's phone call. Somethin's off—I feel it."

Gideon couldn't tell if Chuck believed his story or not. But he was just some random guy who had picked them up—what could be the harm?

"It'll be all right, Jaybird. He's just giving us a ride to the hospital. He could be talking to anyone—his wife, his son, his insurance company. Don't worry."

Jaybird pursed his lips and gave a slight shake of his head but kept his peace. He took out his mouth organ and played "There Is a Balm in Gilead."

Let there be a balm to heal Bigfoot, Gideon prayed. The injured man lay quietly with his eyes closed. He had to be in pain, but he didn't complain.

"The infection is your fault."

"If he dies, it's on you."

"Fool. You should've brought him to the hospital as soon as he was injured."

The effing voices were right, of course. But what was done was done.

During the mournful tune Jaybird played next, Bigfoot stirred. He opened his eyes and turned his head toward Jaybird. He mumbled something indistinguishable. Gideon leaned forward to hear better, but the rich sound of the harmonica and the noise of the truck's motor conspired to obliterate the words. Bigfoot seemed to repeat the same two words over and over, with an intense focus. At last, as the song ended, Gideon heard him clearly.

"See miner, see miner, see miner."

Oh, no. Gideon shook his head. The poor guy must be hallucinating.

The truck slowed, and Gideon realized they had finally reached the hospital, a three-story white stucco building. But to his surprise,

Chuck did not stop at the Emergency Entrance; he turned into a parking area well beyond it, near a helicopter pad. He pulled up beside an ambulance and parked. As Chuck got out, a black van drove up behind the pickup truck. The driver got out of the van and approached rapidly.

Gideon glared at Chuck. "Why did you pass by the emerg—"

"Well, if it ain't Lie-berry Man and Mr. Jaybird Alexander."

"Dang it," muttered Jaybird through clenched teeth. "I knew somethin' was wrong."

Jack Dunham smiled with the satisfaction of an alligator who has just dined on a tasty Chihuahua. He smacked his lips, ran a hand through his scraggy, dishwater blonde hair and hitched up his sagging trousers. "You two vanished into thin air the night of the roundup. Ha! By the looks of those scruffy beards and long hair, you musta been holin' up somewhere in the woods. Lotta good that did ya."

He gave an approving nod to the driver. "Congratulations, Chuck. You done captured some feral humans."

"In your case, Jack, absence does not make the heart grow fonder. You could use a little grooming yourself. Ever heard of shampoo?" Gideon stood up in the bed of the truck. "We got a man here who needs medical attention ASAP. We need to admit him to the emergency room now."

"Whoa, don't be givin' me orders. I'm the overseer for this whole area from Caddo Lake to Marshall."

"Who's your boss?"

"General Huffman, the head of Region VI. And Chuck works for me." He clapped him on the shoulder. "He gets a bonus for bringin' in stray humans.

"So what's this bullshit story you told him about you and Jaybird bein' huntin' guides? Who is this man, and where's his ID? What's the real story?"

"As I told Chuck, he's a New Yorker named Max Grandpied."

"Chuck, run that name through the computer."

"How do you spell it?"

Jack rolled his eyes. "You mean you live this close to Louisiana, your last name is Broussard, and you can't spell a Cajun name?"

"Well, I can spell Arceneaux. That's a hard one. A-r-c-e—"

Jack lost his cool and shouted. "Would you just shut up?"

Max came to the rescue. "G-r-a-n-d-p-i-e-d."

"Thank you." Chuck typed the name into his phone.

"Max came as a tourist to Caddo Lake, and I told him my Bigfoot story," Gideon explained. "Remember back in September when you and me and Reilly Mack hunted Bigfoot out near the lake? When we saw the hairy monster, you screamed and both of you ran away. Left me stranded out there all night."

Jack bent his head and scratched the back of his neck. He stuck his hands in his pockets and shifted his stance. "We, uh, we were just actin', Lie-berry Man. We paid the guy in the furry suit to scare you. That was our plan."

"Really? Did you also spray him with Eau de Putrefaction so he stank like rotted meat? No, I think you were so scared you messed your pants. That's why you didn't show your ugly mug for weeks after that. You quit comin' to the Alligator Gar and the Grocery & Grill. Hard to drop off the face of the earth in little Legend, but you did it, Jack. Haven't seen you since."

He shrugged. "Believe me or not, I don't care. Get on with the story."

Gideon told Jack his tale. "After you turned tail and ran, I spent the night by the dilapidated pier. Jaybird went fishing there the next morning and took me home. After we ate breakfast, we went by the Grocery & Grill so he could drop off some fish. That's where we met Max. He got interested in our Bigfoot stories—"

"*Our* Bigfoot stories?"

Jaybird spoke up. "Yeah, years ago, my dad saw Bigfoot at another area of the lake. And it wasn't no man in a furry suit." Jaybird laughed. "From then on, he kept a gun with him in the boat."

"Max was curious," Gideon continued. "He offered us a lot of money to take him on a hunt for Bigfoot. He paid a lot because he wanted to stay in the wilderness for at least a month."

"So you're tellin' me you were out in the woods on the night of the relocation?"

"It's the truth—we were. No cell service out there. We didn't know anything about it."

"What relocation you talkin' about, man?" Jaybird pursed his lips and wrinkled his brow.

"Oh, you're about to find out. Go on, Lie-berry Man."

"Max surprised a wild hog. It gored him in the thigh, but he managed to kill it."

"Beginner's luck." Everyone looked at Max. "Not many feral hogs in Brooklyn."

"So where's your ID?"

"Probably down at the bottom of a ravine out there. We were up on a ridge when the pig gored me. It knocked me flat on my back. My wallet must have fallen out of my pocket, but it was late and getting dark, so no one saw it. I didn't notice it was missing until a few days later."

Jaybird took up the story. "There was a big thunderstorm later that night. The rain coulda washed it down the hill into the ravine. I went back to hunt for it, but no luck."

"So why did you carry him out to the highway? Why not take him back the way you came?"

Jaybird answered. "I knew our camp was a lot closer to the highway than where we left the boat."

"Well, fellas, while you've been holed up in the woods, there's been a complete change of regime. They arrested the president, and now we got a new military government under General Arthur Pierson. He brought in international troops, mostly Chinese and Russian. We're reorganizing the whole country. Everyone is required to go to a relocation camp. Since you were AWOL, there is the little matter of a $10,000 fine and fifteen-year prison sentences."

Gideon glared at him and hopped down out of the pickup truck.

Jack raised both hands as if to stop him. "Now take it easy. Since I know you, and 'cause naturally, I'm big of heart, I'll have the charges waived due to your extenuatin' circumstances."

"How long are people held at these relocation camps?"

"Depends on their political persuasion. Some people are processed and immediately released, while others have some re-education to do before they can leave. Them that ain't for us are against us. They got a rocky road."

"But Max needs medical help first."

"Oh, he'll get medical help at the camp."

Chuck spoke up. "Uh, Mr. Dunham, there's no Max Grandpied in the database for the United States."

Jack smiled his toothy alligator smile. "Interestin', very interestin'. We got a mystery on our hands. Well, eventually we'll find out who he is. There's ways of gettin' the truth out of a man."

He pointed to the helicopter. A pilot sat in the cockpit, and the rotary blade whirled. A Chinese soldier carrying a rifle approached. "There's your ride, and here comes your personal escort. That bird is goin' to Zabach, Texas, Camp 615, and you're goin' with him."

PART III

CHAPTER 34

PING

October

For Sam, life at the camp shifted between the pseudo-normalcy of her daytime job and her miserable, surreal nights in the barracks. As a writer and editor, she had been chosen to assist the Chinese commander, Colonel Ping. She found herself at the hub of daily operations in the camp office just inside the school's main entrance. For short periods, she was able to lose herself in the work and forget the chaos that had descended on her life. The school building itself comforted her. Reminiscent of her high school in New Orleans, built in the 1920s, it was the familiar in the midst of the strange. The solidity and fine workmanship in its very construction steadied her. She loved the high ceilings and the tall windows that let natural light into the spacious office where she worked—a stark contrast to the narrow, smelly, windowless barracks, crowded with forty women, where she slept.

One day in early October, when Colonel Ping got a fever, Sam called Bertie to the office. He prescribed antibiotics, fluids, and rest for the colonel. Before he left, Bertie and Sam exchanged news in a quick, whispered conversation. She told him Susannah was thinner, but doing well working in the peanut fields with the other women and children. Thankfully, they had put Katie in charge of the kids in Barracks 7, so Peter was in her care. Bertie told her about his partner Adam, a violinist, who helped him with the backbreaking work of clearing trees for the helipad in the cow pasture behind the camp.

The first weeks passed in a chaotic blur. The inmates assembled at 6:00 a.m. for roll call in front of their respective barracks. Due to the scrubs they wore—men in blue, women in green—with their cotton socks and black rubber clogs, they looked like hospital staff. Every person received a tin cup and a spoon. They ate three times a day: portions of rice or stale bread rolls for breakfast, fried rice at midday mixed with eggs, vegetables, bits of pork or chicken, and sometimes a thin beef stew with carrots and potatoes in the evenings. They showered once a week. They had to make their beds and fold their blankets with precision or risk a beating with the wooden batons the BBs carried. The Barracks Overseers were inmates who functioned as spies and live-in supervisors for extra privileges, like WWII-era kapos. The prisoners called them BBs: Barracks Bastards or Barracks Bitches.

To Sam, the peculiar part was the regular medical tests. The nurses drew blood, tested urine samples, and used ultrasound on the inmates' abdomens. There were eye exams, and some people got chest X-rays. It was useless to ask the nurse-technicians questions; they never responded. Rumors circulated that they were testing for AIDS or other infectious diseases.

They attended re-education classes each day at noon, where the instructors mocked and ridiculed the Christian and Jewish inmates, calling them "the deluded ones," "cannibals," "blood drinkers," "stupid sheep." Katie called it Commie-Crap Hour. They were forced to watch videos such as *The Myth of Jesus*, *Gay Jesus*, *Lies of the Bible*, and *Bible Contradictions*. They sang "red songs" extolling the virtues of communism. To espouse atheism and communism was the get-out-of-jail-free card. Deny the Lord and spit upon his name. One microchip later, the gates magically opened and you went your merry way.

Their daily work depended on their experience or physical capabilities, but not always. The three physicians—Bertie and two others—five nurses, and the one veterinarian among the shanghaied throng were assigned manual labor. Most of the male inmates labored to construct the helipad. Under the supervision of the screaming Chinese guards, they had cleared a large area of land with backbreaking manual labor, according to the specifications of the engineer. They had built a frame and would soon pour the thick concrete foundation if the weather cooperated. Bertie came back to the barracks each evening, bent over and aching.

The women and children worked either in the peanut fields, the laundry, or the kitchen. The school basement housed four washers and dryers and four ironing boards at one end. Laundry workers cleaned and pressed the guards' uniforms regularly, but they only washed the inmates' scrubs once a month. The other end of the basement was stacked with the inmates' discarded possessions and clothes, which they sorted and catalogued, down to the contents of the abandoned backpacks.

The commander of the entire enterprise was Colonel Ping. Of course, Ping was not his name. Sam could not make the right sounds to pronounce his real name, Jiao-long, when he introduced himself. But since Jiao-long received innumerable daily text messages on his iPhone, each one heralded by a high-pitched *ping*, Ping he became. The name caught on with all the inmates.

A short, middle-aged man, Colonel Ping had a thick, flat nose, a wide mouth, and a tongue that slithered back and forth between his coarse lips like a cornered pink snake. He combed his black, oily hair straight back over a low, bumpy forehead. His protruding opaque eyes, untouched by warmth or mercy, restlessly scanned his surroundings, like a soldier alert for an ambush. If he ever had a sense of humor, he had either lost it in customs at the airport or left it in downtown Beijing.

Sam sat at the desktop computer, hands poised above the keys. On meeting her, Ping's cordial first words, punctuated by stabs of his short, brownish index finger, were simple. "I dictate—you write."

What a chahmah.

At 5'7", Ping towered over Sam. He used his height advantage to peek down her loose green shirt whenever possible. But today, he was all business. "T-t-t-type r-r-r-r-report to General Huffman." Ping pointed at her and flicked his wrist with an impatient gesture, as if he urged a rickshaw driver to get going—fast. "N-n-now."

She typed: *Thursday, October 15, 2026. Report to General Huffman.* Eyes locked on the screen, she waited.

"Sir, C-c-camp 615 p-p-perfect order."

P-p-perfect order? P-p-perfect hellhole would be more accurate.

"Helipad be finished ten days. Two hundred inmates work twelve hours day."

Ping frowned in concentration, lips pursed, and strode back and forth in the bright, roomy outer office on legs as short and stubby as his sentences. Sam would have to retype the whole report and fill in the missing words once she translated his heavily accented, stammering and preposition-free English.

"Main operation ready b-b-begin Saturday, 31 October." Ping stopped pacing abruptly and grinned. "Ha-ha. Halloween. Perfect."

She had no idea what the camp's main operation would be, nor what Halloween had to do with it. Up to this point, the main operation had apparently been the advancement of human misery. She envisioned the comfortless two-tiered metal bunks crammed into the long, drafty barracks, the thin mattresses and moth-eaten wool blankets, the long hours of work, the brainwashing, and the cruelty of the guards.

After a moment of dead silence, Sam glanced up at his crinkled eyes and display of yellow teeth. She suddenly realized his grimace was a smile. When she didn't respond in kind, the corners of his mouth fell and he resumed pacing. He abruptly raised his voice, startling her. "Continue! M-m-m-medical testing in progress. Will need m-mobile unit OR M-m-m-monday, 19 October."

OR? What was that?

"Statistics!" he shouted.

She jumped involuntarily. As he dictated, she made a list with bullet points:

- Inmates received: 352
- Recanted and released: 218. Microchipped. Issued International ID. Signed affidavit pledging allegiance to new government.
- Deceased: 4
- Abortions: 3
- New inmates: 105
- Current total: 235

He leaned down and shouted in her ear. "End of report."

She grimaced and jerked her head away.

Ping laughed. "Report ready thirty minutes." He turned on his heel and marched through the open door into his lair, the former principal's office. Seated at his desk, he turned on the radio. Sam heard the unmistakable sound of a Mozart piano concerto, one she recognized from Joshua's repertoire.

"You like m-music?" he yelled. He could see her from his desk.

The corners of her mouth twitched as she suppressed an impulse to smile. "Yes, but not that kind."

"Very good." He turned up the volume significantly. "My father musician—play piano. You listen."

Excellent—she could hear it much more clearly now. It was difficult to maintain a frown while her heart cartwheeled in delight.

THE FARM

What spirit is so empty and blind, that it cannot recognize the fact that the foot is more noble than the shoe, and skin more beautiful than the garment with which it is clothed? Michelangelo had it right, thought Bertie. The human body is God's masterpiece, the earthly repository of the soul. A wonder of form and function, of musculature and movement, of proportion, symmetry, and power, the body is a reflection of the Divine. To observe da Vinci's anatomical drawings (as he had in medical school) or the breathtaking kinetic motion of ballet dancers spinning and flying across the stage (as he had in the theater) is to experience beauty and awe.

The wondrous body. *If only it were not mortal and subject to death and decay.*

He was out of shape and breathing hard as he and the other men cleared the area for what was to be an eight-inch-deep concrete pad. The work on the helipad required more strength and stamina than skill. Well, he didn't actually work *on* the helipad—he worked around it. Whyever did this small camp need a helipad, anyway?

The approach area had to be hard and level, and since the pad was situated on the north perimeter of the cow pasture behind the school, they had to cut down some trees and remove the stumps. The guards provided them with hand tools only, a two-man crosscut saw and shovels. Without chainsaws, backhoes, or stump grinders, the work was grueling.

After felling each tree, Bertie and his partner, Adam Chen, sawed the branches and trunk into smaller pieces, then hauled them to a woodpile. To remove the stumps, they dug a deep trench around the base, then rocked the stump back and forth by hand to loosen the roots. It was difficult and exhausting work on hard, unforgiving ground. The oaks and sycamores had shallow roots, but the cedar and pine tree roots grew deep. Bertie's one small compensation was the resinous, sharp odor of the pine and cedar stumps, a relief from the fetid air inside the barracks.

For a seventy-year-old man, the work was backbreaking and devilishly rough on the hands. No gloves were provided, so blisters soon bloomed on Bertie's palms and fingers from the saw, the shovel, and handling the stump itself. It was a painful, long time before his hands developed calluses.

The inmates worked in pairs. Bertie glanced over at Thomas, a lineman for his local power company in his pre-camp life, and Loopy, a thin gangly teenager, who dug around the three-foot-wide stump of an oak. Bertie kept a watchful eye on young Loopy. His face reddened by the sun, the sandy-haired boy was skin and bones. Thankfully, bald Thomas, somewhere in his forties, Bertie guessed, had brawn and weight to spare and did more than his share of the work. He was used to outside work in all kinds of weather, and he had the training and the fitness necessary to climb poles. The older man had a steadiness and patience that helped Loopy.

It wasn't their first time with a shovel; on arrival at the camp, they had been chosen to dig the grave under the stadium bleachers for the murdered young mother and her infant daughter.

They had first called Loopy by his surname, Lupei, until one fateful night early on when he made an unfortunate disclosure. In the barracks, the men had finished their meager dinner.

"I really don't belong here, you know," he said. "I could leave at any time. General Huffman is my grandfather."

Austin Pratt's ugly ears pricked up with interest. "Is he?" Austin, one of the BBs, who always sniffed out advantage, salivated like a wolf on a blood trail.

"Huffman!" Adam Chen had blurted. "That malignant narcissist sonofabitch—what bullshit. You better hope you're not related to him. He's the power-hungry madman who masterminded this camp."

"What are you talking about?"

"It's almost certain he orchestrated the plane crash that killed Eric Tecken. When Tecken died, Huffman took over and the coup began."

"Yeah," said Thomas, "better keep your mouth shut, Lupei, or you may get dumped headfirst into the latrine. Huffman's a traitor; he helped engineer the overthrow of our constitutional republic. You really don't want to be linked to him, especially while you're surrounded by a group of angry guys like us—the people he has illegally imprisoned."

The BB jeered, "What are you gonna do to him, Thomas? Beat him with that piece of rebar you hid under the barracks?"

Thomas spat on the floor. "Never know when something like that might come in useful, Pratt, and not for hitting people. But I tell you, if I ever did whack a person, you'd be my first choice."

Pratt backed away from Thomas. "Keep your voice down. You don't want to draw the guards in. Lupei could get us all in trouble if he really is the grandson of General Huffman."

Adam Chen retorted, "I don't believe it for an instant. Lupei, hell—his real name is Loopy." Adam glared at Constantin and twirled his index finger toward his own right temple.

Worried by the rising anger in the room, Bertie leaned down toward the young man and spoke quietly. "Whether that's the truth or not, boy, if you want to live, keep your damn mouth shut."

Flushed and humiliated, the teenager dropped the subject and stomped off to his bunk. From then on, the men called him Loopy.

Adam Chen was a stocky man, six inches shorter and at least thirty years younger than Bertie. With his low center of gravity and greater muscle mass, Adam could grip the stumps better and bend his back to the job more easily. But it seemed to Bertie that Adam's strength derived more from chronic rage than physical fitness. He was an impressive and creative swearer, certainly in English. When he got carried away with emotion, like a Chinese version of Ricky Ricardo, he lapsed into rapid-fire Spanish with wild gestures to match. Bertie couldn't understand the words, but the musician's red-faced, vehement expressions definitely got the point across.

A violinist with the St. Louis Symphony, Adam raged against the coup—it had taken him from the profession he loved. He hated what the manual labor did to his hands. He hated the fact that the blue-eyed Chinese soldier had confiscated his violin and tossed it like so much junk on the pile of abandoned belongings. But most of all, he hated the fact that he didn't know the fates of his wife back in St. Louis or his son, who had been at college in Michigan. Were they dead? Alive? Consigned to other labor camps? Would he ever see them again?

But Adam's taciturn and surly demeanor melted away when he discovered Bertie was an opera lover. He told Bertie about his early years in Venezuela where his Chinese immigrant parents owned a restaurant in Caracas. As a child, he learned the violin through *El Sistema*, the Venezuelan music education system.

Between grunts of effort, Adam told Bertie about it as they shoveled dirt. "The program, made up of hundreds of music schools for children even includes the Venezuelan Amazon, an area reachable only by boat. *El Sistema* is designed to target those at the poverty level, to take them off the streets, to offer them an alternative to a life of violence, drugs, and gangs."

He stopped for a moment to wipe his brow and stretch his back. He leaned on the shovel, drew in a deep breath, and exhaled noisily. "This great passion for classical music in Venezuela has been built from the bottom up. Most of the children in the program come from the poorest communities, but it also attracts upper-class kids who want a musical education.

"Did you know that Gustavo Dudamel, who conducts the Los Angeles Philharmonic, came out of El Sistema? And Edicson Ruiz, a double bass player, another alumnus, joined the Berlin Philharmonic at seventeen! He was the first Hispanic they ever employed."

"Impressive!" Bertie wiped away some of the sweat stinging his eyes. "But you forgot the third guy—the violinist named Adam Chen." He grinned down at his partner. "You did very well yourself to get a position in the St. Louis Symphony."

Adam's face fell. "Yes, but who knows if I'll ever return to that orchestra or any other ever again." He stopped digging for a moment and shook his head slowly. Then he laughed. "My most useful talent now is my fluent Spanish. The guards come get me when they need a translator for the Mexicans who can't speak English."

He glanced around to check on the nearest guards. Two of them stood about fifteen feet away, chattering in Chinese. Adam bent his head over his shovel as he dug and lowered his voice. "The guards—they talk freely amongst themselves in Mandarin. But what they don't know is that I understand every word."

Surprised as he was, Bertie kept his expression blank, just in case the guards were watching. He spoke quietly. "Really? Do you also speak Chi—" He stopped himself.

"I do."

"According to my friend Sam—she was behind you when they sorted us out at the stadium—you told the soldier you could only speak Spanish and English."

"I did." Adam smiled. "I lied."

"Does this mean you're a virtuoso curser in *three* languages?"

Adam's laugh pleased him very much. "Glad you appreciate my prowess."

"It's a remarkable talent. So, have you learned anything of value from our friends?"

"They call this place the Farm."

"Because it's across from a peanut farm, right?"

"I only wish it were so, Bertie. But . . . " Adam's color blanched. He closed his eyes, passed his hand over his face, and swallowed. "Forget about peanuts. The crops they have in mind are kidneys, livers, corneas, and hearts."

Bertie leaned on his shovel and looked up at the pale blue, pitiless sky. *The human body: image of the divine, repository of the soul.*

The truth suddenly struck him like a punch to the gut. "That explains the helipad." As a physician, he knew the going rates: kidney, $62,000—liver, $130K—heart, $160K. Corneas went for a mere $30,000. *Oh, it all made sense now:* three meals a day to keep the donors healthy. A thirty-minute surgery to remove the liver and two kidneys, pack them in ice and send them on their way, with helicopters to expedite delivery. "We're part of an obscene money-making machine."

Adam nodded. "Yes, and the harvest begins next month, in November."

ANGELS

November

It was the day after Halloween—All Saints' Day. Peter knew because Beano had told all the kids. It was also harvest time. Proud of his job as a shaker, he knelt in the red-brown dirt beside Nathan. Twelve-year-old Nathan dug up the Spanish peanuts with a garden trowel. Once they were unearthed, Peter grabbed the bush, shook off the East Texas dirt, and laid the pods in the sun to cure. His new red wristband glistened in the sun. All the other kids had yellow ones. He didn't know why they chose him to wear it, except maybe because he was the youngest. For some reason, Beano and Donna gave him more hugs than before. But that was okay with him.

He liked the feel of the damp, sandy soil that caked his hands, but he shivered a little in the morning chill. The mornings had gotten colder. Soon they would use the woodstove in their barracks. But in a few minutes the strong Texas sun would warm him up.

The peanut farm was just a short walk across the street from the camp. On the way, they passed the blue farmhouse with white trim where Colonel Ping lived. Peter wondered where the family had gone who had lived there. He wondered if there had been children his age who used to collect the eggs from the tin-roofed chicken coop behind the house. Maybe they swam in the big pond just outside the white picket fence where he had seen wild ducks paddling around in the water. Sometimes he wished he was a wild duck. Then he could just fly away. But he would only do that if his mamma could fly, too. And Beano and Bertie and Susannah and Nathan. And all of them, except Ping and the mean soldiers.

Everyone—well, not everyone, just the women and children—had fanned out across the acres and acres of yellowing bushes. In the distance, he could see Beano and Susannah, and Maria and Lynne, some of the girls from his barracks. Bertie and the men worked on the other side of the school. It used to be a school, anyway. Now it was a prison camp, a prison for all the people who hadn't done anything wrong. Who could understand that? Peter certainly did not.

He liked working with Nathan, who was thin and wiry, but strong. He dug up the bushes quickly. He and Peter had to work fast; each pair of workers, no matter what their ages, had to finish ten long rows by noon. Their rows lay near the edge of the field, against the pine forest. The morning breeze hummed through the tops of the trees and rustled the leaves of the peanut bushes. The sound rose and fell like a thousand comforting voices, singing a wordless song. Peter wondered if it might be the voices of all the saints, an invisible choir. Maybe his father was a saint now, singing with them.

The breeze swept all around him, ruffling his hair, caressing his cheeks and forehead, carrying the clean scent of the pine trees with it. He closed his eyes for a moment and imagined it was his father who tousled his hair and brushed his cheek, just the way he used to do. That made him feel better. But other times when he thought about his dad being gone, his stomach and his chest hurt. When that happened he couldn't eat.

He missed his mother almost as much as he missed his dad. She worked in the main office and lived in Barracks 3. Ping kept the children apart from the adults, so he hardly saw her anymore. The women lived in Barracks 1, 2, and 3; Barracks 4, 5, and 6 were for men. He and Nathan lived in Barracks 7 with the children twelve years old and under. He had counted twenty double bunk beds in his barracks, boys on the right, girls on the left. That was enough room for forty children, but there were only thirty-one now. Some had got orange wristbands. A few days later, all of those ones left, but he didn't know why.

But everybody knew about two of the older boys, Douglas and Tyler. They had tried to run away. They sneaked out one night and dug a tunnel under the fence. When they accidentally set off an alarm, the guards hunted them with dogs. They didn't get very far, and around noon the next day, they brought them back to the camp.

Then the guards marched everyone to the stadium, where they had a black metal machine on the field where everyone could see it. It was shaped like an L. The tall part that stood up high looked like an open window, but there was a pointed piece hanging from the top of it, shaped just like the top part of a K. At the bottom of the window, under the windowsill was a round hole. The flat part of the L stuck out like a narrow table from the base of the window. They made Douglas lie face down on the table and stick his head in the hole. He screamed and fought them.

Once they got Douglas to lie flat on the machine, the top part suddenly dropped down hard and cut off his head. Blood spurted out in a red flood. An electric shock shot through Peter's body—he ceased to breathe and his knees began to shake. Tyler's head got chopped off next. Peter vomited. Ping said they would do the same thing to anyone who tried to escape.

Beano and his mother tried to comfort him that day. His mother had been there in the stadium. She had to sit with the camp director, Ping, but afterward she managed to come and hug him briefly. With tears shining in her eyes, she told him it would be all right. Peter's whole body had trembled so badly he could hardly walk back to the camp. Beano and Donna held him up. Then the bad dreams started.

While Nathan dug up the next bush, Peter kept his eye on Beano. He could see her blonde hair blowing in the breeze several rows over. She was their housemother and the leader of the BCB, the Brave Children's Brigade. That's what she called them. At night, she told them stories and taught them songs. She told the kids the story about the prince and princess and birdcatcher, and the one about Hansel and Gretel. She taught them a song the two children sang at night in the dark forest.

Beano turned her head in his direction and gave a little wave. Today was a day of saints. It was also a day of angels. Angels were so tall and bright. You couldn't really see their faces, but the swords they carried were easy to see. He knew their swords would only be used against the bad people, not against him or the other kids or Beano or Mamma. Two of them stood at the edges of the field. He didn't think the guards knew they were there. Peter wondered where the other two angels were. Maybe they were on the other side of the school watching over Bertie and all the men.

He began to hum the Hansel and Gretel song. The kids sang it every night before lights out, but really it was the kind of song you could sing anytime. It always made him feel better. He wasn't afraid for his mother or his friends when he sang it. Would his mother be safe with Ping? Would Beano, Susannah, and Bertie stay well and safe? Would he ever go home again? Would he ever go to school? Somehow, the music quieted all his fears, at least for a while.

Hearing the melody, Nathan smiled and began to sing the words. He took the lower part to Peter's soprano.

> *Abends, will ich schlafen gehn,*
> *Vierzehn Engel um mich stehen:*
> *Zwei zu meinen Häupten,*
> *Zwei zu meinen Füssen,*
> *Zwei zu meiner Rechten,*
> *Zwei zu meiner Linken,*
> *Zweie, die mich decken*
> *Zweie, die mich wecken,*
> *Zweie, die mich weisen*
> *Zu Himmels-Paradeisen.*

To keep the Chinese guards from understanding, Beano had taught them the song in German. She told them they would learn it by the end of the week. Haha! The children surprised her—they learned it in one night. Beano was so proud of them!

As he worked and sang quietly, Peter imagined fourteen angels descending to watch over him and Nathan. He wasn't sure Beano had got it right, but he sang it anyway. He told her they already had four, and that was probably enough—they really didn't need ten more. She just laughed, patted him on the head, and called him a funny little guy. He could tell she didn't believe him. He knew about the two at the side of the field, and the two who probably watched over the men. He counted the two in the field as two at their heads, like the song said. He imagined the other two at their feet. But the song said they needed ten more: two to their right, two to their left, two to cover them, two to wake them, and two to show them the way to heaven's paradise.

The last two seemed really important.

Of course, his dad was already there. But if those two angels could show him the way to paradise, he might find his dad coming to meet him on the path.

ANCIENT GODS

Constantin lay on his bunk, gazing up into darkness. Sleep refused to come. Mentally, he kept replaying the taunts and threats of the men. His muscles tensed in repressed anger and his throat burned with acid reflux. He had to sit up. He listened to their snores: explosive, comical, and rhythmic, moving in and out of sync like a jarring, endless, particularly ugly minimalist music. The room stank of rancid sweat, dirty feet, stale farts, and unclean bodies. The odors wafted up toward the roof, making the top bunks like his the worst.

He had sealed his own fate on the first day. After he and Thomas buried the young mother and her infant daughter, he returned to the queue. Thankfully, when the guard turned away to take a piss, Constantin had also buried Dumitru's diary, before his backpack was confiscated. When he reached the front of the line, he heard the middle-aged woman ahead of him answer the soldier's questions.

"Religion?"

"I believe in feminism." She lifted her chin with a proud air and straightened the jacket of her pantsuit. She was a corporate attorney. She got a blue wristband.

Of course, at that point, no one understood the color code, but Constantin realized he would have to declare himself one way or the other in a matter of minutes. The sweat from digging had dried up by then, but he felt fat drops of perspiration suddenly spring again from his scalp and run down the sides of his face.

When the woman left, he walked up to the soldier and handed him his Swiss ID, thankful he had had the foresight to leave the National ID in New York.

The soldier grimaced. "What is this? I need your National ID."

"This is all I have. I'm a Swiss citizen visiting the US."

Frowning, the guard spat something out to himself in Chinese. Constantin assumed it was not a compliment. After the man laboriously input information into his laptop by hand, he glared at Constantin.

"Religion?"

He thought of Stella Amore. He thought of the man whose nativity changed the world and time. He thought of Dumitru and the fallen ones who feared that man more than anything. He didn't want to be on their side.

The soldier shouted this time. "Are you deaf or mute? Religion?"

Constantin drew in a deep breath. "I believe in Jesus Christ."

He got a yellow wristband. That answer had led him to this place and these men. He hated this place, and he was furious with these men for shaming him. But he shared one thing in common with them: he wanted out as badly as they did. And he had a way out if he chose to take it. Whether they believed him or not, he could tell the authorities who he was. In no time, *Grand-père*, the governor of Region VI, would free him.

But, as much as he wanted to show the others he was telling the truth, something held him back. The men in his barracks, this slumbering portion of humanity, regarded *Grand-père*, General Richard Huffman, as the Villain of Villains, their Archenemy. He feared they might be right. Would such a man be his refuge? If he aligned himself with the General, would he walk into a trap more treacherous than the prison camp? *It is a sad and hurtful thing,* he thought, *to realize one is closely related to a monster.*

The men would really think him crazy if he told them the long-term plans of the world's elite, according to the Gospel of Dumitru.

At last—the trap is planned and in due time it will be sprung—in the last bastion, save Israel—in the nation most vital to conquer, where power resides: America. The elites envisioned the American coup years ago; now it had come to pass. If he told the men what he knew, no one would believe him, not even Bertie.

Dumitru and *Grand-père* had aligned themselves with evil. He would not. He would not contact the General. Of course, even if he made no attempt to alert his grandfather, it was highly probable that the General would ultimately contact him. In this digital age, Constantin realized his identity and whereabouts were readily accessible, floating in the mysterious ether of cyberspace. Tony had surely reported his absence to the General weeks ago when the turmoil first began. Hopefully, his Swiss ID would delay the inevitable if his grandfather searched for him.

Constantin had set out from New York to confront the General. *Sir, is my father dead or alive?* Either the General knew his father's fate and had withheld the information (the most likely scenario), or he could pull strings on Constantin's behalf to get the answers. But could he trust *Grand-père* to tell the truth? What kind of man—a military man who had sworn a solemn oath to protect his country and its constitution—what kind of man would then participate willingly in the overthrow of said country and the enslavement of its people?

A traitor. A malignant narcissist. A madman.

He wasn't sure what a narcissist was, but it sounded bad. Maybe Bertie, a physician, would know. He would ask him tomorrow. Constantin scratched his scalp. He hoped he didn't have lice. He flexed his blistered hands and stretched. He ached all over: back, biceps, the big thigh muscles. Even his butt hurt. He had never in his life worked like a common laborer. Thank goodness burly Thomas was his partner. A sixteen-year-old, at least this non-athletic one, could not match the power and strength of a grown man. Thomas (who never complained) did more than his fair share of the digging and sawing.

They had finally finished uprooting the tree stumps around the helipad. Now they chopped and sawed the trunks and branches of the felled trees into firewood, more backbreaking work. But they would use it to fuel the woodstoves furnished in each barracks. None of the barracks had insulation, and so far, no coats or heavy clothes had been issued. Winter in North Texas might not last as long as the New York winters or those in Switzerland, but for short spells it could be brutal.

Switzerland. He thought of his mother and Grigori. He wished he could speak to them and tell them he was still alive. He knew they must be worried. On the other hand, Dumitru wouldn't care if Constantin disappeared off the face of the earth and the midget never saw him again. It would affect his day and the course of his life with all the consequence of a bug splat on the windshield of his Mercedes.

He yawned so widely and suddenly that his jaw popped. Then he smiled. He had spotted Cherubino on the very first day, while he dug the grave under the bleachers. Katie Lamb, mezzo soprano. They put her and a young black woman in charge of the children. After roll call, she led them to work in the peanut fields every morning and brought them back each evening. When he and Katie both fled the opera house in Chicago on the day of the coup, he never expected to end up in the same place and same predicament as she. He was sorry she had become a prisoner, too. But since they were here, thrown more or less together, he longed to speak to her, and as improbable as it might be, he especially hoped to hear her sing again.

Katie shone like a lighthouse, a bright beacon in the darkness. Just the sight of her lifted his heart. Her height, the blonde hair, her cheerful demeanor and upright carriage betokened courage and faith. Like the Pied Piper, she had the children completely under her spell; they seemed to adore her. She gave them (and him, too) hope and the promise of freedom somehow. He wished he could meet her, but he didn't know how that would ever happen.

It bothered him that Katie and the women and children were also subject to medical testing. Why had they drawn blood and tested his eyes? They had even used ultrasound on his body. When he asked why, they refused to answer. Were the physical exams meant to weed out the weak from the strong? Were the powers-that-be going to cull the herd? He noticed they only tested the Christians, Jews, Muslims, and political prisoners, the conservatives who had opposed the coup. Those who wore the blue wristbands, the atheists, communists, and turncoats, they released.

Along with Bertie, Thomas, Adam, and the others, Constantin refused to declare himself an atheist or communist. On the first day, he realized the soldiers separated people by religion: Christians, Jews, and Muslims to the right, everyone else to the left. Later on, in spite of the daily brainwashing—the ridiculous, lying videos they were forced to watch—when the full impact of his decision became clear, he still refused to deny Jesus Christ. He only wished he knew more about him. The man was a sword who divided humanity: choose him or not. Choose light or darkness.

He had come to the Valley of Decision—and he had chosen. Such a life as Christ's could not be denied. It was as simple as that.

He supposed their captors thought of him and the others as subhuman. Quite a useful view when one intended to mistreat, torture, and kill people. This was not new—the Nazis had shown the way to justify atrocities, years and years ago.

Did he want to join the side of the current Nazis? *Heil, Grandfather and the Reich.* Did he prefer to be a torturer or a tortuee? His mouth gaped in another gigantic yawn. Neither, of course, but he had to choose sides—no one could remain neutral in these times.

His grandfather was a soldier who had turned on his own country. His father, too, had been a soldier. What kind of man—what kind of soldier—was Gunnar Ross? Was he brave, honest, loyal?

> *Into the valley of death rode the six hundred . . .*
> *Cannon to right of them,*
> *Cannon to left of them,*
> *Cannon in front of them*
> *Volley'd and thunder'd;*
> *Storm'd at with shot and shell,*

Boldly they rode and well,
Into the jaws of Death,
Into the mouth of Hell
Rode the six hundred.

And what kind of man was Constantin Lupei? How much courage did he have? He stared up into the darkness. No doubt the coming days would tell.

The snoring cacophony continued all around him. He laid his aching body down. Fatigue from the physical work of the day and the emotional wringer he had just endured caught up with him. His thoughts slowed, his eyelids drooped, and his breathing grew slow and steady until sleep ambushed him, like a silent, invading army.

In the early morning chill, they walked in pairs, Thomas to his left with Bertie and Adam right behind them. The stiff breeze herded a flock of dark gray clouds across the sky. Now and again, shafts of sunlight pierced the cloud ceiling. They had a day of sawing and chopping wood ahead of them. Constantin did not look forward to that, but the presence of the three older men comforted him. Although they had admonished him for boasting and lying about his relationship to General Huffman (though he most certainly had not lied), they told him the truth about his grandfather, whether he wanted to hear it or not. That fact was very important: because they were truthful, he could trust them.

In terms of age, the stocky, heavily muscled Thomas could have been his father, while tall, gaunt Bertie with his shock of white hair seemed a grandfatherly figure. Constantin's biological father remained a question mark; to his stepfather he was all but invisible, an encumbrance attached to Talyssa, while his maternal grandfather appeared by all accounts to be an ogre with a capital O. A narcissistic one.

"Bertie, what is a narcissist? That's what Adam called General Huffman." (He dared not say *my grandfather*. He was done with that battle.)

"In Greek mythology, Narcissus was a beautiful youth who was pursued by many potential lovers. He treated them so badly that the gods decided to punish Narcissus. They led him to a pool and showed him his image in the water. He fell madly in love with his own reflection. Narcissists are the epitome of self-absorption. Prideful and jealous, like little Lucifers, their goal is power and control, which they try to achieve through manipulation, lying, or any other means necessary. They can't abide criticism or admit error; they take no responsibility for their actions and have little or no empathy." Bertie chuckled. "Consequently, they are some of the most miserable people on the planet."

"Are they strong people?"

"No, although they want you to think so. They project a grandiose façade as a smokescreen to hide very deep-seated insecurities, fear, and shame."

"Do they love other people?"

"No, I don't think so—they're only concerned with their own needs."

"And malignant narcissists?"

"They're like a grab bag from hell: aggressive, cruel, without conscience, regret, or remorse, and they can be physically violent. In fact, they take pleasure in other people's pain. Nasty types."

Thomas and Constantin spoke at the same time.

"Sounds like my mother-in-law."

"Sounds like my stepfather."

Bertie laughed. He put a hand on the boy's shoulder. "So are you going to stay with us here or bust outta this joint?"

Constantin smiled. "Since bustin' out means I flee into the arms of a malignant narcissist, I intend to stay." Constantin glanced up and met the kind, blue-eyed gaze of the older man. He lowered his voice. "But just between us, the Gen—"

Bertie held up one hand like a traffic cop. "Say no more. I suspected as much, but from now on, you'd better be as mysterious and forthcoming as the Sphinx regarding your origins. Understand?"

His origins were a mystery—at least to him—until his grandfather revealed the facts. But he couldn't explain that to Bertie or anyone else. "Yes."

The Sphinx. Constantin immediately recalled the seal in Dumitru's diary: a pyramid surmounted by the all-seeing eye of Horus, enclosed in a circle. The Latin inscription *Novus Ordo Seclorum.* The New World Order. The transition to it was apparently well underway. Years in advance, Dumitru had known the plan to prod this world to a new totalitarian system—by force.

Constantin pondered the image of the Egyptian Sphinx: head of a man and body of a lion, a mythical beast guarding the pyramids of Giza, remnants of a lost pagan tradition. Did Dumitru and his co-conspirators want to bring that tradition back? His diary was evidence of . . . of what? Was the New World Order simply a resurrection of the ancient world order? Would the evil gods, with the help of men, arise once again?

CHAPTER 38

VENOM

Kneeling in the valley between the raised rows of yellowing plants, Susannah dug up the peanuts with her trowel. By the low position of the blood-red sun, close to the horizon, she knew it was almost quitting time. *Thankfully.* She shook the dirt off the plant and laid the exposed pods aside. Then she leaned forward to the next plant. She worked mechanically, wincing at the pain between her shoulder blades and the flaring twinges of sciatica from her right hip down to her knee.

She had to count her blessings, though. At sixty-five, barring assorted but transitory aches and pains, she enjoyed good health. Unlike many in her age group, she needed no medications. Her thick, undyed hair fell in loose, silvery waves to her shoulders. For her largely unlined face and classic bone structure, she gave credit to her Greek mother, who had bequeathed her one of the wonders of the Mediterranean peoples: a light, pearly-smooth olive skin, seemingly impervious to wear. And from her Irish father, she had inherited her large, wide-set hazel eyes.

The skin around those eyes crinkled slightly as she tried to calculate the days spent in the camp: at least a month. In the fifty years of her marriage, she had never lived apart from Bertie for such a long time. Susannah dug into the dirt with her trowel and thought about the marvelous dynamics between men and women, the give and take, the way male and female complemented each other. She enjoyed men, their instinct to protect and defend, their objectivity, their analytical and abstract thinking. She was thankful for her long marriage to Bertie, for his companionship and the steadiness that counteracted her flibbertigibbet tendencies. Men and women: created in the beginning by God, who certainly knew what He was doing. Too bad humankind didn't—if only those rebels Adam and Eve had followed directions, she, Susannah Falkenberg, would not be toiling on her knees in an endless peanut field due to the illegal takeover of a sovereign republic. No, indeed.

Well, too late now. As she reached under the next peanut bush, she heard a rustle and an odd rattling sound. Something half-hidden under the bush bit her hand. Horrible, piercing pain. "Oh God!" She jerked her arm backward and recoiled in horror at the snake still attached to her finger. With strength that surprised her, she flung it off. It flipped lazily through the air, hit the dirt, and disappeared among the bushes two rows over. She watched drops of blood ooze from the two puncture wounds. "Katie!" She waved her good hand to get the girl's attention. "Katie, come here!"

"Coming." Katie immediately bounded toward her over the rows. "What's wrong?"

Susannah lifted her hand and pointed to the punctures on her left ring finger. "Snake bite. I heard the rattles."

Katie opened her mouth, but before she could speak, Susannah hissed. "Shh—don't tell the guards. They'll probably shoot me on the spot."

Katie's eyes were wide and dark with fright. "I'm out of my element with snakes. Bertie's the doctor. What should we do?"

Aware that all rattlers were venomous, Susannah tried very hard to control herself, but she broke out into a cold sweat from fear and the severe pain. She bent forward slightly with her left hand touching her waist; the ring finger had already started to swell. She felt a surge of nausea—whether from her aversion to snakes or from the bite itself, she didn't know.

Years ago, she and Bertie had visited his sister Kristina in Taos. On a hike through the high desert, her brother-in-law Roger had been bitten on the ankle by a rattler. Bertie had taken charge. No ice, no tourniquet, no cutting the wound and sucking out the poison. They kept Roger upright and as immobile as possible. They got him to the hospital in Taos, where the doctor administered antivenom. He recovered, but the frightful incident had seared itself into Susannah's brain.

Feeling a little dizzy, she wiped the sweat from her brow with the back of her hand. She kept her voice low. "I know I must keep the bite lower than my heart. Best to remain still and breathe slowly." *Not so easy when death comes knockin' at the door.*

It was late in the day, almost time to trudge back to the barracks, but Susannah knew she should exert herself as little as possible. "I shouldn't walk," she said, "but I can't stay here in the field either."

"We'll carry you back," said Katie. "As a former Girl Scout, I know just how to do it." Katie beckoned to Donna, the young, black former karate instructor who lived in the children's barracks with her.

Susannah shook her head. "No, they'll see and they'll shoot me for sure. And here comes the Ogler."

The tall, wide-faced woman with prominent Slavic cheekbones was still at a distance, but she covered the ground quickly, stepping over the raised rows with her long legs. The daughter of Russian immigrants, Olga the Barracks Bitch dearly loved her truncheon.

"She's big and perverted, but dumb. We won't tell her a thing. Her main focus is on Donna's bottom, anyway."

As Donna approached, she heard Katie's remark and shook her head. "Oh, tell the truth, Katie, you're just jealous."

Katie laughed. "I freely admit it—you got the best bottom on the Farm."

"'Bout time I got some respect. Although respect, unfortunately, is not what's on the Ogler's mind."

"Hush," said Susannah. "She's coming."

One of the guards blew a whistle to signify the end of the workday. As the women and children stood up, Katie beckoned them to gather around her and Susannah. "Donna, a snake bit her. We have to carry her back to keep her pulse slow."

Donna's hand flew to her mouth. "Oh, my gosh!"

"This is how we'll do it." With her left hand, Katie grabbed her own right arm just below the elbow, making an L-shape horizontal to the ground. Donna did the same. With her right hand, Katie gripped Donna's left elbow. "Now you grab my left elbow with your free hand." Their interlinked arms formed a square. "This is the seat."

"Stand up, Susannah."

Keeping their arms linked, they bent down behind her. "Put your arms around our shoulders and sit." She did. Using their legs, they lifted her. She had always been slender, but like all the inmates, Susannah had lost weight. Katie was surprised at how light she was; it was almost like lifting a child.

When Peter and a little Hispanic girl named Maria saw them lift Susannah, they cried, "Me too! Me too!" In a burst of inspiration, Katie realized the children would serve as camouflage. She hissed to the nearby women. "Pick them up the same way—quickly."

By the time Olga reached them, the women had lifted Peter and Maria off the ground. "What is going on here?" She brushed her dirty blonde hair off her forehead and raised the wooden club she held in her right hand. Pressing her thin lips together, she stared at them with small, pale blue eyes.

The sudden stillness of sound and motion was like a freeze frame in a film. No one moved or spoke—but the fear was as palpable as the clouds moving in from the west. Katie forced herself to smile. "It's a game—a little fun for the women and children after working all day. We call it four-hand horsie."

Susannah managed to grin and nod as if she were enjoying herself. "Giddy-up!"

Olga looked them over and wrinkled her nose, disgusted. "A game. How stupid and childish. Go ahead—wear yourselves out." She tapped the truncheon against her leg and blew a sharp blast on the metal whistle hanging on a chain around her neck. "Just go." She pointed toward the camp.

VIRTUE

As soon as Sam entered the barracks that evening, the women told her about Susannah's snake bite. The long, narrow room buzzed with chatter, while Susannah herself sat white-faced and mute on her bunk, her back to the wall and her long legs stretched out.

When Olga left to take her nightly shower, a privilege granted to all the BBs, Sam approached Susannah and sat down on the edge of the narrow bunk. "Let me see."

Susannah held out her left hand. The ring finger was red and swollen twice its size.

"Good thing they confiscated my wedding ring, or someone would have had to cut it off."

Sam observed the two puncture marks in the horribly swollen finger. "Painful?" she asked, careful not to let her anxiety show in her voice. Her mind whirled, seeking some course of action.

"A bit." Susannah's lips formed a tight white line in her pale face.

Sam guessed the pain was probably severe, but she admired Susannah's self-control.

"Feeling some nausea, and there's a metallic taste in my mouth." Susannah lowered her gaze and her voice. "Wish Bertie were here."

The only real fix was antivenom, but here in the camp, to ask for special medical treatment would be like asking Ping to provide the inmates maid service and breakfast in bed. He would not make the slightest effort to save Susannah's life. No, their captors came to steal, kill, and destroy; they would be happy to snuff her out with a single gunshot.

Sam's stomach muscles clenched as she searched in her mind for a solution. She knew the venom of different rattlers varied in potency. Of course, in the heat of the moment, Susannah could not have identified the snake. Whatever type it was, the only treatment was antivenom at a hospital. And that was impossible.

Feeling hopeless and defeated, Sam sat on the edge of Susannah's bed and her mind just shut down. Her shoulders slumped and she stared at the floor.

You know what to do.

She inhaled sharply and lifted her head. Had she actually heard the words, or did the statement just pop into her head? *You know what to do.*

In her mind, she saw an image of Sitti—not a still portrait, but Sitti in action, praying fervently for Aunt Catherine. With her hands on Aunt Cat's head, she closed her eyes and spoke her petitions aloud. Sam couldn't remember all the words, but even as a little girl she had been struck by the sheer intensity of the prayer. After that, the brain tumor disappeared—no trace of it on the CT scan. The doctors, completely baffled, counted it a miracle.

That was only one of many times she had seen her grandmother pray over people successfully. Known in the community as a healer, Sitti had even healed Joshua. On her deathbed, she had rallied to pray for the troubled pianist who would later become Sam's husband. Sam had laid her hands on Joshua's shoulder as her grandmother prayed. His mental demons left him that night.

You know what to do.

Yes, she did. But she wasn't Sitti. What if she failed? What if she only embarrassed herself? But then she remembered that Sitti never took credit for any cures. "I only pray," she said. "The Holy Spirit does the healing."

Sam prayed silently: *Lord, be with me. Help me in what I am about to do. In Jesus's name, Amen.* She examined Susannah's swollen hand again, the ugly punctures, the bruising. *Better not wait any longer.*

Susannah sat upright with her eyes closed. She appeared to be dozing. Sam didn't want to jar her awake, so she spoke very softly. "Susannah, may I pray for you?"

Susannah's eyes fluttered open and she gave a weak sigh. She met Sam's deep brown eyes with her hazel ones. "Did you think I was sleeping?"

"Yes."

The corners of her mouth lifted slightly in a gentle smile. "I was silently reciting Psalm 91." She wet her lips and quoted. "For He shall give His angels charge over thee to keep thee in all thy ways. They shall bear thee up in their hands, that thou hurt not thy foot against a stone. Thou shalt go upon the lion and adder; the young lion and the adder shalt thou tread under thy feet. Because He hast set his love upon me, therefore will I deliver him." Her eyes held Sam's in a steady gaze. "Yes, darling Sam, please pray for me."

Sam touched the injured hand very lightly, feeling its heat. She realized in that moment that she had no anointing oil. Sitti had always anointed the person first. What should she do? "One moment, Susannah."

Sam retrieved her tin cup from her bunk. She opened the barracks door a crack and listened for the crunch of steps on the gravel path, but all she heard was the distant, mournful hooting of an owl. She stole out into the night, quiet as a ghost. If the guards or Olga caught her, it was all over. But she had to do this right, or at least as best she could. Treading soundlessly on the bare dirt beside the gravel path, she turned into the alley between the buildings and hurried to the back where there was a standing faucet. She opened the spigot a tiny bit, catching the flow of water so it trickled down the side of the cup soundlessly. She filled it only about a fourth of the way.

The night was clear and chilly. She took a deep breath of the fresh air, a great relief from the stuffy, stinking barracks, rank with the smell of sweat, bodies, and fear. The clean, oxygen-rich air lifted her spirits. On the eastern horizon, magnificent Orion rose. Just below him, at his heel, blazed blue-white Sirius, the most brilliant star in the heavens.

The heavens declare the glory of God . . . Their sound is gone out into all lands; and their words into the ends of the world.

Feeling better, she returned to her task. She laid her right hand over the top of the cup, mouthing the words soundlessly: "In the name of the Father, the Son, and the Holy Ghost: Lord, bless this water. Consecrate it. Imbue it with your healing power that it may cleanse, strengthen, and heal. In this hour, Lord, you are our only help—"

She broke off at the sound of approaching footsteps on the gravel path and backed into the shadows against the wall. The guards made the rounds every night, flashlights in hand. Her heart pounded, drumming a frantic cadence—surely it was audible throughout the camp. The crunch came very close. Halted. The light swung toward her, down the alley between the buildings. The beam raked the bare ground two inches in front of her toes. She froze. She held her breath and thought her heart might stop.

For an endless moment, nothing happened. Then the guard turned and walked on. Sam took a shaky breath and waited. She listened without moving a muscle while the sound of the steps faded. The owl hooted three times. Keeping close to the wall, she crept to the front of the building and looked both ways. All clear. She skirted the edge of the gravel and climbed the three wooden steps. She re-entered the barracks, breathless and shaken.

She stood just inside the door on wobbly knees, heart pounding. With an iron grip, she clutched the cup of water—now made holy by the Lord's blessing. She took a deep breath and crossed the room on shaky legs to Susannah's bunk. She asked the other women if they would pray for Susannah. Someone answered, "Of course."

They gathered around the narrow bed in a half-circle. Sam asked those closest to lay hands on Susannah. "You in the back, lay your hands on the shoulders of the person in front of you."

Sam dipped her forefinger into the water, lifted her hand and drew the sign of the cross on Susannah's forehead and hand. "I anoint you with this blessed water, in the name of the Father, the Son, and the Holy Ghost."

She set the cup on the floor and took the older woman's swollen, inflamed hand in both of hers. She gave thanks for Susannah and the fellowship of faithful women. "Lord, you alone are sovereign above all sickness, injury, and death, above all circumstances. You are our only help in this hour." She paused briefly to gather her thoughts and focus all her energy in the prayer. "You have promised that when we call upon your Name in time of trouble, you will answer. Lord, by thy mercy and great power, nullify the effects of the toxins in the body of thy servant, Susannah."

Sam's eyes widened. *A sudden flash, wholly unexpected.*

Her voice broke. "Susannah, be healed in the name of Jesus. Amen."

The women echoed her. "Amen."

Exhausted by their work, they dispersed quickly to their bunks. Sam released her hold. Susannah cradled her left hand in her right and leaned her head back against the wall. "Thank you, Sam. I'll try to sleep a little now." She closed her eyes.

At that moment, Olga returned. "Get to your bunk now." She took four long strides across the room, raised her truncheon and struck Sam between the shoulder blades, knocking her to the floor.

Sam cried out and rose unsteadily. Wincing, she hurried to her bunk, with her mind more on Susannah than the pain. Her prayer seemed to have had no immediate effect. And yet . . . the golden ray. It shot out from her solar plexus to Susannah. With the flash and speed of lightning arcing in a dark sky, it hung for an instant motionless and completely still, then disappeared, leaving the night blacker than before.

She saw it with her inner eye.

Virtue had gone out of her. She knew it—she had felt it. And yet there seemed to be no change in Susannah. *Was she deluding herself?* If Sitti had experienced the same thing, she had kept it secret. Who could explain it anyway?

Disappointment drained her. No instant cure—maybe no cure at all. Sam lay down on her bed, depressed and weary to the marrow of her bones. She wondered forlornly if Susannah would survive the night.

CHAPTER 40

OLGA

Thanks to satellites, mobile phones, and the worldwide web, news travels fast in the twenty-first century. But from time immemorial, the transmission of tidings did not depend on technology. Before it came into being, people found a way. The inmates at the Farm were no different; they had their own communications system. Twenty-four hours after Susannah's recovery from the snake bite, news of the healed one and the healer had traveled through every barracks with the speed of an East Texas wildfire.

When Olga heard the news, hope rose in her heart like a crocus pushing up through the snow: *maybe Sam could help her*. But as soon as the thought entered her mind, doubt and dismay descended, slimy and destructive as a slug infestation in a flowerbed. She had been harsh and unyielding to Sam and the others; she had treated them like garbage. She had struck the small woman with her baton and screamed at her. Sam would more likely spit in her face than help her.

"The Ogler" they called her. She was glad of the nickname; it meant others remained unaware of her illness. At the age of six, she suffered her first epileptic seizures. In the intervening years, her parents had tried every remedy short of brain surgery, but nothing cured her. So far at the camp, she had only experienced petit mal seizures—staring blankly for a few seconds, unresponsive when spoken to, fluttering eyelids—nothing too noticeable.

What she feared was a grand mal seizure—the violent convulsions would be obvious. Her status as Barracks Overseer (she knew they called her the Barracks Bitch) would not save her then. The guards would take her directly to the doctors in the dreaded OR. And from there, no one returned.

But now, emboldened by Susannah's healing, she wanted to tell Sam the truth and plead her case with the diminutive woman. All day long, as she watched the women work in the peanut field, she argued with herself about whether she should or not. She did not want to show her vulnerability to anyone; she did not want her secret revealed, but there was no other way. If Sam spurned her and the others jeered, she would just have to swallow it.

When Sam returned to the barracks that evening, Olga slapped her truncheon against the palm of one hand and barked in her harshest voice, "Sam! Outside now." She jerked her thumb toward the door.

Sam raised her eyebrows, but otherwise appeared calm. She followed the much taller and heavier woman outside into the chill, early dusk of autumn. The wind swooped down from the north, and the air smelled like rain.

Olga faced Sam and swallowed, unable to utter a word. She tapped the stick against her own leg.

"What is it?" Sam asked in a voice barely audible above the wind.

"I . . . uh . . . I know you healed Susannah."

Eyebrows knitted together, Sam waited and watched Olga closely.

"C-c-can you heal me?"

"Of what?"

Sam's question burst the dike. Olga's story spilled through the fissure like the North Sea flooding Holland. Breathlessly, she recounted the history of her illness from the time she was six years old until the present.

"So your staring is not really staring."

"No, and I do not lust after women, no matter what they think."

Sam closed her eyes and sighed. It began to rain, lightly at first and then very heavily. "Let's go in." Olga opened the door to the barracks and they stepped just inside it. The room was dark; the women had already gone to bed. Olga snapped on her flashlight and played the beam around the room to check. In its residual light, she noticed the drawn lines around Sam's mouth and the plum-colored half-circles of fatigue underscoring the smaller woman's eyes. The wind moaned around the corners of the building, and the heavy rain rattled on the tin roof. The outside temperature had plunged, and a cold draft from under the door chilled Olga's feet. Olga pointed the flashlight at the floor to give them some illumination. She shivered and waited.

At last, Sam drew in a deep breath and exhaled through her mouth. She kept her voice low. "In order to be a BB—I mean a Barracks Overseer—you either had to be an atheist to begin with or else you renounced Christianity."

Olga hung her head. "I was scared for my life, so I said the words. I did. But it would be easier to change my blue eyes to brown than to abandon my faith." She gazed into Sam's eyes. "My grandmother, she was Russian Orthodox. She raised me in the church. I believe."

Sam searched Olga's eyes. "That kind come out only by prayer and fasting."

Taken aback, Olga had no clue as to what she meant. Her eyebrows shot up. "Do you mean you won't do it?"

"Don't look so scared." The kindness in Sam's dark brown eyes reassured her somewhat. "Those were Jesus's words to his disciples after he healed a boy with epileptic convulsions—the grand mal type—by commanding the evil spirit to come out of him."

Olga's eyes widened in fear and she laid one palm over her heart. She whispered, "Do you think I'm possessed?"

"*Possessed* is a strong word. I think *oppressed* might be a better description. I think Jesus implied that there are many kinds of evil spirits, and they oppress people in different ways. The kind that afflicted the epileptic boy required the deliverer to prepare himself carefully before doing battle with it."

"Will you help me, Sam?"

"I'll try. Just remember, it will be the Lord that does the healing, not me. But let's wait one day."

"Why not tonight?" Olga's eyes betrayed her anxiety.

"Twenty-four hours gives us both time to prepare." She gave Olga a searching look. "If I tell you to pray and ask forgiveness for all your sins, will you do that?"

Olga hesitated and bit her lower lip. "I am sorry for the times I hit you with the stick. But my other sins, well . . . do I have to tell you what they are?"

Sam laughed. "No, but you have to tell the Lord."

Olga grimaced, but said nothing.

"Look, Olga, he already knows all your sins. You and I—all of us—are completely transparent before him."

"Then why do I have to tell him if he already knows?"

"Because it shows humility and a willingness to change. We admit we have done wrong in thought, word, or deed and ask forgiveness."

"Thought? I got to admit my bad thoughts, too?"

"Yes, you do, and so do I. Thoughts are where it all begins: they're the source of our mean words and evil deeds."

"All right. Do I have to fast?"

Sam smiled. "No, but I do." A great crack of thunder startled them both and they flinched. "Whew, glad we're inside." She smiled and patted Olga's hand. "May I ask a favor of you?"

"Yes."

"Will you request more help in the laundry and transfer Susannah there? I want her to work inside from now on."

"That's easy. This week, three of the women . . . uh . . . selected . . . worked down in the basement. Since they . . . are gone . . . we have to replace them."

Sam closed her eyes and nodded almost imperceptibly. After weekly medical tests—urine samples, blood tests, EKGs, X-rays—the morning selections had begun in early November. They tapped around stomachs and groins, shined lights into eyes, and fed everyone—all to determine who they would slaughter next for the precious internal organs. Two days ago, they had made the latest selection; they put orange wristbands on three or four people out of each barracks, marking them for execution. Sometime within the next week, during the morning roll call, those with orange wristbands, often four to six a day, were escorted away by the armed guards. They never returned.

"Thank you, Olga. Now go and rest. We have a big day tomorrow."

As Sam crawled into her bunk, she had no idea how prophetic her words would be. She closed her eyes and prayed under her breath, barely moving her lips. She prayed for Peter, for Olga, and for her own strength. She pulled her blanket over her head against the encroaching cold. As the rain fell like tears, deep fatigue weighed her down, and she dissolved into sleep almost immediately.

CHAPTER 41

UNTERMENSCHEN

The heavy rain, punctuated by brilliant flashes of lightning and rumbling thunder, soaked the men to the skin and chilled them as they worked. A cold front from Canada had swooped down across the Great Plains to attack the warm, humid air drifting up from the Gulf of Mexico. The resultant clash triggered severe thunderstorms that deluged Texas from Dallas to Galveston. It rained heavily for three days.

The men worked outside despite the cold, driving rain. The armed guards stood to the side, sheltered under a temporary canopy the inmates had constructed. Four tall poles made of pine held up a blue tarp they had staked to the ground on three sides. The edges of the tarp flapped and crackled in the wind. The guards watched Thomas, Constantin, and six others dig a deep, wide trench in the cow pasture, south of the helipad. The rain had softened the ground, but each leaden shovelful of sodden earth strained arms and backs.

Bertie and Adam, as well as other men working in pairs, transported naked male and female corpses to the side of the trench. The bodies had been callously tossed on the ground outside the OR, like so much garbage. Though the men tried to avert their eyes, they could not avoid seeing the ugly holes where body parts had been extracted, the half-open eyes, the rictus grins that told of ultimate agonies. Bertie and Adam loaded their stretcher with the fifth body, a thirty-something man named Rick from their own barracks. His muddied corpse had wrecked eyes and a lungless, heartless chest. They carried him forty feet to the edge of the trench and laid him on the sodden ground. The pile of corpses beside the ragged hole grew. Bertie's leg and arm muscles had begun to tremble. As they returned to the OR, he didn't think he could take much more.

By mid-November, the inmates knew the Farm harvested organs for sale. But only Bertie had seen firsthand exactly how it was done. When two of the OR doctors and three nurses came down with a viral, flu-like illness, the medical team had drafted Bertie to help them operate. He no longer transported corpses; he helped make them. For an endless five days, Bertie assisted in the OR. He would relive the experience in his nightmares.

The first poor soul was a thirty-something male inmate from a different barracks than Bertie's. The nurse gave him an injection before the procedure—whether it was anesthesia or a lethal drug, Bertie did not know. In either case, as he discovered, the dosage was insufficient. They waited about twenty seconds while the same nurse swabbed the man's chest and abdomen with disinfectant—not nearly enough time for anesthesia to take effect.

A thin doctor with a pockmarked face stood on one side of the table. Facing him on the opposite side was a short surgeon wearing bifocals. With a scalpel, Pockmark sliced open the abdomen. Blood spurted and the intestines gushed out with it. The man's legs jerked and twitched—clearly, he was conscious. Bertie's own knees shook and his stomach churned. Pushing the intestines aside, Pockmark removed one kidney very quickly, while Bifocals removed the other with practiced skill. Bertie could see the man still breathed. The procedure was both inhumane and illegal according to American law.

Holding the kidney, still attached to the body by dangling veins and arteries, Pockmark glanced at Bertie. "Cut!"

When Bertie sliced through the blood vessels, a red fountain spurted out. They immediately put the kidneys into an organ transport container.

"Remove eyeballs."

Bertie paled. At that moment, the man's eyelids flew open, and he gazed directly at Bertie in a look of utter terror. The doctors did not care. They wanted the organs fresh, and the best way to harvest them was while the patient was still alive.

Nauseated, Bertie shook his head. "No, I . . . uh . . . I can't do it."

Irritated, Pockmark spat out something harsh in Chinese. He suddenly grabbed the man's head with his left hand, held open the eyelids with two fingers, and used the hemostatic forceps to gouge out the eye in one swift motion.

Bertie turned his head aside and vomited on the floor.

"You clean. Send in nurse."

Bertie went into the antechamber where they kept supplies. A short, tubby male nurse looked up in surprise. He had the drug cabinet open and was counting out pills.

"The surgeon is calling for you right now," said Bertie.

The nurse hurriedly swept the pills back into the container, shut the medicine cabinet, and went into the OR. Bertie glanced around. Lined with cabinets, the small room had a metal counter with a sink on one side. The counter held a box of latex gloves, a jar of cotton balls, a box of tissues, and a jar of tongue depressors. Bertie knew the cabinets stored bandages and other medical supplies. He quickly rinsed his mouth and pulled five paper towels from the wall-mounted dispenser, located beside the drug cabinet.

He expected the drug cabinet door locked automatically, but he gave it a little tug anyway. It opened. He quickly scanned the labels: amoxicillin, seconal, and other barbiturates. With a pounding pulse, he opened the seconal container and took six capsules. He stuffed them into the drawstring opening of his scrub pants, then shut the cabinet door and hurried back into the OR with the paper towels.

When he returned, the entire operation was over; it took only thirty minutes. *Surgery is a snap when you don't have to be careful.* The surgeon had kept the kidneys undamaged, but the rest was butchery. The dumpling-shaped male nurse carried the boxed organs out. He drove a small black van to the helipad where a chopper waited, its rotor blades turning lazily.

As soon as the Chinese medical staff recovered from the flu, Bertie returned to his duties as a body carrier. Though Adam and others asked him about his experiences in the OR, he refused to speak of it.

The now-familiar whirring sound penetrated Bertie's reverie and the din of the pelting rain. As he and Adam trudged slowly back, delaying to give themselves time to recover from the physical exertion, they looked up to see a gray-green helicopter approaching the pad from the east.

"Pick-up time," said Adam. "Get your lungs, hearts, livers, and kidneys here."

"Don't forget corneas." Bertie rubbed his own eyes, thinking of the man they had just delivered to a mass grave. They watched the small black delivery van cover the short distance from the OR to the pad and stop. Before the driver could load the labeled coolers for transport, four men descended onto the pad from the helicopter: an armed guard and three prisoners.

"Now that's different," said Adam. "Not only pick-up, but delivery—a shabby-looking lot." New arrivals came either by train and walked to the camp from the railroad, or sometimes in yellow school buses that parked in the lot by the stadium. "Wonder who those poor fuckers are."

"The shortest one's limping pretty badly." Bertie shook his head and wiped the rain out of his eyes. "I can guarantee he won't be long for this earth; they'll make quick work of him." He turned down the corners of his mouth. "To our captors we're subhuman—walking repositories of organs, nothing more—that's how they see us. *Die Untermenschen.*"

In the meantime, the helicopter, like a great mechanical vulture, lifted off into the clouds with the vital organs. Adam spat onto the ground. "What a bloody fucking business. We're cattle for the slaughter; the designated victims just wear orange wristbands instead of ear tags."

Adam and Bertie watched the three men and the guard pass the OR building on the way into the school, where the processing now took place. As the men walked by the pier-and-beam building, lightning flashed. In that moment, the shortest man, who limped badly, stumbled. The tall black man tried to keep him from falling, but they both went down face first. Adam thought he saw a quick, sideways motion of the black man's left hand, as if he shoved or slung something under the building. But he couldn't be sure in the rain. The black man regained his feet in a smooth, athletic motion and used both hands, now clearly empty, to help the smaller man rise.

Adam was not sure he had seen anything at all. But if he got a chance, he would check under the building to see. *If you had something valuable and hid it, you're a very smart dude. They're about to take everything you own away from you.*

As he and Bertie bent down to slide the remains of a young woman onto the stretcher, Adam peered under the OR. *No way to tell.* It was so dark under there, he couldn't see anything at all.

PIANO

Due to the shortened days and inclement weather, the guards processed new inmates in the choir room. Located on the school's northeast corner, directly across from the stadium and the OR building, it was the first room on the left. Incoming prisoners walked past the desk in the center of the floor and took seats on one of four semi-circular wooden tiers, where the choir members once sat for rehearsals. The piano, a large, black upright Kawai, had been moved out into the hall temporarily.

The three new prisoners walked ahead of the armed guard through the rain, skirting puddles in the parking lot, to the north end of the school. They climbed the concrete steps and waited under the portico while their guard called the main office to buzz them in. Once the door buzzed, Gideon pushed it open and held it for Max, formerly Bigfoot, and Jaybird. Inside, they found the choir room door locked. The guard called the office and spoke to Sam. "Wait there," she told him. "I'll send the processing officer to unlock the door as soon as I can locate him."

Seeing the piano in the hall, Max slumped down heavily onto the bench to rest. Gideon stood tensely beside him, weighing in his mind if he should take action or not. He and Jaybird could make a move on the guard before the other soldier arrived. It might be the only chance they had to overwhelm him. It would be tricky, though, since they were unarmed. Back at the hospital in Marshall, Jack Dunham had taken their guns, knives, and backpacks. He left them the clothes on their backs and their IDs. Poor Max didn't even have an ID.

Hyper-alert, he sensed a change in Max. The injured man suddenly straightened his back and opened the piano's lid. "A Kawai," he murmured. As he gazed at the keyboard, his chin lifted slightly and his nostrils flared. He glanced down at the floor and put his right foot on one of the pedals. Then he raised his hands as if he was going to play.

And play he did. Max struck a deep bass note that resounded in the hall.

The power of the sound so startled Gideon, he took a step back.

He followed the bass note with a rapid series of rising arpeggios ending in a treble trill. Then the notes cascaded downward, to rise again in an upward scale. He struck the bass note a second time and followed it with a splendid flurry of upward notes. Then, a third time, with great authority, his fingers bounded up from the bass in a dazzling scale passage that arced and descended, rose and fell. The music resonated in the hall, filling it with life, filling their hearts with hope and wonder.

"Holy shit," whispered Gideon. "I was expecting 'Chopsticks.'" He glanced sheepishly at the Chinese guard. "No offense, man."

The harsh lines vanished from the guard's face. He smiled and his eyes lost their wariness and anger. With an approving nod, he pointed to Max. "He play Beethoven."

Jaybird's eyebrows almost met his hairline. He laughed softly. "You ain't no harper, Max, you a piano man." He nodded his head. "Now I get it—a harp and a grand piano—they got the same shape."

Gideon heard a high-pitched voice and saw a large group of children approaching. For just a moment, he locked eyes with the tall young woman who led them. Blonde, slim, attractive, with a bright glance. He noticed her cowlick. His breath caught in his throat. He had never seen her before, and yet a spark of recognition arced between them—unexplainable. A knowing—the way Jaybird described it.

She was for him. Done.

Gideon immediately abandoned any thought of struggling with the guard. Gunfire in such a confined space could very well kill her or one of the children. He would not risk it.

Jaybird broke his reverie with a nudge in the side. He pointed at Bigfoot. "Look."

Max sat with bowed head, his hands resting limply in his lap. Tears streamed down his face. "I remember, I remember, I remember . . . "

The children's barracks had an invisible overseer. Katie and Donna were left unsupervised, but Ping insured their absolute cooperation by designating a scapegoat. That child had to wear a red wristband. After the two boys, Douglas and Tyler, tried to escape, he explained to the two women that if there were any more escape attempts or incidents requiring correction, the child wearing the red wristband would be publicly beaten and then decapitated. Naturally, he chose the youngest for the honor—Peter Brightman.

When Ping ordered Peter to wear the red wristband, Katie and Donna decided to tell Peter and the other children that the new wristband designated him as the musical leader. Katie explained to Donna that the little boy had perfect pitch. In the absence of a piano, Peter could sing the correct starting pitch for the children's songs. "And from now on," she told the children, "we are going to be the best behaved barracks that ever the world has seen."

"Why is that?" asked Nathan.

"Because our circumstances will not defeat us. No matter how difficult or chaotic things are on the outside, we will hold onto an inner peace. We are going to have order and cleanliness in our barracks. We are going to treat ourselves and each other with the greatest respect and courtesy. We are going to follow the rules and walk with our heads held high."

The gymnasium was behind the main building beneath the second-floor auditorium. The children, watched by Katie and Donna, had spent an active, noisy hour there. The older ones played with basketballs, shooting and dribbling on one side of the court, while the younger children jumped rope or kicked a soccer ball back and forth at the other end. Shouting and laughing, they enjoyed themselves. At the end of the play session, Donna led them in a short series of exercises: sit-ups, jumping jacks, running in place.

Afterward, they headed toward the cafeteria for their supper, two-by-two in an orderly queue, youngest and smallest first. Having exercised well, they were tired, but in good spirits, and mostly quiet as they walked toward the main corridor. Katie was glad of that, since they had to pass Ping's office. He had only recently allowed the children a daily hour of exercise, and she did not want that privilege revoked.

Even before they turned the corner into the main hall where the colonel's office was located, they heard the music. At first, Katie thought it must be Ping's radio; the door to his office stood open. Sam told her he played classical music all the time. But when she looked down the hall toward the cafeteria, she saw the source: a red-bearded man with shoulder-length, tousled auburn hair played the piano at the end of the corridor. A guard and two other men stood beside him.

She locked eyes with the bearded, sandy-haired man standing beside the pianist. His gaze, so intense, pierced her in some unfathomable way. He was a complete stranger, but on some primal level, she recognized him. At the same time, the rich music, played with such passion and authority, enveloped her, stopping her in her tracks. Impossible as water gushing from a rock in the desert, it flowed where it should not. The music had such abundant life—it touched her and made her realize how deeply she had missed singing and performing. Hot tears pricked her eyes.

It came to a close all too soon. Immediately, another sound took its place: a high-pitched child's voice, excited and shrill. "Beano—look! The prince and the birdcatcher!" Peter pointed at the pianist and the slender black man standing beside him.

"What?"

Ping charged out of his office into the hall with Sam trailing him.

"Mamma!"

Ping was already ten steps down the hall with his back to her, so Sam seized the opportunity; she bent down and hugged her son. It was a rare moment to even see him. Fright, anger, and sadness swirled within her at the sight of his red wristband. She lifted him in her arms as she stood up and kissed him on the cheek. Peter threw his arms around her and buried his face in the crook of her neck.

There was a sudden scuffle at the end of the hall. The pianist collapsed to one side, but the young black man and the sandy-haired prisoner caught him before he fell off the bench. They carefully lowered him to the floor.

The blue-eyed processing officer, the one who had ogled Sam, dashed past the children, caught up with Ping, and saluted him. The two men marched down the hall to confront the new inmates. Once the officer unlocked the door, the two new prisoners carried the pianist in, and Ping followed after.

Katie and the children proceeded in the same direction. Donna led the children to the left into the short hall where the cafeteria entrance lay. They would eat supper there before returning to the barracks. Katie stationed herself at the corner to make sure none of the children strayed. Sam, still holding Peter, lingered a moment with Katie.

Katie spoke very softly. "Did you hear him play? He's the real thing."

"Yes, most of it—I could tell he was a professional. Ping was bending over my desk pointing something out on the computer screen when he heard the music. He straightened up in one jerk, like a mechanical doll and said, 'Who play piano?' Then he bolted."

"Mamma—"

"Shh, Peter, you have to whisper."

He lowered his voice. "I know who they are. The piano player is Tamino from the story Beano told us. He's with the birdcatcher Papageno. I think Sarastro put them in prison with us."

"Tamino and Papageno?"

"Yes, remember Tamino the prince has reddish, messy hair like Daddy, and Papageno is black like Isaiah. That's who they are. The story is real."

"I see." He was convinced. Sam smiled, kissed him on the cheek and set him down. "Go on now with Beano and eat your supper." She touched Katie's arm. "Thanks for taking such good care of all the children. But to change the subject, do you know Olga, the BB?"

"The Ogler? Yes, she tends to fixate on female bottoms, Donna's being her favorite. I'm just glad she's not in my barracks." Katie rolled her eyes.

"Well," remarked Sam, "she lives in Barracks 3 with me, but there may be more to her story than an attraction to women. She told me she has epilepsy, with short seizures that cause her to stop and stare. We may have completely misjudged her."

"Really? Donna will be relieved to know that."

Sam glanced nervously down the corridor. "Go on to the cafeteria, Katie. We don't want Ping to see us talking."

"All right." Beano took Peter's hand and led him away. Sam watched them wistfully until they turned into the cafeteria entrance. Before she returned to her office, she glanced at the upright piano, a far cry from Joshua's seven-foot B model Steinway at home in Brooklyn. And yet, her heart had leaped when she heard the pianist play—it was so familiar. How strange to hear the Emperor concerto in this place. She had recognized the opening of the first movement, a piece Joshua had played many times, the piece he was supposed to play with the Houston Symphony. The piece he would never play again.

Blinded by tears, she turned abruptly and hurried back to her office before Ping returned.

CHAPTER 43

DELIVERANCE

Austin Pratt, the Barracks 4 BB, was a thin, nervous man who resembled a rat with spectacles: brown eyes set close to a ridged nose that rode high over a lipless mouth and a receding chin. Physically, he was as fit and athletic as Olive Oyl, who probably had bigger biceps. The inmates weren't sure if the former accountant really regarded his wooden baton as a weapon, or simply clutched it nervously as a means of self-defense in case they attacked him.

Early that evening, Pratt introduced two of the newly arrived men, who had been assigned to his barracks. He showed the men, freshly showered, their beards shaved and hair trimmed, to their bunks. There was no overcrowding, due to four newly vacated beds whose occupants, minus a few vital organs, now slept in a muddy mass grave in the pasture behind the school.

Gideon, the fair, gray-eyed one, said the guard had taken Max, who had the leg injury, to the OR. He coughed into his elbow. "What's the OR?"

"The operating room," answered Bertie. "Just as I predicted." He gazed resignedly at Gideon and Jaybird. "If he's your friend, I hope you told him goodbye. He's now part of the harvest."

"The harvest?"

Adam Chen explained. "This is Camp 615, but everyone calls it the Farm. When we first came, we thought it was named for the big peanut farm across from the school. But the primary crop is us—our internal organs. By now, Max has probably involuntarily donated his liver, kidneys, heart, and lungs."

"Dang it!" Jaybird sat down heavily on an empty bunk and dropped his head into his hands. "We found him wanderin' like a beast in the woods by Caddo Lake. He was so wild lookin' we thought he was Bigfoot at first. Both his shoulders were dislocated, he was half-starved and dehydrated with matted hair. Full of scratches and bug bites. Poor dude didn't even know his name. Didn't have no ID. We finally just made up a name for him. He didn't know how he come to be wanderin' there. And now, today, he plays the piano in the school like . . . like . . . uh, Rubenshine, the prince of piano players."

Adam smiled. "You mean Arthur Rubinstein."

"Yeah, him. I seen a video of him in school one time. Little dude with a big nose and fluffy white hair. The man played with his whole soul."

"He sure did," agreed Adam. "He was a great musician, a legend."

Gideon was astonished at Jaybird's long speech among strangers, clearly prompted by the younger man's affection and pity for Bigfoot.

Jaybird sat up straight. "Well, see, today, walkin' into the school, we didn't have no idea Max could play the piano. The dude sits down without a word and plays so amazin' it touches your heart. We couldn't believe it. When he finished playin', he cried. He said, 'I remember, I remember.' Then he collapsed from his infected leg." Tears leaked from Jaybird's eyes, and his voice broke. "He finally remembered who he was, and now they gone and killed him."

The conversation broke off. The men stood around the woodstove to warm themselves and dry their clothes after the day's downpour. The only sounds in the chilly room were the ticking of rain on the tin roof and the deep, rattling coughs of one of the inmates in a nearby bunk.

"Where are you and Jaybird from?" Bertie asked Gideon.

"The teeming metropolis of Legend, Texas, population two hundred fifty."

"I've heard of it—that's where the plane crashed, isn't it? Near Caddo Lake? No survivors."

Gideon nodded.

The barracks was silent, except for one man who coughed. After a while, Gideon said, "Sounds pretty bad, that cough." He smiled. "Even worse than mine."

"That's Loopy, the deluded kid who tried to make us think he was related to General Huffman, the psychopath." Adam rolled his eyes. He pointed his index finger toward his temple and twirled it. "That's how he got his name. He's loopy."

Bertie explained. "He got sick working outside in the cold rain the past three days." He lowered his voice. "He's exhausted, got fever and chills and that deep cough. He might have pneumonia."

"Can he get some medical help?"

Bertie gave a short bark of a laugh. "I wish. I'm a doctor, Gideon, but a doctor can't do anything without medicine, and there won't be any forthcoming. Those in charge here don't give a damn about a young boy's life. They only care about the money they can make from selling his organs. The sonsabitches doing the operating don't even wait for the anesthetics to kick in before they make their incisions. It's barbaric."

Adam scratched his head. "Wait a minute, Bertie, there's another alternative."

"Such as?"

"Such as the healer next door in Barracks 3—the one who healed your wife from the snake bite."

"I know that's the news going 'round, but honestly, how can we know if it was prayer that healed Susannah? We don't even know what kind of snake bit her. I doubt it was even venomous."

"But she said she heard a rattle. All rattlesnakes are venomous."

"To varying degrees. Some more than others."

"But all her symptoms were gone the next morning: the swelling, the inflammation, the pain, the nausea. Why don't you believe it?"

Bertie sighed. "My scientific training makes me skeptical of so-called 'healings.' I admit I can't explain how it happened, but Sam's just a writer, not a miracle worker; I came here on the same train she did. She's not Madre Mio."

"Who?" Adam and Gideon spoke simultaneously.

Bertie grinned. "My joke—a female version of Padre Pio. He was an Italian monk and one of the greatest Catholic saints of the twentieth century."

"Do you believe Padre Pio healed people?"

"Well, yes, Adam. But he was an extraordinary case."

Jaybird lifted his head. "Hold on. Don't healing depend partly on the sick person's faith? Least that's what Jesus said. *Your faith has made you whole.* He said that to the woman who bled. She reached out and touched the hem of his robe. He said the same thing to the ten lepers and a blind man he healed." Jaybird cleared his throat. "I'll bet you a boatload of catfish that no doctor could explain his miracles either. Just goes to show that the spirit is heaps more powerful than the flesh—or any medicine for that matter."

Adam looked at Gideon. "What do you think?"

"Well, although I call myself a Christian, I'm not that religious. So, I'm in the skeptic's boat with Bertie."

"Bertie! Can the new man come here and talk to me?" Loopy coughed with the effort of speaking.

"Which one? There are two of them."

"The one who knows the stories about Jesus."

Bertie glanced at Jaybird. "Will you?"

Jaybird rose from his bunk. "Sure."

Bertie pointed. "That's Loopy. Second bunk on the left, the upper one."

Jaybird peered down in the darkness at the thin boy lying there. "Hey, Loopy. My name is Jaybird."

The boy turned on his side to face the young black man. Two tired gray eyes stared at him out of a sickly pale face topped by a short stubble of wheat-colored hair. Jaybird had the oddest sensation that he had met the boy somewhere before; he seemed so familiar. Loopy held out a hand to shake. When Jaybird took it in his, it was hot, and the boy's eyes had a fevered look. Jaybird felt almost overcome by the waves of loneliness and longing radiating out from Loopy. *Just like me, bro. You don't fit in anywhere, do you?*

"All the men in this barracks are supposed to be Christian, Jaybird, but you're the only one I heard actually talk about Jesus. Would you tell me the stories you mentioned about him, the ones about the woman and the lepers? I know very little about him, and it seems to me he must have been one of the most incredible men that ever lived."

Feeling a strong kinship with the boy, Jaybird smiled and released Loopy's hand. "You got that right. You just lie back and get comfortable. I'll be glad to tell you those stories. I was raised up readin' the Bible."

At day's end in Barracks 3, Sam had a quiet conversation with the BB. "Olga, when I pray for you, I'll have to reveal your illness to the others. Do I have your permission?"

"Do the others have to be there?"

"The prayers of a group are more powerful. It will be more effective for you."

Olga mulled that over, eyes downcast. She whispered, "They will mock me. They already do."

"I promise they will not. I won't allow it."

When Olga remained silent, Sam asked, "Have you forgiven the ones who have hurt you?"

The Ogler's icy blue eyes slowly filled with tears. "Yes, I named them in my mind and forgave them all. And I asked the Lord to forgive me all the things I've said and done and thought wrong."

"All right, then. Let's begin." Once again, Sam invited the other women in Barracks 3 to gather around. Only this time, no one came. The silence in the room, filled with ill will and tension, hung heavy. No one moved.

While Olga stood with downcast eyes and slumped shoulders, Sam addressed them all. "Listen to me—Olga is not the enemy. Remember, we do not fight against flesh and blood, *but against principalities, against powers, against the rulers of the darkness of this world, against spiritual wickedness in high places.*

"She has epilepsy. Those moments when she stares are actually small seizures. She could have a grand mal seizure at any time. If she does, you know they will cart her off to the OR to be butchered. Would you deny her healing? None of the people the Lord healed were perfect, and neither are any of us. If we want mercy, we have to show mercy. Come now and pray for Olga. Watch and see what the Lord can do."

After a moment's hesitation, they came. Those closest to the rangy, blonde woman placed their hands on her, while those farther away placed their hands on the shoulders of the person in front of them.

Sam had fasted for twenty-four hours and made her own private confession. In terms of sinful thoughts, she had harbored many malicious ones toward Olga herself, the guards, Ping, and the unethical doctors who chopped up human beings like so much meat. She had to remind herself that forgiveness was not an emotion—it was an act of will.

The atmosphere remained edgy. Susannah, newly healed herself, seemed unaffected by the tension in the room; she was almost joyful. Her healing had been the spark that set them all on fire, even the Ogler.

"It takes humility for anyone to ask for healing," Sam told them. "Remember that. We cannot have any negative thoughts or wishes towards Olga now. If you feel that way, please leave us."

Two women walked away: Meredith Miller and Carol Bredner.

"Sit on this bunk, Olga, or I'll never be able to reach your head."

The corners of the tall woman's mouth curled up slightly and she sat. With bowed head and closed eyes, Sam anointed Olga's forehead with olive oil she had blessed. Olga herself had got it from the kitchen and brought it to Sam in a little glass bottle. Sam placed her hands on the woman's head and began to pray.

To calm herself, Olga concentrated on breathing slowly. She closed her eyes and focused on the warm touch of Sam's hands on her head. Little by little, a deep relaxation overcame her. She imagined herself seated in her grandmother's garden in DeKalb, watching the dappled light filter through the canopies of the apple trees, listening to the rustle of the leaves mixed with birdsong carried on the wind. She let herself expand into a place of rest and quiet.

But all was not well—there was a serpent in the garden. She was aware in a distant way of Sam's words and commands, summoning the darkness out of her. She could tell it did not want to leave; it tried to hide. But she knew it was there. As the prayers became more intense, it fought to stay inside her. She did not want it to stay. Her mind became a single plea, repeated over and over: *Jesus, help me . . . Jesus, help me.*

Everything suddenly came to a head. Her heart rate sped up; it felt like a bass drum pounded in her chest. The sensation frightened her and she gasped for breath. A sharp, painful, wrenching sensation wracked her. Her head snapped back and her whole body stiffened. From very far away, she heard someone wail. Then everything went black.

GIFTS

Austin Pratt, overseer for Barracks 4, had one redeeming feature, as Gideon discovered—he was susceptible to bribery. By offering Pratt the Rat a pint of whiskey miraculously obtained by Olga, Gideon got thirty minutes alone in the Zabach High School library. He only needed fifteen. He stole *The Secret Garden*, *The Lion, the Witch and the Wardrobe* (how that escaped purging he never knew), and *The Adventures of Tom Sawyer* (a flamethrower in the faces of the politically correct). "Long live Mark Twain!"

That evening, he took Adam's place in the last task of the day. He helped Bertie deliver firewood to the children's barracks. Adam was delighted to be relieved of his duty when Gideon requested the change. "Oh, hell yeah." He flopped down onto his bunk and sighed with relief. He flexed his aching back and shoulders. He and Bertie had chopped wood all day.

"Why are you so eager to help me tonight?" Bertie asked as he and Gideon walked to the woodpile.

Gideon bent to gather an armful of wood. "Katie Lamb."

Bertie smiled. "Ah. Did you know she and I traveled on the same train to this camp?"

"Lucky you."

"She's an opera singer, a mezzo soprano." His breath smoked in the cold air.

Gideon grunted with the weight of his burden as they walked from the woodpile toward the barracks.

"She was in the midst of singing a Mozart opera in Chicago when the coup took place. She fled the opera house on foot—still in costume—and ended up on the train to Texas. She and I and Susannah traveled in the same compartment as Sam Brightman and her son, Peter. Peter calls Katie "Beano," after the role she sang in the *Marriage of Figaro*—Cherubino."

Gideon said nothing. He pressed his lips together and shifted his grip on the bulky bundle of split wood and kindling he carried.

Bertie continued his monologue. "On the train, she told Peter a story and taught him a song to keep his mind occupied. In fact, she helped distract us all from the uncertainty and fear. And she shared food from her backpack with us." He smiled again. "A lovely girl." He paused and glanced at Gideon. "I can see why you're interested."

As they approached the children's barracks, a sudden fear gripped Gideon. What if she wasn't there? He and Bertie were delivering a ten-day supply of wood. If he missed her, he couldn't come back for an eternity of 240 hours—if he could even arrange it then.

Then, faintly, he heard the children singing. Surely she led them. The sound floated on the air, ethereal and distant as the song of angels. Bertie knocked. The music stopped and Katie opened the door. Shyness paralyzed Gideon; he stood stiff and mute as a tree rooted to the ground.

For sixteen years he had lived like a monk. He had noticed attractive women, but he had never felt anything for any of them but a passing twinge of lust. Now, although he had longed for this moment, he couldn't even lift his eyes to her face.

Bertie stepped into the room ahead of him. With a backward toss of his head, he said, "Katie, this is Gideon."

His body betrayed him. His knees wobbled; his hands grew slick with sweat, and his mouth was dry as the sands of Afghanistan. He hadn't been this flustered since ninth grade when he asked pretty

Elizabeth Jenkins to go to the movies with him. (She turned him down.) He kept his eyes on the rough wood floor.

"Come in, Gideon. It's cold out there."

She had no idea. The invitation and her voice, low and mild, unlocked his paralysis. He took a step over the threshold and beheld a semicircle of children. A pretty black girl, probably in her twenties like Katie, stood behind them. The children sat cross-legged in three rows, watchful and unnaturally still, Gideon thought. But of course, they lived in a web of tension and uncertainty—at any moment the spider might come for them. Fear enlarged their solemn eyes and drained the blood from their faces.

"They're just bringing wood to keep us warm." Katie reassured them.

Bertie set his load down onto the floor at the base of the woodstove with a clatter. Gideon followed suit, but as he bent to release the wood, a heavy object fell out of his bundle and hit his foot. "Ow!" He almost lost control of the load as two more rectangular objects dropped and slid partway across the floor.

"Books?" exclaimed Katie.

He lowered the logs onto the pile. "Uh, yes." His mind was so fixed on Katie that he completely forgot he had hidden them in the pile.

Her smile lit up the room and warmed Gideon's heart. "Look, kids!" As she picked them up, she announced their titles: "*The Adventures of Tom Sawyer, The Secret Garden*, and my all-time favorite *The Lion, the Witch and the Wardrobe!*"

She gazed at him with a sparkle in her eye. "Where did you get them?"

"The school library."

"Really. How did you get access?"

He shook his head very slightly. "Better if I don't tell you."

"So when are these due?" She smiled.

"Well, as a former librarian, I would tell you three weeks." He shrugged. "But these I filched. Books are meant to be read—no reason for them to gather dust on the shelves. So keep them as long as you like—just not in plain view. I don't think our captors will miss them."

"Thank you, Gideon, what a wonderful gift. We are going to enjoy these." Clutching the books to her chest, she leaned in, surprising him, and kissed him on the cheek.

To his chagrin, he blushed. *How could he, a combat veteran, turn to mush like that?* He had to restrain himself from reaching out to embrace her.

He mused on his predicament. In the camp, men and women mutually attracted had almost no possibility of courtship. Longing, held in check, could only smolder in eyes and hearts. But somehow, Gideon discovered, the enforced separation magnified the desire and purified it into something holy.

She faced the children. "Let's sing a song for Gideon and Bertie."

And so they did. Bertie watched the children, but Gideon's eyes never strayed from Katie.

Later that evening, when Gideon described his visit to the children's barracks, Jaybird smacked a fist into his palm. "Dang it, Shadow Man, I gotta go next time."

"Why's that?"

"Why's that! Didn't you see Donna in there?"

"The pretty brown-eyed girl?"

"No, the *beautiful* brown-eyed girl. Vo-cab-u-lar-y, man."

Gideon covered his mouth with one hand, but it didn't hide the grin. "Yeah, I sure did see her."

"Well then, don't ask me why I want to deliver firewood next time."

"I brought them more than firewood. I brought three books—children's classics I stole from the school library."

"Hmmm. Now you done launched yourself into the world of crime: librarian turned book thief."

Gideon laughed. "It was for a good cause, bro. I'll steal some more if I get a chance."

Jaybird wondered what gift he could bring. Before he could explore his options, Loopy tugged on his sleeve.

"Jaybird, can I talk to you?"

"Sure." He followed the boy to his bunk where there was a little more privacy. "What's on your mind?"

Loopy coughed a little, then lowered his voice. "What would you say if I told you there is a group of extremely rich men—many of them unknown to the public—who are conspiring to take over the world? I'm pretty sure my stepfather Dumitru is one of them. They may be planning this with . . . uh . . . with the help of supernatural beings. Maybe fallen angels, maybe Lucifer himself."

When Jaybird remained silent, Loopy blushed. He swallowed and explained. "I know it sounds crazy, but Dumitru wrote about it in his diary. There is a group called the Nine—I think those are the supernatural ones. It seems like the men get their orders from the Nine, who give them power and authority to do their work. But I don't know much more than that." He searched Jaybird's face, trying to gauge his reaction. "So . . . uh . . . well, what do you think, Jaybird?"

"Most people would think you gone off your rocker, for sure."

Shamed, Loopy dropped his head and stared at the floor. His mouth worked and he felt hot tears prick the back of his eyes.

"But I ain't most people."

Loopy's head bobbed up, and he gazed hopefully at Jaybird. He coughed violently into his elbow. After the coughing fit passed, Jaybird noticed how rapidly and shallowly the boy breathed.

"See, this time we're livin' in was foretold thousands of years ago. Ain't nothin' surprises God. He knew it all from the very beginning, down to the last detail, and He told us about it in his book. That's why the government banned the book—they can't stomach the truth. The battle between good and evil has been goin' on since the Garden of Eden. Proud Satan roamed around Paradise with honey on his tongue and pure malice in his heart. He thought he could spoil God's plans, right under his nose. But when Adam and Eve disobeyed the Lord, God looked ahead and made a new plan.

"Meanwhile, Satan and his fallen angels went to work on earth. They lusted after human women and had children with them. They even messed with the animals. They tried to taint all human DNA with their own, and they damn near succeeded. They gave men knowledge that wasn't for their good."

"Like what?"

"Like weapons, witchcraft and sorcery, occult knowledge. It was an evil time, like now. After many years of interbreeding, only Noah and his family had pure blood. God decided to wipe out the bad guys and start over, so he told Noah to build an ark, and he did. Everybody laughed at Noah and called him a fool, but he did what God said, no matter what. When the rain came down from the sky and water gushed up from inside the earth, the mockers didn't laugh no more. But then it was too late. Only Noah's family and the animals in the ark survived. In the worst of times, God protected them.

"See, Loopy, in every age the battle goes on between the children of the Lord and Satan's children: the wheat and the tares, the sheep and the goats. Sometimes, for us—but not for the Lord—it's hard to tell which ones are goats. But now, as it was in Noah's time, the differences are clearer. What most people don't understand is how deeply hateful and malicious Satan and his children are. They want to destroy life. They come to steal, kill, and destroy. This place is a perfect example."

"I know. Who would have thought there would be concentration camps in America?"

"Satan's malice and hatred for us goes deep as the ocean and high as the Milky Way."

"Why is that?" Loopy's shoulders slumped. "Jaybird, I think I need to lie down."

"Okay. Do you want me to finish this later?"

"No, keep on." The boy climbed into his bunk and lay on his side, facing Jaybird.

When he was settled, Jaybird continued quietly. "Satan's chewed up inside with jealousy and spite for the Lord and all his creation. Since God made us in his own image, and Satan can't win against God, he's goin' after us. We're the targets. He can sure destroy us if we let him. He tries every which way to tempt us and get us off track. There's an unseen battle goin' on for our souls, Loopy. But the Lord has his angels, too. They're fightin' for us.

"Now, I have no way of knowin' exactly what the devil and his evil men conspire to do, but it won't surprise me if they are workin' behind the scenes to destroy us and take control of the world. This coup is part of their plan, no doubt." Jaybird laughed and shook his head.

Loopy wrinkled his brow. "Why are you laughing? What's funny about that?"

"They a little behind the times. See, the war was won two thousand years ago."

"How's that?"

"Jesus Christ was the second Adam, a perfect man who *obeyed* his father all the way down to death. He made things right again. He took our sins on him and nailed them to the cross. He paid our debt with his blood and sacrifice. By doing that, he reconciled us to God and re-opened Paradise. If we believe on him and repent of our sins, we are forgiven. The devil has no power over us."

"But people still suffer and die."

"They do. The war is won, but the battles still go on. See, Loopy, every person has to choose. You choose the Lord, you suffer with him a little while. You choose a life of sin and the flesh, you enjoy yourself—for a little while. But the reckonin' is comin'—and nobody knows it better than Satan himself—when the Lord will return. *For the Lord himself shall descend from heaven with a shout, with the voice of the archangel, and with the trump of God: and the dead in Christ shall rise first: Then we which are alive and remain shall be caught up together with them in the clouds, to meet the Lord in the air: and so shall we ever be with the Lord."*

Jaybird's grin was infectious. "Whooee, I can't wait for that! And I sure wouldn't wanna be in the other camp when that goes down. The prince of lies is due for a fall. A terrible fall. One word from the Lord, and it's over for him."

"But when will that happen?"

"Don't know exactly—nobody does. But I know this: the Lord is gonna let Satan have his way for a very short time. He's gonna allow evil to take over the world, just like your stepfather and his buddies want. And right when Satan and all the evil men get total control, when they think they've won, and they're sittin' around back-slappin' each other, drinkin' bourbon and smokin' cigars, that's when God's gonna lower the boom. He's gonna squash 'em like bugs. And guess what God's gonna do then?"

"What?"

"Why, he's gonna laugh. He's gonna have the biggest belly laugh of all time while he watches them suckers squirm. The Lord is gonna claim this earth as his and he's gonna reign."

"And what will that be like?"

"That's gonna be like a kid's expectation of Christmas ten times over. Better than anyone could ever imagine—a time of peace and justice and righteousness and truth. The wolf will dwell with the lamb, like Isaiah said. The cows and the bears will feed together, and the lion will eat straw like the ox. *They shall not hurt nor destroy in all my holy mountain: for the earth shall be full of the knowledge of the LORD, as the waters cover the sea."*

"Hard to imagine, Jaybird. But who will rule?"

"None other than the Prince of Peace. We gonna be in the best hands there is, Loopy. The government will be on his shoulders." Jaybird grinned. "That should help you sleep easy, boy. Go ahead and lie back. It's late and we all need to rest."

Jaybird left the boy and climbed up to his own bunk. He lay down and closed his eyes. *Faith. Gotta believe even though we're walkin' in the dark here. The Lord keeps his promises. Ain't no one more faithful and true.*

Then his mind returned to Donna. He hoped to visit her in a few days. Jaybird's heartbeat jumped like a rabbit flushed out of hiding—he would have a chance to be with her—maybe talk to her—if he didn't go completely tongue-tied in her presence. Huntin', fishin', playin' music, memorizin' Bible passages—no sweat. But small talk, and God forbid, flirtin' were as foreign to him as ballroom dancin' was to a beaver.

But what gift could he bring? He stretched out his arms behind his head and bumped the warped board at the top of the wall. The hiding place for his pouch, his slingshot and ammo. Bertie had retrieved it all from under the OR.

His mouth organ.

He sat bolt upright and grinned. *Problem solved—he would bring the gift of music.*

PLANS

Full of scarcely repressed excitement, Ping had Sam comb the data on the current inmates to find any musicians among them. Like a kid about to take a rollercoaster ride at the county fair, he practically hopped up and down beside her while she searched. She found three musicians: Katie Lamb and Adam Chen were the only professionals, but a piano teacher from Chicago, Annette Alba, lived in Barracks 2. Ping took the list of names, chuckled, and seemed to float into his office on a wave of bliss.

A few days later, on Monday, November 16, Ping made two announcements at morning roll call. The regional governor, General Huffman, was coming to visit in two weeks, and to honor him, the inmates were going to give a concert on December 1. He didn't stutter once. "Preparations begin immediately!"

Galvanized by his love of music, Ping moved his magic wand, and miracles happened. He authorized a piano technician to tune and regulate the grand piano in the second-floor auditorium. (The inmates didn't even know it was there.) Adam Chen's violin suddenly reappeared. When the three musicians were summoned to the office to receive their new assignments, Sam laid the instrument on her desk before Adam without a word. He froze for a moment. With a visibly trembling hand, he opened the case slowly, as if he were afraid someone might have splintered the instrument. To his great relief, the violin appeared to be in perfect condition. He lifted it reverently from the case, tightened the bow, applied rosin, and tuned the strings. He began to play a slow, unaccompanied piece—Sam guessed Bach—while tears streamed down his face.

Ping told them they had two hours a day to prepare for the concert—eight to ten every morning—and to give him a list of pieces or arias they needed. He would provide the sheet music. Annette Alba blanched and protested that she was not really a performer. To everyone's surprise, Ping reassured her. "You d-d-do best. Do not w-w-w-worry." He rubbed his palms together briskly and laughed. "I have special p-pianist coming."

Katie suggested the children could perform. She had already taught them several songs.

"I listen. N-now."

A guard accompanied the three musicians back to their respective barracks. Katie gathered the children and rehearsed their three best songs. She returned with them to the office, where they sang their pieces.

She had taught them well. When children sing in tune and lightly in their head voices, there is no sweeter or purer sound in the universe; it is the aural distillation of innocence. But like a laser, it cuts to the heart. Peter, standing in the front row with the younger children, smiled proudly at his mother. Sam, touched by the music and the presence of her son, struggled to control her facial expression and willed herself not to cry.

"Excellent. They sing too."

"Thank you, sir. We look forward to it. Right, kids?" They cheered. Katie raised her index finger. "Uh, but I do have one request."

There was a tense silence. Despite the chilliness of the day, Sam felt sweat break out on her forehead and under her arms, but Katie's blue-eyed gaze at Ping never wavered. Fearless and calm, she faced him.

"What that?"

"To make the performance the very best we can, it would help the children to increase their food rations, at least until the concert, and provide them with jackets for the cold so they don't get sick."

Another silence. Sam held her breath while her pulse attempted to deafen her. It was a brilliant move, but a dangerous one; she hoped Katie had not overstepped her bounds.

The corners of his mouth dived, his tongue flickered back and forth, and his serpent-like, opaque eyes glittered as Ping weighed his choices. At last he spoke. "Okay, we do that. Now," he raised his voice and pointed a stubby finger at the center of Katie's chest, "you sing."

She did not even blink. She gestured for the children to sit on the floor, then she announced her aria. "Che farò senza Euridice?" from Gluck's *Orfeo ed Euridice*." She addressed the children, though Sam knew she was setting the scene for her and Ping as well, without appearing to. "Orfeo is a young man who sings a lament over his lost love, Euridice, who died of a snake bite on their wedding day. While he sings, he holds her in his arms, even though she is dead."

Ping pointed to himself and raised his chin. "I know this one. I s-s-see it Los Angeles."

Sam did not recognize the name of the aria; she had no idea what to expect. Before Katie sang, she beckoned the oldest girl. "Lynne, I need a little help." A gaunt adolescent, with a sprinkle of freckles and long, chestnut-brown hair stepped forward. Katie whispered instructions into the girl's ear. "Can you do that?"

The girl nodded and gave a shy, pleased smile. Immediately, the child lay on the floor, eyes closed, as if she were dead. Katie glanced at Peter. "Give me an E, please." Peter glanced proudly at his red wristband and sang the pitch for her. Katie, the gregarious, blonde farm girl dropped to one knee and took the girl into her arms.

In an instant, Sam beheld a surprising transformation. Before them all knelt Orfeo, a vulnerable, heartbroken young man. In her green scrubs, without costume or makeup, something in the way the singer held herself suggested masculinity and great grief. Orfeo cradled the head of the delicate Euridice in his left hand, while his right arm encircled her waist. Eyes closed and head turned toward his chest, the girl lay limply in his embrace. In a rich, plangent voice, Orfeo poured out his sorrow. He was lost for he had lost his love.

The children sat transfixed. They watched the scene solemnly and intently. Their eyes grew large and their mouths formed little O's.

Toward the middle of the aria, Orfeo cried out, "Euridice, Euridice." Little Maria began to cry. As young as they were, these children had already suffered terrible losses, beginning with loss of freedom. Sam wondered how many of them were now orphaned; how many of their parents lay in a mass grave, their organs ripped from them?

When the last note faded away at the end of the aria, no one moved. Finally, Katie lifted her head and smiled. The children erupted into applause and cheers while Katie and "Euridice" stood up and took a bow.

Ping announced they would recreate the same scene for General Huffman's concert. He would provide costumes and makeup. Katie told him that she had arrived at the camp dressed as Cherubino, the pageboy from *The Marriage of Figaro*. She would only need that costume if he could recover it, and she could also sing two arias by Mozart. "I can describe the clothing to Sam." Of course, she said that only for Ping's benefit; Sam had seen her in the costume on the train.

"Yes, do that and make list of arias now. I get m-music. You rehearse with p-pianist Annette until my p-pianist ready. She not play concert."

To Sam, he said, "Get names of p-p-pieces from violinist."

After Katie specified the vocal and piano scores she needed, Sam left to find Adam. She located him and Bertie outside near the OR. With pad and pen in hand, she asked Adam to name the pieces he wanted for the concert. He asked for a piano arrangement of Vivaldi's "Spring" from *The Four Seasons* and the Beethoven Spring Sonata, op. 24. He winked at Sam. "We're in Winter now, but it can't last forever."

"Speaking of music," said Bertie, "I retrieved the gear the new guy stashed underneath the OR on his first day. He brought a harmonica, of all things. Sam, did you know he's supposed to be a virtuoso? Maybe he could play on the concert, too."

"All right, I'll tell Ping we found another musician and see if he'll listen to him play. But I'd better get back . . . "

She turned to go, but Adam placed his hand lightly on her arm. "Sam, there is a sixteen-year-old boy in our barracks who is very sick. Bertie thinks he has pneumonia. He got chilled in the cold and rain the last three days. If he's too ill to work, they'll butcher him. Would you be willing to lay hands on him tonight or tomorrow? I think prayer is his only hope."

The pleading in Adam's dark eyes was intense. Sam dropped her gaze and stared at the muddy ground. "I would, but how can I even get to him? It's death to be caught outside the barracks at night."

"I know it's a great risk, but there's no other way to save him. We've got a plan to smuggle you in. It's better that we don't move Loopy— that's his name." He quickly gave her the details and told her they would put the plan in motion the next night. "After lights-out, wait for the signal: a mourning dove call twice in a row. *Coo-ah, coo-coo-coo. Coo-ah, coo-coo-coo.*"

Sam smiled. "Yes, I recognize that call."

"As soon as you hear it, leave your barracks and go toward Barracks 4. Jaybird, a young black man—the harmonica guy—will escort you."

"How is the Ogler, by the way?" asked Bertie.

"I think the Holy Spirit healed her. As I prayed, I saw a black mist rise out of her and disperse. The unclean spirit was rough on her; it didn't give up without a fight. She had a convulsion just before it left. Her head snapped back, her body went rigid, she screamed, and then she became limp as a corpse. I thought she had actually died, but after a long couple of minutes she opened her eyes and said, 'It's gone. I know it.' We were so thankful."

Sam lifted a hand in parting with a casual air, as if she would meet them for a drink after dinner. "All right, see you tomorrow night."

Adam glanced at Bertie. "I pray God will have mercy on poor Loopy and heal him, too." He patted the empty stretcher with his free hand. "I never want to see him laid out on one of these damn things."

Bertie simply shook his head. "Remarkable. Maybe she is Madre Mio. She's healed two people now and takes no credit."

"No, she has the humility to know the healing power is not her own."

A guard shouted at them to get moving and do their work. They walked to the OR, set the stretcher on the ground, and laid another mutilated corpse upon it.

CHAPTER 46

RISKS

Gideon told all the men in Barracks 4 that Sam would pray over Loopy, but only he, Adam, and Jaybird knew the whole plan. It would be a high-stakes performance with no dress rehearsal. Everything hinged on Jaybird, the hunter. If he succeeded, Adam, the lone wolf, would prowl. "Once you step outside the barracks," Gideon warned, "you're on your own." They would provide Sam a scant eighteen minutes with the boy. There would be no second chance.

Despite their best efforts to keep him in the dark, Austin Pratt overheard two of the men talking about Sam coming to their barracks. Pratt immediately told them she could pray for Loopy, but not in his barracks. Gideon placated him. "No problem, Austin. You rule here. We'll figure out an alternative."

The next evening, Jaybird and Adam asked Pratt if they could go out to use the latrine. Jaybird clutched his stomach and grimaced. "Think we got a stomach virus, man. I got the runs, and Adam—"

Adam vomited on the floor.

"Eccch! Get out, damn it!" Pratt shouted, pointing to the door. He gagged and turned away from the brown puddle of puke dotted with rice grains. "You're gonna clean that up when you get back!" he shouted.

"This may take a while," Jaybird said, as he and Adam rushed out the door together.

"You look a little pale, Pratt," said Bertie. "Let me get you a cup of water." He poured some from the plastic jug beside Austin Pratt's bed, one of the perks given to BBs. The powder from the capsule he emptied into it dissolved nicely. He was gratified when Pratt drank it all down.

Outside in the cold night air, Jaybird whispered, "How'd you throw up on cue like that?"

"I kept back a mouthful of our crappy rice-soup supper and spewed it."

Jaybird laughed quietly. "Good job." He fingered the three steel ball bearings in his pocket. He hoped he would only need one. But no matter what, he had to succeed. Adam smiled. "Good hunting, Jaybird." They parted and moved quietly to their chosen places.

The night was overcast. Between the pools of light in front of each barracks lay twenty feet of darkness. The armed guards walked the gravel path between the back of the school and the barracks, then followed the perimeter around the school grounds. The circuit took nine minutes. Every few minutes, the soldiers manning the north and south watchtowers swept the school yard with powerful searchlights.

Adam Chen stood in the shadows with his back against the side wall of Barracks 4. The crunch of gravel signaled the guard's approach. Adam peered at the barely discernible figure crouched in the rear exit of the school. Jaybird had already climbed up and loosened the light bulb above the doorway. In the darkness he was practically invisible.

As the footsteps grew nearer, Adam waited tensely, listening. He heard a slight whoosh, then *clonk*. The footsteps halted abruptly. A heavy *thunk* followed, as if someone had dropped a sandbag onto the gravel.

Jaybird vaulted down the concrete steps and met Adam on the path where the body of the fallen guard lay. They dragged him into the shadows between the barracks and stripped him of his uniform, boots, and cap.

"Is he dead?"

Jaybird shrugged and stuffed his slingshot into the waistband of his pants. "Not taking time to find out. He's going into the latrine. He'll either sink or swim." They carried the man and dropped him into the foul-smelling latrine. Quickly, in the darkness behind the barracks, Adam stripped off his own clothes and changed into the guard's uniform. It was a surprisingly close fit. He buckled on the holster and the loaded pistol.

"You scary, man. You look like one of them."

Adam smiled. "That's the point." He handed Jaybird his clothes. "Go get Sam right away, and stow these in the barracks. I'll make at least two rounds, which gives you about eighteen minutes." Sweating despite the chill night air, Adam picked up the guard's flashlight and pulled the cap low over his forehead to conceal as much of his face as possible. He set out on the gravel path.

When the two men exited the barracks, Gideon decided to speak to the boy for whom they would risk so much. He had greeted Loopy in passing, but never really chatted with him. He and Loopy worked in separate areas by day, and at night, Gideon was so exhausted from work and his own illness that he often fell asleep as soon as he had eaten. He sat on the edge of the lower bunk where they had moved the boy.

"Hi Gideon." The words sparked a coughing fit that racked Loopy's whole body. When he recovered, he watched Gideon solemnly, but did not speak.

Feeling awkward, Gideon coughed into his elbow. "Listen, if all goes well, Jaybird'll bring Sam in here pretty soon to pray over you." He rambled on to hide his unease. "That Jaybird's quite a guy. In addition to knowing the Bible, he's also a harmonica virtuoso. He can play any tune, and he can mimic all sorts of birds. He taught us how to imitate the bluejay—his namesake—the cardinal, and the mourning dove. He's also a handyman. Seems like he can fix just about anything. He's only a few years older than you, maybe twenty or so."

"What about you?"

The question surprised Gideon. "Me? I'm a librarian—or was—in a small town called Jefferson here in northeast Texas."

No response. "And before that, I was in the Marine Corps. I served in Iraq and Afghanistan."

The boy's eyes lit up. "My father was a Marine in Afghanistan. But he got killed, or at least that's what my mother and stepfather told me."

Gideon grew curious. "Sounds like you don't believe them."

He turned his head away and coughed into his elbow. "I don't. I think they lied to me. There's a detailed list online of the soldiers killed in that war. It gives the name, rank, date, and cause of death for each person. But my dad wasn't on the list. I searched through three years of casualties."

"Hmmph." Gideon coughed again.

"You're coughing almost as much as me. Do you have pneumonia, too?"

"Naw, just allergies."

Loopy turned on his side to face Gideon. "My grandfather is . . . he is . . . well, he's a high-ranking military man. I believe he knows where my father is, and if I can someday just talk to him—" He coughed so violently and long that tears leaked out of the corners of his eyes.

Gideon patted him on the shoulder. Poor kid, so sick and all alone, maybe about to die, unless Sam could heal him. Of that, Gideon remained skeptical. "Listen, you'd better rest now and save your strength. We can talk later when you feel better." He walked back to his own bunk, hoping all was proceeding according to plan outside with Jaybird and Adam.

Austin Pratt staggered up beside him, unsteady as a drunk. He would have fallen if Gideon had not caught him by the arm.

"You know, Gideon, bringing that woman into our barracks would have put us all at risk." He rubbed his eyes and yawned. "I mean, if the guards found out, we could all be punished—or killed. Not worth the risk. Don't think she can save him anyway; he seems pretty far gone to me." His eyelids drooped and he yawned again. "Why help one man at the expense of thirty-six others?"

"Think about it, Austin—what if *you* get ill? Do you recommend we just shrug our shoulders and let you die so as not to endanger ourselves?"

Austin pursed his non-existent lips.

"You know, in Afghanistan, we risked our lives to recover the dead bodies of our men. Shouldn't we take the same risk for the living?"

Austin shrugged.

"And secondly, buddy, if you do want to go on living, you'll keep your mouth shut about Sam and Loopy, unless you want that baton of yours to find its way up your rectum and out your mouth. You know *nothing*—understand?"

Austin muttered something incomprehensible. He clutched the truncheon to his chest and threw himself down on his bunk with his back to Gideon. Two minutes later, the BB lay submerged in sleep, snoring and oblivious.

Bertie came over and inspected the slumbering man. He gave Gideon the thumbs-up sign. "The skinny bastard won't surface till morning. And when he wakes up, we'll tell him nothing happened— the whole thing got canceled. He'll never know."

Gideon smiled and sat tensely on the edge of his own bunk, jiggling one leg. He counted the minutes until Jaybird reappeared with Sam.

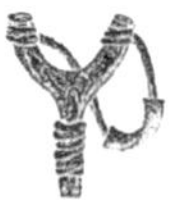

In Barracks 3, Sam and Olga stood with the door slightly ajar, listening. "At the signal," Olga said, "I'll go to the shower. You'll have about twenty minutes."

"Thank you, Olga. You're a good person."

"*Pshaw*—no I am not, but I am a healed person thanks to you. No more seizures. Just remember, I can know nothing about what you do tonight."

"Agreed." Sam knew Olga risked everything to look the other way. She rubbed her finger against the small glass jar of olive oil in her hand, the anointing oil blessed for healing.

Coo-ah, coo-coo-coo. Coo-ah, coo-coo-coo.

The signal. It sounded so much like a real bird, she almost hesitated. Sam let Olga walk out first, then counted to twenty before she slipped out the door and glided quietly to the dark area between Barracks 3 and 4. Jaybird materialized out of the shadows and took her hand without a word. They hurried across the gap and up the stairs to Barracks 4.

She found Loopy in a lower bunk where the men had laid him. She sat on the edge of the bed. "Hello, Loopy, I'm Sam."

The boy opened eyes glazed with fever. His cough was deep and phlegmy. Underneath her hand his forehead was hot.

"Jaybird told me you would come. He's been telling me about Jesus." He stopped and panted for breath.

She stroked his forehead. "Good. Think on Jesus; he's the one who is about to heal you. Now tell me your real name."

"Constantin Lupei."

"Oh." *Loopy. Lupei.*

She immediately recognized the name. General Huffman's office had emailed a bulletin to all the camps in Region VI, looking for him. She found Constantin in her database and responded. Shortly after, Ping announced the General's visit. Coincidence, or not? Was the General's visit simply part of a camp inspection, or was the boy so important the General was making a special trip for his sake? If so, she hoped it meant they were going to release him. She smiled at him. "A dignified and beautiful name."

Sam glanced at the men who stood nearby. "Gather round him quickly, lay your hands on his body, and pray silently." Taking a little oil on her middle finger, she anointed Constantin's forehead and chest with the sign of the cross. She gave thanks for his life. She thanked the Lord for his healing power and his sovereignty over all sickness. Then with faith and authority, she commanded his lungs to clear, his fever to break, his strength to return. "I cast out all bacteria, viruses, or infection from him. Be healed, Constantin, in the name of Jesus."

He gazed at her with hope in his gray eyes and spoke in a low voice. "Something changed." He smiled weakly. "I felt it."

Sam laid one hand on his burning cheek and the other in the center of his chest. "It's going to be all right. Close your eyes and rest. You'll be fine by morning."

A tear slid down from the corner of his eye. "Thank you." He wiped his face and breathed a full, clear breath. He sank into sleep almost immediately.

"I'm going to see if I can get him transferred to indoor work," said Sam, "maybe to the laundry or the kitchen." She grinned knowingly at the men. "Somehow, I think Ping will write an order to make that transfer this week."

As the men dispersed silently, a great longing emerged in Gideon's heart. When Sam passed by him, he reached out and gently took hold of her wrist. "I . . . uh . . . could you . . . " Abashed and tongue-tied, he pleaded with her through his eyes, which never left her face.

She stopped and gazed at him intently. "It's your lungs, isn't it? Cancer."

His request burned in his heart, but still he could not speak.

"I will pray for you, too, if that is what you wish."

He pressed his lips together and nodded. He wanted to tell her about the voices, but somehow he could not.

"She can't help you, fool."

"You deserve eternal torment, you piece of shit."

"Sit down on your bunk and tell me your name."

His knee creaked when he sat. "Gideon Marsh."

She smiled. "Nice name, that. Gideon was an unlikely warrior of the Old Testament."

Jaybird, who with Bertie, had followed them, said, "He don't know the story, but I'll fill him in later." Smiling, he shook his head and clicked his tongue. "What we gone do with these 'educated' people who ain't educated?"

Sam laughed softly, then addressed Gideon. "Your namesake was a bit hesitant to believe God, so he tested him." She gazed directly into his eyes. "You are a little unsure about God, aren't you?"

Gideon finally found his voice. "I want to believe. In Afghanistan, in combat . . . well, believe me, every breath, every hammer-stroke of the heart was a prayer."

"Do you have PTSD?"

Gideon squeezed his eyes shut and a single tear pushed out from the corner of his eye. Grit and rocks ground against each other in his throat; he couldn't utter a word.

She touched his arm gently. "It's going to be all right, Gideon." Sam glanced at Jaybird and Bertie. "Please lay your hands on him." She anointed his forehead and chest with the sign of the cross. Laying her palms on his chest, she prayed with an intensity that astonished Gideon. She commanded the cancer, every cell of it, to leave his body. *If she had commanded a platoon with the same confidence and power, the men would have gone out and died for her.* "Be healed, Gideon, in the name of Jesus."

Then she laid her hands on his head. "Lord, we know there is no sin that you cannot forgive if the sinner repents. Forgive Gideon all his sins, and help him to forgive himself. I cancel all assaults of the enemy against his mind. I declare an end to the mental torment and guilt. Make him clean by your blood, and protect him with a wall of fire from all demonic attacks and evil spirits. In Jesus's name, amen."

Gideon felt a shift within himself, a lightening, as if a burden had lifted. He wanted to tell Sam and thank her, but he could not trust his voice. He simply nodded as she took her leave. He lay down upon the bunk and tensed, waiting for the taunting voices, but they did not come.

Jaybird held out an elbow. "Miss Sam, it is my honor to take you back to your barracks."

She smiled and took his arm. "Thank you, Jaybird. Are you the harmonica player?"

"Yes. How'd you know that?"

"Your reputation precedes you."

They slipped out the door and quickly crossed the ground between the two buildings. He waited until the door closed behind her before he spoke softly. "Good night, Miss Sam. You a wonder." Soundlessly, he returned to Barracks 4.

Adam Chen had made his second circuit. Apparently, he had reached the end of his duty. As he passed the south watchtower, another guard met him and spoke to him in Chinese. "Nine o'clock. Your duty is over. How could you forget, silly egg?"

"Too tired to think." Adam lowered his head and rubbed his eyes with his fingers, managing to cover most of his face with his palm.

"Go back to the barracks. Have some Snow Beer. Wǎn ān."

"Wǎn ān." Feigning fatigue, Adam walked slowly toward the south entrance of the school where the guards' living quarters were located on the second floor. He entered the building, bypassed the stairs to the upper floor and continued through the main hall, praying he would not meet anyone.

He turned left into the short hall that traversed the center of the building and halted at the exit where Jaybird had unscrewed the light. Standing back against the wall, he watched the new guard pass by outside. Shortly after, he saw Olga return to her barracks. Adam forced himself to wait three minutes before he exited the building. Standing in the shadowy area between Barracks 3 and 4, he gave the mourning dove signal. *Coo-ah, coo-coo-coo. Coo-ah, coo-coo-coo.*

Jaybird immediately opened the door to Barracks 4 for him. In the darkened room, Adam hurriedly changed back into his own clothes. Jaybird took the uniform to the latrine. He wet the clothes and filled the boots with water before he dropped them into the pit. He listened for any stirring or sounds of life in the pit, but heard nothing. He peered into the latrine and saw the whites of the guard's eyes, staring at him. The hair stood up on Jaybird's head. The corpse—the man was stone cold dead—had not sunk. Anyone looking down into the latrine would see it.

He stripped off his own clothes and laid them on the ground. Naked, he gripped the plank over the cesspit with both hands and lowered his body into the stinking hole. It was the most disgusting thing he had ever done. He felt with his feet for the corpse and used his legs and weight to push it far under the surface into the reeking, slimy depths. When he got it down as far as possible, he hung chest deep in the pit. Using his arm muscles, he slowly pulled himself up. His feet made a sucking sound when he lifted them out; his lower body was coated in shit slime. At the outside faucet behind the barracks, he rinsed himself as best he could.

Shivering in the cold night air, he donned his clothes. At that moment, the reality of what he had done struck him hard—he had killed a man and buried him in a cesspit. "I'm sorry," he whispered. He glanced at the scudding clouds above him. *Forgive me, Lord, but what else could I do? We're in a war down here.* The clouds parted momentarily and he glimpsed Orion low on the eastern horizon. At the same moment, he heard a voice. "The battle is the Lord's." Whether it was audible or simply resonated in his mind, he did not know. He smiled. *Yes, it is, Lord, and no one can defeat you.* He blew out a breath and murmured to himself, "Time to get my ass inside before the guard comes back and uses it for target practice." He hurried back into the building with spring in his steps.

Inside, he found Adam and Bertie conversing. "How's the boy?" Adam asked.

"He hasn't coughed since Sam left. He seems to be sleeping peacefully." Bertie smiled. "And so is our dear BB—sleeping like a drunk who downed a bathtub of bourbon."

"Only bourbon ain't what he drank," said Jaybird.

"No, indeed. By the way, Sam also prayed for Gideon."

"Why?" said Adam.

Bertie touched his own chest. "Somehow she knew he had lung cancer. And PTSD. He's sleeping like a baby."

"Good. I hope she succeeded in both cases." Adam blew out a breath. "Whew, I don't know how peacefully the rest of us will sleep, but we've done all we can tonight. Wǎn ān."

Jaybird and Bertie spoke simultaneously. "What?"

"It means *Goodnight*. Time you learned a little Mandarin."

CHAPTER 47

THE UNEXPECTED

With muscles strung as tight and tense as an E-string, Adam Chen did not sleep well at all. He dozed in short snatches and had a nightmare that the guards burst into the barracks and took him out to be shot. He woke in the darkness, feeling gray and heavy-lidded, but even that could not dampen his anticipation of the eight o'clock rehearsal. He rose and paced back and forth like a captive lion, bursting with energy.

After roll call and his breakfast of stale bread and water, he and the other musicians hurried to the band hall. Woodwind, brass, and string instruments in their cases were stored against one wall. Two dusty tympani, a bass drum, and a xylophone sat abandoned in a corner. On the opposite side, there were practice rooms where he and Katie could warm up. The guards had moved the chairs aside and set the upright piano in the center.

Adam reveled in the pure pleasure of playing his own violin, of feeling like a musician again. He hadn't felt so energized about practicing since the very beginning of his career as a bright-eyed first violinist in the orchestra. He discovered another deep pleasure in Katie's singing. The dark, rich timbre of her voice unlocked him and filled him with happiness, as if she turned the key to time and took him back to childhood, where he first delighted in the sound and wonder, the magic of music.

And maybe it was more than magic. Here, in this place of death and dismemberment, the music remained above it all in a sphere untouched by malice or ugliness or cruelty. For a few blessed hours it enveloped them in its serenity, purity, and peace. If there was ever a balm in Gilead, this was it. Without a doubt it made the wounded whole; it healed the sin-sick soul.

And then there was Katie herself: in her beauty and youth she moved him and heartened him. Her spirit shone as brightly around her as the golden aura of a saint. The memory of her and the music carried him through each day and studded his dreams with more bright stars than a winter's night.

When she sang Cherubino's arias, she moved and gestured like a boy. Of course, (and it pained him to notice, since it brought his wife to mind) she had all the lovely attributes of a woman: curves more beautiful than a violin, high breasts, cornsilk hair, and such blue, blue eyes, shining with mischief and delight. It would be so easy to love her, and yet he could not. He maintained a physical distance from her, else he might give in to temptation and take her in his arms. He hoped she would be more bearable once she was costumed and made-up as a boy—believable and still attractive, but a boy. *You are not attracted to boys, Adam Chen.*

The other woman in the room was pudgy, middle-aged Annette Alba. Her graying, curly hair framed a round, lined face with small, brown eyes. Her nearly transparent skin color bore out the name Alba: white. She was a good-natured, cheerful teacher, but a nervous and highly inaccurate performer, completely lacking in self-confidence. She was at least malleable. Whatever they asked of her in terms of tempo, dynamics, and nuances, she tried to do. *Try* was the operative word— she generally missed the mark by miles.

Adam secretly called her Polly. She couldn't play eight bars without a*pol*ogizing. Squinting despite her spectacles, she would grimace and declare, "Oh, sorry, that should have been an F-sharp. I a*pol*ogize, the triplets were twice too slow." Katie voted otherwise. "As the Queen of

Wrong Notes, I crown her Klinkerella." Needless to say, the rehearsals bounced and lurched along like a tank on rocky, treacherous terrain. Eventually they got where they were going, but they all had bruises to show for it.

The two professionals looked forward to working with the new pianist. When that would be, they didn't know. After Annette left, Katie said, "Maybe the mystery pianist is Ping's father. He's supposed to be a professional."

"That could be awkward, but if he's an excellent pianist, I'll take him." Adam held up his right hand with crossed fingers. "Here's hoping."

Here's also hoping they don't find the missing Chinese guard. After a thorough search of the school building and barracks, no body and no evidence turned up. They had not yet begun interrogations, but the prospect seemed inevitable. In any case, for the time being, with one week to go before the concert, Adam believed he and the other musicians would be exempt.

Although the days went by in a dreary sameness, nothing stays the same, not even in a concentration camp. Loopy recovered, and thanks to Sam's front-office manipulations, got transferred to the kitchen, much to his chagrin. He and Arthur, a fourteen-year-old, were the only males amongst all the women. They chopped vegetables and meat for the cook and washed dishes.

The business of the camp went on as usual, but the number of new inmates increased. So did the number of corpses. To deal with the disposal of more bodies, two new incinerator trucks arrived. Jaybird and Gideon fed the bodies, one at a time into the metal ovens housed inside the trucks. Jaybird closed the hatch and waited while the guard inside the truck activated the intense flames.

Jaybird scratched his head. "Why do you think they chose this place to harvest organs?"

"A rural small town is perfect for secrecy," said Gideon. "It's out of the way, but close enough to Dallas-Fort Worth for quick delivery by helicopter. No major highways nearby, and the train only passes by twice a week. Who ever heard of Zabach, Texas?"

"Well, where are all these busloads of people coming from, two months after the roundup took place?"

"There are probably a limited number of organ-harvesting sites, so they cull people from other camps and process them here. The new arrivals are mostly young and healthy—perfect specimens for harvest."

They walked back to the OR for another body. The incinerator trucks were parked at the far northwest corner of the school, about fifty feet from the building. "You know, Jaybird, they're not gonna let any of us go. To keep this business secret, they'll have to silence all of us. We'll either be slaughtered for our organs or just murdered, sooner or later. I was in the Marines—I know how military minds work." He spat on the ground. "I guarantee you, we're dead men walking."

Jaybird grimaced. "I been payin' attention to the kids' choir." *And especially that beautiful, doe-eyed Donna who helps with them.* "I heard 'em singin' this mornin.' They sounded so sweet I almost cried." He gazed at Gideon. "Them, too?"

"Every pair of eyes and ears, every mouth that can bear witness."

They worked silently for a few minutes until Jaybird couldn't stand it anymore. They delivered another body, loaded it into the oven and started back. "Dang it, man, we got to break outta this joint."

Gideon nodded. "Yes, indeed, we do. I've had my fill of wholesale slaughter." He smiled at Jaybird. "Besides, I just got healed." He was still a little weak and underweight, but he was definitely on the mend; his cough had disappeared, and deep inside he felt the change—he felt life inside him. He wasn't the strongest he'd ever been, but if he got a few good meals, he would be. And thank God, the voices had quit tormenting him, his personal Greek chorus of persecution. But it was an adjustment: despite their absence, he kept anticipating their acid comments. "I don't want to die here; I'm hungry—for the rest of my life."

"Can't call you Shadow Man anymore. The Lord made you well, he sure did. I can sense it. When we got here, you looked about eighty. Now you only look sixty-five or so."

"You smartass." Gideon aimed a swat at Jaybird, but the younger man laughed and feinted to one side, so the blow struck only air. Gideon blew out his breath in a whoosh. "You know, Jaybird, we *are* going to break out of here. We'll come up with a plan. Those children will not die here, and neither will we, if I can help it. After all, we outnumber the soldiers—there's only fourteen of them. Even if we're weaponless, we got people with all kinds of skills and abilities here; we just have to figure out how to use them to coordinate an escape. Maybe my time in the military will serve us well."

"Gideon, bro, if the Lord is on your side, it ain't about numbers. You prob'ly don't know this, but the Old Testament dude named Gideon, he defeated 120,000 Midianite and Amalekite warriors with 300 men."

"With air strikes and heavy artillery?"

"Ha—he didn't need it 'cause God was his secret weapon. Here's how it went down. Before the battle, Gideon had 32,000 Israelites on his side, but God told him that was too many. God said, 'Tell the men who are scared for their lives to leave, and the next mornin' 22,000 hit the road.'"

"Why did God want him to reduce his fighting force?"

"To show what he could do. He didn't want the Israelites to think they won the victory on their own. See, God is a specialist in doing the impossible." Jaybird grinned. "It gets better. Now Gideon had only 10,000 men left, but God told him that was *way* too many. He had to whittle the number down to three hundred."

"How did he do that?"

"God told him to bring the men down to the water to drink and to separate the ones who lapped water from their hands from the ones who knelt down to drink directly from the water. God said to take the ones who lapped from their hands, and those were the three hundred."

"So how did three hundred men overwhelm 120,000?"

"It wasn't by brute force. Gideon split them into three companies and gave every man a trumpet—probably a ram's horn—and a pitcher with a smolderin' torch in it. The torches wouldn't catch fire until the air hit them. It was night, and the enemy was camped down in a valley. They snuck down and surrounded them. When everybody was in place, Gideon gave a signal, and they blew the trumpets, smashed the pitchers, and waved the lighted torches.

"They yelled, 'The sword of the Lord and of Gideon.'" Jaybird grinned. "The Midianites crapped their pants. They thought they were surrounded by a tremendous army. They panicked so bad, they even fought each other with swords. Then they ran, and that was all she wrote." Jaybird laughed. "The battle was won. The Israelites chased 'em down and killed their generals."

"How many casualties?"

"Zero."

"Hmmph. They won the battle against overwhelming odds without a single casualty." Gideon smiled. "In any age, in any war, it doesn't get better than that."

Jaybird returned his smile. "Expect the unexpected when the Lord is on your side."

"No talking!" One of the guards shouted at them and gestured impatiently with his rifle.

They picked up the body of a once-beautiful young woman and laid the desecrated corpse on the stretcher. They walked back to the incinerator trucks on the well-worn path. Out of earshot of the guard, Jaybird said in a barely audible voice, "Well, Gideon, my friend, if I was a guard in this camp, I'd be nervous as hell."

"Why's that?"

"'Cause the Lord sure ain't on *their* side."

MEMORY

He awoke on a tiled floor, wet and shivering. He recognized the tiered risers of a choir room. A large, framed wall hanging caught his eye. The white letters stood out against a deep blue background:

Orpheus' lute was strung with poets' sinews,
Whose golden touch could soften steel and stones,
Make tigers tame and huge leviathans
Forsake unsounded deeps to dance on sands.

(The Two Gentlemen of Verona, 3.2.79–82)

Shakespeare understood the power of music. He did, indeed: it could soften steel and stones, make tigers tame and leviathans dance. It could also heal and restore memory. It certainly had for him: playing the piano had returned him to himself. He was Joshua Brightman, concert pianist, husband of Sam and father of Peter. He had a history and he remembered it all.

He blinked and realized two Chinese soldiers stood over him. The taller one had startling blue eyes. The short, squat one seemed excited about something. To his left he saw Gideon and Jaybird, looking relieved and concerned, standing just inside the door, guarded by a third soldier. He groaned and squeezed his eyes shut again; with consciousness, pain returned.

The short Chinese soldier looked at his infected wound briefly and then asked him his name, age, profession, and religion. Ten minutes ago, he would not have known the answers. "Max Grandpied," he lied. *Not on any database, according to Chuck Broussard.* He didn't want them to know who he was. The rest was true. "Thirty-nine. Musician. Jewish." Then the commander in his halting, stammering way asked about his career and education as a pianist—what was in his repertoire, of all things. The man's eyebrows lifted when he listed his solo performances with major orchestras.

With his curiosity satisfied, the commander gave the guards rapid orders in Chinese. Thanks to Li Ling, Max caught a little of it: *operating room . . . blood . . . report . . .* Without a word, the guards brought in a litter and carried him out. He barely had time to lift a hand in farewell to his friends.

They bore him from the school building to a temporary building he had passed earlier in the day on the way in—where Jaybird picked him up when he fell. His joy at the return of his memory eclipsed any worries about his own fate. Even if he was going to his death, he remembered: *I am Joshua Brightman.*

Then his thoughts turned to Sam and Peter. They must still be in New York; he had last seen them at home in Brooklyn before his flight.

He had boarded a Monday-morning flight to Houston at 10:30 on a brisk, sunny September day. The plane took off from LaGuardia and made a U-turn to the south at low altitude, directly over the borough of Manhattan. An early cold front had swept the skies clean. He took advantage of the few empty seats to move from the center aisle to a window seat.

He had a splendid view of his native city, framed by the East River and the Hudson. The morning traffic surged up and down the avenues and the long diagonal of Broadway: cars, trucks, yellow cabs, and lumbering buses, clearly visible from his bird's-eye view. Plumes of steam rose from the buildings, a dense, spiky stone forest which appeared to rise out of the water. At the center of the narrow island lay the long, green rectangle of the Park. Its crown jewel, the Reservoir, caught the light and sparkled like a blue diamond. The noble bridges, Manhattan and Brooklyn, stood tall to his left, illumined by the rising sun. In all the years he had taken flights to and from the city, he had never seen New York in just this way. Its energy and pulsing life excited him and pleased him enormously. He wanted to fix the vision in his memory forever because it was so vivid and beautiful, and because he had a premonition that he would never see it that way again.

When they reached cruising altitude, the captain assured them they had a smooth flight ahead with good weather conditions all the way to Houston. The seatbelt lights went off, and the flight attendants headed down the aisles with drinks and snacks.

He drank a glass of orange juice and ate one of the energy bars he had stowed in his briefcase. He hadn't eaten breakfast, and he was tired from his predawn trip to LaGuardia. When he finished the snack, he locked his wallet, mobile phone, and keys inside the briefcase and stowed it under the seat. He had three hours to rest, and he intended to take advantage of the time. He eased the seat back, turned up the collar of his bomber jacket, zipped it up, and closed his eyes. Minutes later, he slept soundly.

The next thing he recalled was the moment he awoke on the forest floor, face down, in pain. A line of ants marched across pine needles and blackened leaf debris onto his hand and disappeared under the cuff of his jacket. All memory of the flight had vanished, and with it, all memory of his past.

How had he gotten from a plane in mid-flight to the forest floor—alive? Quite a mystery. The plane had probably begun its descent for landing when he fell. Maybe he was ejected at a very low elevation as the plane dropped out of the sky, and the forest canopy broke his fall—either that, or the hand of God. When Jaybird and Gideon found him, he was still clad in the bomber jacket, although he was barefoot with a sprained ankle and two dislocated shoulders.

During their sojourn in the woods, they told him about the plane crash in Caddo Lake, Legend's most spectacular news ever. But that was before his memory returned. Neither they nor he made the connection between the plane crash and his mysterious appearance in the woods. Why would they? According to the news, everyone on board had perished. Now he knew he was the sole survivor.

But what a thrill to recover his identity. Playing the piano had jump-started his memory; it had restored him to himself. Whatever his fate in the hands of his captors, he was grounded now. The irrational fear had vanished; he could face his future with courage.

Under orders from the camp commander, the OR doctors had worked hard to save his life. They re-opened his thigh wound and cleaned it thoroughly. They gave him fluids and powerful antibiotics intravenously. After a few days, he had graduated to antibiotic pills twice a day. They housed him in an empty second-floor room adjacent to the auditorium and made sure he had three meals a day.

Isolated from the other inmates, he spent the first few days recovering from the infection. As soon as his strength returned, one of the guards brought him into the auditorium and showed him the old seven-foot grand Steinway. "Colonel fixed piano. He say practice. You play concert soon."

Nothing, other than freedom and reunion with his family, could have pleased him more. He surveyed the auditorium from the stage; he guessed the building had been constructed in the first or second decade of the twentieth century. The wooden seats sloped upward from the base of the stage to the back wall. The seating area had a large center section flanked by two wide aisles with narrower sections to left and right. The acoustics in the hall seemed very live, but that would be tempered with an audience in attendance.

The beautiful grain and feel of the yellowed ivory keys, slightly textured and cool under his fingers, was a pleasure in itself. The piano had been tuned, and Joshua liked its warm, deep tone. Like a wanderer home after a long and wearying journey, he felt a profound relief to sit at the keyboard again, to play the music he loved. He slept better, his appetite improved, and a new, youthful energy suffused him. Time ceased to exist as he played. He would sit down to practice in the mornings and in what seemed five minutes, the guard brought his lunch. To amuse himself, he played the mournful tune Jaybird had played in the truck on the way to the hospital. "C minor, C minor, C minor." He laughed: his perfect pitch had kicked in, but they thought he was hallucinating.

Left to himself, on his breaks from practicing, he explored the auditorium and found one exit that led to an exterior metal staircase. It was a long way down to the ground; he had almost forgotten the auditorium was on the second floor. In the wings he found the light box and tested the three spotlights, the row of multicolored lights above the stage, and the house lights, all in working order. A heavy blue curtain, smelling of mold and dust, framed the rather small stage. He drew it all the way open on either side so its thick folds would not mute the sound of the piano out in the hall.

The camp commander, the strange little man who had interviewed him the first day, came often to hear him practice. Joshua knew the name Jiao-long meant "looks strong like a dragon." Unfortunately, Jiao-long's parents had miscalculated. Maybe the baby had looked strong like a dragon, but the man looked squat like a frog: wide-mouthed with a flat nose and opaque black eyes. "You play c-c-concert here for General Huffman—soon. You tell me what m-m-m-music you want. I get it, quick." Squatfrog told him about the singer and the violinist who would share the program, but he had yet to meet them. He had received the accompaniments to their arias and pieces, all of them familiar, especially the works for violin, which he had performed with Li Ling. He had never performed the Mozart and Gluck arias, but he had heard them many times.

For his part, he had decided to play a Scarlatti Sonata in D Minor and the Chopin C-sharp Minor Scherzo. As he practiced the Scherzo, he became aware of someone listening in the hall—Squatfrog, of course. No one else ever came in. At the end of the piece, he turned his head expecting some comment from the man. But it wasn't Squatfrog at all. Standing halfway down the left aisle was a small, brunette woman with tousled hair. Dressed in green scrubs, she stood stock still. She held sheet music in one hand, but her other hand covered her mouth.

Recognition struck him like lightning, rendering him mute. He heard her whisper, "Joshua?" She took a step forward and he rose from the piano bench at the same moment. Without regard for his injured leg, he ran three steps to the edge of the stage and leaped to the floor. She extended both arms, the music fluttered to the floor, forgotten, as she ran to meet him.

Long and wordlessly they embraced. Time and the turning of the world seemed to stop. He smelled her skin, felt its smoothness, the softness and warmth of her body. She felt his strong arms enveloping her, the solidity of his chest, the scratch of rough whiskers against her cheek; she remembered how perfectly they fit together.

She pulled back from him. "But how?" She searched his eyes. "How is it possible you survived?"

He kissed her gently on the lips and enfolded her again in his embrace. "I have no idea. I was asleep on the plane, and the next thing I knew, I awoke on the ground, in severe pain, in an unknown forest. How I got there is a complete blank. I had amnesia for weeks—I didn't even know my name. Two men found me wandering in the woods near Caddo Lake. I looked like a wild man—they mistook me for Bigfoot at first." He laughed. "They fed me and took care of me. But that very evening, the relocation took place, so we fled back into the woods. They later changed my name to Max Grandpied."

Sam laughed. "Max Bigfoot."

"It was when I played the piano in the school here that my memory returned."

"Oh my gosh! I was down the hall but didn't recognize you, even though it sounded like your playing. But Peter did." Sam's face crumpled and she began to cry. "He was right, and we didn't believe him. I thought you were dead."

Joshua brushed away her tears. "Peter is here, too? I can hardly believe it." He gazed into her warm brown eyes. "It's pretty miraculous, my love. Against all odds, I guess God wanted us to be together, and he wanted me to live."

A great lump formed in her throat; it hurt to speak. The words came out in a strained whisper. "Not half so much as Peter and I."

CHAPTER 49

TRIALS

The interrogations began on Monday, two days after the Chinese guard went missing. Sam did not know the guard's fate, but she guessed he was very likely dead. He disappeared on Saturday, the same night the men sneaked her into Barracks 4. She prayed the two events were not connected. If they were, the soldier had paid an awful price for the healings of Constantin and Gideon. She feared a dreadful reprisal from Ping; more suffering was sure to come.

Her reunion with Joshua was the light in her darkened universe. She mused on it with hope and sadness. Against all odds, he was alive. Peter would be overjoyed when he found out. He would soon see his father at the concert Ping had planned—for of course Joshua was Ping's special pianist. But would they—could they—ever escape this camp? Could they ever be a family again, or would they die here—slaughtered for their organs?

Thankfully, as crazy Ping's musical prize, Joshua had a chance to avoid that fate. Peter's fate was far less certain. Children had little to no value in the context of a concentration camp. He wore the red wristband; the threat of death hung over him like the suspended blade of a guillotine. One misstep, and Ping would retaliate mercilessly against the most helpless . . .

To keep her mind focused on something else that morning, Sam informed Ping that there was another musician at the camp, an excellent harmonica player. "Perhaps he could play at the concert, too."

"No. Classical music only."

"Well, the pianist might need a break during the program. After all, he will be accompanying the children, the violinist, and the singer. Then he has to play his own solo pieces. He'll probably give a better performance if he gets a rest."

Ping pursed his lips. "What k-kind of harmonica?"

"I don't know, but he had it with him when he came, so it should be down in the basement with the other belongings." (Of course it was not. Bertie had already retrieved it.)

He answered grudgingly. "All right. Find the harmonica and give the p-pianist a rest at the c-concert." Appearing preoccupied, Ping disappeared into his office and closed the door.

She thought it odd that he gave in so easily and didn't ask to hear the man play. Maybe his mind, like everyone else's in the camp, was on the whereabouts of the vanished guard. Sam gave a mental shrug and sent a note to Jaybird Alexander to inform him of his role in the concert.

While Ping holed up in his office, Sam seized the moment to do an internet search for the German name *Zabach*. From the moment the train passed the town station, she had wondered what it meant. To her surprise, *Zabach* was not German in origin, it was Hebrew. Her mouth dropped open when she read the meaning: *to slaughter, kill, sacrifice.*

That same Monday morning, unbeknownst to Sam, they interrogated Meredith Miller, one of the two women in Barracks 3 who refused to pray over Olga. Less than an hour later, two guards came for Sam as she worked in the office. They burst through the door, grabbed her by the arm, and jerked her out of the chair. Ping came out of his office to watch. He knew. Leaning on the door jamb, he smirked and shook his head. "Bad egg." The men wrenched Sam's arms behind her back and handcuffed her. They hustled her out the door and down to a room at the south end of the hall. She had to run to keep up with them. They pushed her down into the chair, the only piece of furniture in the bare space, then tied her arms and feet to it.

She recognized the blue-eyed soldier who had ogled her the first day. He stood very close in front of her. "Inmate Miller tell us you lead religious services in the barracks." He smiled. "Not allowed." As Sam opened her mouth to respond, he backhanded her violently across the face. The blow snapped her head to the side and split her lower lip.

Sam cried out in shock. "I prayed for people who were ill. That's all."

"Praying not allowed." Blue Eyes backhanded her again. This time she refused to cry out. Her cheek stung and she tasted blood.

"The guard who disappeared—where is he?"

"I have no idea; I know nothing about him."

"Who killed him?"

"I don't know."

For that, the other guard, who had a wide scar under his eye, struck her hand with a truncheon. She cried out and squirmed in pain.

"Where is the body?"

"I don't know. If there is no body, maybe he isn't dead. Maybe he deserted."

He slapped her face and screamed, "He not desert! Who killed him?"

She knew they wanted any lead they could get—she tried to block out the names of the men in Barracks 4 by mentally reciting Psalm 23.

The interrogation seemed endless. Blue Eyes covered the same ground over and over. Sam denied all knowledge of the crime. She could not tell if minutes had gone by or hours. Finally, she ceased to answer. Scarface, however, did not cease to strike her. When her arms were swollen and blue with bruises, he beat her legs. Blue Eyes screamed at her. "You tell who killed the guard. You tell where is his body."

"I told you, I know nothing about the guard."

Scarface changed batons. With the first shock to her mouth, she lost control of her bladder. By the time they got to her genitals, she had soiled herself. The stink enveloped her.

Blue Eyes again: "You tell who planned this murder."

Not now or ever. She would never implicate Jaybird or Gideon. Head lolling on her chest, clothes soaked with sweat, urine, and feces, she retreated inwardly. *Lord, help me. Christ help me.* She had no idea how long it went on. At some point she must have fainted. When she came to, her tormentors had gone. Only one guard remained with her. He sat on a metal folding chair beside her.

She had an overpowering thirst. She him asked for water.

"No water, no food."

She closed her eyes and drifted into sleep. She snapped awake when she felt a sharp prick in her thigh.

Smiling, her captor held a long needle before her eyes. "No sleep."

On Wednesday, the body in the latrine emerged from its depths. Jaybird, Gideon, and Adam had scanned the surface of the cesspit on every visit. They knew the body would rise eventually due to the decomposition process; the gases formed inside the corpse would cause it to float. If they could puncture the body and release the gases, it would sink again.

Unfortunately, they never got to enact their plan. One of the boys from Barracks 7 saw the corpse before they did. His shrill cries of alarm drew the guards, who forced two men from Barracks 5 to get down in the muck and lift the nude, partially decomposed body out. The news rushed through the camp with the speed and force of a flash flood. Rumors and hearsay swirled.

Ping had released Sam the day before, late on Tuesday afternoon. After thirty hours in the chair, the guards untied her, but she could neither stand nor walk; she had lost all feeling in her hands and feet. Supporting her on either side, the soldiers dragged her back to the barracks. They intended to dump her on a bunk, but Olga interceded. "Stop! She's soiled and reeking. I cannot have that filth in this barracks. It will make us all sick."

She pointed at Susannah and Valentina, a young Hispanic woman, newly arrived. "Take her out to the water faucet and wash her." Olga handed Susannah a small bar of soap. "I will get her clean scrubs." Olga stormed out, and the two men handed Sam over to the women.

Sam mumbled something inaudible. "What did you say, dear?" Susannah asked, appalled at the smell and the frail, battered state of her friend.

"Water. So thirsty."

Valentina held onto Sam while Susannah picked up the petite woman's tin cup from her bunk. "We're going to the water faucet now. You're so thin. Did they feed you at all?"

"No food, no water, no sleep."

"Oh my God," said Susannah. "Meredith Miller gave your name to them. But it sure didn't do her any good. She's a goner—yesterday they took her to the OR."

They half-carried Sam to the water faucet. Before they washed her, she drank three full cups of water. As quickly as possible, they stripped off her clothes. Blue, green, purple, and yellow bruises covered her swollen arms and legs. Edema had set in, and her lower legs resembled those of an elephant. The ankle bones were completely hidden by the fluid-filled flesh. "When we put her to bed, we'll elevate her legs so the swelling will go down."

The water was cold, and even in the afternoon there was already a chill in the air. They worked quickly to lather her body with soap and scrub off the dried excrement and old sweat. Her clothes were ruined. Sam spoke very little. Indifferent to her nakedness, she let them handle her as if she were a baby. She was so dazed, exhausted, and numb she didn't even care about her own fate.

Valentina wadded up her soiled clothes and tossed them into the latrine. Olga appeared with a towel and clean scrubs. "Let's dress her quickly and get her into the barracks under a blanket." As the sun sank into the west, the temperature dropped quickly. They fed her the evening meal of rice soup and put her to bed. Olga provided an extra blanket to help elevate her legs. Sam dissolved into sleep.

At roll call on Thursday morning, the day after the body was discovered, Ping addressed the inmates as they stood at attention in front of their respective barracks, except for Sam who rested in her bed according to Olga's orders. The day was gloomy, the sun a distant radiance that had not broken through the thick clouds.

"One of you m-murdered our g-g-guard. That person c-c-c-come forward now. *Now!*" he screamed. No one moved. Ping's face flushed with anger. "I wait fifteen minutes. Fifteen minutes! Then executions begin. T-t-t-ten people per day. Four men, four women, two children. Guards select."

Rainclouds massed above them, and a chill wind picked up. Lightning flashed, followed seconds later by the deep, prolonged rumble of thunder. The rain swept in from the west, a thick gray curtain that drenched them where they stood: men, women and children. Ping and two of his guards sheltered under an overhang at the back of the school, but even so, the long fingers of rain wet their shoes and pants legs.

"Get my v-v-violinist!" Ping bellowed. Adam trotted to the front. "Get violin and play."

He disappeared into the school and picked one of the student violins. He was not about to risk his own instrument in the damp weather. Hopefully, Ping wouldn't know the difference. He quickly tuned the instrument and returned. Ping let him stand under the overhang, against the wall.

"Play!"

For the most bizarre concert he had ever given, Adam played the J. S. Bach Partita in E Major. The piece for solo violin had seven dance movements. In order to fill up as much time as possible, he took all the repeats and kept conservative tempos. As he played, standing on the concrete stoop, he faced the thirty-six men of his own barracks. They stood at attention in four rows of nine on the gravel path, miserable and shivering in the rain.

Adam gave his best. He did not play for a petty tyrant and his minions; he played for the captured and enslaved people of a once-great nation. With all his skill, experience, and passion, he made the student-level violin sing. He drew more rich and beautiful sound out of the instrument than it had ever produced or likely ever would again. He spoke to his fellow captives wordlessly in tones they could all understand. Like a benediction, the music bestowed blessing and strength upon them, the promise of love and freedom, the certainty of an abiding joy at the heart of life: unaffected by pain, unbowed by cruelty, arising in the darkest circumstances.

Every woe has an end—and each person standing on that field of misery knew it. The music inspired them to square their shoulders and stand a little straighter. It touched them all—even the captors—but for the captives, it was a call to rise above fatigue and fear, pain, sadness, cold, and hunger. *Let not your heart be troubled, neither let it be afraid*, proclaimed the music: *Death is only a door that leads from Life to Life.*

The piece came to an end. Ping bellowed once more, "Who killed the guard? Step f-f-forward!"

Jaybird sweated despite the chill rain. The pressure to confess, to take the punishment, rose within him like steam confined in a kettle.

He had fired the silent shot—he had killed the guard. He alone should pay the price, and then it would be done. He didn't want to endanger the other men or God forbid, Donna, his beautiful brown-eyed girl. That was the tune he had played for her and the kids, "Brown-Eyed Girl." Her smile had warmed him, and her eyes, dark and liquid and deep as those of a doe, had shone. He had looked forward to playing many more songs for her at the concert, but forget about that. To keep her and the others safe, he had to forfeit his chance of that and of any future together with her. He ached to take one last look at Donna, but he kept his gaze straight ahead. He feared any movement might set off Ping or one of the guards.

Such a great pressure built up in him, he thought his head would explode. He blew out a breath—he would do it. Jaybird straightened his back and shoulders, but before he took a step, Gideon, who stood beside him, immediately sensed his intent. He grabbed Jaybird's arm to stop him and shouted like a drill sergeant. "Men, two steps forward!" The men of Barracks 4, all thirty-six of them, obeyed.

Then, like echoes overlapping, the responses sounded left and right: "Men, two steps forward . . . forward. Women . . . women . . . two steps forward . . . forward. Children, two steps forward!" until the inmates of every barracks had turned themselves in for the crime.

The heat of salt tears mingled with the cold rain on Jaybird's face and ran down his cheeks. He shook his head and blinked them away. *Now what? Will he kill us all?*

The corners of Ping's mouth descended and he clenched his fists. Frustrated and enraged, he spat on the ground. At the same time, a tiny part of him admired their courage and singleness of purpose. *Damn the Americans.* Although it would have given him pleasure, he couldn't slaughter them all—it would be a waste of precious organs. Too many for four surgeons to handle.

His mind churned. General Huffman would arrive on Sunday. The day after arrival he would inspect the camp; the concert would take place the next evening, on Tuesday, December 1. He did not want Huffman to know about the guard's murder. It would seem like he, Jiao-long, was not in control of the camp. No, better to act as if nothing had happened and go on with the concert he had arranged. A magnificent concert. He swelled with pride at the thought of it and felt some of his anger dissipate. He would get to the bottom of the guard's murder in time, but for now it could wait.

"Dismissed!" he screamed. "Get to work! Clean barracks, clean school—everything spotless for General! S-s-see to it!" He turned to Adam. "Musicians excused. You practice in auditorium—now!" He pointed to the second floor. "First dress rehearsal tonight. I come."

Jiao-long stalked off to his office on his short, stubby legs. When he entered the office, he remembered Sam had been gone since Monday. He turned back to the guard who stood in the hall. "Get S-s-sam Brightman," he demanded. "No cleaning for her. She works here." The guard hesitated. "Go now!" Ping screamed.

CHAPTER 50

THANKSGIVING

Adam Chen sat midway back in the auditorium while Katie and Max rehearsed. Their chaperone, a single guard, sat yawning in the last row. The three musicians had introduced themselves before the rehearsal began. The pianist's name was unfamiliar to Adam, but he had a very strong hunch he had met the man somewhere before. But where? The question nagged at him as he watched and listened to them work on the Gluck and Mozart arias.

The auburn-haired pianist far exceeded Adam's expectations. One cannot hide mistakes in Mozart's transparent music, and Max played the aria accompaniments flawlessly. He and Katie had an instant rapport. His crisp, clean playing supported her beautiful voice perfectly; it was a delight to hear them. As they worked, Max gave Katie some very good suggestions. She made the adjustments willingly, and the quality of the performance improved.

As he walked up to the stage to take his turn, Adam finally remembered where he had seen Max before. After tuning the violin to the piano, Adam asked, "Did you by any chance play the Ravel Concerto with the St. Louis Symphony about three years ago?"

Max smiled. "Yes, in October of 2023."

"Thought so. I played in the first violin section." Adam set his music on the stand and lowered his voice. "You know, they call this place the Farm because the goddamned sonsabitches here harvest organs from the inmates. That makes us all dead men walking. But you—you're the only one who was dead before you ever showed up."

Max's eyes widened and he cleared his throat. "I think you found me out." He opened the score to the Vivaldi Spring Concerto and laid his hands on his thighs.

"So what's the story?" said Adam.

Max regarded the violinist with a mixture of amusement and resignation in his hazel eyes. "Adam, let's play first. Afterward, I'll try to explain."

What followed was the most satisfying hour Adam had spent in years. "Max Grandpied" knew the violin repertoire, and he played with the utmost musicality and skill. Adam could have wept with pleasure.

Katie, who had been listening in the auditorium, joined them onstage when Adam and Max finished rehearsing the Vivaldi and a Beethoven sonata. Adam shook the pianist's hand. "Thank you, I'm looking forward to the rehearsal tonight and the concert. It's a great pleasure to work with you."

"Likewise."

The guard stood up as if to escort them back to their barracks. Adam addressed him. "We have a few minutes left in our rehearsal, so we're going to talk through a few passages."

The guard shrugged and slumped down in his seat again.

Adam turned back to the others. He pointed out a passage in the piano score as if discussing it. He spoke quietly and rapidly. "And by the way, I saw you arrive in the rain with the other two guys a few weeks ago. Gideon and Jaybird—they live in my barracks now. When they found out you had been sent to the OR, they thought you were dead. Everyone did."

Max pointed at the same passage and nodded. He too kept his voice low. "Actually, the OR doctors fixed me up. They cleaned my wound and gave me some strong antibiotics, thanks to the camp commander, who is crazy for piano music. When I played the Kawai in the hall that day, he heard it and came running. The music not only saved me, but it restored my memory."

Adam gazed pointedly at Max. "You and all onboard supposedly perished in the plane crash at Caddo Lake."

"That's the part I can't explain. I was on the flight, but I don't know how I survived. I don't even remember the explosion."

"But you are Joshua Brightman," whispered Katie. "I met Sam and Peter on the train coming down here. She told me you were her husband. I actually saw you perform the Tchaikovsky First in Chicago." She laughed. "You're the best and only deceased pianist I ever worked with."

Max smiled. "Katie, if I were dead, your singing would bring me back to life." His smile faded and he gazed at them earnestly. "For the time being, I have to be Max Grandpied. I don't want the colonel to know I survived the plane crash or discover my relationship to Sam and Peter. I'm afraid he might try to use it against us."

"He might." Katie thought about the red wristband Peter wore and the brutal torture Sam endured. Ping could use Joshua or Peter as leverage to coerce Sam into confessing what she knew, or to work against each other or their friends to do his nefarious bidding. As isolated as Joshua was, she guessed he didn't know about her torture. Sam would recover, so Katie decided not to upset him—he would find out later anyway.

"No problem, Mr. Grandpied," said Adam. "But I'm gonna deliver the news of your second miraculous survival to your friends."

"Please do. They only know me as Max."

Katie smiled. "Don't worry, Max, Adam and I will keep your secret."

"Time to go," announced the guard.

The agent of blunt force trauma, a 5/16" steel ball bearing, rested at the bottom of the latrine under a five-foot-deep shit stew. After the deed was done, Jaybird had recovered it on the gravel path and dropped it into the opposite end of the foul-smelling latrine from the body. No one would ever find it. The murder weapon, Jaybird's slingshot, lay hidden in its black pouch, along with more steel balls and his harmonica, above his bunk. Because the barracks had been hastily constructed with cheap materials, the board at the top of the wall had already warped, creating a small gap between two of the open rafters. It was just large enough for the pouch to squeeze through into the soffited eave.

On entering the barracks after Ping's dismissal, Jaybird's legs almost betrayed him. He opened his mouth to thank Gideon, but his throat constricted and words failed him. He simply laid his hand briefly on the other man's arm in passing. He wiped his eyes with his sleeve, walked carefully to his bunk, and climbed up into it. He had managed fine outside, but now his whole body trembled in a delayed reaction. He turned on his side and closed his eyes.

The men had been careful to show no emotion outside when Ping dismissed them. Adam went straight to his rehearsal in the auditorium, but the others, once inside the barracks, laughed in relief and smacked each other on the shoulders. Many of them congratulated Gideon. "That took balls, man." He sighed in relief that his plan had worked— at least so far—and that the men and women of the other barracks had spontaneously followed suit.

"Thankfully, we have a reprieve," he said. "It may be due to General Huffman's visit two days from now. Imagine that—for once, his presence will actually help people. He would be so disappointed—the only person that sonofabitch ever works to help is himself."

As the other men dispersed, Loopy appeared at his elbow. The boy had fully recovered from the pneumonia. "How do you know that about him? Have you had dealings with him before?"

In the aftermath of the terrible tension he had just endured, Gideon's guard was down. He spoke quietly without thinking, as if to himself. "I sure did. Way back, I was married to his daughter. A lifetime ago." He glanced at Loopy, or rather Constantin, as they called him after his cure. The blood had drained from the boy's face.

"Are you okay? Not feeling ill again, are you?"

"No, I'm all right. Gideon, did you and your wife have any children?"

The older man laughed harshly and looked away. His nostrils flared and the muscles of his jaw tensed. "She was supposedly six months pregnant when she left me—or thereabouts, I should say. I was overseas when she moved out. Edie didn't tell me about the pregnancy—one of the neighbors did. I came home from Afghanistan to an empty apartment. She had fled, and her father, the effing general, wouldn't tell me where she and the baby went. He knew, of course."

"What year was that?"

"2010."

"Did you search for them?"

"Yeah, for months, not that it did any good. The private detective I hired quit after three weeks. The General really didn't want her and the baby found. His goons threatened the detective's life, burgled his house, and killed his dog. He advised me to give up the search if I valued my life; he even advised me to go into hiding. You see, this is the way the General operates: he has a long arm, and he is totally ruthless."

"I was born in 2010."

Gideon peered at the boy, expressionless.

"My mother is General Richard Huffman's daughter."

The revelation superheated the air like lightning, producing a thunderous shock wave that rocked them both. Afterward, neither one of them remembered moving, but they found themselves locked in a fierce embrace.

"They told me my father's name was Gunnar Ross," Constantin whispered, gripping Gideon with arms like steel bands. "They tried to throw me off so I could never find you."

Gideon smiled. "You know what I just realized? This is the last Thursday in November. It's Thanksgiving."

Austin Pratt jarred them out of it. He dropped a box of brushes and cleaning supplies onto the floor. "Get to work, men. We're gonna clean this barracks first, and then the auditorium. When General Huffman inspects this place, the walls and floor better shine like gold."

That afternoon, they had the pleasure of seeing—and hearing—Bigfoot play his solo pieces in the auditorium. The men of Barracks 4 were assigned to clean the space, but Jaybird was so spellbound by the music he hardly moved. Gideon had to nudge him three times to do his work. Max practiced intently, ignoring the noise of brooms, mops, and one outdated vacuum cleaner. The inmates worked without speaking. The music, if only temporarily, washed away their sadness and provided a respite from the ugliness and monotony of their days.

That evening, as soon as Austin Pratt left for his shower, Gideon called a meeting in Barracks 4. He stood with the woodstove at his back, facing the rows of tired men who sat on the floor before him, like the children at library story time. As he stood to address them, he knew it was time for bitter reality, not tall tales.

"Men, it's my opinion, if we just continue to do our work here and hope for some kind of deliverance, we'll all be dead within a year. They will never let us go. We've witnessed the greatest atrocity ever to take place on American soil. They're going to get rid of all of us, either by harvesting our organs or by straight-up murder. They have no mercy. They're going to murder the women and children, too. Does anyone disagree? If so, speak up now."

He gazed at the men and waited. Silence.

"All right. I called this meeting to plan an escape. My goal is to get us all out without a single casualty."

Thomas snorted and shook his head. "Gideon, are you nuts? You expect almost 300 people to walk out past armed guards through an electrified fence without getting shot or fried? That's impossible."

"Maybe or maybe not, Thomas. With God all things are possible. Believe me, I've been thinking about this nonstop. We have to try. If we do nothing, we're all dead." His motivation had tripled in intensity since his reunion with his son. He wanted to free Constantin, Katie, all the children, and every last man and woman in the camp if he could. "The night of the concert, everyone will be gathered in the auditorium: Ping and the General, inmates, doctors, nurses, and most of the guards. Today is Thursday—Thanksgiving, actually. The concert is next Tuesday; we have five days to get ready. I've got a plan, and some of you are going to play crucial roles. Adam, Thomas, Jaybird, Constantin, and Bertie, we have to talk details. The rest of you men, go on to bed. The fewer details you know, the better, in case it all goes sideways and there are interrogations." The men rose wearily and headed for their bunks.

"Huddle around," said Gideon. Constantin was the first to receive his assignment: it made him glad of his kitchen-boy career, as the task fell to him because he had access to the stove. Thrilled, and yet terrified he might fail his father, his heart thundered in his chest, like the sound of approaching cavalry.

Gideon kept his voice very low. "Timing and strict obedience are essential to our success. And we are going to keep this among ourselves. We can't afford any leaks about this plan." Gideon glanced at the five men. "We do have to get word to Katie Lamb so she and Donna are prepared." *Katie Lamb. Just to speak her name charged the atmosphere.* She never left his thoughts.

The mention of Donna's name conjured her image for Jaybird. The cropped, curly hair framing strong cheekbones and a prominent nose, the lovely mouth. Slender yet strong, she stood with an upright posture.

I am black, but comely, O ye daughters of Jerusalem, as the tents of Kedar, as the curtains of Solomon. He searched for her each morning during roll call as she and Katie stood amongst the children. Gentleness in the eyes, but strong will and fierceness in the bones. *Behold, thou art fair, my love; behold, thou art fair . . .* He read her. With certainty, he knew her from afar.

"Susannah told me Donna was a karate instructor in her former life," said Bertie.

That's the fierceness, all right, thought Jaybird.

"Hmm. Those karate skills could be very useful." Gideon nodded thoughtfully. "And deceptive. The guards won't expect a woman to be a physical threat."

"You *ain't* gonna put her in combat." The words leaped out of Jaybird's mouth in a commanding tone before he knew what happened.

Everyone regarded him with surprise. He conversed often with Gideon and Constantin, but he rarely spoke to the other men, and never so forcefully.

Gideon raised his eyebrows. "Of course not. But it's good to know she could defend herself and the children if necessary."

"All right." Jaybird dropped his eyes to the floor.

Gideon ran a hand through his sandy hair. "Jaybird, since you're gonna play your mouth organ at the concert, you'll be backstage with the other performers. More on that later. We'll need a guard's uniform and boots, Adam's size, hidden backstage by the night of the concert."

Bertie spoke up. "Susannah works in the laundry—she can get the uniform. Olga can probably bring it to the auditorium. She's wholly on our side ever since Sam healed her epilepsy, and she seems to have free access everywhere."

"Excellent." Gideon continued. "I also need a diagram of the auditorium showing where all the exits, staircases, and restrooms are located." He laughed. "Sam can probably get that intel from Max, Ping's musical hamster: the auditorium is his cage and the piano is his exercise wheel. Since he spends all his time in there, he'll know the layout."

"I can get messages to Sam," offered Constantin. "She comes into the cafeteria every day either to eat or to get food for Ping."

"Good. Tell her tomorrow. We need to get this plan underway." Gideon smiled at Constantin. Then the corners of his mouth dropped and he sniffed the air. The smell of cigarette smoke drifted into the barracks, the signal that Austin Pratt had returned. One of his privileges for snooping on the inmates was his cigarette ration. He always stood outside the barracks and smoked after his nightly shower.

"Okay, meeting's over. Everyone back to your bunks."

When Austin Pratt entered the dark barracks ten minutes later, all he heard was the sound of snoring.

But not everyone slept. With his arms behind his head, Jaybird lay in the dark, eyes wide open, envisioning a future he prayed would come to pass, but one he knew he might never see. His lips moved, as under his breath, almost soundlessly, he spoke into the atmosphere an ancient song:

> *For, lo, the winter is past, the rain is over and gone.*
> *The flowers appear on the earth; the time of the singing of*
> *birds is come, and the voice of the turtle is heard in our land;*
> *The fig tree putteth forth her green figs, and the vines with*
> *the tender grape give a good smell.*
> *Arise, my love, my fair one, and come away.*

If they survived the escape, where would they go? How would they live? How and where did not matter, Jaybird decided, as long as they were together. He could live off the land the rest of his life. As long as they were together.

Arise, my love, my fair one, and come away . . .

Gideon lay on his side, his breathing irregular and shallow, his muscle tension so tight he felt incapable of movement, like a toy soldier made of lead. He needed a sign. He needed a sign from God, who had never ever spoken to him. He implored the almighty being he had ignored his entire life outside of combat: *Tell me this is the right thing to do. Please tell me that I am not leading a latter-day charge of the Light Brigade. Lord, do it not for my sake, but for the sake of my son and the innocent children, Katie, and all the men and women I do not want to harm.*

A sign, Lord, please give me a sign . . .

GRAND-PÈRE

On Sunday afternoon, two days before the concert, they sat in Jiao-long's office, drinking the best Chinese tea the colonel had to offer. General Huffman would inspect the entire facility the next day, but he already knew of the camp's efficiency. He complimented Jiao-long on the number of harvested organs. "Colonel, your operation here is small, but you should be proud. Your medical staff has done excellent work. Percentage-wise, you are the most profitable camp in Region VI. My congratulations to you all."

"Thank you, General." With that, Jiao-long relaxed slightly. Very slightly—as much as he would have in the presence of a king cobra. The General's reputation for violent rages and volatility preceded him. Jiao-long forced a smile at the hulking man across the desk, while his collar grew damp from perspiration.

"Now, I have a special matter to discuss with you," Huffman said. Jiao-long sipped his tea nervously. Secretly, he wished he had served whiskey. He needed a drink to face this giant. In the company of the General, he felt as small and undistinguished as a gray pebble at the base of a mountain. The cup in Huffman's enormous hand looked like a toy, a dollhouse miniature. The man's cold eyes were like the dark portals of hell; he seemed to fill the office and take up all the oxygen. Jiao-long felt suffocated. He was glad the desk separated them.

"I want to see Constantin Lupei as soon as possible."

Jiao-long's brows drew down in puzzlement. "Who this C-c-c-constantin?"

"My grandson. He's an inmate here."

Jiao-long stopped his cup halfway to his mouth. Sam told him the General's office had enquired after the young man, but he had no idea he was the grandson of Region VI's governor. He broke into a clammy sweat. *Had they already harvested the young man's organs? Oh, please, no.*

"The woman from your office notified me that he is here, in Barracks 4."

Jiao-long quickly set the cup down to hide the trembling of his hand. It clattered on the saucer. A brown surge of hot tea washed over the edge like a rogue wave and burned his thumb. He winced. "I send for him now. You will t-t-t-take him home?"

"Yes, on Wednesday when I leave, but first I want to speak to him—privately."

"Certainly. Excuse me a m-moment."

Jiao-long closed the door carefully behind him and hurried over to Sam's desk. She was back at work, inputting information into the database. Post-torture, she moved slowly and avoided eye contact, whether out of fear or loathing, he didn't know. Nor did he care.

"C-c-c-c-constantin Lupei. Find him quick. He still l-l-living?" His heart raced—how could he have known the General's grandson was among the inmates? Sweat ran down both sides of his face. He knew Huffman would rip out his Asian heart and eat it raw if he thought Jiao-long had killed the boy.

Even with her peripheral vision, Sam could see the sheen of perspiration on Ping's face. "Let me check." She had the joyous job of recording the names and death dates of all the inmates Ping butchered. It was possible Constantin had died while she was absent from the office, during the days of her torture or in the aftermath when she recovered. She suspected not, but she feigned difficulty in finding the information. She rubbed the sore tendons in her arms and dragged the process out as long as she could to keep Ping stewing. *Be afraid, you short, chunky pissant tyrant. Have a dose of the poison you deal out to the innocent every day.*

"Ah, yes. He's still alive and living in Barracks 4."

Ping let out a repressed breath, visibly relieved. He wiped the sweat from his brow. "Send guard to get him now. Have g-g-g-guard take him to choir room and wait there for General Huffman. He talk to him privately."

Prior to his imprisonment, Constantin had never set foot in an American public school, much less one in such a rural setting. An alumnus of expensive Swiss and New York private schools, he was surprised by the plainness and shabbiness of the choir room: its battered upright piano (*not a shiny black Steinway or Bösendorfer?*), the worn linoleum, the cracked, peeling, yellowish paint, the lone wall hanging with its Shakespeare quote, and the cheap metal folding chairs that must have created a literal pain in the collective asses of the Zabach High School Choir.

"Sit," said the guard. He placed one of the metal chairs beside the chipped and battered teacher's desk.

Constantin sat. He wiped his hands, damp from washing dishes, on his pants while his heart thumped like a kettledrum. When he asked the guard who had summoned him where they were going, the man said, "Big honor. General Huffman will talk to you in the choir room."

Oh, no. He had hoped to evade his grandfather during the visit. The kitchen inspection, scheduled for Monday, would have been his riskiest moment for discovery. He had planned to hide behind the gleaming silver refrigerator or flee into the pantry, but it was too late now—the General had summoned him.

On Ping's orders, the whole camp had been spruced up for the honorable general's visit. Constantin had personally scrubbed the kitchen floor yesterday, while Arthur, the other kitchen boy, wiped down all the counters and cleaned the electric stove, outside and in. Both the men and women had cleaned and painted the barracks. The inmates worked during the day, but at night in Barracks 4, Gideon and the other men made plans. Constantin had an assignment he had to complete for them on the day of the concert. They hadn't filled him in on all the details, but he knew his part was important. That made him more nervous than this meeting; he would rather die than let them down.

As he fidgeted on the hard, cold metal chair, he wondered how the General had discovered his whereabouts. At the moment he wasn't sure if his palms were damp from dishwater or fear. *Il faut du courage pour avouer la peur.* It takes courage to admit fear. *All right, I admit it: to be perfectly honest, I am very, very afraid.*

On the opposite side of the wooden desk, a single empty chair waited. He knew his grandfather would soon arrive and fill it, all six-feet-six and two hundred eighty malevolent pounds of him. Neither he nor the guard spoke. The silence pressed on his ears. What was the purpose of this private conference? No doubt his grandfather would berate him for running away from New York. *He hadn't followed orders.* Everyone in the General's world followed orders—especially if the orders came from the General. Two days before all hell broke loose, the General had warned Tony Amore that he, Stella, and Constantin were to gather supplies and then remain in the brownstone until further notice, while the military action took place.

Some military action—a complete overthrow of the United States government. And General Richard Huffman, the traitor, had been a part of it.

On the first day he had come to the camp, when he realized the guards would strip him of all his possessions, he had hidden Dumitru's diary and the three letters from his grandfather. What seemed to be misfortune became an excellent opportunity. They chose him and Thomas to bury the murdered woman and her wailing child, now forever silenced. As they waited under the stadium for the guard to bring them shovels, Constantin removed the diary from his backpack, still wrapped in the plastic liner from the Chicago hotel. He laid it on the ground and covered it with his blazer.

Once the guard returned with the shovels, he and Thomas dug the grave. They laid the bodies in it, with the baby girl lying on her mother's breast. A bloodied pink bow remained clipped to the child's thin brown hair, what was left of it—half the infant's head had been blown off. As they filled in the grave, he remained hyper-aware of the guard. When the man turned away to take a piss, Constantin reached under the blazer and placed the bundle into the hole. He quickly covered it with dirt before the guard resumed his watch.

Heavy, rapid footsteps out in the corridor interrupted his thoughts. The guard snapped to attention, and Constantin's pulse accelerated. He straightened his back for the confrontation with *Grand-père*—he had better keep his wits about him. The door opened, and one of the most dangerous men in the world strode into the room, dark and tall and menacing as the Angel of Death.

Constantin rose as the General entered. Huffman spoke gruffly in the deep, raspy Texas accent Constantin remembered so well. "Guard, you may go. Close the door and wait outside." As the guard exited, the General crossed the room in four long strides.

"Constantin." He held out his arms in a stiff, stilted fashion, leaned down, and embraced his grandson awkwardly. Their chests did not even make contact. "We have a lot to discuss. Sit."

Constantin resumed his seat while the General settled his bulk upon the teacher's chair. His eyes, dark and opaque, bored into Constantin's. "Why did you run away from New York? Tony and Stella were frantic when they couldn't find you. And how in hell's name did you end up here?"

No pleasantries, no display of concern, no *How are you? I've missed you.* Welcome to Antarctica: the General radiated as much affection and warmth as the Ross Ice Shelf.

"For a long time I've wanted to know more about my real father— what happened to him in Afghanistan. I searched for records of him online, but I found nothing. You knew him, and you have the highest rank in the military, so I thought you might be able to fill in some of the blanks. I decided to come to Texas to ask you all my questions. I knew Tony and Stella would never allow me to leave during the academic year, so I ran away. I was impulsive—it was no fault of theirs."

"They were distraught when they couldn't find you—especially in light of the civil unrest that followed."

Civil unrest. Quite a euphemism. "I know. I am very sorry I worried them. I thought the military action you mentioned to Tony would be limited to the city. I had no idea it would encompass the entire nation."

"Tell me how you got to this camp."

Constantin outlined his route, the long bus ride to Pittsburgh, the brief plane trip to Chicago, his overnight stay there, and the chaos at the train station. "I boarded a train to Dallas. En route, some general announced the cou—I mean the change of government—over the train's speakers. That's how I found out what was happening. When we got to Texas, the train just stopped in the middle of nowhere. The soldiers forced us to get off and walk through the woods to this school."

"And why did you not immediately tell the camp commander you were my grandson?"

"It was all confusion at first; I had to do as I was told. After I was assigned to a barracks, I told some of the other inmates, but they didn't believe me. They thought I was grandstanding. They mocked me, and one or two threatened my life. I was the youngest person in my barracks—no match for three dozen grown men—so I just dropped the subject. There are some really angry patriots in this camp."

General Huffman raised his voice. "Don't you think I'm aware of that?" Irritated, the General tapped the desk with the fingers of one hand.

"I thought you were a patriot, too, Grandfather. Why overthrow our government?"

The General smiled. "To create a better one." He sniffed. "Government by the people, for the people, and of the people—how asinine. It is ridiculous and naïve to think the American people know what's best for this nation. Most of them are morons. Their goals are a full belly, a roof over their heads, and twenty-four-hour entertainment. Whether they know it or not, the day of the nation-state is over. The plan is underway to merge all the nations into a single entity with a sovereign lord and his Council of Nine. The peasants will have their needs met, but the elite will rule."

The Nine again. But a sovereign Lord? *The Prince of Darkness, by any chance? Or are we reverting to a medieval monarchy?* "And you are part of that elite?"

"Of course, and by extension, so are you, your mother, Dumitru, and Grigori. Life is about to get much better for the average Joe." The General smiled pleasantly. "No more responsibilities, no more deciding where to live or what work to do. Superior minds will make the decisions. Go along with the program and follow orders—there the common man will find the road to utmost security. Eventually, the morons will understand how much better life will be. They will be taken care of, and they will like it."

Taken care of—as in the genocide common to every totalitarian regime in history. "Will they continue to enjoy being butchered for their internal organs?"

The General sat dangerously still, like a viper ready to strike. His dead, snake-like eyes bored into Constantin, who, in a tense contest of wills, refused to look away. Finally, the General dropped his gaze and produced a forced sound meant to be a laugh. "My grandson has a sense of humor." He cleared his throat. "We reserve that honor for the Christians, the Jews, and political dissidents: the Deluded Ones, Purveyors of the Great Lie." The General sat back in his chair and crossed his arms over his chest. "We made sure to bring you up free of that delusion. Believe me, the world will be a better place without them."

"I see." Constantin studied his hands, trying to control the overpowering impulse to launch himself across the desk and rip out the throat of the smug, evil bastard. *The Deluded Ones, such as Sam, who had prayed over him and brought him from near death by pneumonia to perfect health, who had healed Olga of epilepsy and his father of lung cancer.* "Well, what can you tell me about my father? Did he really die in Afghanistan?"

General Huffman pursed his lips. "Sad to say, he did."

Interesting, since he seems to be alive and well in Barracks 4. "How did he die?"

"He was killed, along with two other soldiers by a roadside bomb. He had only been there three weeks. The vehicle he rode in was destroyed, and we only recovered parts of his body." The General paused and arranged his features into what he imagined was a picture of real sorrow. "Just damn bad luck, boy."

"Where did it happen?" *Tell me, you lying, ridiculous fool.*

"Qazi Bandeh."

"Why didn't you tell me the facts sooner?"

The General's smile, which never reached his dead eyes, was as grotesque as the rictus of a corpse. "You were so young. Your mother and I wanted to spare you the ugly details of his death."

General Huffman suddenly sat up straight, placed his hands flat on the desk, and leaned forward. "Well now that I've answered your questions, Constantin, there is an important matter we must discuss. Dumitru informed me that his diary is missing from the house in Geneva. He suspects you took it with you when you left Switzerland and returned to New York in August."

Constantin froze. Should he admit the truth? Should he deny all knowledge? Thank God he had had the foresight to bury the diary where no one would ever find it. He stalled for time.

"Why does he think I took it?"

There was a bitter quality in General Huffman's laughter. "He has closed circuit cameras everywhere, including the library. He, Talyssa, and Grigori had gone out for dinner, but you stayed in the chateau."

Constantin tried to remain impassive, but he felt a rush of heat in his cheeks. *No point in lying now.*

"Recently, when he couldn't find the diary, he played back the video footage. Took him a while, but he figured it out. Why did you take it?"

"For the same reason I ran away from New York—I was curious about my father. I took the diary to see if I could get information about my . . . uh . . . origins."

"Did you take it with you to New York?"

"Yes."

"Is it there in the brownstone?"

Constantin did not answer.

"Dumitru wants it back."

"Why is it so important to him?" Constantin tried to appear nonchalant. "All I read was some dumb stuff about him eating an apple and watching a fly walk on his hand. Boring as hell. I didn't think he would miss it, so I dumped it."

"Why did you do that?"

"It was a load of self-absorbed drivel—pure bilge. Excess weight in my backpack."

"Where and when did you dump the diary?"

"September. In the river."

"What river?"

"The one in Chicago."

The General blew out a breath. "Two months in the water. It must be ruined by now." He tapped the desk with the fingers of his right hand. "Probably not worth it to dredge the river. They may have disintegrated, and if any pages are left, they're probably illegible."

Constantin agreed. "He used an old-fashioned fountain pen with water-based ink." He smiled. "No one can read his diary now—not even the fishes or the crabs."

For a moment, the General lowered his head, closed his eyes, and massaged his forehead with one hand. Then he drew in a deep breath and lifted his gaze to his grandson. "Let me give you a warning, Constantin. Your stepfather is an immensely wealthy man with unlimited resources and very powerful friends. Very territorial. He is neither sympathetic nor sentimental; he will eradicate his enemies without compunction. He would kill his mother if she got in his way."

A disturbing thought entered Constantin's mind. "Would he kill Grigori, his own son?"

"Depending on the circumstances—yes, I think he would. No one, including your little brother and your mother, are exempt from his murderous will."

He let Constantin digest that for a moment. He leaned back in the chair. "What happened to your backpack?"

"I don't really know. They stripped us of all our personal possessions when we arrived here. I left it on a heap of suitcases, purses, briefcases, mobile phones, and laptops just outside the football stadium. Where it went from there, I have no idea."

"I intend to find it. And I hope for your sake, you are telling the truth." Had his eyes been lasers, he would have vaporized Constantin. "If you lie, boy, you die." The General stood so abruptly that his chair screeched backward and almost fell over. "Believe it—I'm your judge, jury, and executioner."

"This is the way your new, better government works, I suppose. The only laws are the ones you create and observe for your own purposes, to protect your power. Very convenient—streamlined to destroy one's enemies. In the new America, dissent equals death."

Richard Huffman's eyes gleamed with a smug, cruel pleasure, and he smiled. "Exactly." He thrummed his fingers on the desk. "I inspect the camp tomorrow. Tuesday is the concert, which I imagine will be excruciating, don't you?" He chuckled.

"Oh, I'm looking forward to it." Constantin smiled. "It may surprise you, Grandfather. It may very well be smashing."

Huffman sniffed. "I doubt it. And by the way, when I leave here on Wednesday morning, you're coming with me."

Like hell I am. Far from cowing him, the General's words created an implacable resolve in Constantin's heart. *I found my father despite your lies and manipulations, and no matter what, I will not leave him now.*

"Guard!" the General shouted. The man stepped quickly into the room. "Take this inmate back to his barracks."

CHAPTER 52

ADVENT

Olga's freedom of movement and her new fealty to Sam made her a perfect courier. She conveyed Sam's latest message verbally to Katie Lamb. She found the singer in the gym supervising the children's exercise. The shouts of the children, the noise of their running, and the thumps and smacks of basketballs resounded off all the hard, flat surfaces, creating an excellent cover for her words. "When you take the children to rehearse with Max the pianist for the first time, allow Peter ten minutes alone with him before the other children enter."

"Why?" asked Katie.

"Sam said Max is his father, but Peter doesn't yet know he's here at the camp. They'll need private time."

Katie realized it would be safest if Peter and his father reunited privately. "Max" could explain the necessity for subterfuge. Otherwise, the five-year-old might blurt out Joshua's true identity and put the whole family in jeopardy. "I understand. I can arrange that."

Olga hurried away, intent on her next errand.

As she watched the children play, Katie mused on the meandering road fate took in their lives to bring them all together. She, Sam, and Peter met on the train, and now Sam's husband and Peter's father—the pianist everyone thought was dead—had turned up alive here at the Farm. *The Lord knows the end from the beginning, he sure does.* And what a bonus for her and Adam: they had the great privilege of collaborating with Joshua Brightman, one of the world's best pianists—in a concentration camp, of all places! Unbelievable.

Mentally, she set about planning everything for Tuesday, the day of the concert, and also the day of the children's only rehearsal with Max. She and Donna would take them to the piano rehearsal ten minutes early. In the foyer, the kids could go over the lyrics and practice marching in time as they pretended to play trumpets. She would send Peter in to Max with a note. She smiled to herself as she composed the note in her head:

Max —

Peter is one of my best singers. After you speak to him (take your time), please send him back to me. Then we will rehearse the children's choir. We are gathered in the foyer.

– Katie Lamb

Tuesday was the first of December. A Lutheran for all her twenty-eight years, Katie knew the past nine weeks in the camp had brought them to the beginning of Advent: a time of double-barreled expectation. In the life before the coup, she and all Christendom would have prepared themselves for the approaching Nativity. The hymn tunes and words ran through her mind:

O come, O come Emmanuel and ransom captive Israel.

Come thou long expected Jesus, born to set thy people free…

But just as Christ's birth had been foretold, so had his second coming, his triumphant return in power and great glory. The readings this time of year came from the prophecies of Isaiah and Matthew, the promises that the Lord would return to save his people and smite the wicked. But of course, no one but God himself knew the day and hour. So there was always the call to be ready: *for in such an hour as ye think not the Son of man cometh.*

She secretly harbored the hope of release, of freedom, soon. How they could ever achieve that, she did not know, but the longing for it grew with every passing day, with every act of cruelty and injustice she witnessed. Every generation had looked for that time, the return of the King. *Let it be soon, Lord. Let it be soon.*

On Tuesday, Katie and Donna led the children up the stairs to the auditorium. They stopped in the rectangular foyer outside two sets of double doors corresponding to the two aisles inside. They heard the sound of the piano, somewhat muffled by the closed doors. The children were very excited, and Katie heard one child whisper, "He's playing a march!"

"That's *Marche Militaire*," said Peter. "My dad used to play that for me . . . before . . . " His voice trailed off and he stared at the floor. *He said he would come back . . .*

"Can we go in?" asked another.

"Not yet. We're a little early." Katie took a notecard out of her pocket. "We'll wait here until the pianist is ready. Here, Peter." She handed him the card. "You go in and take my note to him. Come back and get us when he's ready."

"Me?" The sadness in Peter's blue eyes gave way to hopefulness.

"Yes, go on now. Walk straight down the aisle. You'll see him up on the stage."

Donna opened the door for him, but he hesitated. The cheerful music, louder now, suddenly spilled into the foyer. The children smiled and marched in place, keeping time with their feet. She grinned down at Peter. "Scoot!"

Clutching the note in one hand, Peter stepped over the threshold, and Donna closed the door quietly behind him. He found himself in an enormous room with rows and rows of empty seats. The aisle before him sloped downward. It was a long, long way to the stage, maybe a mile. The ceiling seemed almost as far away. *I am a tiny mouse in a giant's house.* His stomach felt funny, kind of fluttery, and he chewed on his lower lip, uncertain. Why hadn't they sent one of the bigger kids? He almost turned around and pushed open the door to run back to Katie and Donna.

The pianist kept playing. *He doesn't know I'm here yet.* Peter took a few steps forward and noticed the seats had letters on the arms. He read them as he slowly walked down the aisle. T, S, R. Spider webs stretched between rows T and S from the top of one seat to another. Q, P. *P for Peter.* He glanced at the stage. He could only see the side and back of the pianist's head as he played, his face toward the keys. His curly reddish hair hid his face as he bent forward. *Like daddy.*

Now came the dancing, floating butterfly music in the middle of *Marche Militaire*, the high notes fluttering, just like his stomach. *Just like daddy played it.* Peter walked faster. O, N, M, L, K, J. Here was the march again with deep bass notes, the very high notes shimmering and golden as the sunshine streaming through the high windows. Peter moved in time to the music, humming under his breath. I, H, G, F, E. He touched the next letters with one finger, leaving a faint, damp trail. *D—Daddy, C—Come, B—Back.*

A—

The music stopped, and so did Peter. He found himself up against the stage. It stood slightly above his head. Feeling fluttery and shy, he kept his eyes on the floor and clutched the card tightly. He heard quiet steps coming toward him. He crumpled the note in his hand. *He didn't want this pianist; he wanted—*

"Peter."

—Daddy. He blinked. He knew that voice. His heart beat in his throat. He slowly raised his eyes to the black shoes, the blue pants and shirt, to the face and the warm, green eyes smiling down at him. His

heart somersaulted. "Daddy!" He dropped the card and raised both arms. And suddenly he was lifted up and Daddy hugged him so tight. He buried his face in his father's neck.

"You came back," he whispered, "you came back." And that's when his face crumpled up like the card, and he started to cry.

Joshua laughed and cradled his son's head. "Yes, my little man, I did. It just took me longer than I expected." He stroked Peter's hair with one hand. "You've grown since I saw you in September."

"Have I?" Peter pulled his head back so he could look into Daddy's eyes. He sniffed and wiped his face with his sleeve. He gazed solemnly at his father for a moment. "Daddy, you've got a lot of white hairs now."

Joshua smiled. "I imagine I do."

"Daddy, where have you been? Did you know Mamma's here at the camp, too?"

"Yes, Peter, I know she's here. I have been on a great adventure and it's a very long story—"

"I know, Daddy. You met the dragon, didn't you?"

Joshua thought of the coup. "I . . . well, actually . . . I did."

"I know. We're all in the story now, aren't we? Katie told it to me on the train when she and Mamma and I came here. Sarastro made the prince and the birdcatcher walk through fire and water."

"Were they brave?"

"Yes, and the prince led them through it all with his magic flute."

"Then what happened?"

"The giant Sarastro let them go, but—" Peter gazed at his father and wrinkled his brow.

"But what?"

"The dragon was still alive. Will the dragon win, Daddy, or will everything be all right?"

His father blew out a deep breath and looked Peter in the eyes a long time. "Dragons are very powerful and very evil, my son, and sometimes they rule for a time." Here he pulled Peter to him again and hugged him hard. "But in the end, they never, ever win."

"I knew it, Daddy." Peter felt a little scared, but the fluttery feeling was gone.

"We're still in the middle of the battle, though. And there's something you've got to do to help us, Mamma and me."

"What?"

"You've got to keep my real name a secret and pretend you don't know me. And Mamma and I have to pretend we don't know each other either."

Peter's brows knit together.

"Can you do that? Just for the time we're here in the camp."

"Okay, Daddy."

"Thank you, Peter. And from now on, you've got to call me Max, like everyone else." He set his son down on the stage. "Now is that a note for me, down there on the floor?"

"Yes, I'll get it." Peter scampered down the steps to the auditorium floor, picked up the crumpled card, and handed it to his— "Here, Max."

Max nodded his approval. "Perfect." He read the note and smiled. "All right, Peter, go tell Katie and the troops to come in. It's time for a rehearsal. Quick! Run!"

Peter laughed for the first time in ages. He ran so light and fast, he wasn't sure if his feet touched the floor. It seemed to him that he flew—as if he held the hand of an angel.

CHAPTER 53

ASSIGNMENTS

On Monday, the day before the concert, the inmates lined up in the chill darkness for roll call at 6:00 a.m. The guards had removed five people who wore orange wristbands that morning. One woman screamed and fought, to no avail. The soldiers overpowered her and dragged her away. Gideon kept his eyes on Orion the Hunter shining above them, with brilliant Sirius, the dog star, at his heel. After the five prisoners were taken away, the inmates shivered and waited. Finally, when the stars had faded in the growing light, Ping, wearing a blue beret and his full uniform, came through the door at the back of the school. Flanked by two armed guards, he announced (as if everyone did not know) that General Richard Huffman would inspect the camp that day, and the concert would take place the next night. Everyone would attend. He expected "excellent behavior" from all.

As Ping harangued them, motion above and to Gideon's left caught his eye, a small black dot moving against the rosy sky. A bird, some kind of raptor, very high up, glided in lazy circles above the camp. It descended and suddenly shot down toward the camp in a fierce, purposeful dive. As it came closer, Gideon realized the bird was huge—a bald eagle. He thought its prey must be another bird or a rabbit out in the pasture, but it seemed to dive directly down at the assembly.

The raptor pulled in its wings to increase speed, and at the base of its dive, the legs reached down and the talons connected with Ping's head with such force that it knocked him backward. Badly startled, Ping shrieked in fear and ducked, but the eagle scratched him and snagged his blue beret. The colonel screeched an order in Chinese. The flustered soldiers flanking him reacted sluggishly; they fired several rounds at the departing raptor, all of them wide of the target.

A murmur of surprise and stifled laughter swept through the assembly of inmates. Ping's oily black hair stood up in random spikes like a punk rock drummer. Flustered and embarrassed, he smoothed his hair with his hands and swiped at a long, bloody scratch on his forehead. The eagle had shattered his dignity.

Gideon suppressed a laugh. *The eagle bested the dragon.*

His sign! There it was, clear and unmistakable. Later that day he put the plan in motion.

When Olga noticed Austin Pratt smoking outside his barracks that evening, she asked him for a cigarette.

"Here," said Pratt, and handed her a smoke and his lighter. She lit the cigarette and took a drag. At the same time, Susannah opened the door to Barracks 3 and stepped outside. Olga shouted, "Hey! Get back in the barracks. You do not have permission to go out."

Susannah said something unintelligible and remained where she was. "Shit," said Olga to Pratt, "gotta go take care of the morons in my barracks." She stamped out the cigarette and walked toward Susannah, drawing out her truncheon.

"Get back in the barracks," Olga screamed, threatening the older woman with the stick.

"Don't hit me!" Acting cowed, Susannah quickly opened the door and disappeared into the building with Olga at her heels.

Inside, Olga lowered the baton and smiled at Susannah. She stowed the cigarette lighter underneath her bunk beside the pint of cooking oil she had stolen from the kitchen earlier that day.

On his way to the latrine, Thomas retrieved the piece of rebar he had hidden under the barracks. It was the wee hours, when Pratt was asleep and the guard had just made his round. He walked behind the latrine and came within a foot of the electric fence. He shoved the rebar into the damp ground, leaving about eight inches showing and then used the primitive facilities. He was back in his bunk in three minutes.

The following day, around five o'clock, fourteen-year-old Arthur carried a large pot of vegetable soup to the refrigerator, but tripped and fell as he passed the stove. The soup ran all over the floor and under the stove. The guard punched him in the back and screamed at him and Constantin. "Clean now!"

Arthur groaned. "Sorry, sorry, sorry!"

"I'll help him." Holding a serrated knife in one hand, Constantin stood beside the sink. He volunteered to clean under and behind the stove while Arthur wiped up the four-foot puddle stretching from the stove to the refrigerator. While the guard cursed at Arthur, Constantin slid the knife up his sleeve and laid a dish towel over his arm. He pulled the electric stove out slightly from the wall so he could wedge himself behind it. Lying on his left side, he was almost completely hidden from the guard. He unplugged the stove and found the Phillips-head screwdriver Olga had left against the wall. With trembling fingers, he took out two screws and quickly removed the metal cover panel on the back of the stove. Sweat rolled down the sides of his face as he removed the nuts holding the three-prong cord in place. He drew it out and then replaced the cover panel. Quickly, he used the dish towel to wipe the tiny bit of spilled soup that had trickled under the stove. He wrapped the power cord and the knife in the dirty dish towel.

"Hurry up!" the guard shouted at him.

"Finished."

Leaving the screwdriver under the stove, Constantin stood up, came around front, and pushed it back in place. Arthur had used up three dish towels cleaning the larger mess. "Give me those," said Constantin. He wadded them up together to further conceal the cord and knife.

He offered the dripping, messy towels to the guard. "You want to take them to the laundry?"

"You idiot—you take them now!"

They marched down the hall to the laundry room where Constantin handed them to Susannah.

With Ping's approval, Sam had ordered the children matching concert outfits, according to the sizes Katie gave her. When the clothes arrived, Katie stored them in the children's barracks. The adults' dress clothes came from the massive mounds discarded by the inmates on arrival to the camp. The laundry women found and cleaned dress shirts, ties, jackets, trousers, shoes, and socks for the three male musicians. They located Katie's opera costume and shoes, as well as a dress for Lynne, the girl who would play the role of Euridice in the scene from *Orfeo*.

On the day of the concert, under Olga's supervision, Susannah delivered clothes for Adam and Jaybird to Barracks 4. Hidden between pants and shirt was the serrated kitchen knife and power cord, as Gideon had instructed. With Olga chaperoning her, Susannah brought Katie's costume and Max's clothes to the auditorium late in the day. She stacked them carefully on a towel they laid on the floor in the wings. The towel concealed a uniform, a truncheon, and a black pouch.

The musicians were allowed to shower before they dressed. Jaybird donned shirt, trousers, jacket, and tie in wonder. He had never owned such finery in his life. "Whooee, gents, lookee here. Jaybird Alexander is purty as a peacock."

Pratt wrinkled up his nose at Jaybird. "Why are you all dressed up? You're not a musician."

"Beggin' your pardon, Mr. Pratt, but I sure am." He pulled his mouth organ out of his jacket pocket and played a riff.

Pratt pursed his lips and sulked off, tapping his baton against his thigh.

When Adam returned to his barracks, he found the blazer, pressed pants, and clean shirt on his bed. Thomas came over to look at Adam's fine clothes. He stroked the blazer and felt the telltale lumps underneath. "Nice."

While Gideon and Bertie distracted Pratt, Thomas removed the knife and the power cord. He concealed them the best he could in his pants. "Going to the latrine," he yelled at Pratt. "Diarrheeeea!"

He held one arm against his abdomen as he dashed out the door. In case Pratt followed, he ran directly to the latrine where he sat in princely solitude. Using the knife, he stripped the power cord at both ends, exposing the copper wire. When he determined the coast was clear, he went around back to the place he had left the rebar. He laid the cord and the knife in the high grass behind the latrine and then ran back to the barracks where he gave the thumbs-up sign to Gideon.

CHAPTER 54

CONCERT

The auditorium buzzed with quiet conversations and laughter. The inmates, excited by the prospect of a concert—of an hour of real pleasure in the hellhole that was the Farm—sat in the center section: women in front and men in the rows behind them. The children sat closest to the stage, bunched together in the narrower seating areas left and right of the wide center. The medical staff sat in the back of the center section, keeping several empty rows between them and the inmates. Colonel Ping and General Huffman sat alone, unguarded, in the single balcony, confident that the eight armed soldiers on the main level had everything under control. There was one guard at each exit in the back, two on each side wall, and two others at the front, on either side of the stage. The remaining six guards manned the two towers and searchlights outside.

Constantin leaned toward Thomas. "Do you think we'll be able to purchase wine and *hors d'oeuvres* at intermission?"

Thomas snorted. "I'd be happy with beer and pizza, but that ain't gonna happen in this joint."

They sat two rows behind and to the right of Bertie and Gideon. Gideon did not want Huffman to recognize him during the concert, even if it was highly unlikely. The General would not expect his former son-in-law to be present; they hadn't seen each other since the wedding, seventeen years ago. From the balcony, Huffman would only see the back of his head. The inmates were all dressed alike—it would be like identifying one sheep in a herd of hundreds—or so he hoped.

Someone backstage lowered the house lights, and an expectant hush fell on the audience. The high-gloss finish of the black Steinway gleamed in the bright stage lights. Its open lid flared up like the wing of a great bird, banking in flight. *If the plan fails, maybe we can all get in it and fly away*, thought Gideon. Adrenalin surged through his body—combat readiness. The players knew their parts, and everyone was in place. *Be with us, Lord, 'cause here we go.*

Gideon watched the children march up the stairs to the stage from either side. Dressed alike in white, long-sleeved turtlenecks, bright blue vests, navy-blue slacks, and dark rubber-soled clogs, they stood in a double semicircle in front of the grand piano, smaller ones in front. Katie Lamb, tall and blonde, stood at the stationary microphone. If, by the grace of God, his plan worked, he would free her and then, in as courtly a fashion as the wilderness permitted, he would woo her. And win her.

"Good evening, and welcome to our concert. My name is Katie Lamb, and our superb pianist is Max Grandpied." As she gestured toward Max, her slightly crooked smile revealed the charming gap between her front teeth. The auburn-haired pianist returned her smile and nodded to acknowledge the audience's applause.

Max Bigfoot—completely transformed from the wild man who had emerged out of the woods. Gideon smiled, but his attention stayed riveted on Katie. Her shoulder-length flaxen hair seemed made of light, like the mane of a palomino horse. Slender and lithe, she seemed completely undaunted by the guards or the bloodthirsty executioners, Ping and Huffman. Her good-humored smile radiated cheer and energy—as though she knew everything would be all right—as if the world had not descended into madness and death. Her buoyant spirit was infectious: people in the audience smiled; they sat straighter—the heaviness in hearts and minds lifted. The children were no exception. Like the Pied Piper, she had obviously charmed the little ones; they adored her. Katie seemed to glow onstage, as if she had been made for it.

"Our first piece is the children's chorus from Bizet's opera *Carmen*. We'll sing in French, but the translation is this: 'We arrive, here we are. The dazzling trumpet sounds. We walk with our heads up, like little soldiers, marking time. Shoulders back, chest up, arms by our sides.'"

She faced the children, and at her direction, Max began the introduction. On the surface, the rhythmic march music was charming. Played in the bright, high register of the piano, it brought to mind a band of toy soldiers. But within the context of the Farm, it tore at Gideon's heart. Marching in place and swinging their arms, the children kept time to the music. The sound of their feet was steady as a snare drum: *Tap-tap, Tap-tap.*

Avec la garde montante,
nous arrivons, nous voilà.

Marking time, they lifted their arms and pretended to play trumpets.

Sonne, trompette éclatante!
Taratata, taratata!
Nous marchons la tête haute
comme de petits soldats,
marquant sans faire de faute,
une, deux, marquant le pas.
Les épaules en arrière
et la poitrine en dehors,
les bras de cette manière
tombant tout le long du corps

With rising tension, Gideon watched the children, who marched with heads high like little soldiers: one-two, marking time. Shoulders back and chests up, playacting. How could they know they sang their future? They stood on the precipice of a change so great it would forever mark a dividing point in their lives. In a very short space of time, every one of them would march into the wilderness to the trumpet call of hunger, cold, and danger. It would be no game—they would be required to be as obedient and brave as soldiers. He would have spared them if he could, but it was not possible. This was the time they lived in, and they all had to face it.

After a big round of applause, Katie addressed the audience. "We'll sing our second song in German. It's called . . . uh . . . the 'Evening Song' from Humperdinck's fairytale opera *Hansel and Gretel*. Lost in the woods as night falls, the two children sing this song for comfort and courage before they lie down to sleep."

Bertie shook his head and leaned toward Gideon. "That's not the name of the song," he whispered. "It's the 'Evening *Prayer*.' She didn't want to say the P-word in front of our atheist captors. Fourteen angels protect the children, two standing guard at their heads, their feet, to their right and left, and so on."

Max played a gentle, melodic introduction, and then the children sang:

> *Abends, will ich schlafen gehn,*
> *Vierzehn Engel um mich stehen:*
> *Zwei zu meinen Häupten,*
> *Zwei zu meinen Füssen,*
> *Zwei zu meiner Rechten,*
> *Zwei zu meiner Linken,*
> *Zweie, die mich decken*
> *Zweie, die mich wecken,*
> *Zweie, die mich weisen*
> *Zu Himmels-Paradeisen.*

The sound, light and pure and hopeful, floated into the hall. Their youth and innocence might as well have been a sword; it pierced all Gideon's defenses. A painful lump grew in his throat, and he noticed tears in Bertie's eyes. Peter Brightman, marked with the red wristband, the five-year-old designated victim, stood in the first row.

The peril of the little ones and the sound of their innocent voices fueled the white-hot lava of Gideon's outrage—that this regime even targeted children for butchery. He vowed silently to protect and defend them—and with the help of God, to free them. In an hour or less, they would make the attempt. Once they were out, there were stretches of wilderness in America where men could live and survive for years if need be.

The last song was a light, rhythmic piece called "Little Innocent Lamb." The refrain stayed with Gideon long after the concert ended.

> *Little Lamb, little Lamb, little innocent Lamb,*
> *I'm a-gonna love you 'til I die.*
> *Little Lamb, little Lamb, little innocent Lamb,*
> *I'm a-gonna love you 'til I die.*

Katie Lamb. As the children returned to their seats, Gideon murmured under his breath, "I'm gonna love you 'til I die. I'm gonna shield you." *Or die trying.*

Adam Chen, the Trilingual King of Curses, performed next. Bertie muttered under his breath. "Good Lord, he actually looks civilized."

Jaybird, standing backstage, hardly noticed the clothes the musicians wore—he found himself immersed in the violin and piano pieces. He remained aware of Donna, whom he could see from the wings, sitting in front with the children. He loved music, but a live concert played by musicians of this caliber was a revelation. In "Spring" by Vivaldi, the music clearly imitated the trilling and chirping of birds, the flow of water, smooth and swirling. He could see and hear a storm—thunder in the piano, with brilliant flashes of lightning in the violin. It matched the storm in his chest over what he had to do within the hour.

Adam began the Beethoven sonata alone, playing harmony with himself in the slow, mournful beginning. The piano entered in the same mood of longing and sadness, quiet and subdued. The piece reminded Jaybird of Caddo Lake at dusk, still and lonely, overlaid with muted colors glowing like mother-of-pearl. He had been lonely almost all his life, isolated by his painful sensitivity to the thoughts and emotions of others. He had fished and hunted alone; after his father died, he had kept to himself in the small cabin. The music seemed to call forth his own longing for human companionship. He let his glance rest on Donna. He had spoken to her only once, when he got his chance to deliver firewood to the kids' barracks and played his mouth organ for them. But even so, he sensed her strength and also her gentleness. Somehow, he knew she was a giver, not a taker, and he wanted more than anything to get to know her.

Abruptly, the music flickered and flashed, erupting like a fish breaking the surface, arcing in the air, splashing down, and then leaping again, bursting with life and energy. The notes raced headlong and brilliant: piano and violin precisely together, as if the two players were one. Back and forth the music went, alternating from quiet shadow to sparkling sunlight.

Adam's true self shone. The middle-aged, foul-mouthed griper's façade vanished to reveal a true artist. Handsome in a black suit with a pale yellow shirt and black tie, his salt-and-pepper hair newly cut and combed back from his forehead, he projected a striking stage presence. With dancing fingers and varied strokes of the bow, he played confidently with elegance and style. In his hands, the violin, a hollow wooden box with four strings, produced, as if by magic, sounds of such resonance and beauty that Jaybird forgot to inhale. When the piece ended quietly, it seemed as if the audience held its collective breath. Then boisterous applause broke out; whistles and shouts of approval rocked the house.

Sam could not take her eyes off her husband—she drank him in as if he were the Elixir of Life. Joshua wore a white shirt and sky-blue tie, a gray blazer, and black slacks with black, shiny shoes. His curly hair formed an auburn halo around his head. To her he looked wonderful. Though words and language were her métier and her passion, Sam could not begin to articulate the emotions swirling in her heart. It still astonished her to see Joshua alive and well, if thinner than before and limping slightly.

When the piece ended, Joshua and Adam took their bows—and there were many. The audience did not want to let them go.

As Adam closed and latched his violin in the case backstage, Cherubino made her entrance. Dressed in a red vest over a white, puffy-sleeved blouse, yellow knee pants, white hose, and black patent-leather shoes, she beamed at the audience. Constantin immediately recognized the costume. There stood the singer he had followed from the opera house to the train station. And wonder of wonders, his wish was about to be fulfilled: he was actually going to hear her sing again.

For the first aria, Katie beckoned to Lynne, one of the older choristers, to come onstage. As she had acted out the scene for Ping, Katie, playing a young man, knelt on one knee and held the girl in her arms. In Orfeo's lament for the lost Euridice, her mezzo soprano voice rang out rich and dark as grief: *What will I do, where will I go without Euridice, my beloved?*

The applause was deafening.

After a shy bow, Lynne returned to her seat. Max set the scenes for Katie's two Italian-language arias from the *Marriage of Figaro*; he described the adolescent Cherubino's mad infatuation with women. When he began the accompaniment, Katie, who looked about fourteen onstage, stalked back and forth across the boards with such a masculine air, it was easy to believe she was a lovesick boy. After uproarious applause, a beaming Katie finally left the stage.

Standing at the microphone, Max introduced Jaybird. "Now we have a special musical surprise. Please welcome Mr. Jaybird Alexander and his magical mouth organ."

As the applause rose, Olga grimaced and left her seat, one hand held protectively over her stomach. She appeared to be ill. With her authority as a BB, she tapped one of the male inmates on the shoulder and beckoned him to help her as she left. He took her arm, and they walked rapidly toward the doors at the back of the hall.

The house lights came up as the tall, slender black man walked out onto the stage. Inexplicably, the guards on either side tensed and pointed their rifles at him, but he held up his hands, one empty, one holding the silver, rectangular musical instrument. He smiled. "It's a har-mon-i-ca. Not loaded."

That got a laugh from the audience.

Jaybird, who had never been the center of attention for so many people, stood at the microphone feeling awkward and out of his element. His backstage butterflies had morphed into helicopters. He leaned forward and spoke softly, half-startled by the sound of his own amplified voice. "This one's for Max, our Piano Man." With sweaty hands, he put the harmonica to his lips, and played Billy Joel's song of the same name. His nervousness faded as he concentrated on the music. He glanced now and then at the audience, gratified to see the smiles on the inmates' faces. He segued into "Swing Low, Sweet Chariot."

Hope it chaps your butt, Huffman, you traitor atheist.

After the applause, he announced, "This one's for a gracious lady." He gave them a rollicking version of "Oh, Susanna." Susannah beamed and blew him a kiss. Bertie gave him a thumbs-up sign with a grin that could have encompassed the state of Texas. Again, without stopping, Jaybird moved into Bob Dylan's "Mr. Tambourine Man." He could hear the audience humming along.

"For my special one." Jaybird dared a glance directly at Donna, who dazzled him with her smile. He launched into the Van Morrison song "Brown-Eyed Girl." Finally, in prayer and homage to his Maker and defiance to the enemy, he played a blues version of "He's Got the Whole World in His Hands" as the audience clapped in time. *Well, why not, what could they do to him—put him in a concentration camp?* In the rousing applause that followed, he made a stiff, self-conscious bow and then disappeared into the wings.

His part had only just begun.

Joshua returned to the stage, determined. He knew that for Colonel Ping his piano solos were the climax of the entire concert. He also knew what Ping had done to Sam and Peter. Adam had told him all at the last rehearsal.

He announced his pieces, then sat at the keyboard. Before he began, he glanced directly into the wings. Adam, now in uniform, and Jaybird gave him the thumbs-up sign; they were ready to go. Max gave a faint, purposeful nod. The small gesture belied his passion: he burned to personally deliver death blows to the slaughter-masters who had tortured his wife and threatened to sacrifice his son. But in Gideon's plan that task belonged to others; it was his role to lend them cover. And he would. He lifted his hands and played the Scarlatti Sonata in D Minor with the greatest focus and intensity of his life. For just under four minutes, he made it sparkle and flash through the air like a diamond-headed mace.

After the applause, before he launched into the Chopin C-Sharp Minor Scherzo, Joshua glanced again at Adam, Jaybird, and Katie. Together, they stood poised in this last hushed and pregnant moment, like alpine skiers on a cold and windy height, about to give themselves to the elements, to go off-piste on a steep, unpredictable, and dangerous course. There would be no going back. The charge and tension in the air was palpable; the moment had come.

Joshua dropped his glance to the keyboard, resolved. With all his training, talent, and long experience, he would rise to the occasion. In a small-town high school auditorium, next-door to a cow pasture in rural Texas, Joshua Brightman, concert pianist, was about to give the greatest performance of his life.

He lifted his hands and played.

CHAPTER 55

A SWORD FOR THE LORD

When Olga, feigning nausea, and Thomas, her chosen escort, left the hall, the armed guard who accompanied them was Blue Eyes. Olga and Thomas, along with everyone in Barracks 3 and 4, knew he had threatened to burn Adam's violin on the first day, and he had led Sam's interrogation and brutal torture.

"I have to vomit," Olga told the men, grimacing. They quickly descended the stairs to the restrooms. She rushed into the women's room, but she did not throw up. She turned on the tap in one sink and let it run. Then she turned off the light and climbed up onto the third sink, situated nearest the unlocked window. She levered herself onto the ledge and glanced outside where now, about seven in the evening, it was fully dark. Cautiously, after glancing left and right, she crawled out the window, dropped down onto the ground, and walked swiftly to her own barracks.

Once inside, she quickly gathered the container of cooking oil and Pratt's lighter. She eased out of the building and made her way cautiously to the dark, deserted OR. She edged around the building to the side farthest from the school, where she intended to break a window with her truncheon. Luckily, she found one of the horizontal slider windows ajar. She opened it wide, climbed up, and managed to squeeze herself through the narrow space into the anteroom.

After the searchlight from the north guard tower made its eerie pass, she opened the window on the opposite side, then unlocked the exit door deadbolt. In the OR itself, she pulled the mobile operating table forward and used it to wedge open the doors to the anteroom. Beginning at the far wall of the OR, she coated the floor with oil. In the anteroom she doused the floor and cabinets. Standing at the exit, she waited for the next pass of the searchlight before she lit the oil with the lighter. The instantaneous flames gave a satisfying *whoosh* as they spread away from her like dragon fire to the center of the building. She quickly exited out the door and hurried back to the school where she stood in the shadows and watched. The windows flickered with an orange light as the flames flared and grew in intensity.

As they waited for Olga, Thomas asked Blue Eyes if he could use the men's room. The guard adjusted his glasses and nodded. "I'll go too." As they peed side by side at the long urinal, Thomas gasped and pointed toward the ceiling in surprise. "Oh, my God, what's that?"

When Blue Eyes looked up, Thomas kneed him in the balls. The man screamed in pain and doubled over. Thomas yanked the rifle out of his hands and swung the stock with all his strength at the guard's head. The blow produced a sickening crunch and knocked the guard's glasses across the room. Blue Eyes collapsed.

Breathing hard, Thomas regarded the dead man sprawled on the tiles. "You won't torment Sam or Adam or anyone ever again, Blue Eyes. Violence you gave, and violence you have received."

Rifle in hand, Thomas quickly moved down the deserted corridor and took the main stairs down to the basement. Thanks to Susannah he knew the main breaker box was located in the laundry. He flipped on the light switch. The time on the large round wall clock was 7:15. He had about twelve minutes until the concert ended.

The breaker box was locked and he had no key. He knew he could pop it open with a screwdriver, but he didn't have that either. He took the rifle butt and struck the metal door in the middle. The sheet metal bent in and the edges pulled up. A little more and he could grip the edge with his fingers. He gave it another sharp blow that did the trick. He set the rifle down and gripped the edge of the door. In two hard jerks, he had it open. He pulled the main breaker. The building went dark.

He noticed a flickering orange light through the narrow windows high up on the basement wall. *Olga must have done her part.*

He heard shouts outside the building. As soon as his eyes adjusted to the darkness, he ascended the main stairs. He exited through the back door in the transverse corridor. Outside, a single guard ran past him in the direction of the OR fire, but the man never looked up. As soon as his footsteps faded, Thomas ran to the grassy area between the latrine and the electrified fence. He located the piece of rebar sunk in the ground and wound the bare end of the copper cord securely around it. He formed the other end into a hook, pulled the cord taut, and then dropped the hook around one of the horizontal wires of the fence. There was a spark, followed by a loud pop and crackle.

"Thomas." He jerked involuntarily, startled by the soft voice behind him. Olga huddled in the grass next to the latrine. "What do we do now?"

He pointed toward the fence. "You should go quickly. Skirt the helipad on the left side so you're not out in the open, and once you get to the trail, go down a ways and then cross over to the right, the north side. Wait there until we all come."

"But the fence . . ."

"I shorted it out." He stood beside the fence and pulled two of the wires apart so she could squeeze through. "Go, now, Olga. You're a very brave woman, and you've done your part."

Inside the auditorium, Joshua infused the intense, turbulent opening of the scherzo with drama and drew as much sound from the piano as the instrument could produce, determined to keep all the attention on himself. Droplets of sweat formed on his head and rolled down his cheeks as he played the impetuous, surging notes. In the major mode section, he played the noble theme followed by swiftly cascading arpeggios, light and glittering as fairy dust. After the brief respite of quiet contemplation, while his heart thumped in his ears, Joshua drew a deep breath and reprised the rushing, impassioned music of the beginning.

Even at a distance of fifty feet, a human head is a much bigger target than that of a squirrel or a rabbit. Standing about two feet back in the wings, Jaybird peered out through the eight-inch gap between the stage curtain and the wall—Max's doing, pre-concert. The two targets, backlit by the lighted Exit sign, had their eyes fixed on the stage. The General scowled and slumped in his chair, but Ping the music-lover sat upright and beamed with pride and pleasure at Max's performance. Jaybird stood ready with the handle of his slingshot in one hand and the pouch enclosing a steel ball bearing in the other. Beside him, Katie held the truncheon and a second ball bearing. As Max neared the powerful, fortissimo ending of the Chopin, the pianist glanced directly backstage at Adam and gave a nod.

"Now!" Adam whispered.

When the crashing piano chords began, Jaybird Alexander inhaled, held his breath and drew back the sling with all the power he had. The first shot flew at the bigger man. Katie immediately handed him the second steel ball. As soon as he saw the head snap back, before the body went limp, Jaybird shot again.

Over the music, Ping heard a sound like a bowling ball striking a pin. Startled, he turned his head in surprise. The General sat slack-jawed and stunned. "G-g-general Huffman, are you all r—"

The second steel ball drilled through Ping's temple into his brain. His neck snapped to the left; his pupils dilated in shock, and he slumped toward the other man. Like a girl with her date at the movies, he laid his head on the shoulder of the most feared man in Region VI.

At precisely that moment, the hall went dark.

"Done," Jaybird whispered, and lowered the slingshot.

Katie said nothing, but she stepped close and took Jaybird's arm in hers. She felt the trembling of his body in a delayed reaction. Jaybird leaned into the comfort her presence and physical touch provided him.

Adam whispered, "Bravo, Jaybird. Superb."

Max finished the last few measures of the wild, surging music in the dark. A smattering of applause and a buzz of excited, confused chatter rose from the audience.

"Showtime," said Adam. Dressed in a captain's uniform, he strode out onto the dark stage with a bravado he did not feel. Speaking Chinese, he announced himself in a tone of command. "This is Captain Chen, aide to General Huffman." He shouted at the young officer standing at stage left. "Junior Sergeant, dial the camp commander and give me your phone. Now!"

Rattled and unsure of himself, the junior sergeant immediately obeyed. He speed-dialed the number and handed Adam the phone. Holding it to his ear, Adam pretended to speak with Ping. "Colonel, this is Captain Chen, standing on the stage. What are your orders?" He listened for a few seconds, then responded. "Yes sir, yes, I will take care of it."

Keeping the phone in his hand, Adam shouted in Chinese. "Men, Colonel says we have an emergency—the OR is burning; we must take care of it immediately. Do not fire weapons here in the dark." Adam could see a flickering orange glow through the auditorium windows. "Guards on the sides and in the back, go to the fire. Guards in front, stay with me. We will take the prisoners back to their barracks through the side door near the stage."

The junior sergeant had flicked on his flashlight and pointed it at the exit to the exterior staircase. "Hold your position," Adam shouted at the other guard on stage right.

Switching to English, Adam screamed to the murmuring audience. "Silence!" He waited a beat until they complied. "Children, stand!" He turned to the others backstage. "You musicians," he shouted, "follow junior sergeant out the side door. Children next, then women, then men. Back to barracks. Now!"

Joshua, Jaybird, and Katie followed the junior sergeant to the door. It opened onto a metal staircase with a railing on one side that led from the second floor straight down to the ground. Katie told the children to walk in single file. "Put one hand on the shoulder of the person in front of you and follow me."

At the head of the stair, the junior sergeant stopped, took out his sidearm, and said, "Boy with red wristband, come here."

Joshua, standing right behind him, froze. This was not part of the plan.

The junior sergeant screamed, "Boy with red wristband, come here now!"

Peter came forward, wide-eyed, but as he passed his father, he gazed at him solemnly and said softly, "It's okay, Max. Mamma said, 'Let courage rise with danger.'"

Joshua watched his son in wonder as the boy stepped forward to do the guard's bidding. *Let courage rise with danger.*

The junior sergeant shouted at Peter. "Silence! You hold this. Show where we walk." Peter took the flashlight and directed the beam toward the staircase. The junior sergeant gripped his shirt with one hand and leveled the gun at the boy's head. He addressed the musicians. "Any trouble on way out of building, boy dies. Understand?"

Fear, rage, and a tsunami of adrenaline sent tremors through Joshua's whole body. He swallowed hard and tried to control his voice. "There won't be any trouble."

Katie turned to the children behind them and spoke in a clear, loud voice. "Hold onto the railing as you go down the stairs, and step slowly and carefully. Everything is okay. We are not going to rush." As they exited onto the staircase from the dark hall into the chilly night, Katie surreptitiously handed the truncheon she held to Joshua, who walked right behind the Chinese guard.

The junior sergeant led the way down the stairs. He had to bend over slightly to keep the 9mm at Peter's temple, making their descent snail-paced and awkward. If he rushed, the boy might trip and they would both fall. Behind the guard, Joshua gripped the truncheon with a sweaty hand, holding it close to his leg. Through the roaring in his ears, he tried to figure out how he could bash the guard without the man pulling the trigger. Every breath was an agony of indecision. He steeled himself as he looked at the back of the junior sergeant's head. *Let courage rise with danger.* If ever there was a time, it was now.

The descent to the ground seemed to take hours: slow, cautious step by slow, cautious step, forcing everyone behind them to proceed in a lugubrious, dirge-like rhythm. Finally, Peter's beam of light illuminated red dirt. When the guard and Peter stepped forward in the same rhythm, Joshua inhaled and swung the baton at the soldier's head with both hands like a major league power hitter. At the same moment, something dark flew by him. The sickening crunch when he connected was punctuated by the ear-splitting roar of the gun.

With the assurance and aplomb of a ringmaster, Adam controlled the order of events in the auditorium. Using the light from the mobile phone, he stepped down from the stage and walked up the aisle to the men's section.

"You, you, and you!" he screamed at Gideon, Bertie, and Constantin. "Lead the women." They stood up immediately and moved into the aisle. The women filed out, and the remaining male inmates followed them. The doctors and nurses had already fled out the back. The only other people left in the hall were the two corpses reclining in the balcony. *And may those two bastards rot in hell,* thought Adam.

He spoke to the remaining guard. "Keep the men covered and give me the flashlight. I check to see no one hiding."

He heard a shot from outside and fear gripped his guts. *Oh, God— not the child. Please, please let him be all right.*

"Want me to check?" asked the guard.

"No, you stay here. Junior Sergeant in control outside." *He hoped the hell not.* Maybe Joshua or Jaybird had wrested the gun from the bastard and shot him. He would find out shortly, but in the meantime, he had to keep control of the auditorium. He directed the flashlight's beam down each row, pretending to look for strays while he monitored the men's progress.

As the last few men filed out, the guard kept his rifle leveled at their backs. Adam came up behind the soldier.

"All clear."

Keeping his eyes on the men in front of him, the man simply grunted in reply.

Perfect. Adam gripped the foot-long, metal-cased flashlight and bashed him in the temple. The guard staggered to the left, and Adam hit him again, harder. When he collapsed, the rifle fell from his hands. Adam grabbed it and the 9mm sidearm. He dashed backstage and got his violin from the wings. Using the straps, he carried the case on his back, and then he left the building—the last man standing.

Joshua stood paralyzed with fear. The guard lay crumpled on the ground at his feet, the pistol still grasped in his hand, his head split like a melon. The flashlight Peter had held lay at a perfect angle on the ground to illuminate the blood and brains leaking onto the red dirt.

Where he expected to see his son, there was only a dark, coiled, unmoving lump. In the ambient light from the flashlight, he saw liquid trickling onto the dirt. His hands went slack and he dropped the truncheon. Faintly, through the buzzing in his ears, Joshua heard Gideon's voice.

"Children, stop and stay in place until we tell you to move."

Gideon rushed past the children down the staircase. A much smaller figure followed on his heels. Once on the ground, he could see the guard was dead. He grabbed the flashlight and trained it on the immobile heap beside the fallen soldier. He knelt, reached out gently, and touched the highest point. His hand came away wet. "Jaybird? Are you all right?"

A low groan emerged. "If *all right* is hurtin' like sin, then yeah, I am."

They heard a muffled, high-pitched voice. "I'm all right too, but my head hurts."

"Sorry, boy. Had to knock you down. That mean dude woulda shot you, but he only grazed my butt." With another groan, Jaybird rolled off the boy.

"Hope we have a big enough Band-Aid," said Peter, sitting up.

Joshua dropped to his knees and folded Peter into a fierce embrace. "Oh, thank God." Sam's small arms encircled them both.

Gideon laughed in relief. "Bigfoot, didn't know you had a son, but apparently you're raising a comedian."

"I was scared, Daddy. Why did he call you Bigfoot?"

"We were all scared, Peter, but we're okay now. I'll tell you the story of Bigfoot later."

"Good job . . . uh . . . " Gideon gazed at Max. "I don't even know your real name."

"Joshua Brightman. My son, Peter, and my wife, Samantha."

Gideon grinned. "Nice to finally meet the real you, man. And what a pianist you are!"

Quickly, he turned to the business at hand. He took the guard's rifle, handed Joshua the flashlight, and removed the sidearm from the soldier's limp hand. "Samantha, keep Peter with you. He seems okay, but his head took a hard hit. Jaybird, can you walk?"

"Oh, yeah."

"Okay, take the pistol. You, Joshua, and Katie get the children and everyone else down onto the ground, backs against the building. Keep them silent and still. I'm going to take out the south searchlight. Once it goes out, lead them fast as you can—without running—to the back of the latrine behind Barracks 4. Thomas is there. He'll show you the way out."

Gideon's glance lingered on Katie. He brushed her cheek with his hand and looked at them all. "Be safe and God bless."

Gideon glided into the darkness, hugging the school building. The automatic rifle, similar to the M16A4 he had used in the Marines, felt right at home in his hands. In fact, the whole scenario felt familiar; he couldn't count how many times he had approached a target in Afghanistan under cover of darkness. He intended to move in close in order to take down as many guards as possible before he shot out the light. He wanted to give Constantin, the children, and his friends as much insurance as he could. He had been in firefights before; he looked forward to this one.

With all eyes on Gideon, no one saw Constantin sneak away in the opposite direction.

When Adam emerged at the top of the staircase, the searchlight made a pass. He heard three shots in quick succession, followed by a fourth and the sound of shattering glass—then silence and darkness. He heard Joshua's voice below him. "All right, we're going to walk quickly to the latrine behind Barracks 4. Form three columns with children in the middle, men to the right, women to the left."

Gripping the rifle, Adam hurried down the stairs toward the front of the line. Some of the women shrank back in fear. Jaybird whipped around and pointed the pistol at him.

Adam smiled and played air violin until Jaybird realized who he was.

"Dang it, man, you scared the sh—uh . . . the heck outta us." Jaybird lowered the pistol and wiped his brow with his sleeve.

"Glad I fooled you, but most guards don't carry violins on their backs. Jaybird, please take this for me."

"Let me take it," said Joshua. "Jaybird here just saved the life of my son and got shot in the ass for his good deed." Joshua hoisted the case on his back. "You scared me, too, Adam. You look way too authentic."

Adam's glance shifted to the right and his tone was grim. "Let's hope it's authentic enough to fool the soldiers coming this way." He pointed in the direction of the OR where they could see two guards approaching, backlit by the orange glow of the fire. "They're probably coming to investigate the shots."

"Yeah, man, that was Gideon," said Jaybird. "He took out the searchlight. I guess the guards returned fire. Hope he's all right."

Adam lowered his voice. "Walk towards the barracks now, and let me handle them."

Two soldiers approached at a dead run, their footsteps explosive on the gravel. They halted when they saw Adam. One spoke in Chinese. "Searchlight out. What happened, sir?"

Before Adam could reply, two enormous explosions, followed by a third came from the OR, startling everyone. Then the screams began. "Go back to the OR now!" Adam shouted. "I'll take care of the prisoners. *Run!*"

As the men sprinted back the way they had come, Adam asked, "What the hell was that?"

Bertie answered. His white hair gleamed in the darkness. "Oxygen tanks, I imagine—in intense heat, they can explode like bombs."

"Perfect!" Adam laughed in relief. "All right, let's go, everyone! Walk quickly!"

Jaybird glanced at Joshua. "Sure hope Gideon comes back soon."

Not as much as I do, thought Katie.

CHAPTER 56

DEPARTURES

Constantin hoped that later in life—if after this, the good Lord allowed his life to continue—his current mission would be considered brilliant, brave, and daring—not foolhardy, as he feared it very well might be. As he slipped away and ran in the direction of the OR fire, his heartbeat rivaled a hummingbird's wings for speed. His shallow breaths and soaking sweat betrayed his fear.

No matter—he had to have it. He wanted proof.

First, he had to get past the group of guards battling the OR fire, and then he had to clear the fence. He could feel the heat as the temporary building burned, engulfed in orange flames and billowing smoke. The soldiers, armed with fire extinguishers taken from the school building and small water hoses, appeared to be losing the fight. They faced the fire, and he was able to sneak behind them.

He bent low and hugged the school building until he got to the north entrance where the music rooms and cafeteria were located. He hurried around the high concrete stoop to the side farthest from the OR and rested a moment. So far, so good. But somehow he would have to cross about thirty feet of open space to get to the electrified fence. Thomas should have shorted it out by now—at least he hoped he had. Otherwise, once Constantin touched it he would be fried like a shrimp, minus the cornmeal. He needed some kind of metallic—

Just above him and to his left, the door to the darkened school slammed open and a guard rushed out with another fire extinguisher. The man flew down the steps and ran toward the fire. Like an invitation, the door stood open. Quiet as a shadow, Constantin slipped into the building.

The choir room door opened when he tried it. He walked forward in the dark and stumbled over a metal music stand. He caught it before it clattered to the floor. Suddenly inspired, he pulled the rack off and gripped the base. This would do—now he was ready.

Boom! Boom! Something exploded outside.

Without thinking, Constantin bolted out of the building, down the steps, and across the open space. *Boom!* By the time he reached the fence, he heard screams coming from the OR.

God help me. He placed the three-footed music stand's base against the ground and tilted it so the pole fell against the wire fence—and nothing happened. *Bless you, God, and thank you, Thomas!*

Taking the stand with him, he crawled through the fence in two seconds and ran for the stadium bleachers. At this distance from the fire, he was far less likely to be seen, but here was the tricky part: he had to find the two-month-old grave in the dark. Hopefully, the grass had not grown over it.

He set the stand down and dropped to his knees, feeling the ground with his hands in the approximate area he and Thomas had dug the grave. After a moment, he found a depression with sparse growth and a few bare patches. As he felt along the edges, it became clear the sunken area had an oblong shape. *This had to be it.* He used the pole of the music stand to dig on the side where he had hidden the diary.

Thankfully, the dirt was moist and somewhat loose. He and Thomas had not packed it down when they refilled the grave, and apparently the guards had never done so either. He knew he had to dig two or three feet down, so he bent his back and tunneled like a fear-crazed gopher. He broke up the soil with the pole, then shoveled it out with his bare hands. When he had a hole about three feet wide and two feet deep, a putrid smell filled his nostrils, and he almost gagged. He knew the remains of the mother and child lay buried deeper down, but from that point on, he used the pole more like a probe, poking and testing for any hard object.

At last, he felt an obstruction, and he cleared away more soil to uncover it. When a white patch appeared, his heart leaped; he knew he had found his mark—the plastic bag enclosing the diary. He unearthed it in less than a minute.

He refilled the hole rapidly and whispered a short prayer for the two buried victims. He shook most of the dirt off his hands and tucked the diary, still in the plastic bag, under his left arm. He took the music stand base, too—he could swing it like a mace if necessary; the three metal feet would do most excellent damage against a human skull. He knew his father and friends would make for the woods on the west side of the camp, and he intended to meet them there—if he could find them in the dark. He decided to go north first and then west, to keep the stadium between himself and the school building.

Thomas, Jaybird, Joshua, Bertie, and men from each barracks stepped on the lowest wire of the fence and pulled up on the wire above it to open up large gaps where the children and adults could pass through quickly. As soon as all the children had assembled outside the fence, Katie and Donna lined them up in a double file, holding hands. They admonished them to be silent. Walking rapidly west, they skirted the woods on the south side of the helipad. The adults followed right behind. When they came to the end of the helipad, they hugged the tree line and walked westbound, parallel to the double trail toward the fire lane. After about a hundred yards, they crossed over to the north side and entered into the shelter of the woods where they met Olga.

By the time all the inmates had passed through the fence, Thomas had almost given up hope of Gideon's return. Every minute seemed like an hour. When he and the others were ready to leave, at the last moment, Gideon materialized out of the darkness, rifle in hand. "Is everybody out?" he asked.

"Yes," said Thomas, "except for us. Are you all right?"

"I am, but I dispatched the two watchtower guards into the next life. Only one of them had time to return fire, and he missed. I've been your backup—standing guard from behind Barracks 5, but let's talk later. Time to go!"

"But first," said Thomas, "I'm taking the evidence, so they don't know where we got out. You guys go through the fence now." When they stood on the other side, Thomas lifted the copper wire hook from the fence and then gingerly touched it to the wire again. To his great relief, it did not spark. He immediately wrenched the rebar out of the ground and wrapped the cord around it. He climbed through the fence and smiled. "Ready."

Gideon grinned. "All right, let's get out of this shithole."

Adam faced the camp and gave a salute. "*Comer mierda*. Or as they say in Beijing: *Cào nǐ mā*."

As they ran toward the safety of the woods, Jaybird's curiosity got the best of him. He caught up with Adam. "Was that Spanish and Chinese?"

Adam smiled. "Yes. I gave a fond farewell to our captors."

"Really?" Jaybird was taken aback. "What exactly did you say?"

"I said, 'Eat shit and fuck your mother.'"

The Trilingual King of Curses and the Slingshot Sharpshooter laughed all the way into the woods.

THE PATH

Gideon estimated their meeting place in the woods was just under a mile from the camp, far too close for comfort. When he and all the men arrived, Gideon found all the family groups had reunited: parents with children, husbands with wives. As if launched from his own slingshot, Jaybird ignored the pain of his burning butt and flew toward Donna. Bertie found Susannah, and the former Max Grandpied swooped up Peter in one arm and embraced Sam with the other. People hugged and kissed each other all around. With his thoughts on freedom and his family, Adam kissed his only nearest and dearest present, his violin. Then he and Thomas traded accounts of their separate adventures. Hovering near Sam and Joshua, Olga spoke quietly to a chastened, sheepish Austin Pratt. Gideon found Katie easily—all he had to do was locate the cluster of orphaned children. The others had reunited with their parents.

She still wore her opera costume; her white shirt and yellow knee pants gleamed in the darkness. He embraced her tentatively—he had watched her from afar, but never touched her. Her iron grip around his torso gave him all the encouragement he needed. He planted a chaste kiss on her forehead, wordless with relief. But she drew his head down and kissed him full on the mouth. "I've been wanting to do that for weeks."

He smiled. "Just so you know, you're the first pageboy I ever kissed."

Katie's throaty laugh pleased him. "Your plan worked."

"By the grace of God." Gideon gazed into the blue ocean of her eyes. "I have so much to say, Katie, but it must wait. We're not really safe yet. I have to find my son and maneuver nearly two hundred fifty people out of harm's way." He held her to his chest briefly and then turned away. He smiled to see the people embracing and talking quietly as he walked among them looking for Constantin.

His search came up empty. He asked the men if anyone had seen Constantin pass through the fence, but no one had. Where could he be? Surely the guards hadn't captured him. Gideon groaned inwardly. Had he pulled his people out of captivity, but lost his own son a second time? Could God be that cruel?

His desire to return to the camp to search for Constantin almost overwhelmed him, but the discipline he had learned in the Marines held him back. He would not endanger the lives of so many adults and children for one boy—even if that boy was blood of his blood. Time was critical. To evade the enemy, they had to move north within minutes. They had a few weapons and the clothes they wore—but no food or water.

Somehow he had to lead and sustain them through the piney woods, a tract of forest covering several thousand square miles where the northern borders of Texas and Louisiana met the southern corners of Oklahoma and Arkansas. They could roam the area, with its many creeks, lakes, and abundant game, for years if need be. At least that was his plan. He knew it could be done; during WWII, large groups of Polish Jews escaped into the forests and survived on the run for years in a much harsher climate. He and Jaybird had the survival skills to lead the people, but for every minute the company stayed in place, they risked discovery. They had to put many miles between themselves and the Farm without delay.

He organized the company into a narrow, inverted V formation similar to a flock of migrating geese. He and Jaybird would take turns as leaders, while the other men lined up to form the outer arms. The women and children would travel inside the V. "To survive," he told them, "we must move as silently and cautiously as deer. No talking, and you must obey any order instantly. We will travel mostly at night and sleep during the day."

Someone asked, "What about food?"

"We'll hunt and gather once we make camp, but for the time being, we'll have to do without. Our immediate priority is to stay alive and outrun pursuit."

Gideon gestured forward with his arm and raised his voice. "Let's go!" The company moved out, with Gideon leading the way and Jaybird just behind him. Thomas, Adam, and Joshua brought up the rear, spanning the open space between the wide ends of the inverted V. The heavens had cooperated; the clouds had cleared, enabling Gideon to find the Big Dipper and its pointer stars. From them, he located the North Star and led the company north and slightly east.

His shoulders drooped, and his heart might as well have been an anvil, it was so heavy in his chest. Every step took him away from the son he had so lately found. The more he pondered the situation, the more questions he had. Why had no one seen Constantin? When had he disappeared? If the soldiers had captured him, there would have been shots and some sort of outcry, but as far as he could tell, that hadn't occurred. If he had not been captured, then where was he? Had the boy foolishly returned to the school auditorium to check on his grandfather—*may that SOB rot in hell*. Had he returned to the barracks for some reason and gotten trapped? Gideon prayed not. If they reset the breaker for the electric fence, he wouldn't be able to get out, and if they caught him, they would torture the boy until he spilled his guts.

They walked through what appeared to be an open-air telephone pole warehouse: the dark, bare trunks of the pine trees rose fifty feet or more before the needles appeared. The ground was littered with pinecones, and trees seemed to go on forever as they trudged through the sparse undergrowth. Through the gaps in the overhead canopy, he could see the North Star often enough to keep his bearings.

It was possible he might never see Constantin again, and he might never learn his son's fate. The thought skewered his heart like a twisted dagger. Gideon did the only thing he could do: he prayed. *Thank you, Lord, that I found my son and got to know him a little. He's only sixteen, not fully grown, malnourished and weak. Please send your angels to help him and bring him to safety. Guide him through all dangers and keep him from evil. In Jesus's name, Amen.*

And then he did the thing he had to do. He trudged on.

Constantin entered the woods well north of the stadium, about one hundred fifty yards north of the helipad, he estimated. He hoped if he kept due west, his path would intersect that of the others. They would have entered the forest quite a bit south of his position. He didn't know the full plan, but he knew his dad's goal was to stay in the forest and move north and east toward Arkansas.

He trod as quickly as possible, hoping he wouldn't walk in circles. It was disorienting amongst the trees, especially in the dark. The shouts from the soldiers at the camp grew more and more distant. The fresh scent of the pine resin filled his nostrils. The farther he advanced into the forest, the quieter, colder, and spookier it grew. An owl hooted repeatedly in the distance. Constantin thought about the other creatures roaming the woods at night: raccoons and possums, cougars, black bears. Not too reassuring. Hopefully it was too cold for snakes.

He gripped the diary in one hand and the pole of his trusty music stand nervously in the other. He held it upside down so he could club any predators with the three-footed end. Of course, in all honesty, if he met a cougar he would probably pee his pants. An outdoorsman he was not.

How could he keep a straight course? He had read about *l'étoile du nord*—something about finding it by keying off of Ursa Major, *La Grande Ourse.* In daylight he would be able to distinguish east and west roughly by the sun. If he kept the morning sun on his right, he would be heading north. But, *mon Dieu*, he had ten hours to go before sunrise—plenty of time to get completely and royally lost.

After Arthur, the kitchen boy, told Katie (in whispers) the story about spilling the vegetable soup and how it had given Constantin time to cut the oven cord and how Thomas used the oven cord to help short out the electric fence and how he, Arthur, stepped on the leaked-out brain matter of the guard that Max bashed in the head and how he might still have blood and gunk on his clogs and did she want to see? she put a polite finger on his mouth to stem the tide. "Not now, Arthur. I have an important errand for you."

"Really? What?" He smiled and raised his head like a dog expecting a treat. If he'd had a tail, he would have wagged it.

"Run ahead and ask Gideon to stop for five minutes. Tell him we need a bathroom break badly." The last time she and the children had relieved themselves was around 5:00, more than three hours ago. If they didn't stop soon, there would be wet pants, followed inevitably by red, rashy bottoms.

Wide-eyed and seized with purpose, Arthur dashed toward the front of the V formation. Two minutes later, he galloped back—almost breathless—*thank God.*

"He said we'll stop now for five minutes. We should only walk ten paces into the brush. When you hear the mourning dove call, we have to be back in place."

"All right, you lead the boys to the left, and I will lead the girls to the right. Come directly back and do not explore. Count your steps."

"Okay!" He and the other boys gleefully veered off toward the west. Katie didn't worry because the men on the west side would be with them. She and the seven girls, ranging in age from six to twelve, had to go through the line of men on the east side to gain a little privacy.

Past the human fence, she counted ten steps. The undergrowth was not thick, but she was waylaid by unseen spider webs, and she had to push aside the thin branches of small understory trees and hope that none of the low, bushy plants or vines happened to be poison ivy. In the first clearing she found, she told the girls to pee. When they finished, she had them turn their backs, stand together, and hold hands while she squatted and relieved herself for what seemed like a minute. She rose and pulled up her underwear and knee pants and fumbled with the blasted buttons. *Buttons! Why didn't the costumer just put in a zipper?* Here she was in a dark forest, fleeing for her life just as she had through the streets of Chicago, dressed in the same pageboy costume. Too bad Cherubino hadn't worn hiking boots. These patent-leather shoes were not the most practical footwear for the trek.

Coo-ah, coo-coo-coo. Coo-ah, coo-coo-coo. Coo-ah, coo-coo-coo. The signal to return. She extended her arms out to either side like a hen waving her wings, shooing all her chicks toward home. As they picked their way through the underbrush, Katie was startled by a cracking sound as a branch snapped behind her. She froze. She heard the unmistakable sound of something large moving through the brush. An animal? Or had the guards tracked them through the woods?

Despite the fact that midwinter approached, his predicament reminded Constantin of *A Midsummer Night's Dream.* An owl hooted plaintively:

whoo-whoo? He stopped briefly and gave an old-world bow in the direction of the sound.

"Good evening, Mr. Owl. *Whoo* am I? My name is Bottom."

He certainly felt like an ass, wandering about in the forest at night. He had definitely trudged over hill and over dale, through bush and brier—he had the scratches to show for it. He thought his westbound path and that of the northbound company should have intersected by now. Had he missed them? Was he still headed west?

As he walked on, doubts welled up in his mind, thick and oily, blacker than the night. He had just as much chance of finding Titania, Oberon, and Puck as he had of finding his father and the others. *A Midsummer Nightmare,* it was. He tried to suppress the persistent, insidious voice that taunted him: *You are lost, you idiot. You are wandering in circles. You will never find them. In fact, you'll probably walk right back into the camp.*

He had no way to gauge the time, but it felt like hours since he had unearthed the diary. He would be with his father now if he hadn't slipped away to retrieve it. He inhaled sharply and stopped— it struck him suddenly that his father might have gone back to the camp to find him. *Oh, please, no, no, no.* He could have endangered his father and the whole company. If anything happened to his dad, it would be his fault. The inner voice mocked him: *You fool, you ass.* Shame washed over him; he bowed his head and winced. *Father, forgive me.*

Weary, hungry, and cold, he walked on, assailed by a rising panic. He tried to fight it. *The Lord is my shepherd; I shall not want.* He groped in his mind for more of the words. *Yea, though I walk through the valley of the shadow of death, I will fear no evil. I will fear no evil. No, I will not. I will not be afraid. For thou art with me, thy rod and thy staff, they comfort me. For thou art with me, the Lord, the maker of heaven and earth. I am not alone. I am not alone, for thou art with me.*

It was his litany of hope, a lantern to disperse the darkness. As he repeated the words, a calm descended on Constantin. He suddenly noticed a silvery light all around him. He looked up and caught a glimpse of the half moon. His heartbeat slowed and he took deeper breaths. The moonlight illuminated an animal trail leading forward, but veering off to the right from the direction he had been walking. He stopped for a moment, trying to decide if he should follow the path. In the psalm, there was something about "He leads me in the path . . . " He bowed his head in frustration; he couldn't remember the words.

He took the path. After a few minutes, he began to doubt himself. Should he go on or turn around? Finally, his indecision brought him to a complete stop. Close to panic, he heard a bird call. *Coo-ah, coo-coo-coo. Coo-ah, coo-coo-coo. Coo-ah, coo-coo-coo.* Three times. A mourning dove, off in the distance. Constantin lifted his head. Did mourning doves coo at night? Was it a bird, or a signal? He peered intently through the trees and caught a glimpse of white. It moved.

Electricity shot through him and he charged forward on the path, stepping on dry branches, brushing aside limbs, heedless of the noise he made. *Could it be* . . . His heart leapt: he saw a white shirt, bright yellow knee pants, blessed blonde hair. *A lifeline—just like in Chicago.* His voice broke on her name, "Katie!" Wet-eyed, but weary and cold no more, he waved his music stand in the air and ran to meet her. "Katie!"

EPILOGUE

There are two histories of the world. I learned of them both during the years we roamed like nomads through the American wilderness, hunting and foraging to survive. My mother, a gifted writer, recorded this history. She chronicled our stories, our experiences in the camp, and later, our wanderings. She kept a record, so the world would know.

Even though we lived in constant fear of discovery and death, life went on. In the new year, we celebrated the marriages of Jaybird and Donna and Gideon and Katie. Constantin was his father's best man. I think he loved Katie, too. Adam and Thomas left the company the next spring to travel north in search of their families. Three babies were born in the second year of our wanderings, including my sister, Miriam, and Jaybird's son, Isaac. My mother continued to heal the sick through prayer. Like her sitti, she had the gift. Death came for some along the way. We grieved for them. We had to bury them and move on.

North America is a large continent, well-populated. Or at least it once was. But even in the time before the depopulation by plagues and the wholesale slaughter of its citizens during the coup, there remained vast areas where few, if any, people lived. America's very size, and the untamed spirit of its people (well, many of them, at least) made it a formidable place to conquer, even by the traitors from within.

We avoided the cities, but in the rural areas we found many houses abandoned by the inhabitants at the time of the coup. Like us, they had only been allowed to take one suitcase, so they left behind larders full of foodstuffs, pots and pans, and closets stocked with clothes and shoes.

We thanked them each time we ate their food or dressed ourselves in their shirts and pants, coats, sweaters, and boots. We thanked them for each blanket and quilt, for needles and thread, for the tools in their work sheds, for the hidden Bibles, the classic books, for the medicines and antiseptic salves, and for the windup emergency radios that gave us contact with others.

And there were many others. Gideon counted on that fact. Other veterans like himself led pockets of resistance almost everywhere. Southerners, Westerners, and those from the small towns in the heart of the nation had hunted and fished its forests, rivers, marshes, and swamps; they had hiked its mountain ranges, its plains, and the backcountry. They knew the land intimately, in a way its invaders could not.

Having lived all their lives in freedom, having absorbed it in their bones and blood, Americans could not give up liberty without a fight, no matter how overwhelming the odds. Since the very birth of America, its people always prided themselves on independent thinking, on taking initiative. They believed hard work and ingenuity could surmount any obstacle, and that they, not the government, were responsible for themselves.

Clear-eyed and angry, they had watched and listened for years as those in the highest offices—craven, amoral addicts of money and power, pissants in everyone's mind but their own—sold out their country and its people to foreign tyrants. Americans saw through the blatant lies and thefts; all along they perceived the colossal arrogance and condescension, the veiled malice behind it all.

And they resisted.

Of course, I learned this history much later. I read the books we scavenged. I listened to the adults who told tales beside campfires and related accounts of kingdoms and wars during the long treks over back roads and logging trails, and on other days when we waded through creeks and marshes. I heard the conversations in winter, when they thought I was asleep, as we gathered for warmth in caves or in the underground bunkers we dug. I loved history, the chronological record of important events. Whether carved into stone or written in books, it is an account of what has happened, a tale of civilizations, conquests, explorations, rulers, and nations.

We believe the accounts that have come down to us through time. But are they all true? Finite beings with limited perspective record a history like themselves, fragmented and flawed. The scribe writes what the king tells him to write. The conqueror's narrative may not match the tale the conquered would tell if he could speak through his shattered teeth and bloodied mouth. And there is so much we do not know. There are histories of ancient peoples written in languages we cannot even decipher: What do they say? There are monuments so mysterious and colossal, no one knows their purpose or how they were built. If only the Sphinx could talk . . .

But there is another history of the world, the *true* history. It is the Creator's story, written by the hand of man, yes—but divinely inspired. Its author is all-knowing and everywhere present, inhabiting past, present, and future. His story tells of all he made and his interaction with his wayward people. It describes the ancient, ongoing spiritual battle between a powerful, prideful adversary so filled with envy that he would spit in the face of his Creator and usurp his place. He would destroy creation and enslave the souls of men.

The war began in a most unlikely place, a perfect garden, where the adversary lied to human beings and tempted them. They listened to his seductive voice and disobeyed the one rule their Maker gave them. Their fall was instant and irreclaimable. With Paradise lost, the battle for the souls of men began. It has raged ever since.

Many people, some of whom have not read or studied this account at all, hold it to be largely unbelievable. They do not perceive that our earthly story takes place in a spiritual framework, that unseen presences influence the visible world. How do I, Peter Brightman, know it is the true history? Because it terrifies the powers-that-be. It exposes their evil; it threatens their puffed-up arrogance and their merciless, iron-fisted rule. It shines an unwavering light on all those who seek to conceal their deeds in darkness—they cannot bear it. Throughout time they have always sought to suppress this history and destroy its adherents.

And now that our country, the last bastion of light in the world, has fallen to the tyrants, the culmination is very near. Evil will triumph. The dragon will have his day, his years, and he will crush all opposition.

But just as his victory has been foretold, so too has his swift destruction. It is inevitable, and it will unfold exactly as it is written in the true history of the world. This is our consolation and the source of our joy. We hold this truth in our hearts. We know the dawn will break and sudden light will destroy the deepest, heaviest darkness once and for all. The dragon cannot keep that day from coming. It approaches, and we rejoice. Thus, the darkest of times has become for us the time of noblest mirth.

I recall a song from the early days of our journey. Like my father, I have an excellent musical memory. The day was damp, cloudy, and cold, with a persistent north wind that cut through every layer of clothing I wore. We ascended a hill—probably somewhere in Arkansas. As Constantin and I walked behind Katie and Gideon, she began to hum a tune. The melody made a good, duple-time marching song. It began with an upward leap, like the first step into the future, clear and hopeful, with a middle phrase that rose and arched. Gideon listened for a time until his curiosity got the better of him. "What is that song?"

"It's an Easter hymn."

"Easter in December?"

She laughed. "Yes, indeed."

"Isn't that out of season?"

"We are an Easter people, Gideon, my love. Redemption is never out of season, even though it took place two thousand years ago."

"What are the words then?"

"Well, I only remember one verse, probably the last." She sang the words in her rich mezzo soprano, and everyone matched their steps to the beat. Somehow the music warmed us and made the uphill going easier. Unable to resist, the other musicians joined in; my father hummed a bass line, while Jaybird filled in the harmonies with his mouth organ.

> *Now let the heavens be joyful,*
> *Let earth her song begin,*
> *The round world keep high triumph,*
> *And all that is therein;*
> *Let all things seen and unseen*
> *Their notes together blend,*
> *For Christ the Lord is risen,*
> *Our joy that has no end.*

We sang with Katie as we reached the top of the hill. And then a great flock of blackbirds alighted in the trees above us, chirping and trilling a garlanded descant. We laughed to hear it. The song seemed to rise up in the wind and spread out over the land. Perhaps the angels, unable to resist the marvelous singer, magnified it with their voices. Beautiful, it was. It rang out like the pealing of many bells, signifying a victory already won, a blessing upon us all.

ACKNOWLEDGMENTS

Many thanks to editor Zachary Gresham, whose comments and insights helped me improve the story tremendously, and who encouraged me by his belief in the novel.

I am indebted to Jacob Sweatt for relating some of his Marine combat experiences in the Middle East, the ensuing PTSD, and the difficulties veterans have in readjusting to civilian life. His experiences are not recounted exactly, but recreated with fictional characters to approximate what he saw and suffered.

My brother Neal F. Isaac (gun-enthusiast extraordinaire) shared invaluable knowledge and advice about electricity, guns, and slingshots. (As a boy in the wilds of Louisiana, our dad actually did hunt with a slingshot to save ammo.)

Thanks to my opera orchestra friends, violinist Johnny Chang and oboist Erin Tsai, who advised me on Chinese speakers of English, and the Chinese language. Johnny helped me with specific Chinese and Spanish phrases. His Central American background, his talent and trilingual ability inspired me to create the character Adam Chen.

Maria Grazia Repetto helped me with the proper way to swear in Italian.

If you would like to listen to the piece Bigfoot heard in his mind in Chapter 25, it was Handel's Concerto a due cori No. 2 in F Major, HWV 333: V. Allegro ma non troppo.

My idea for the book's title came from a hymn text by Edward Hayes Plumptre (1865). The words *noblest mirth* occur in verse 3: *With all the angel choirs, With all the saints of earth, Pour out the strains of joy and bliss, True rapture, noblest mirth.*

The poem in Chapter 16 is "The Lamb," by William Blake.

The Easter hymn in the Epilogue is verse 3 of a text by John of Damascus (8th cent.), translated by John Mason Neale (1853).

Both the depiction of torture in the camp and the operating room experience are based on eyewitness testimony from *China Tribunal Judgment: Independent Tribunal into Forced Organ Harvesting from Prisoners of Conscience in China (2020)*.

And credit to whom all credit is due: *Soli Deo Gloria.*

ABOUT THE AUTHOR

Wendy Isaac Bergin, a Louisiana native, is a lover of language and music, and the genre that combines them both: opera. She gets to indulge her passion regularly as principal flutist of Houston's Opera in the Heights Orchestra. A seasoned veteran of the halls of academia—another hotbed of high drama—she has served on the music faculties of Prairie View A&M University, the University of Houston-Downtown, Blinn College, and Lee College. Wendy is the author of three novels—*The Piper's Story: A Tale of War, Music and the Supernatural, The Threshold of Eden,* and *Lessons in the Wild.* She has lived in Brooklyn, Stockholm and Houston. Now, she enjoys the adventures of bucolic life among bobcats and coyotes in the almost-hill-country of Texas.

More about the author and her work can be found on her website: www.wendyisaacbergin.com

THANK YOU

In this age of social media sharing, without social proof, an author may as well be invisible. So if you've enjoyed *The Time of Noblest Mirth*, please consider giving it some visibility by reviewing it on the platform of your choice. A review doesn't have to be a long critical essay. Just a few words expressing your thoughts, which could help potential readers decide whether they would enjoy it, too.